No more lies

R.S. Etchells

Published in 2017 by FeedARead.com Publishing

Copyright © R.S. Etchells.

A CIP catalogue record for this title is available from the British Library.

With thanks to all who have encouraged & believed.

You know who you are.

Chapter 1

The room was silent. The older man stared at the middle-aged woman before him. She held his gaze, no longer afraid to face him, knowing that for once she could be the strong confident woman she really was, even though the whole of her material life; her job; her home; and those for whom she cared so deeply were all, in this moment slipping from her grasp. There would be no turning back.

The older man broke the silence. "So, you've have been living a lie for the past twenty years."

"Not exactly. I've never lied, just never been allowed to be completely honest and it's time for that to change. I'm not prepared to live such a fragmented and disjointed existence anymore. Part of me has been hidden for far too long as if it is some dark and sordid secret. It's about time I began leading an honest life, life with complete integrity."

The woman paused, waiting for some response. When none came, she continued. "I'm choosing to leave behind the deception; to be fully visible and alive for who I am as a whole person. It's as if I've been forced to dampen down or even disown a vital part of me for years, only allowing it to surface when it's convenient. How can that be honest?"

She had made the journey early that morning, having thought long and hard about what to wear. She'd decided against the uniform, but went for a smart suit and blouse with an open neck. She'd lost count the number of times she'd draped the delicate silky scarf across her shoulders and then taken it off again. In the end, it stayed on. And now the ends gave her something to wind round her ring finger as the silence continued to fill the room. It was a crisp bright day in the first half of

January. The winter sun was surprisingly strong and had quickly dispelled the grey mist that had shrouded the early part of the morning. The natural light caught the edge of the stained glass nestling high in the medieval windows of the sombre room creating a colourful display of light against the imposing oak panels.

Man, and woman sat opposite each other on sofas that had long since lost their firmness. The glowing embers of the log fire warmed the room in a desperate attempt to melt the stony atmosphere that had now developed between these two respected individuals. It could have been a scene from a late Victorian novel, rather than an awkward moment at the end of the first decade of the 21st century.

The man raised himself from the sofa turning away from the woman before him; she followed him with her gaze as he went towards his desk, buzzed the intercom and spoke to his secretary.

"Sally, can you bring in a pot of coffee please? And ring through to Catrin and tell her I shall be delayed."

"Oh Bishop, Catrin has only just been down to ask how long you will be."

"It can't be helped we need more time to......" there was a pause, as if Bishop David couldn't quite work out what he needed time to do. ".......time to discuss things more fully," he concluded.

"Er, if you'll pardon me for saying, but Catrin asked me to remind you that your grandson will be in school uniform before you've even laid eyes on him if you don't make the trip soon."

"Yes. I suspect Catrin and I will have that conversation when I see her in a little while. Thanks Sally," he sighed.

The intercom had been on loudspeaker. Whether this was on purpose or not, Charlotte couldn't work out. Bishop David turned back to her. "I take it you could do with a coffee? I should have offered you one sooner." Charlotte sensed that the Bishop had consciously taken steps to control his anger during that long period of silence that had hung between them. She was herself still struggling with the mix of emotions that threatened to spill out, so simply nodded, adding a quiet, "please" to be polite.

David moved some of the magazines and books that were strewn across the coffee table between the sofas to make space for the tray of coffee that was on its way. He didn't sit down but walked around the room towards the window. 'This was not how the morning should have gone', he thought to himself. He had written to Charlotte one month earlier asking her to consider an important role within the diocese. She was an experienced minister, well respected amongst her parishioners and colleagues alike. She had been priested in 1994, as long as any woman could have been, Rector of the East Dartmoor group of parishes for eight years and Rural Dean for three of them. At forty-eight she was ready for this position, more than ready.

"Charlotte," David had turned to face his friend from across the room, but then stalled, suddenly aware that he was looking at a stranger for the first time.

"Coffee, Bishop," interrupted Sally as she knocked on the door and opened it all in one swift movement, before walking into the room with an air of assurance that for a moment swept aside the heaviness that had now filled every splinter of those old oak panels. She placed the coffee on the table in front of Charlotte, glancing up at her and then frowning slightly before reaching to the shelf beneath and pulling out the box of tissues that had remained hidden, secreted for the more difficult discussions.

The brief frown had been one of bewilderment for this was to have been a joyous occasion. The Bishop would have briefly discussed the arrangements before leaving Charlotte and Sally to work out the details. Nothing had been agreed of course, nothing was set in stone, there was still an official process to go through, but it was a foregone conclusion, everyone was in agreement, she was the best person for the job. Intelligent, hardworking, dedicated, no family ties, practical, confident, resilient, good sense of humour, which was an essential trait, quite attractive too, although of course that would never come into it – made a change from the boring bald headed blokes that were usually invited to apply for such positions.

Charlotte caught Sally's eye and thanked her with a brief smile. Her hands had been in her lap still fiddling with the silk scarf that she was now very glad she had decided to wear. She hadn't quite known what to expect, but strangely, the long drawn out silences had not been part of her forward thinking.

Bishop David thanked Sally for the coffee, and almost as an afterthought added, "most kind, and digestives too. You do think of everything," and noticing the discretely placed tissues gently emphasized, "everything". Sally then handed the Bishop a small folded piece of paper, which he took and read.

"Any reply Bishop?" For the first time in the past half an hour, which was unlike David, he smiled. "Just a moment Sally" and taking his pen he scribbled on the reverse of the note.

I love you too. Thank Lizzie for being so understanding and yes we'll definitely make it for an early supper, love D x

"Do you mind popping up to Catrin with this?" He asked the ever-obliging Sally.

"I don't need to, she is waiting outside."

"Oh well, in that case, Charlotte will you give me just a moment?"

"Of course," her voice stronger than she had anticipated and glad that somehow Sally had managed to lift the atmosphere, simply with coffee, a slip of paper and a knowing look.

So, for a brief moment Charlie was left alone with her thoughts. She could hear murmurings outside, but they seemed civil enough. It must be difficult trying to juggle family life, wife, children and grandchildren, with the pressured life of running the diocese. Charlie, along with several of her colleagues, suspected that it was Sally who probably did most of the running, leaving the Bishop to chair numerous committees, preside at civic occasions, attend the House of Lords and write the occasional book, in between Radio 4's "Thought for the day", and occasional appearances on TV. And then of course he had meetings like today, with his clergy.

Charlotte knew that this meeting was nothing like the one the Bishop had anticipated. She wondered for a brief moment if she was, in a strange way, proud of the way she had managed to surprise him. But how could she be proud of throwing away the best career move ever offered to her? Yet, she had chosen this moment to surprise her Bishop by throwing her principles at the poor unsuspecting man. Even that wasn't strictly true: He had suspected for a long while and had even challenged her once just before she took up her role as Rector, but she had managed to slip the noose, answering as always, truthfully, but not completely. After all, Bishop David didn't want to hear the whole truth.

The murmurings outside the door stopped and David walked back in, more at ease than he been a few moments before. 'Yes,' thought Charlotte, 'family life did have something going for it, no matter how difficult the juggling act.'

"Coffee?" he asked again.

"Yes, please, white no sugar," remembering a time in the nineties when political correctness went mad and one had to say "with milk" rather than "white".

Bishop David poured the fresh coffee into the plain white mugs and he remembered a time when his secretary wouldn't have dreamt of bringing anything other than bone china cups and saucers; some things had certainly changed, but others would take a long while before being accepted.

"Here's what we are going to do..." said David, as he handed over the coffee, clutching the hot mug in his large hand so that Charlotte could take the handle. He blew briefly on his glowing fingers, thinking, there was something rather useful about saucers. "... we'll forget the last half an hour ever existed, we'll forget what you've just told me and pretend it never happened and carry on exactly as we would have done had you not told me."

Charlotte stared at David through the steaming coffee as she took a sip. Then she placed the mug on the coaster strategically placed on the coffee table. Very slowly as if in a trance, all the time controlling a growing anger. She lifted her right hand towards her mouth and slowly rubbed her index finger across her top lip, supporting the underside of her chin with her thumb. David was almost mesmerized by the confidence of the woman sat in front of him. He had just completely let her off the hook, but rather than the huge sigh of relief he was expecting she was sitting playing with her top lip.

"Do you understand what I just said?" David once again felt the anxiety rise in his stomach.

Charlotte couldn't quite believe that she was still prepared to throw everything away, but she continued, stubbornly. "I don't think you have understood what I tried to tell you less than ten minutes ago."

Since she was just sixteen years old, Charlotte had felt the inner longing to the call of the priesthood. Long before the church had agreed that women could ever take up such a position. Now thirty years on, she had, more or less, been offered a senior post. As an Archdeacon, she would have pastoral oversight of over a hundred churches in six deaneries. And yet, this was the moment she had chosen lay aside the mask.

"I have understood perfectly well." The Bishop's voiced had a hard edge, "and I am giving you a chance to take back what you have divulged and we shall never again speak of it."

"I can't do that."

"You have been doing it for over twenty years."

She took a moment to calm the growing anger and to compose herself. She chose her words carefully before responding to the man that she had grown to deeply respect over the years.

"Many years ago, Bishop, I was asked to come and see you, by Archdeacon Robert after he had discovered that I had been granted permission to have a lodger in my home. Your one and only question was to ask if there was anything you should know about. I said I didn't think so. You also told me on that occasion that if anything ever came to light I was on my own and there would be no backing from the diocese. I had hoped that as the years went on there would come a time when the church that I have grown up in and served all my life would recognise me as a wholly integrated person." Charlotte leaned forwards slightly. "I have never lied to you Bishop David. You and I both know, that sadly, all too often the Church of England has survived by shoving things beneath the carpet, by papering over the cracks and by pretending that some things don't exist at all. Priests that burn out and then turn inwards and allow their parishes to flounder through lack of leadership. I'm sorry to have to say this, but it's nothing we don't know. And I can't be part of this deceit any longer, which means I can't pretend I am someone I'm not. I don't want to be just another problem to be hidden away and never discussed." She sat back into the sofa, her heart pounding in her chest.

"Quite a speech." David could feel the anger deep in his stomach, and regrettably felt the acid threatening to overwhelm him from the ulcer that he'd been battling with for the past six months. "I'm beginning to think you were right and I was wrong – I shouldn't be encouraging you to apply for the post. I'm not sure what advantage you think you will gain by trying to make out that we are all a corrupt bunch of....." he stopped himself from saying what he might regret. "This isn't just about your honesty is it! This isn't just about your righteous integrity!" He had raised his voice but paused briefly expecting a response. Charlotte just stared ahead of her. "What shall we expect? Journalistic whistle-blowing? What are you trying to do? Clear the air so when the shit hits the fan you'll already be long gone? Why Charlotte, why? Why do this? Have you finally flipped? Will you go to the press with your 'poor little me story of victimised lesbian? Get in there first with some pointless slander of your colleagues? It won't wash!" Then as if in a state of shock from his own behaviour his anger suddenly dissolved as abruptly as it had bubbled up. He rubbed his hand through his thinning air and looked directly at Charlotte, blowing out a deep long sigh "I'm sorry, I shouldn't have raised my voice. I've…….. I don't know." He picked up his coffee and sat right back into the sofa. Still Charlotte said nothing.

The silence hung like a heavy sodden curtain between them.

Charlotte stared ahead of her. David watched as she rubbed her eye-brow back and forth. Another nervous gesture like rubbing her lip. David felt sorry for her. He knew that the church she had portrayed in her little speech was in many ways much more of a truthful portrayal than most ministers would ever admit. He didn't like it any more than she did. Her honesty was one of the reasons he wanted her as part of his inner team. She would cut through the pretence, or so he thought. He had suspected she was gay for years. But whilst there was no evidence and whilst no-one made waves he had been able to turn a blind eye which was exactly what Charlotte had just ranted on about.

After a few moments, Charlotte eventually broke the silence.

"Bishop David, don't you see it is because of the truth that rather than accepting the invitation to apply for archdeacon I am offering my resignation? I am fed up with not being able to be totally honest with

11

people. It's about me not the system." She paused again. "Well, maybe it is about the system. Yes, if I'm honest part of me is fed up with our inability to challenge colleagues that just don't seem to pull their weight."

Bishop David interrupted "And with new capability reviews that is going to change."

"Maybe," Charlotte didn't sound convinced, "and as an Archdeacon one of my jobs will be making that happen."

"Exactly!" said Bishop David

"Which is why I can't do it! Always in the back of my mind will be that niggling feeling, how can I judge others when I'm living a lie? Living a double life; carrying on a relationship in secret. I guess if I was single...... but even then, I'm fed up with just not being open and honest. If I was offered the post I would be drawn even further into this secretive life. And if it was to all come to light.... well then, we'd definitely have the press on our backs. I can't live with that in the back of my mind all the time. I am who God created me to be. I've known that since I was fifteen years old. I have tried to change. I was even engaged for a while, but that would have been the ultimate lie – denying who I am and a disaster for the bloke involved."

Charlotte expected a response but David remained silent. He called to mind Psalm 46 *"Be still and know that I am God"*. What made this even more difficult was that deep down he had no problem with what Charlotte had confessed. In fact, he didn't regard it as a confession. How could he when he didn't regard it as a sin? He knew the rules as well as Charlotte, but rules are not always correct, which was why as long as Charlotte was prepared to continue with the charade he would simply deny the conversation ever took place. But she was a better woman than he was a man. She was sitting there willing to give up everything she had worked for because of her integrity and she chose this morning to tell him.

For a moment, he was suddenly mesmerized by the coloured shapes of light on the dark oak. How could God create such simplistic beauty yet make life so complicated at the same time? Why did Charlotte wait till now? That's what made him angry. He had sat in three staff meetings discussing potential candidates and even though many agreed that Charlotte was the best person for the job, even now after nearly twenty years of women in the priesthood he still had to persuade some of those on Bishops staff that a female Archdeacon was absolutely the right thing for the diocese. Charlotte was perfect. Strong enough to cope with the prejudice, gentle enough not to put people's backs up. She had even fought to maintain the license of a male Reader in her parish although he refused to receive communion when she presided, preferring to attend when the male curate (a trainee) took the service or go to one of the other churches in the group who had one of the other three male priests, all of whom Charlotte oversaw with integrity, wisdom and discernment. He had to finish this meeting soon. Catrin would go spare if he didn't get a move on. His new little grandson was already three weeks old, and although he'd seen him over the webcam hadn't actually made the four-hour round trip to meet him face to face and do the traditional changing of the nappy, just to prove that Bishops were not above such things. And, of course to remind Lizzie, as he had reminded his other daughters and son, that he had also changed their nappies, although admittedly he was only a curate and a humble vicar in those days. He pulled himself away from his momentary day dream and turned to face Charlotte once again.

"Charlotte, I accept that you don't feel taking on the role of Archdeacon is the right step for you at the moment. I don't have another meeting with Bishops staff for three weeks. I want you to take some time to think about this some more. I would like you to take a retreat, get away from the parish for a few days, three at the minimum. I'm sure your colleagues will cover for you, they will understand why. Have you told them about my letter?"

"No, I've only discussed it with my partner."

"Your partner! Don't rub it in – please, I'm trying to be fair."

"It is not my intention to 'rub it in,' I'm simply telling you the truth. She is just as supportive now as she has always been. She doesn't want me to give up everything any more than you do – or actually any more than I do. But this is the catalyst – the epiphany moment if you like........" David interrupted her, before she expected him to endure another speech. He also had a grandson he wanted hear.

"I'm sorry, please, no more – just go away for a few days, try to include a Sunday, will you? Ask that wayward Reader to say matins for you instead of a communion service – it will make his day. If anyone asks, be honest – well nearly. I've asked you to take on a position of responsibility and need your answer within three weeks and have suggested you go away to pray it through. That should get the village drums doing overtime." And then as an afterthought added "I never asked this question, because you've never told me but…. how shall I put it?" He thought for a moment then came up with, "Will your partner mind being in the house alone?"

"Bishop, the lodger who lives with me is just that, my lodger. She also happens to be gay – but she is not my partner. My partner, thankfully has her own home just outside Plymouth and as far as I'm aware is known only in the parish, as an acquaintance of mine. She hardly ever visits the parishes, apart from the occasional call out as the vet or if she pops into the new organic farm shop when she wants something a bit special, usually on a Friday night when I've got an evening free. She worships at a church in the city centre, is a committed Christian but not a member of the Church of England. No, my partner won't mind me going away, she's used to it. But my going away, won't make any difference Bishop. I've thought of nothing else since your letter. I won't change my mind."

"Just go." David was not angry any more, just tired and a little upset. He had jumped to certain conclusions and had been wrong. Here was a person he respected and perhaps, he had to admit, even loved in a fatherly sort of way, being totally open and honest. He could do nothing but probably accept her resignation. His only other option, given all that she had divulged was to enforce a clergy discipline measure leading to the withdrawal of her licence and all that went with it. That, or join in with the lies and deception. She knew it and he knew it. "On your way out, don't forget to make an appointment with Sally so that we can meet again before February 25th." Charlotte realised he had still not accepted that she had made her final decision. "That's the date of the next Bishops staff. We will discuss the post again then."

Charlotte nodded. She knew when David had had enough. She wouldn't argue. She was also conscious of his beckoning family commitments. And she was grateful, that at least he had shown some

15

recognition that she had a family, even if it was outside his immediate experience, and even if he had drawn the wrong conclusion, but he wasn't alone in that. It had all been part of the elaborate and painstaking detail that she had developed over the years to put people off the scent. An overtly gay lodger, who she can absolutely with honesty say she is not sleeping with, is quite a good decoy.

David stood up, as Charlotte made her way to the door in the opposite corner of the room, but just as she placed her hand on the old brass handle he faintly called after her "Charlotte...." She turned, her hand still resting on the latch. David held his hand out to her. "Give yourself some time, please. Thank you for being honest. I respect you for that."

Charlotte took his hand, and Bishop David responded by grasping it in both of his. "You are a good priest Charlotte. We need people like you." But he allowed his voice to slow and fade as he uttered the last few words. The hypocrisy of them, just a little more than he could bear. He released his grasp, reached over and opened the door to allow Charlotte to go.

David went to the coffee table and picking up his now lukewarm mug of coffee took it back to his desk and slumped down in the modern blue ergonomic chair that Catrin had insisted was good for his back, but that he maintained looked totally out of place in his seven-hundred-year-old study. He thought about the last ninety minutes, then reached down to the bottom right hand drawer of his desk and took out the battered old brown leather notebook. Opening it up at the next blank page he wrote:

January 8ᵗʰ 2009.

'Be still and know that I am God.' I wish you'd stop telling me to be still when there is so much to sort out. Why couldn't the psalmist say 'Be busy and still know that I am God?'

Then he put the book back in the drawer, moved the chair back away from the desk, spun around briefly on the axis, before standing up to head out the other door and up the back stairs to his own flat where Catrin was no doubt waiting with a cheese sandwich. As he reached the door, he suddenly remembered he hadn't prayed with Charlotte before she'd left and at that moment realised just how emotional he felt. She was probably still with Sally, but rather than rushing to find her, he simply stood where he was, opened his hands in an act of submission and prayed.

"Lord, thank you for Sally, give her the right words to say to Charlotte and the wisdom to know when to be silent. Keep Charlotte safe on her journey home and grant her the motivation she needs to take time to think this through. And, Lord I pray that Catrin is not too annoyed about the delay. In Jesus' name. Amen"

Chapter 2

"So how was the chat with the Bish?"

"How do you know I was seeing the Bishop?" Charlotte had come in through the back door and was slipping off her shoes in the scullery when Sasha called out from the kitchen.

"It's circled on your monthly planner above your desk. 'Bishop'."

Sasha made a gesture as if underlining the word in the air. She was unloading the dishwasher when Charlotte eventually got home having made a detour to the supermarket for a sandwich and to pick up a couple of beers to have that evening with the fish and chips she was planning to buy from the mobile chippy. Mr Baker only managed Tuesdays and as Charlotte had a wedding rehearsal at 6pm, chips seemed a good idea.

"I saw it yesterday," continued Sasha, "when you demanded I sort out the rubbish for the dustbin men this morning."

"Only because you haven't done it since last year!"

"Give me a chance its only one week in."

Sasha had lodged with Charlotte for three years. She worked in London three days a week and had a flat just off the Old Kent Road, but had been born and brought up in Cornwall and preferred to live away from the city as much as her work would allow. She'd known Charlotte for just over ten years, when she had been a student at Exeter University where Charlotte had worked as Chaplain. Sasha had been a mature student, well in years at least, if not quite in attitude and experience, studying business development and majoring in marketing. She'd found her way to the chaplaincy on numerous occasions partly because she felt lonely and had difficulty fitting into student life and partly because she had a soft spot for Charlotte, although she had never let on. Charlotte had taken her under her wing and had given her a part time job managing the room bookings when her secretary took maternity leave and she was left with limited support from the typing pool.

"So, you still got a job, or did he give you the sack?" quipped Sasha, with no idea that her comments were not so far from the truth.

"Drop it Sash and just put the kettle on." Charlotte sat down at the kitchen table, probably her favourite room in the house.

"Oh come on Charlie, I'm only joking. Lighten up, this isn't like you."

"Sorry, long tiring morning. It was very foggy across the moors on the way over, quite icy in places. Do you fancy chips tonight? I've topped up the beer supply."

"Great – if he comes."

"Should do – it's Tuesday."

"Yeah, but old grumpy doesn't like the cold weather and without the tourists he might just decide it is not worth the trouble."

"Joys of rural living!"

"You got a meeting tonight?"

"Wedding rehearsal at St Agnes, 6pm."

"I'll put the oven on for 7pm – and get the plates hot."

"Domestic bliss- what would I do without you?"

"Go and live with that long-suffering partner of yours no doubt!"

Charlotte smiled. She'd been lucky to find a good friend in Sasha, someone to trust, without the emotional baggage. They were good for each other, each living their own lives, each enjoying their own space but providing a bit of company when needed. And in a large old rambling rectory, with half an acre of land, in the middle of the Devon countryside, there was plenty of space.

"You had lunch?" asked Sasha.

"I grabbed a sani' and an apple at Tesco in Exeter and had it up on the moor on the way home. The fog had cleared by then. Haven't you got work to do?"

"Slave driver! Yeah, I'm just waiting for a response from the boss about some art work I've sent across." Sasha was leaning against the sink waiting for the kettle to boil. "Tea?"

"Cheers, I think I'll get out of this suit. Back down in a tick." Charlotte slid across the kitchen floor in her tights, into the tiled hall and spun around the newel post at the bottom of the stairs, but rather than go on up, she sat down on the second step put her head in her hands and let the tears that she'd been keeping back, since David had grasped her hand at the end of their meeting, flow down her cheeks and course a salty path across her lips and onto her tongue. She stayed there for a few minutes before the parish phone broke the silence. She let it ring, the answer phone would pick it up. Then she rallied herself, ran on up the stairs and quickly changed into some dark grey trousers, a black clerical shirt and pulled on a warm beige-coloured jumper. St Agnes Church would be freezing at 6pm and it wasn't worth firing up the old boiler for a wedding rehearsal.

Sasha was calling up the stairs. "You got lost up there? Tea's on the table, I'd better get back to work."

"Thanks Sash." Charlotte glanced at her watch. 3pm already. She'd need to go at 5.30pm to get to St Agnes in the next village. Why people wanted to get married in old cold churches in the middle of winter she didn't know! She knew they'd be keen to decorate with candles and make it look mystical. It'd be mystical alright if the Dartmoor fog came in and if the fuse box blew like on Christmas Eve: Thank goodness for the musical talents of the churchwarden's daughter home from Bristol University, 'Carols by candle light *and Flute!*'

Charlotte picked up her tea from the kitchen and made her way to the study at the front of the house. It overlooked the front gate, which meant she could see any visitors before they made it as far as the front door, which just occasionally was quite an advantage. She picked up the post from the hallway table and pushed open the door with her foot, plonked the tea on the desk and looked over to the machine; seven messages. Not too bad seeing as she'd been out all day. She was tempted to leave the post for Linda who'd be in the next morning to help out with the parish admin, but she quickly looked through to spot the junk she could throw out immediately and made sure there was nothing private, before putting the rest into Linda's tray on the other desk. They shared the study with ease, as Charlotte was rarely there for any length of time during the day and even if she was, it was big enough to accommodate both of them. When Charlotte had first come to the parish there had been no secretarial support at all. The previous Rector had managed with the help and support of his wife. She had been paid a nominal sum on his expenses, but nothing official. Charlotte had changed all that. She'd been used to running a busy chaplaincy with three part-time staff including an excellent secretary, when she wasn't busy producing more babies to populate the county. The first few months in the parish had been a nightmare. No secretary, no broadband service, limited mobile phone connection, no digital TV network, an ongoing battle against a long-

21

held prejudice towards women priests from some sections of the community, desperate feelings of loneliness in a huge house, and an overwhelming sense of looming bindweed in the patch of land that had once been a well-kept garden. Five years on most of those problems were a thing of the past, apart from the bindweed.

Her thoughts were interrupted by the sound of digital bird song. Her "home" phone was ringing.

"You still alive?" Max was ringing on her 'hands-free' between clients and the line was appalling.

"Just about!"

"Any chance you could come over tonight? Asked Max, "Whatever happened I know you could do with a hug!"

"I'd love to b...."

"But you have a meeting," sighed Max.

"I've got a wedding rehearsal at 6pm, promised to have fish and chips with Sash and I really ought to prepare for tomorrows delegation visit about the disabled loo at St Nicks. I've not even looked at the plans Mrs Harlow sent over. Oh, and I promised to speak to Sam later about that funeral he's doing."

"You mean I have to wait till Friday?"

"'Fraid so. This line is terrible, can you ring me later? Sometime after ten?" But the line went dead. If Charlotte had been overly sensitive she'd have thought Max had put the phone down on her, but she knew better than that, more than likely she'd simply got out of range down a country lane. She got her own mobile out of her briefcase, texted

'Ring after 10. Promise long chat, luv Cx,'

and pressed send. Max would be able to pick it up when she stopped. "God," she prayed out loud, "I'm lucky to have her!"

Charlotte listened to the messages on the machine. *Two callers who left no message*. She liked messages like that; another message from the couple about the rehearsal asking if they could bring candles to set up in the church. 'No surprises there then' she thought to herself. A long and drawn out message from an excitable woman, who wanted to arrange a wedding at St Judoc because her boyfriend had proposed over Christmas and although they thought about their own parish, really liked the look of St Judoc and wondered when they could meet up to make all the arrangements and would tomorrow evening be alright because her boyfriend had to go back to the army barracks in Kent on Friday because he was about to go back to Afghanistan......... Charlotte was exhausted just listening to the message and immediately felt a small weight descend across her shoulders. It would be a difficult conversation when she spoke to the poor young woman later that evening. She doubted the couple would have the right legal connection to marry in the picturesque church of St Judoc.

Next message revealed that the organist at St Bartholomew wanted to change one of Sunday's hymns, and had then rung again about hymns for a funeral at St Hilda's in Sheepsgate later that week. The last message was from Jack, husband of a fellow priest who was ringing around on Gill's behalf trying to arrange a get together for her birthday on the 30th in Plymouth. It always made Charlotte giggle to think that a couple actually existed called Jack and Gill, especially with a surname like 'Hill'. Poor Gill she'd known her for years ever since theological college. You should have heard the jokes at their wedding – the vicar could hardly keep a straight face. She quickly rang Jack and left a message saying that the 30th was okay. She knew it was the day before she was due to see the Bishop again, but that wasn't until noon. Then she got out the wedding file and checked through the paper work and service sheet for the rehearsal that evening. She knew that for the next few hours she would have to put the morning's meeting behind her and concentrate on the more immediate business of running the parishes. She also had a chapter meeting the following day and quickly rang Rupert, the vicar of the parish hosting the meeting. Then she rang the Director from the new eco-friendly funeral services company who was giving the talk at the meeting. He was out on a funeral visit but his secretary confirmed the arrangements.

She glanced at the clock. 4.45pm, just time to check some emails. Fourteen since she'd checked them earlier that morning. Four from the school all entitled 'Collective Worship' all sent at the same time. 'I wish they'd get that server problem sorted out,' she thought to herself. Her reply confirmed that she would be at St Nicholas School at 9.15am on Thursday and would bring her guitar. An e-mail from the Archdeacon about the delegation visit, asking Charlotte to bring the most up-to-date plans, as if she would forget! One from the chair of the committee also asking her to bring the plans. 'Who do these men think I am?' One from the PCC secretary asking her if she should bring the plans! Charlotte sent one e-mail responding to all, copied to all the other members of the delegation and members of her own planning group confirming that she would bring the paper plans as well as her lap top with the 3D drawings from Mrs Harlow, the architect, in case she was running a little late. She spotted another email from Max and one from her nephew, but she'd leave those till later. Three were obviously spam, so got deleted. One from the magazine editor reminding her to include a note on the weekly notice sheet about payment, which she printed off and left for Linda and one from Derek a 'house-for-duty' priest asking her if she could drop by to discuss some changes to the rota.

It was not always easy accommodating Derek, but he and Helen, his wife, give as much time and support as they possibly can so she hardly ever allowed her own frustration to show. Derek is still of working age, but is financially supported by his wife, who is head-teacher of the local comprehensive school. Derek had a serious road traffic accident ten years previous just after he had turned forty. He had been ordained priest when he was thirty-four but had continued teaching RE whilst helping out in his parish, so he had never been full time in a ministry post and never been paid for it. He had been knocked off his push bike by a motorcycle. Derek hadn't been wearing a helmet and suffered a severe head injury. It had left him partially paralysed down the left side of his body as well as slightly slurred speech. It meant his teaching days were over. When the house for duty in the sleepy village of Mutton came up, he applied and was delighted to be given a chance. Not paid for what he does in the parish, and only receiving expenses is a huge commitment, but 'House for duty' means they live rent free, giving he and Helen an extra income from renting out their old house whilst living in the delightful Victorian vicarage. It gave Derek back some of his self-confidence and sense of self-worth. The mental pain of becoming disabled had been worse than any physical pain he had endured whilst in hospital.

Another member of the team is Roger, a recently retired priest in his late sixties. An absolute God send. He is very active in the benefice, but never pushy and has a huge amount of respect for Charlotte. He and his wife, Jean, thoroughly enjoy their retirement in Southbridge and know they are very lucky to enjoy good health and make the most of it whilst they can. They have two sons both with extremely well paid jobs, one in America and one in Canada. They pay for their parents to visit them twice a year for about a month at a time. Once between Christmas and Easter and once over the summer, fitting in with the major Christian festivals but always ensuring they are around to give Charlotte a well needed break from time to time.

The fourth member of the team is Sam, a twenty-four-year-old unmarried man in his first post following ordination and still learning the trade. He had trained at Cuddesdon. Sam is extremely bright and enthusiastic, with a very promising career ahead of him. It is up to Charlotte with the assistance of Roger, Derek and the rest of the parish to mould him into a well-rounded priest before sending him out to face his own churchwardens, organists and funeral directors. Sam had a habit of introducing new and fantastic ideas, but not quite managing to work out how it would happen in the reality of a scattered group of rural parishes on the edge of Dartmoor. Charlotte hoped Sam would make it to the wedding rehearsal as he would be conducting his own weddings later that year, but he was also trying to arrange a funeral visit with a family on the other side of the benefice in one of the farms just outside Upton and might not make it back in time. She'd ring him later.

Charlotte's palm top suddenly bleeped a warning that she only had half an hour before her next meeting. She could get to most of her benefice from most places within half an hour, so it was generally speaking a good system, unless she hit milking time!

"Sash" She called upstairs, "I'm off, don't forget the plates". No answer. "Sash..." The flush went.

"Give a girl some privacy – I heard you," she called out as she opened the bathroom door. "And you'll bring home chips for 7pm?"

"Make it 7.15 by the time I get back."

"More like 7.45 knowing you, you'll end up arranging a baptism in the queue waiting for your mushy peas!"

"No way – it's too cold – see you later."

"Bye."

Sasha went back to her newsletter. The company she was working for wanted the reviewed proofs that evening. She hoped they could do all the work via email but it looked as if she would still have to go up to London on Thursday and probably have to stay till Saturday morning. Business was going well. Most of the companies she had contracts with were London based, but a couple were in Plymouth and one in Exeter. She was working on a new contract in Taunton and possibly one in Bristol and hoped she could soon be totally based in the South West. So many companies were moving out of London. She could sell the flat, make a packet and commute from a little place in the country, but it would mean letting Charlie down. Working from home meant being disciplined and keeping her mind on the job so she returned to sorting out the new layout trying to keep a clean professional look whilst still including the two new articles the company had just sent through.

Chapter 3

Lizzie looked at her watch. She would try her mother's mobile one more time. She couldn't imagine what would be keeping them. Sally assured her they had left just after 2pm and hoped to be in Gloucester by 5.00pm. Catrin had promised to pop into the mall to pick up the new Thomas the Tank Engine curtains for Joshua that Lizzie had ordered from John Lewis. It was gone six and no message. Lizzie wondered if Michael would get chance to ring and say goodnight to Heather but he would probably be too busy at the launch until way after midnight when she would get the usual text. Something he always did when working away from home.

The door-bell went. "Thank goodness," thought Lizzie. She admitted to herself that she had started to get quite anxious. She opened the door and froze. She stared at the two women standing on her door step, one was in police uniform, the other in a long overcoat. The woman in plain clothes took out a small black wallet and said something, but Lizzie's mind went into turmoil. She heard Joshua crying in the background and Heather came running to the door, probably expecting her much loved granny and grandpa. She saw the strangers and immediately hid behind her mummy, pulling the folds of her skirt around her and clutching her manky old blanket which was never far from her grasp. Joshua carried on yelling.

The woman in uniform spoke. "Mrs Tannin?"

Lizzie nodded. "Perhaps we could come in?" and gently but firmly reached out her right arm as if she was reminding Lizzie what "in" meant. Little Heather grabbed her mummy's knees, Lizzie reached down and picked her up, holding her close. She felt something deep inside her tighten forming a constricting knot preparing her insides to receive what she innately knew was to be bad news. A strange thought crossed her mind and she found herself hoping it was not going to be both her parents. She wished Michael was not all the way down in London. It would take him three hours to get back, even if she could get in touch with him immediately, which was unlikely.

She led the two women into the toy strewn lounge and for once didn't apologise for the mess.

"Is your baby alright?" asked the women in the long coat.

"Oh goodness, yes," as if Lizzie had only just heard her baby's cry. "Yes, please just sit down for a moment, I'll go and get him. Heather stay here with the nice ladies. Why don't you show them your new dolls pram?" Lizzie rushed out of the room, before the women had chance to say anything else. She ran up the stairs and into her room, where little Joshua had only just woken up for his feed. He desperately needed his nappy changed. David would have taken pride in doing that, but he wasn't there. It was strange how she seemed to operate on automatic. She didn't even know why the women were there. She had left her little daughter alone with them. As if in a trance, she carried on changing her son's nappy. It was as if she needed to hear whatever the news was in her own time. She knew what it was going to be. Her mum and dad would always ring if they were going to be later than twenty minutes and they were well over an hour overdue.

Joshua was as good as gold and appeared to smile at his mum as she cleaned him with wet wipes and put on a fresh nappy. Then she picked him up in her arms and slowly went back downstairs, to hear Heather

29

telling the two women all about her own baby and how she took her out for walks in the new pram that Granny had brought when she had come to meet her new brother. Lizzie swallowed back the tears. How hard it must be for the women, knowing that this little granddaughter would never see her grandparents again.

"I'm sorry, I haven't even offered you any tea." It was a situation that Detective Wilson had been in twice before, but it was the first time for Constable Barrow. Wilson took the lead.

"Is there anyone who could look after the little ones for a short while? A neighbour perhaps?"

For one awful moment Lizzie wondered if she was about to be arrested for something in a case of wrongful identity. Then in a strange almost mischievous goading manner, as if pushing the women into saying what they had so obviously come to say she said. "My parents will be here soon, they're coming up from Exeter but they must have been delayed."

Barrow glanced at Wilson who kept a strong composure.

"Mrs Tannin, I'm afraid we have some bad news."

Lizzie braced herself for the news. She still had Joshua in her arms and sub-consciously held him close, realising that her dad had never seen him and was never going to. She heard the woman's voice but couldn't quite understand what she was saying.

"Your husband's car has been involved in a serious accident this afternoon." Detective Wilson looked quickly down at Heather who seemed pre-occupied with her doll and pram and was taking no notice of the conversation. She added quietly, "Your husband is missing, Mrs Tannin. We can't locate him."

Lizzie looked at the women in shocked disbelief.

"My husband is in London," she said simply.

Wilson continued. "Mrs Tannin this is very difficult, can you tell us if your husband was driving his car this afternoon?"

"He's in London."

"Mrs Tannin have you spoken to your husband since about 3pm this afternoon?"

"No of course not. He was driving to London and then straight into a meeting. He'll ring later at the children's bed time."

"Mrs Tannin," Wilson persisted in trying to get her message across. "There has been a terrible accident, many cars were involved, including a transporter and a coach and we fear your husband may have been involved. What time are you expecting your parents?"

"Michael is in London." Lizzie was pale and clammy in a state of shock.

"Mrs Tannin, is there a neighbour?" Detective Wilson repeated her earlier request. She kept an air of firm reality on the situation. Barrow had turned her attention to Heather, who had climbed up onto her mother's lap alongside a little baby brother.

The front door opened. "Lizzie, we're here," called Catrin. "We're so sorry we're late love. There was a dreadful accident just after Bristol. We saw it happen, it was awful. Those poor people. We couldn't do anything. The police were there within seconds and turned us back. We were diverted along the A38. Your dad was late leaving as usual, but we managed to get the curtains. Get the kettle on love we could both do with a good strong cuppa. Did you know there's a police car outside your...... Oh!"

31

Wilson met David's eye first, a little taken aback at the cerise coloured shirt and dog collar. He had been running so late that Catrin hadn't even let him change.

"What on earth has happened love?" Catrin fell into the sofa next to her daughter putting her arm across her shoulders and gently pulling her close, as if she was still just a small child, even though she was clutching both her three-week-old son and her four-year-old little girl.

David held out his hand and rather formally greeted first Detective Wilson and then Constable Barrow, an action born out of habit. He looked over at his daughter, who was in shock. She was staring straight ahead of her, holding her children close. Joshua started crying again, sensitive to his mother's anxiety and Heather joined in, not understanding what was going on, but distressed by her mother's reaction. Then she suddenly climbed down and ran to her grandpa, who lifted her into his arms and held her close.

"Is it Michael?" he asked.

Wilson nodded to Barrow, who picked up the cue and attempted to explain, trying to be brief and clear, just as she had been taught. "Mr Tannin has been involved in a fatal car accident sir." She hesitated and then stumbling over her words, "er, …. his car sir, his car has been involved. We, er…. we can't track him down…..I'm sorry sir, but he is feared dead, Sir."

Lizzie, gasped.

"I beg your pardon?" asked David, "Did you say dead?"

"NO! NO!" Lizzie screamed and Catrin held her daughter tighter than ever.

Detective Wilson took over again "Sir, my colleague said feared dead. We don't know. We found his car down an embankment, but it was engulfed in the fire. I'm sorry, but we are not too sure what we've found. I am so sorry."

Lizzie suddenly turned and started sobbing into her mother's shoulder.

"Dead?" was all David could say, as he held his beloved granddaughter closer than ever, as if shielding her from the horror of the news.

Barrow seemed to gain a new confidence. "Feared dead, yes sir. This afternoon a terrible accident on the motorway involving......" But Wilson stood up placing a restraining hand on Barrows shoulder. There would be time enough for explanation and Barrow hadn't quite grasped that the older couple already knew about the accident, and by the sounds of it might even have seen it, perhaps thankful not to have been involved. Tragically they had been wrong and it was slowly dawning on them they were now very much involved as they tried to comfort their daughter and grandchildren.

"All we are trying to ascertain at this stage is whether any of the family have had contact with Mr Tannin since 3pm today, the time of the accident." Wilson addressed her question to David, leaving the two women to comfort one another, but Lizzie yelled out.

"He's Michael, Michael, my Michael – not Mr Tannin and no I haven't heard from him. You just said he's been killed…….."

"We don't know. That is what we are trying to find out." Constable Barrow was trying hard to keep her voice under control, to stay strong.

"Sorry to ask you this Sir, but perhaps you could confirm for us what sort of car Mr Tannin owned?" David just shook his head.

Turning to his wife he said, "I'll take Heather into the kitchen, this is no place for a child." Heather was crying now, not for her daddy, she hadn't fully understood what had been said, but was upset because her mummy had shouted and was crying. She started to struggle and began pummelling her granddad on his chest. David simply held her closer as he carried her back into the hall. She started kicking, so David changed his grip and held her legs close to him too. The physical pain a four year could inflict was nothing to the pain he felt at that moment for his middle daughter. He had supported hundreds of bereaved people in his time and amongst them quite a few bereaved parents. He didn't feel bereaved himself in that moment, his grief was for what his daughter had lost.

He sat on one of the hard kitchen chairs, still holding on to Heather. She had calmed down, stopped struggling and put her arms around her grandpa's neck whispering, "Why were those ladies' naughty?"

"What makes you think they are naughty poppit?"

"Mummy shouted at them, and she only shouts at me when I'm naughty."

David stood up again from the chair and turning around sat Heather gently down onto it. He knelt down beside little Heather and put his hands either side of the chair.

"I don't think the ladies were naughty. Mummy was shouting because she is sad, big people do that sometimes." As soon as David had uttered the words, he knew what was coming next, but hadn't had time to think about what to say, and didn't even know what Lizzie would want him to say.

"But why is Mummy sad?" asked a very concerned and confused little four-year-old.

David found himself thinking about all the things he once counselled parents not to say. He had encouraged parents and grandparents to be honest with children. When asked, he had suggested children attend funerals and not hide death from them. But now, he took the easy route, and would work out the more difficult one later. "Mummy's sad because Daddy's gone away." David winced waiting for the next question about when Daddy might be back, it didn't come.

"Grandpa, can I have a biscuit?" David was just about to say that it might spoil her tea but stopped himself. There would be plenty to spoil tea that evening, so found the tin and let Heather choose one of the chocolate animal ones. She picked out an elephant and sat happily licking off the chocolate and wiping her fingers down her *'here comes trouble'* T shirt, the irony of which was lost on her. David made a pot of tea. He had only caught a brief glimpse of his grandson, and knew that he would never forget that the day he had first met him was the same day the little boy also lost his daddy, a daddy he would only ever know through photos and other people's memories.

"Grandpa, why are you crying?" Heather reached up a chocolate covered hand and wiped it on the Bishops shirt, but it didn't matter.

David hadn't even noticed his own tears, "I'm a little bit sad too."

"Because of Daddy?"

"Yes, because of Daddy."

"Don't worry Grandpa, he'll be home tomorrow," and reached into the tin for another chocolate elephant. David turned wiping his eyes with his hankie and carried on preparing the tea. 'Time enough', he thought to himself, 'for explanations about where Daddy had gone and why he wasn't coming home later. It would wait until little Heather was being held close against the warmth of either her mother's or her grandmother's breast'.

Chapter 4

'Mr Grumpy' as Sasha had described the mobile fish and chip man, had decided it was worth the trip to Langford on a cold January evening. The villagers made sure it was worth his while and a short queue had formed much to Charlottes surprise and slight annoyance. It was nearly 7.30pm and Charlotte was famished. Her feet felt like they had blocks of ice attached to the soles. The wedding couple had indeed spent most of the first thirty minutes discussing candles with their florist who they had also invited to the rehearsal. Charlotte had spent the time practicing relaxation techniques to control the growing anger as she stood waiting for the couple to make their decorative arrangements before deciding to turn their attention to the small matter of the actual ceremony.

There was the usual gossip in the queue, which Charlotte largely ignored. One or two were chatting about some accident up near Bristol. It sounded serious, but Charlotte's mind was still on the safety of four little bridesmaids carrying lit candles, which was what the couple had in mind! Bridesmaids usually had hair rigid with spray with bits hanging out. Highly flammable! Charlotte physically shuddered at the thought.

"Ev'ning Rector, haddock or plaice tonight?" Old Grumpy sounded quite upbeat.

"If you have two pieces of haddock ready I'll take those and a large chips."

"Right' y'are", the new improved version of 'Grumpy' threw the chips into the bag, added an extra scoop and threw on a piece of haddock. "You want them wrapped separate love?"

"No thanks Mr Baker, I'll put them on plates when I get back." She watched as the second piece of haddock was added to the mound of chips. "You sound up-beat today."

"So I should, aint y'heard? My Ned's become a dad. I'm a granddad at long last. Still wish they'd gone and gotten wed first. Yer, pr'aps, you'd do 'em and little'n all at same time?"

"Perhaps I could Mr Baker. Ask them to come and see me sometime." Charlotte stifled a giggle, remembering what Sash had said about arranging baptisms in the queue whilst she waited for the chips, maybe she'd secured a wedding at the same time.

Charlotte paid for her chips. "Congratulations Mr Baker, have you seen the little fella yet?"

"Met him this afternoon, 'andsome."

Charlotte smiled as she took her well wrapped package.

"Yer maid 'ave one o' these on the 'ouse." And Mr Baker handed over a pickled egg.

"That's very kind of you Mr Baker, thank you very much" She'd have preferred a pot of mushy peas, but took it graciously.

A few minutes later she arrived home. "Chips!" She shouted, "and guess what, 'Grumpy' isn't any more, he's a granddad." Her grand entrance was met with silence. "Sash, where are you?" Charlotte had come in through the front door and kicked her shoes off in the hall before going through to the kitchen. She felt the oven. It was cold. This was unlike Sasha, she may emit an air of scatter brain academia, but was in fact these days very organised which was why her business was going so well.

"Charlie." Sasha was framed by the kitchen door. Her eyes were red and swollen and she clutched a very soggy tissue.

"Sash, love, what on earth is wrong? What's happened? Come on, come and sit down and I'll make us some tea." Charlotte began fussing around. She turned on the oven and put the plates in to warm and added the chips to keep them from getting cold. Then she turned her attention to making tea, but still Sasha stood in the door way, not saying a word. Suddenly realising Sasha was still pinned to the spot, Charlotte went over and put her arm gently across Sash's shoulders, drawing her close. "Sash, whatever is it? Come and sit down."

She led her to one of the kitchen chairs. "Now please, tell me what's wrong. You're frightening me." Charlotte knelt down in front of Sasha, her hands holding the side of the chair. How could she have known she was echoing the actions of her Bishop who had done just the same, when comforting his little granddaughter just a short while ago.

"There's been an accident." Sasha suddenly blurted it out looking straight at Charlotte and holding her gaze for as long as she could, before breaking down again and sobbing into her tissue. Charlotte took another from the box and handed it to Sasha. She had been alongside so many others who had received sudden and shocking news, and she knew well enough to take things at their own pace and let it come when they were ready. So, she waited. It took Sasha a moment to compose herself before trying to speak. In that short pause, several possibilities shot through her mind; Sasha had a brother in Iraq; her grandmother had only recently come out of hospital after a fall. She wondered if Sasha had accidentally damaged something, but that wouldn't make her this upset. If it was somebody in the parish, the queue at the Fish and Chip van would have been buzzing already, word gets around fast in the country. She remembered somebody saying something about an accident on the motorway, but that was miles away. Then Charlotte's heart froze and she felt herself go rigid with fear. When Max had rung, she had got cut off. She took her mobile from her pocket – no text, no voice mail.

She looked at Sasha and with a faltering voice urged her "Who is it Sash? Please tell me."

Sasha took a gulp of air through a sob and clutched Charlottes hand but still said nothing. "Oh, dear God, Sasha please – is it Max?" Charlotte wasn't blaspheming, it was a genuine prayer.

"No, it's Michael."

"Michael?" Charlotte slumped back onto her ankles, with some relief that it wasn't Max but in that moment, couldn't think who Sasha meant. Her look must have betrayed the confusion.

"Michael, Max's brother. Charlie, he's dead."

"Dead? What do you mean dead? How? What's happened?"

"The accident on the M5. Max rang about ten minutes ago. She's going over to her parents in Plymstock. Can you go across? The police are still with them."

"Dead? His poor wife! The kids! I can't believe it. Of course, I must go. I can't imagine……… Mo and Vince…. They must be in a state. Yes. I must go. I'll just ring Sam tell him.... What do I tell him?"

Charlotte was still sitting in front of Sasha. But now it was Sasha's turn to offer some comfort. She slipped down onto the floor next to Charlotte and held her close. "You'll think of something. Just tell him you've been called away. I'll ring him if you like."

"No, I'll ring him. Thanks Sasha, but I can't really have the lodger ringing the curate, can I?"

"To be honest I don't see why not." Sasha often struggled with Charlotte's insistence on keeping her away from any parish business. Charlotte didn't respond to her but just continued. "I can't believe it…….. I must get going."

"Then take your mobile," said Sasha, "Ring Sam on the way. You'll think of something. Just say you've been called out. You don't have to say why. He's the curate not your boss!"

"He'll want to know more."

"For goodness sake Charlie, just go. For once put Max first, before your precious parish."

Charlotte turned and hugged Sasha. On automatic pilot, she ran to her study, picked up her pastoral services book and bible stuffing them into her brief case along with her diary, phone and then in a ridiculous moment of management madness squeezed in the plans for the St Nick's development that she'd need in the morning and grabbed her laptop.

The phone went. She hoped it might be Max, but she'd ring on the mobile. The answer phone clicked in. Charlotte waited to listen to the message being left. They'd have to wait she thought. She heard the voice of the young excited woman wanting to arrange a wedding. Charlotte hesitated, then picked up the phone.

"Hello….. Yes, I'm Reverend Northern…… Yes, I got your message but I'm afraid I've been called out on an emergency, I'll have to ring you tomorrow…… No I really can't speak now I'm so sorry, I will you ring tomorrow. Are you in early evening? I'll try you then….. Yes, I promise, sorry I really must go. Bye for now…… yes it is exciting, but

41

we will have to discuss it tomorrow before your fiancé leaves for his base, bye for now, yes bye." Charlotte put the phone down and saw Sasha in the doorway.

"I don't know how you do it. Your would-be brother-in-law has just been killed and you find time to talk as cool as a cucumber to some blond bimbo wanting to arrange a wedding."

"That doesn't sound like a compliment."

"It isn't." Sasha had gone from distraught to angry in the space of a couple of minutes – "for goodness sake Charlie, get your ass over to Plymstock where your family need you." Her voice was unexpectedly forceful.

"Thanks Sash." Charlie's thanks was far from sarcastic. Sash's reprimand was the kick she needed.

Charlotte left, briefcase in one hand, car keys in the other and still managed to peck Sash on the cheek before dashing to her car.

"But drive carefully," called Sash, before she went back to the kitchen and turned off the oven leaving the chips to go cold.

Charlotte took the narrow lane and onto the B3459 which would take her onto the top moor road and eventually down to Plymstock. She turned on the radio and waited for the 8pm news. She knew nothing of the accident, but remembered Sash had said something about the M5. She was sure a fatal accident on a motorway would feature. It was a way of preparing herself before she got to the family. It would take about forty minutes to get to Plymstock. She suddenly realised she was treating this like any other pastoral emergency. Trying to gather as much information as possible, wondering in advance how best to approach the situation thinking about what she would say and at which point to offer prayer. It then hit home to her exactly what had happened and she was momentarily ashamed by what she had been thinking and feeling. This was not a professionally removed pastoral visit. She pulled into a farm gate entrance, and turned off the engine.

'Max has lost her brother,' she said to herself. 'Michael, who we both love is gone.' She still she felt little more than the professional emotion of empathy. It was the sort of feeling she often felt for a family before a bereavement visit. She took her mobile out and was thankful that she had a signal. She rang Max's number.

"Charlie, where are you? Are you on your way?"

Charlotte didn't answer but asked "Max, oh Max I'm so sorry. Is it true? Is he….. dead?"

"*Feared* dead, we don't know for sure," Max was talking fast, her voice full of anxiety. "There was a fire involving three of the cars. Michael was in one of them, we think, but the police can't say for certain. One of the cars they think it's Mike's but…" her voice trailed off for a moment, "….. there's not a lot left of it, all burnt out and……"

"It's OK Max, don't say any more. How are your mum and dad?" asked Charlotte.

"Dad has made about six cups of tea in the past hour, mum is talking non-stop, thinking of every reason why Michael might not have been in the car." She took a deep breath. "Can you get here?"

"Yes, I'm on my way I've just pulled in to ring you. I'll be there in about thirty minutes. Are the police still there?"

"No, they are going to ring with any news. Just get here Charlie please I need you, and get here safe."

Charlotte rang off, 'Feared dead.' She felt an insane sense of hope. 'Maybe he wasn't in the car. Maybe he had lent the car to somebody else'. But she stopped herself, she was wishing harm to someone else by thinking such things. She just had to concentrate and get to Plymstock. But first she texted Sasha.

"There is hope. He may not be dead. They haven't actually found him."

She looked at the message, thought about ringing instead, but pressed send. Then she put the phone back in her brief case, started up the engine and pulled out. She'd forgotten to ring her curate.

On the journey, she shed no tears, her only thought was for Max and her parents. At least they knew about her and Max. They wouldn't have to pretend that Max had called her as a friend who happens to be a priest. She thought about Michael and his young family. He also knew about his sister's relationship and was a great support, although felt he had to keep his own family in the dark, which was sad. Charlotte knew that, in the eyes of Michael's in-laws, whom she'd never met, Max was a successful single vet, with a flourishing practice in Devon. Charlotte hadn't been invited to Michael's wedding and was ashamed to admit she couldn't even remember his wife's name. So many random thoughts were crisscrossing Charlottes mind. She had to concentrate. She would be needed both as partner and professional tonight.

Eventually Charlotte drove onto the Tannin's drive, just as a police car pulled up outside the house. The officers didn't get out immediately so Charlotte knocked at the door and was greeted by Max's dad. "You didn't have to come in uniform love." Charlotte looked behind expecting to see one of the officers. Vince pointed to his neck.

44

"Oh, sorry," apologised Charlotte, as she pulled out the white clerical collar and undid her top button, "I've come straight from work!" Vince smiled, even in the midst of such crisis he still had such a gentle nature.

"Any more news?" asked Charlotte.

Vince pointed to the police car, "Not yet, but I think you may have got here just in time. Do you want a cup of tea?"

'Why was it,' Charlotte thought to herself, 'that the British always drink copious amounts of tea in times of crisis?' Vince led Charlotte into the front room where Maureen and Max were sat on the sofa with Max's two Collies at their feet. Max got up, disturbing the two dogs who immediately started wagging their tails excitedly when they saw Charlotte.

"Charlie thank goodness you're here, I'm so glad to see you," said Maureen jumping up as fast as her arthritis would allow and hugged Charlotte, before Max had chance.

The doorbell rang again.

"A police car drove up just as I arrived," said Charlotte, bending down and making a fuss of the two dogs. "I'm so sorry Maureen."

Maureen had moved away from the sofa and stood waiting for her husband to answer the door to the officers. She knew they were about to bring the worst news of her life. Charlotte sat down next to Max, who so far hadn't said a word. Max simply clutched Charlotte's hand.

"Are you sure?" They heard Vincent's voice in the hallway. "Which hospital?"

Maureen stared towards the hall, not daring to hope that it might not be the news she had feared. Max however, still holding onto Charlotte's hand, lowered her voice so Maureen couldn't hear and whispered in

Charlotte's ear. "Maybe there is something to identify him. Will we have to go?"

"Let's just wait," replied Charlotte.

Vincent walked back into the room where his daughter and wife were waiting. He was white, his eyes wide, his heart was pounding. "We have to go to Bristol. They found Michael in some ditch. He's in intensive care, in a serious but stable condition. Oh Maureen, he's still alive. Charlie – I don't know if you prayed – but it's a miracle, an absolute bloody miracle. He must have somehow got out before the car caught fire. They think there were two impacts, one from the transporter and then seconds later from the oil tanker. Somehow, he got out of the car, but he might have been struck by another vehicle throwing him over the embankment. That's where they found him. He's been air lifted him to Frenchay Hospital. He's still with us. It'll take a couple of hours to get to Bristol, but we must go."

"Look, you can't take the dogs, I'll take them back with me."

"Charlie, no please you must come, the dogs can wait in the car."

"Max, Michael's wife will be there and her mum and dad possibly, let's not complicate things, not now. He was always so adamant that we shouldn't meet them – well not as a couple anyway."

"Charlie please, I need you there. You can wear your collar, come as our parish priest if you must."

"Michael has his reasons. Let's just see. I can do my bit with the dogs. Just go, but ring me, let me know what's happening. Please Max, it'll be for the best."

But Max persisted. She didn't want to do this without Charlie. "He doesn't mind, not really. He loves you as a sister. It's just his wife's family – come on Charlie this is about Mum, Dad and me."

"I think Charlie has a point love, leave it." Maureen could be very firm. Max looked at her father, who shook his head and then said "We should go, let Charlie take the dogs. You can come in our car."

"Might be best if we take two cars mum. I'll have to get back. You and Dad will probably want to stay. Why don't you take the Land Rover Charlie? It'll be easier with the dogs."

"And have the neighbours gossiping about a strange car in the driveway! No, you'll have to cope with your fuel guzzling monster on the motorway. The dogs will have to slum it in the hatchback, they'll be fine. Come on you'd better get going."

Max and Charlotte loaded the dogs into Charlotte's car, whilst Maureen and Vince shut up the house.

Once the dogs were secured in the car, Max turned to Charlotte, "He's going to be okay isn't he Charlie?"

Charlotte took Max in her arms and again held her tight. "Let's hope so Max. Make sure your dad doesn't get too tired. Why don't you all have a break at Exeter? Have a coffee or something."

Max buried her head into Charlotte's shoulder. Charlotte held her for a brief moment longer before saying "Your dad's waiting. Give Michael a hug from me if you can. Tell him to be strong."

Maureen and Vince slid into their Ford Mondeo and Max clambered up into her K Registered Land Rover. Charlotte watched as the two-car convoy left the side street heading for the main road as a salty tear escaped from the corner of her eye. She wiped it away wishing she could have gone with the family, but knew she'd be more useful as a dog sitter.

Charlotte attached the dogs to the discreet rings she and Max had installed in the back of the hatchback. It was still only 9.30pm, but Charlotte felt as if a whole lifetime had passed in those two short hours. She rang Sash.

"Charlie, oh my God. What's going on? How's Max? I didn't think I'd hear from you for ages. Your bloody work phone's been ringing like mad. Can't they leave you alone?"

"He's not dead Sash. They found him."

"Fuck!"

"Sash!"

"Sorry, but that's incredible. How can he be alive?"

"Nothing short of a miracle by the sounds of it. Look Sash, I'm on my way home and I've got Patch and Stitch with me. I'll fill you in when I get back."

"Yeah fine, I'll get their bowls out. See you in a bit."

Charlotte arrived home at 10.30pm having picked up some dog food from a supermarket in Plymstock. She let the dogs out into the back garden to do what they needed to do. Poor things were not getting a late-night walk, she was too shattered. She and Sash talked over a large whiskey in the kitchen, only interrupted by a call from Max at about midnight saying that they had arrived at the hospital but that Mike's wife and her mother were with him so they'd wait in the relative's room and would ring if there was any change. He was unconscious and had suffered multiple injuries from the second impact, but they didn't know

48

much more. Shortly after, Sash went to bed, knowing she had to drive to Exeter and catch the train to London the following day. Charlotte left the dogs in the kitchen and went to her study. She couldn't respond to any messages, so for once left the answer phone to flash in the darkness.

Chapter 5

At about 5am the next morning Charlotte was woken up by a scratching sound at her door. Patch or Stitch had obviously managed to open the kitchen door and were demanding attention. Charlotte dragged herself out of bed, annoyed that she had forgotten about the early morning exploits of her two charges and made a note to change the central heating clock to come on half an hour earlier. Pushing her feet into her slippers she shuffled across to the bedroom door and opened it to the delight of not one but two boisterous dogs, who nearly pushed her over in their excitement. 'Nice to be loved,' she thought.

She padded down the stairs and led the dogs to the back door to let them out for an early morning pee in the back garden, closing the door quietly behind her so as not to wake Sash, only to be startled by the phone extension suddenly bursting into life in the kitchen.

"St Nicholas Rectory," answered Charlotte.

"Oh good, you're up. I thought you might be. Did the dogs wake you?"

"Max. Why didn't you use the mobile?"

"I did, but it rang through to the voice mail."

And with that she heard Sash, "Charlie where the hell are you? Your mobile's been ringing. It might be Max."

"Sorry Sash," said Charlotte calling up the stairs, "Yes, it is Max. She's on the landline."

And then turning her attention back to the phone, "How's Michael?"

"No change. We've been up all night. They've got him sedated. His pelvis is shattered along with his right femur and his left shoulder looks bad."

"Oh no! What about his wife? Sorry I can't even remember her name."

"Liz. Shocked of course. Her mum is with her. Her dad stayed behind with the children."

"Good for him. Does anyone know what really happened?"

"They think Mike got out of his car but was hit by the tanker which threw him completely clear of the fire. That's what caused all the damage, but if he hadn't been hit....." She went quiet. "Well not a lot would have survived that fire."

"So........" Charlotte hesitated, not quite knowing how to ask. ".....what's the prognosis?"

"Well, he's already proven himself to be a fighter. They have every confidence he's going to pull through. As far as they can tell there's no significant head injury, just cuts and grazes across his face from where he fell, but his pelvis is in a right state. That's the most serious. He was in intensive care overnight to make sure he was stable. He'll be going up to theatre to reconstruct his pelvis and right leg. They've put the shoulder back in already. It dislocated when he fell. He's in quite a mess Charlie."

"And what about your mum and dad?"

"Exhausted, they haven't slept. They're going to stay up here for a few days. I'm going to book them into the Travelodge, but then I'll come back and go up again tomorrow with some of their things. They can buy the basics. What about the dogs?"

"Fine, well actually hold on, I need to let them back in." Charlie opened the back door and damp dogs left paw prints over the kitchen floor and wagged soggy tails over the cupboards. "Yes, they are absolutely fine. I'll take them for a walk in a minute."

"Can I call in on my way back?"

"You'd better."

"I'll be in the Land Rover. I'll leave it in the lane so it won't be recognised."

Charlotte suddenly realised just how facile the sham sounded. "At the moment, I really don't care. Bring it in. What time do you think you'll be here?"

"Changed your tune. Good! Can we have lunch? I'll need to get back for a 4pm surgery."

"Of course! Max, sweetheart, please take it easy, you've not had much sleep if any."

"I grabbed a couple of hours in a chair – I'll be fine, I'll be really careful, promise."

"See you soon. I love you Max. Don't forget it."

"Love you too." And with that Max hung up leaving Charlotte to find some old towels for the dogs, before giving an update to a bleary-eyed Sasha.

Charlotte loved the early morning, so as soon as it started to get light she took the dogs down her drive into the lane and back along the footpath behind the rectory and church. It would take them across the fields for about a mile before crossing back towards St Agnes church, about an hour's walk in total. It was damp but not cold. The walk would give Charlotte some time to think and even pray. The dogs enjoyed the freedom and chased each other, walking about three times the distance of Charlotte. She could hardly believe the events of yesterday. The tense morning with the Bishop, the wedding rehearsal, which seemed to concentrate far more on where to place the candles than on the actual lifelong promises the couple were going to say to each other, the conversation with Mr Baker about the birth of his grandson and then the roller coaster of emotions over Mike. She found herself thinking about Liz. She'd never met the poor woman, but she felt so sorry for her. It was a shock for all of them, but even more so for her and two little ones. She obviously had supportive parents nearby. She'd need them even more whilst Mike was recovering. He was so lucky to be alive, but it would be a while before he was back on his feet. She hoped the family would accept some help from her and Max, and hoped it would be as a couple for once, after all, she would soon have a bit more time on her hands. But those thoughts would need to be put to one side for a few days. She certainly didn't want to go on retreat, but how would she explain that to Bishop David? Honesty was probably the best policy, but no need yet, it could wait. There were more important things to think about.

The birds heralded a new day. Even with everything going on Charlotte still felt an immense gratefulness for life. She loved the countryside. She loved rural life. It was true some parishioners had a habit of thinking they knew everything about her and telling everyone else what they thought they knew, but apart from that, she enjoyed being part of a close-knit community and secretly enjoyed hearing the rumours that were so far from the truth. The only truth was that very few people knew very much about her private life at all.

When she got back to the rectory Sasha had already left. Charlotte gave the dogs their breakfast and made herself a large bacon butty, feeling ravenous after her walk and remembering that she hadn't actually had supper the previous evening and with the same thought peeped into the oven and found the now cold, but still wrapped fish and chips. She glanced at the dogs, but shook her head and decided last night's supper was destined for the bin.

She had an hour before the planning meeting. The doorbell went. It was Linda ready to do her morning in the office.

"Morning Vicar!" Linda's usual greeting. "You're looking a bit peaky. You're not sickening for something I hope. Can't have you off sick, the parish would never cope!"

"They would as long as you're around Linda. I'm just a bit tired." And with that both dogs bounded out from the kitchen only to be met with a firm "down" from Charlotte, which much to Charlotte's surprise, met with immediate obedience.

"That's impressive," admired Linda. "Your friend away on her hols again?"

"Er yes, sort of, just for a few days. I'll just barricade them in the kitchen."

"Oh, don't mind me, I love dogs" and she stooped down to make a fuss of them.

"I'm sure you do, but you haven't seen the pile of work I've got stored up for you."

"Slave driver," smiled Linda.

Charlotte dealt with her two charges, whilst Linda took off her coat and looked through the work on her desk.

"You want a coffee Linda?" Charlotte called out from the kitchen.

"Lovely."

Charlotte made a pot of fresh coffee, partly to give herself another injection of caffeine and partly because she knew Linda would get through a pot in the course of the morning.

"Your answer phone's flashing twelve messages Charlotte," said Linda when Charlotte came back with the coffee. "Do you want me to go through them?"

"Uh? Oh no, it's okay, I've got a good half an hour before I'm due at St Nicks. I got back a bit late last night and couldn't face them."

"No need to explain love," but Linda saw Charlotte wince. She hated being called love, or dear, especially by people younger than her. "Sorry Charlotte, I forgot."

"I'm just a bit touchy this morning, lack of sleep. Ignore me........ *love!*" And both women chuckled before getting on with their work.

Charlotte plugged the headphones into the answer phone, a helpful innovation when sharing an office.

As she went through message after message she could hardly believe what she was hearing. Apart from the young woman ringing again about her wedding, just wondering if Charlotte had got back from the emergency, all the messages were from members of her chapter wondering if she had heard the news that the Bishop had been involved in the massive pile up on the M5. Nobody had any details, but something had been said on the radio late last night. Charlotte stifled a gasp, just as Linda glanced across. She immediately got up from her chair and rushed over to Charlotte. "What's the matter, love?" Ignoring protocol.

"Linda, have you heard the news this morning? The accident?"

"Pile up on M5? I assumed you knew."

"Was the Bishop involved?" Charlotte's voice sounded panicked.

"They were saying something about his son, or son-in-law. Had some sort of miraculous escape. You know what these reporters are like jumping on the band wagon for a good humanity story. Mind you they made a humongous mistake last night on the local Radio, said the Bishop himself had been part of the pile-up and was feared dead. Is that what all those messages were about?"

"Hmm," Charlotte only grunted as she grappled with a cascade of thought. How many people could have escaped such a terrible accident? "Did they say what happened?"

"No," Linda was struck by Charlotte's concern. "It was very brief. Once they found out it wasn't actually the Bishop it wasn't really news any more, they were just putting the record straight. Do you need me to ring anyone?"

"Uh? Oh No. I'm sorry Linda, I'm only half with it this morning."

"Anything I should know?" Adding, "you know, in case anyone rings whilst you're out?"

"No, you're okay. But if Sam rings apologise for me. I said I'd ring him last night and never got around to it. Oh, and could you ring this lady?" Charlotte handed over the number of the young woman about the wedding at St Judoc's. "Can you get some more details from her if possible, I'm ashamed to say I don't even have her name, she just kept saying 'I'm the person about the wedding at St Judoc.' Arrange for them to come over this evening to see me between 5.30pm and 7pm. But whatever you do, don't give the impression it is to arrange the date. I'm not even sure I can actually marry them, she doesn't live in the parish and he's stationed in Kent. I think all the other messages have been answered by the great British media!"

"Sure!"

"And could you could let the dogs out in the garden about eleven?"

"No problem."

"Help yourself to coffee."

"No need to remind me about that one. Is it alright if I go at about midday? I've got to take Poppy to the dentist? I can be back at two for an hour."

"Yes, that's fine." Secretly Charlotte was relieved. She had already wondered how she would explain Max visiting the dogs, but not taking them back with her.

It was cold in St Nicholas and Charlotte was annoyed that she hadn't thought to turn on the heating earlier that morning. The Archdeacon kept his big heavy coat on for the whole of the meeting, only the hardy PCC secretary braved wearing just a jumper. Mrs Harlow, the church architect was late as usual turning up at 10.45 when the meeting was nearly over, but Charlotte had explained the plans as best she could with the help of the 3D computer reconstruction that the clever assistant at Harlows had sent by email. All this fuss just to convert a broom cupboard into a disabled loo to comply with new recommendations. No-one denied that having a toilet that everyone could use was a good idea, but it would have been a lot easier to have built on a small extension at the back of church and to have included the little kitchenette they wanted. But agreement for an extension on a listed building was a rare accomplishment and the diocesan committee dealing with such matter had, in their wisdom shunned the idea before any plans could be drawn up. The brooms would have to find an alternative home. Trouble was to give enough room for wheelchair users, the existing cupboard was about six inches too short, eight inches too narrow and not near enough to an existing drain to be of any use. Shame the efficient Mrs Harlow hadn't worked out that little problem before dragging out an Archdeacon, a representative from the Heritage Trust, an archaeologist, an over-enthusiastic curate (who, having not spoken to Charlotte the night before had decided to track her down at St Nicholas) and a busy church warden away from her day job managing a local doctor's surgery, all to a cold church in the middle of January.

'Still,' thought Charlotte, 'at least she had done her bit. Now we know where we stand.' By 11.00am toes and fingers were far too numb to hang about to discuss alternative sites, so Charlotte invited the delegation back to the rectory for coffee and biscuits, hoping it would be a quick meeting.

Poor Mrs Harlow only managed five minutes before doggy fur had her spluttering and wheezing for the front door with the promise to revisit the plans and find a suitable alternative. The chap from the Heritage Trust munched his way through three biscuits whilst spraying the assembled gathering with numerous ideas about alternative sources of funding, including an ingenious idea about the use of a reclaimed

58

lavatory that would invite money from an ecological fund as long as the church agreed to only use recycled toilet paper. Charlotte thought back to her college days when training included discussion about the merits of the biblical oral tradition and which Ancient Fathers had lived in caves. Try as she might she could not recall at any point being told how to approach the small group of church members that made up the Church Council, about the issue of what to shove down the lav' in order to attract the right sort of funding. Times had changed!

Eventually the only people left were the Archdeacon and young Sam. The Venerable Clive King was anxious to speak to Charlotte about vacant Archdeacon's post. Sam was still hovering to discuss the forthcoming funeral. Charlotte had no intention of divulging to Clive King the contents of her discussion with the Bishop, no matter how supportive he thought he was being. Unfortunately, Clive, who could be rather brusque at times, simply told Sam that he had a discreet matter to discuss with Charlotte so would he mind leaving. This annoyed Charlotte intensely, but she didn't have the energy to argue. Poor Sam flustered his way out. Charlotte knew she would have a hard job reassuring him later that day that it had nothing at all to do with his performance as a curate.

By now it was 11.30am giving Charlotte just half an hour before Max was due to arrive, so she would have to subtly move the conversation on.

"I suppose you've heard about the Bishop's son-in law?"

This was not what Charlotte had expected. "Ur, no, I don't think so."

"He was caught up in the accident last night on the M5. He's in a terrible state."

Charlotte didn't quite know how to respond. Clive wasn't to know she also had a loved one who had been caught up in the same accident, and she certainly wasn't going to discuss it with him. On the other hand, she was shocked to hear that David would also be feeling something similar. Son-in-law and Brother-in-law, or at least as near to a brother-in-law as she could get. She pondered how both held a similar sense of emotion and involvement. The difference was that for the Bishop it would be made known. Earlier that morning, for one fleeting moment, she had wondered if there was any chance that they were concerned about the same person. She had dismissed the idea. If Mike was the Bishop's son-in-law, she would have known.

"Is he badly hurt?"

"I don't know, he was taken to Bristol by air ambulance, so it sounds serious enough."

"Clive, I'm sorry but I don't understand why you sent Sam away just so that we could discuss the accident. It will surely get around the diocese quick enough."

"Oh, I'm sorry, that's not why I wanted Sam out of the way. I wanted to discuss the Archdeacon appointment."

Here it comes she thought. "With me?" Charlotte tried to sound coy, but it didn't work, it was well known that she had been asked to consider applying.

"Of course. We would be colleagues if you got the job. I just wondered if you had put in an application?"

"Not yet."

"But you will, won't you?"

"Clive, I'm just not sure, it's a huge commitment I don't know if I'm cut out for it."

"Don't talk rubbish, of course you can do it, but do you want to?"

Charlotte found herself looking at Clive for a moment, before declaring with a degree of unexpected emotion and surprise. "Yes, I do."

"So, what's stopping you applying?"

Charlotte would not give him the real answer. "The Bishop has asked me to take a retreat to think it through. I'll make a decision after that." She was still at a loss as to how she would juggle parish, retreat, dog-sitting and running up and down to Bristol.

The dogs had been quietly sitting at their feet during the conversation, but decided they were bored and needed the great outdoors, so started head butting both Clive and Charlotte against their knees.

"I suppose I should go," was Clive's response to the renewed doggy interest in his smart black trousers. "How long have you had dogs?"

"Oh, I'm just looking after them for a few days. They're good company though."

'And good at annoying archdeacons so that they get going before lesbian partners arrive at the door,' thought Charlotte wickedly to herself.

"Don't underestimate yourself Charlotte, I'd like to have you as a colleague," and with that he pulled on his big heavy coat, and walked to the front door, calling a cheery goodbye to Linda as she was coming out of the study, also with her coat on.

"Is it okay if I disappear too? I'll be back about 2.00pm to do the wedding register for Saturday. I managed to ring the woman about the

61

wedding. All the details are on your desk. Her name's Zoe. You've got a couple of messages too. Rupert Jenkins wants to talk to you before chapter about including the Bishop in the prayers."

"Oh, right, I'll give him a ring. That's great, I may be gone before you get back, so don't forget your key."

Linda shook her bunch of keys above her head, "Right here Vicar! Bye." And off she went to be a mum.

Within seconds of Linda leaving Charlotte heard the back door open and the sound of very excited paws sliding on the kitchen floor and tails wagging against the cupboard doors. She knew it was Max and hurried back to the kitchen.

"I parked round the back," was all Max could say before Charlotte had scooped her up in an enormous hug which only enticed the dogs into a barking frenzy. Moments later the dogs won and both women stooped down to make a fuss of them. The few minutes of laughter was short lived as Charlotte interrupted the play fights with the more serious matter of how Michael was.

"Probably still in surgery, I'm going to ring this evening. Mum and Dad are being amazing. The children are the biggest worry. Lizzie's mum and dad live in Exeter so it sounds like Lizzie will stay with them so they can help out with child care and she'll drive up and down to Bristol."

"Exeter?" asked Charlotte.

"Yeah. Why?"

"Oh nothing. Do you know much about Lizzie's parents?"

"No, not much. I've only met them once at the wedding. They seem nice enough."

"Don't suppose you know what he does for a living?"

"No idea, haven't asked. I never felt the need to know what my brother's father-in-law does to earn his keep. For all I know he could be a managing director of an international company earning millions or a school caretaker. What's with the interest about my sister-in-law's family all of a sudden?"

Charlotte waved her hands in the air in a dismissive way, "Sorry, it's nothing. I was jumping to a conclusion." But the thought was growing in her mind. She scratched her ear in the same nervous action she had used just over twenty-four hours later when she had been speaking with Bishop David.

Max reached up and took her hand from her ear, "Spill the beans, what's on your mind?"

"Did you hear that Bishop David's son-in-law had been involved in the pile-up?"

"No, how would I know that?" Max poured herself a coffee from the pot, only to discover it was cold.

"It was on the local news, late last night apparently."

"I wasn't really listening to local news last night, I was concerned that my own brother was fighting for his life." Max had sat down at the kitchen table.

"Don't be like that."

"What's his son-in-law's name?" asked Max, dropping her slight irritation as immediately as it had arisen.

"Well that's just it, but something tells me it might be Michael."

63

"Mic.... you mean our Mike? Don't be ridiculous. If he was married to a bishop's daughter don't you think he would have told us? Your imagination is running wild."

"So, what's his father-in-law's name?"

Max hesitated before answering. "Yeah, okay it's David, but there are loads of Davids"

"And I don't suppose Lizzie's mum is called Catrin? Not such a common name."

"Oh, bloody hell!" Max responded immediately.

"Max, that's not like you!"

"No, but it's not every day you discover your partners boss is your brother's father-in-law!".

"You really think so?"

"Got to be. Surely. That's why Michael wasn't keen for us to meet them. The little sage has been protecting us for the past ten years. Do you remember the fuss I made when he wouldn't invite you to the wedding? I nearly didn't go myself. Oh Charlie, can you imagine the scene if we had both turned up last night?"

"David wasn't there. He was looking after his grandchildren."

"Granted."

"But your mum and dad must have known he was my Bishop."

"You know what they're like when it comes to church. They probably don't even know what a Bishop is, well maybe, but they certainly wouldn't know a bloke in Exeter would be your boss. Even if they did, they wouldn't think much about it. She paused for breath before adding. "Charlie...." now Max had a doubt in her voice "How can we be positive it's him?"

"Get real! Of course it is, it has to be. It might have made more sense for Mike to have warned us though."

"He's in a coma!"

Now it was Charlottes turn to tut her annoyance, "I don't mean now you fool, I mean years ago, when he first knew. We could have arranged our own avoidance tactics."

"Yeah and you would have been even more on edge than you are already. Come on it's only been the last year or so that you've let me stay here for the odd weekend. That wouldn't have happened if you thought Mike might let something slip to your boss. You've had enough wobbles about us over the years."

Charlotte fell quiet. She had struggled on and off about being in a relationship and had even broken it off with Max once. She wasn't proud of her insecurities, but it was part of the package when leading a double life and the main reason she had had enough of it and had made the decision to come clean with the Bishop.

"Come on Charlie, stop thinking too much, we'll cross the next bridge when we come to it, just like we always have. What's for lunch? I've only had a slice of toast since yesterday lunchtime."

Charlotte prepared ham and tomato sandwiches but disappeared back to her office to ring Rupert, leaving Max to sort out the tea. By the time she came back, the dogs were happily tucking into bone shaped chews and the pot of tea was brewing on the kitchen table.

"I've just lied to Rupert and understand a little more about why Michael had never let on."

"How come?"

"Rupert, vicar in Okehampton wondered if I had heard anything more about the rumour that the Bishop was somehow involved in the accident yesterday afternoon."

"What did you tell him?"

"What the Archdeacon had said this morning, that as far as we know the Bishop was not directly involved but that a member of his family had been badly injured. And all the time I was talking to him I wanted to yell down the phone that it was a member of my own family, well nearly - one day!"

Charlotte sat back down at the table disturbing one of the dogs who had managed to lie underneath it. "Sorry Patch, but if you will get under our feet, what do you expect?"

She started pouring the tea. "We're going to pray for the Bishop and his family at the Chapter meeting. I won't even be able to pray for Michael, I'm not supposed to know him."

"Don't let it upset you."

"I hate the lies and deception, you know I do. It's plagued me my whole ministry. I hate not being able to tell them all how much we're worried about Mike, and then I'll have to carry on with the meeting as if nothing was wrong." She thumped the table in her frustration, making the dogs jump.

Max took her hand. "And you will be brilliant, like always. It's what Sash most admires about you, that professional front of yours. Where is she by the way?"

"Oh, doing her day job in London, she'll be back on Saturday I think."

"Friday night at your place then?"

"Seeing as I'll have the dogs, yes!"

"Are you sure that's okay?"

"What Friday night? Yeah sure, I'm not going to get all jumpy again, I've already told the Bishop about us any way."

"You did? I didn't think you'd go through with it."

"I told you yesterday."

"No, you said we'd talk about it when you rang later in the evening, but other things took over, remember?"

"Oh, yes of course. Well I told him that I wouldn't be going for the archdeacon's post, told him I was fed up of the double life and mentioned that I would resign my orders rather than going down a discipline route which would no doubt roll on for a couple of years."

"Bloody hell Charlie! What did he say?"

"Suggested I go on retreat for a few days to think it through. He had the audacity to suggest the conversation never took place and for us to go on just as before being utterly discreet. But I said it was time I made an honest woman of you."

"You didn't!"

"No I didn't. I meekly agreed to the retreat and to meet him again on the 31st, but that might change now. Can you imagine his reaction when he finds out that Mike has known about us all along?"

Max ignored the rhetorical question. "So, what about the retreat?"

"I haven't thought any more about it. Like you said, other things have taken over. But I'm not going anywhere whilst I've got Patch and Stitch."

"I was thinking about the need to think about it more. I thought you'd done all your thinking."

"I have. I don't think a retreat will change anything, unless I decide to continue with the hide and seek game."

"Hide and seek?"

"I keep my true self hidden and everyone else tries to seek it out. I'm through with that. It's dishonest and falls too far short of the Christian message of truth and honesty. You know that better than I do. You've found a church who knows you're gay and they're fine."

"They still don't know I'm nearly married to a priest. One rule for laity, another for the white plastic brigade."

"I don't wear my white plastic at your church."

"Exactly! And even they don't know we're an item. You won't let me tell them."

"I know, I'm sorry," glancing up at the kitchen clock. "Oh, Max look at the time, it's nearly half past one. I've got to go by two at the latest. Let's take the dogs for a quick run in the back field. Linda will be back soon, it might be best if you disappear before then, otherwise she'll wonder why I've still got the dogs."

"Come on then. Patch, Stitch – walkies!" And with the long-awaited command from their mistress both dogs shot out from under the table, nearly knocking it over in the process, sloshing the left-over tea from the mugs and generally causing a brief moment of mania. Charlotte feigned annoyance, but had to laugh as both dogs, in their excitement, stood on their back legs with their front paws pinning Max to the spot. One had her paws on Max's chest and the other half way up her back. Just a sharp "DOWN" from Max had them both under control and off they went, not bothering with leads, for a quick run around the church field that normally had sheep grazing, but thankfully, they were being kept in the farmer's barn during early lambing.

●

Chapter 6

The police car sitting outside Lizzie's house had attracted much attention. It was unfortunate that an unsuspecting Constable Barrow had been a little too helpful when Lizzie's inquisitive neighbour showed apparent concern for the family. The neighbour just happened to spot the Bishop's purple shirt and clerical collar when he was on the door step and asked Constable Barrow if the cleric was a friend of the family. Barrow was far too quick with an answer.

"The Bishop is Mrs Tannin's father, I'm afraid her husband was involved in the accident on the M5 earlier today. Who can I say is asking?"

Unknown to the inexperienced Barrow, the supportive neighbour also turned out to be a freelance journalist. The constable had given her enough information in just one sentence to make the late-night news and the early morning papers.

All the neighbour said was, "Oh the poor love, I'll drop by tomorrow." And was gone.

The journalist had managed to somehow ascertain using that small snippet of information, that the Bishop concerned was Bishop David Graham of Exeter diocese. By ten O clock, it was on the local news but had got skewed in translation, reporting that the Bishop himself had been directly involved, much to David's shock. By then the first editions had made it to the presses.

Sally, the Bishop's secretary, was tossed headlong into managing a media frenzy.

David had phoned Sally first thing to warn her. She arrived at the Bishop's palace at eight fifteen in the morning to find a dozen messages already on the answer phone. She didn't have chance to deal with them before the phone started ringing again. A mixture of concerned colleagues and the media wanting official statements, as well as less scrupulous journalists posing as clergy who got very short shrift from the conscientious Sally who had no trouble seeing through such scheming ways.

Lizzie had complete trust in her father and had left him to cope with her two tiny children whilst she and her mother went to be at Michael's side. But after a fractious few hours, David had admitted defeat and driven to Frenchay Hospital with a sleepy Heather and a very grumpy little Joshua secured in his carry cot. He wanted his mother's breast, having ignored the expressed milk Lizzie had left the previous evening. David and Catrin arrived back in Exeter at around midday with a rather tearful and tired Heather, leaving Joshua with his mum. The plan was for Lizzie to drive down later that day once Michael was out of theatre, leaving Vince and Maureen at Michael's bedside until he regained consciousness. It was complicated, but life was like that.

Sally had managed to rearrange the Bishop's diary for the next two days. Most of those cancelled had already heard the news so were very sympathetic. Sally decided the media has its uses after all.

One morning paper, however, had still got its information wrong and had printed a story about the Bishop lying in intensive care fighting for his life. This was the reason for so many phone calls from very concerned friends and colleagues and even some family members who hadn't been able to get an answer on the Bishop's private phone.

71

The valiant Sally found herself confirming rumours, dispelling others and gently clarifying with members of the family that it was actually Michael and not David who was hurt, which was of little comfort and even more shocking for some.

The most difficult conversations were with Ruth and Naomi, David and Catrin's two daughters, who had been trying to contact their mother and sister, but of course both their phones had been turned off in the hospital. Neither daughter had thought about trying their dad, assuming the worst. Their brother John, on the other hand, had a healthy suspicion of the media and managed a long conversation with his father late the previous night. For some strange reason neither men had wanted to disturb the girls assuming that they wouldn't have heard, not living locally. Sally couldn't stop herself strongly suggesting to David that he made Ruth and Naomi his first priority when replying to some of the calls that needed his personal attention.

By four O clock, David had also managed an official press release, with the help of his diocesan press officer. The simple statement would be circulated to all agents, meaning that by tomorrow the family should be left alone.

"After all Bishop," said his press-officer, "a story about a Bishop's son-in-law, is far less news worthy in the eyes of the media, than the Bishop himself."

One unthinking rooky of a journalist actually said to Sally that it was a shame, 'a dead Bishop was much more exciting', she had put the phone down on him before he uttered another word. In fact, she had probably slammed the phone down.

72

The release read:

On the afternoon of Tuesday 8th January, a serious and horrific accident occurred on the M5. My heart goes out to those concerned especially to the families of those who so tragically lost their lives. Many others were injured and we owe a great debt to the professionalism of the dedicated police, fire-fighters, paramedics and hospital staff who have worked tirelessly to rescue and treat all those caught up in this terrible incident, my son-in-law included. I would like to take this brief opportunity on behalf of all who find themselves drawn together by this tragedy to thank you for your continued prayer and support.

Catrin had rearranged her own day, so rather than speaking at a Working Women's luncheon she had taken Heather to the local toy shop to buy a bathroom set for her doll. Heather had spotted a nurse's outfit whilst they were there so they bought that and a pretend first aid kit too.

"So that I can look after Daddy," little Heather had announced. Still not understanding just how poorly her daddy was. Before Lizzie and Catrin had rushed down to Bristol, they had taken a few minutes to try to explain to Heather that Daddy had been hurt and that is why she had to stay with Grandpa while Mummy and Grandma went to see how he was. Of course Heather wanted to see her daddy too, but they wondered if she could stay and help Grandpa with her little brother, because he didn't know where everything was. Catrin was adamant that a night in a hospital corridor was no place for a four-year-old child whose father's

73

life hung in the balance. Lizzie was too much in shock to argue. David was willing to do whatever his wife suggested.

Later that afternoon Sally, Catrin and David sat down in David's study with the diary, whilst Heather, dressed in her nurses uniform, happily bandaged first her doll, then the leg of the desk, before turning her hand to her grandpa's hand and arm, whilst he carried on with the conversation simply holding his arm out ahead of him, only intervening when his beloved granddaughter decided Grandpa had a poorly nose which also needed bandaging, at which point Heather went back to giving injections to her doll with a running commentary to the pretend doctor helping her.

"Tomorrow is fine," Sally informed them both. "As it was supposed to be your day off anyway, although you had both agreed to attend the retired priests' annual dinner in the evening, but Tim Geech rang enquiring after you, following the news report. When I told him the real story he suggested you needed time with your family so they are not going to expect you."

"He's a good soul," replied David, as Heather pretended to inject her grandpa's leg.

"Friday. You have appointments here all day, so I'm sure we can keep an eye on Heather if Catrin wants to go up with Lizzie."

"That's very kind of you Sally," said Catrin. "Are you sure?"

"I've got grandchildren of my own. It's no problem at all, just don't expect me to finish that diocesan report before Monday, I can always do a bit of work at home."

"No," said David. "You do more than enough already. By Monday we'll try and get something else sorted, I think Ruth is trying to get home, and Mike's parents said they would take Heather down with them for a few days."

"And any way, as soon as Mike is out of immediate danger and onto an ordinary ward we'll take Heather up to the hospital," reminded Catrin.

"So, shall I free up what I can?" suggested Sally

"Postpone the clergy reviews for next week, apart from Kenneth Tween, I do need to see him, but see if he could do first thing. I'll do the memorial dedication in Ivybridge, unless Clive King could do that. Bishop's Council next Tuesday. Is that here?"

"No, you were all going to Lee Abbey for the day."

"If the Abbey children's team would look after Heather you could take her with you. She'd love it," suggested Catrin

"I'll give them a ring and ask," said Sally.

And before long the two women had the next fortnight planned and David wondered if Vince and Maureen were going to completely lose out on the opportunity to have their granddaughter to themselves.

Heather had become a little bored and Sally had by now been at work for over ten hours, so they called the meeting to a halt.

Michael was still sedated in intensive care, but he was stable. They had saved the badly broken leg and reconstructed his pelvis. He had lost a lot of blood internally and they hadn't saved the spleen although both kidneys appeared to be working well.

Lizzie arrived at the Bishop's Palace at 7.30pm, exhausted but determined to spend a little time with Heather before putting her to bed.

75

She handed Joshua to her father, "Sorry Dad, nappy needs changing." Even though her life had been turned upside down, she still had a glint in her eye. Joshua was usually a contented baby and happily went to his grandpa to be bathed and changed ready for bed.

Catrin prepared the adults a meal and opened a bottle of red wine.

Once Heather was settled, they sat down for their meal.

"Thanks for letting us stay I'm not sure I'd cope on my own with the children."

"You don't have to, we've got it all arranged," Catrin reassured her, although as she did, Lizzie glanced over to her father for extra confirmation. He simply nodded saying "Tomorrow is my day off, so we can all go up to Bristol and take it in turns to keep Heather occupied."

"But Dad, I don't really want Heather to see her daddy like that."

"There's a whole night to go before then. We can stall her until the afternoon. I thought I could take her to that place on the harbour, the nature museum." Her father was quite looking forward to the prospect of another day with his little granddaughter.

"You mean that science place - Explore-at-Bristol? She'd love that. Are you sure?"

"Of course he's sure, he can't wait. You know how much of a kid he is at heart. It'll do him good to do something different. And you and I can concentrate on Michael and Joshua between us."

Catrin was often at risk of tipping over into 'bossy' mode, but just kept enough in reserve to allow those around her to feel secure, but not overpowered, most of the time.

"I'm sure Mike's parents would like to spend some time with the children too. They'll need a break," offered Lizzie.

"How long are they intending to stay in Bristol?" asked David. He'd only seen them briefly that morning, when he dropped Joshua off at the hospital to be with his mummy and to pick up Catrin.

"They want to stay until Mike is awake obviously, and probably over the weekend. Max has gone back home."

"Max?" David frowned.

"Mike's sister," answered Catrin.

"I didn't even know Mike had a sister."

"Yes you did. She was at the wedding. Don't you start losing your marbles Dad!"

"Max? Was she one of your bridesmaids?"

"No Dad, she is about ten years older than Mike and decided she would look a bit out of place." Lizzie decided to keep the full story from her parents. Mike and his sister had fallen out over the invitations. Lizzie wasn't quite sure what it was all about, and Mike had never let on. She suspected Max had got in with the wrong sort of bloke and Mike was adamant that he was not going to get an invite. It got so fraught that Max had threatened to boycott the wedding completely. But sisterly and brotherly love prevailed much to Lizzie's relief. Mike was very attached to his big sister, despite the huge age difference and he had been like a bear with a sore head until Max had resigned herself to coming alone only about a week before the wedding.

"Could she look after Heather? Has she children of her own?" asked David.

"They'd be teenagers," said his wife, "Oh, maybe they could help?"

77

"Mum, Dad. Just wait before you go in organising overdrive. Maureen and Vince have offered to have Heather any time I want. I'm just a little bit worried about being away from her too long though. She'll be upset enough with Mike in hospital without her mum disappearing too. So I'd be grateful if we could keep the next week as it is, and perhaps Heather could go down to Plymouth next weekend to see how she gets on. She's done that before, so it should be okay. As for Max, she's not married and she hasn't got any kids, just two dogs that, according to Mike, are substitute children. She's a vet on the edge of Dartmoor somewhere and she's already offered to look after Heather and Joshua for a few hours whenever she can get time off work and get back up to Frenchay."

"What about the dogs?" questioned Catrin, "She couldn't possibly juggle two dogs, a four-year-old and a young baby."

"Mother, will you stop trying to oversee every little detail. Max has already dropped the dogs off at a friend of hers before she even left for Bristol. They'll stay there for as long as necessary, apparently."

"It's good to have friends," said David very quietly. Whenever Lizzie used 'Mother' or 'Father' it was a signal that she was annoyed. In the same way that whenever they used Elizabeth Ann, Lizzie knew that however grown up she was, she had overstepped the mark.

"Yes Dad, it is. Come on let's finish off this wine, I could do with a good night's sleep."

Just then the phone went. "Michael" yelled Lizzie. But David put a constraining hand on her daughter's arm, whilst Catrin answered the phone.

78

"Oh that is good news...... yes of course do you want to speak to her? .... Yes, alright..... I'm sure she will. Thank you so much for ringing." Catrin came back into the dining room. "It was Vince. They've reduced the sedation and taken Mike off the ventilator. He's breathing unaided and beginning to respond."

"I should go back, I should be there when he wakes up."

"Love, you can't, you're shattered. You have to stay here with Joshua and Heather." David was not going to let his daughter drive all the way back to Bristol and didn't much fancy the idea himself.

"We'll go back first thing in the morning," reassured Catrin. "We can be there by eight if you really want to. We can all go together."

David wondered what he would do with a four-year-old in Bristol at eight o clock on a Thursday morning.

"You're right, sorry. We'll go in the morning. It's okay, we don't need to leave that early. Make it an 8am start here. We'll still be in Frenchay by about 9.30am and Dad can go straight into town with Heather.

"Vince suggested you ring him on his mobile later on and he can give you the full details," said Catrin. "They are going to get something to eat now, and his phone was nearly out of battery, so wait till they are back at the hotel about 10pm they thought."

"Alright."

"You do look tired love," Catrin was concerned about her daughter and the pressure and stress she was feeling. "Why don't you take your wine and have a bath. We'll listen out for Joshua."

"Now that is a very good idea. Did you pick up those things for me Dad?"

79

"In the big holdall on your bed."

"Thanks, I won't be long."

But it was nearly ten when Lizzie emerged from her long luxurious soak using some of her mum's aromatic bath foam.

Chapter 7

Earlier that same day, the deanery chapter meeting had gone well, except that Charlotte and Sam were nearly late due to Charlotte was past the little village of Winstone and out onto the A382 towards Okehampton when she realised she had forgotten to pick up her curate. She turned around and found him waiting on the corner. Neither Roger nor Derek were able to attend due to other commitments, so on the twenty-minute trip, Charlotte eventually had an opportunity to discuss the funeral Sam would be taking.

Rupert had led the short act of worship including prayers for the Bishop and his family 'during their time of great trial.' Charlotte was asked if she had any more news about the accident. She just repeated what the Archdeacon had said confirming that the Bishop himself had not been involved although he had been on the motorway at the time. She felt slightly sick and briefly excused herself to visit the ladies having introduced the speaker. She felt she was deceiving her colleagues and hated it.

When she came back one of the other female priests whispered asking her if she was okay, as she looked a little pale.

"Just a bit tired. Pat, I'll be fine. Thanks for asking."

The eco-friendly funeral director was quite comical which might have seemed disrespectful to some, but it was all in good taste and offered light relief to those who dealt with death on a weekly basis. It emerged that more and more people were concerned about the environment, even in death, so faster bio-degradable coffins were becoming very popular. He also talked about a crematorium which was trying out new more energy efficient methods of cremation. His hearse was run by rechargeable batteries as it didn't need the sort of power offered by more traditional engines. With some jollity, he shared a story about a funeral just outside Moretonhampstead, when the hearse was struggling so much up an extremely steep hill that a rather fit young cyclist managed to overtake the cortège.

Over tea and cake Charlotte conducted a brief business meeting reminding the gathered clergy about deanery and diocesan events, as well as reminding them of certain documents that the diocese needed before and immediately after annual meetings in April. The men and women shared anything of significance from their own parishes and discussed one or two matters of concern, including the continued theft of lead from church roofs. The diocese and ecclesiastical insurance were still debating about the use of anti-vandalism paint on drain pipes to deter the thieves. The paint meant there was no grip for an unsuspecting thief. The problem was if they went down that line, there was a risk that if a thief fell from a drain pipe the churches would be liable for personal injury. At that point there was a loud groan from the assembled throng. The best solution at the present time, was for locals to keep an eye on their churches and report anything suspicious to the police. In the country that meant about a forty-minute response time, so the meeting decided praying for miracles would be more effective!

At half past four, Charlotte drew the meeting to a close, leaving Rupert and the ladies who had provided the refreshments to clear the church hall and get it ready for the keep fit group. 'Proving', thought Charlotte, 'that community cohesion was alive and well in rural Devon.'

She dropped Sam back home, reminding him of the pastoral meeting that evening and their supervision meeting at the Rectory the following morning.

She was home just after five, leaving her time to let the dogs out before the appointment with Zoë Carmichael and Thomas Whiteacre to discuss their wedding plans. Linda had left a couple of messages as well as some letters for Charlotte to sign. At twenty-five past five, the doorbell went, just as Charlotte was rubbing down the damp dogs after their brief run. She left them in the kitchen, and answered the door to a young woman of about nineteen with long blond hair dressed in tight jeans and a large chunky sweater and a man who looked as if he was well into his thirties, dressed in a smart blue suit with what looked like a regimental tie. Charlotte showed them into her study offering them tea or coffee. Both accepted the offer of coffee, which meant that Charlotte could return to the kitchen to finish drying off Patch and Stitch.

It turned out that Captain Whiteacre had been married before and had two children by his first wife. She had apparently got fed up with army life and had left him three years previously taking the children with her. He was still fighting the courts to gain access. He was very open about his situation. Zoë sat on the edge of the sofa and hardly said a word, which slightly worried Charlotte.

"How long have you known each other?" enquired Charlotte.

Zoë looked at Thomas, almost as if asking permission to speak, but Charlotte wondered if she was being a little over sensitive given the age difference.

"It's been a bit of a whirlwind romance to be honest," she said. "We met in August at a friend's wedding, but seeing as Tom is going out to Afghanistan so soon, we wanted to get some things in place."

Charlotte hated these conversations and hadn't even known about the added complication of the divorce before they had got there. Her mobile rang in her pocket. She glanced at it quickly. It was Max. Charlotte was torn. She wanted to speak to Max knowing that Mike was due out of theatre but she needed to be utterly professional with this couple. "Will excuse me for one moment? I'm afraid it is connected to the situation last night. It's rather important." Zoe and Tom both nodded.

"Max, what is it? What's happened? Is Mike okay?"

"Steady on, yes Mike is doing really well. That's why I phoned. He's out of theatre and back on the high dependency ward. He's still poorly but is off the ventilator and doing well."

"Thank God. Max, I'm in a meeting at the moment. Can I ring you back about seven?"

"You can try. I've just phoned between clients. I'm supposed to finish surgery at seven, but it's quite busy."

"Well, we'll speak later, sometime."

"Love you babe."

"Love you too," and Charlotte added a kiss for good measure.

Charlotte returned to what turned out to be a very difficult conversation. She wasn't able to give them an answer that evening. She tried to explain that a marriage following a divorce was not always possible in the Church of England, at which point Zoë burst into tears. She also explained that because neither of them lived in the parish, and had no immediate connection through the parish, the only way they could get married at St Judoc's was for that one of them, which would mean Zoë, to become a regular worshipper so as to qualify for the electoral roll and that would take six months. Zoë looked uncomfortable when Charlotte explained what being on the electoral roll meant. It then turned out that Zoë was not baptised, which she would need to be before being able to be accepted onto the roll. To top it all a fretful Zoë then blurted out that she was pregnant and wanted to get married before she began to show. Charlotte was rather surprised at Capt. Whiteacre's reaction. It was obvious this was the first he had heard about it.

Just for a brief moment Charlotte found herself wondering if the baby was his. She put the thought out of her mind. It was obvious she would not be able to conduct the wedding so prying further would serve no purpose that evening. The couple needed to go away and think things through. Captain Whiteacre was leaving for Afghanistan just four weeks later. Charlotte did offer them something to think about. If they were to marry at a registry office, perhaps they would like to come back for a wedding blessing. If they were prepared to wait they could even combine it with the baby's christening and maybe Zoë would like to think about baptism for herself.

The couple left, very unhappy and Charlotte didn't think she would see them again. She then reminded herself that it would be very unlikely she would be the one conducting any blessing and baptism. She scribbled a note in the back of her diary reminding her to pass the couple to Derek. She would use the scenario with Sam during the supervision session, as a pastoral example. She also prayed that young Zoe would not be left widowed with a young baby to bring up alone, or even worse, left with nothing if Thomas was lost, before being able to marry her. It was like turning the clocks back seventy years. But Charlotte could not dwell on the conversation. She had an hour to have something to eat, feed the dogs, get ready for the pastoral visitors meeting and try to ring Max.

She fed Patch and Stitch first and let them out in the garden whilst she put some pasta on the stove. Then she used her mobile to ring Max, but only got the voice mail. Less than a minute after she put the phone down it rang. Assuming it was Max she picked up, "Missing me or the dogs?"

"What?" Came a puzzled reply. It was Sasha.

"Oh Sash, I'm sorry I thought it might have been Max."

"Thank goodness, I thought you'd gone gooey eyed over the lodger." Sash had felt her heart flutter briefly, but would never admit to her lingering infatuation with her good friend. "I'm just ringing to see how Mike is."

"He's out of theatre and it looks as if he is stable for the time being."

"I didn't know he needed surgery."

"They needed to do some work on his pelvis. It doesn't sound great Sash, but at least he's out of danger. Are you staying in London this weekend?"

"I was, but wondered if you needed a hand with the dogs."

"That would be fantastic."

"I'll probably be finished by Friday afternoon so I'll come back sooner if it's a help."

"Er, Max is coming over on Friday."

"Ah, in that case I'll make it Saturday!"

"Thanks Sash," grinned Charlotte pleased that she and Max would have a bit of time to themselves. Changing the subject, she asked, "Had a good day?"

"Not bad, Ms Naomi Goldsmith was like a bear with a sore head. I don't think she liked anything I'd produced. She certainly wasn't her normal efficient self. I'm going back tomorrow with some fresh proofs, so it's a night at the computer this evening and I'd *sooooo* wanted to visit that posh new wine bar in Kensington."

"As if!" Charlotte had heard the sarcastic tone in Sasha's voice. She was definitely a pint of real ale and a bag of crisps sort of chick. You'd never get her anywhere near posh frocks and tall delicate wine glasses. "Thanks for ringing Sash. See you on Saturday."

"Let me know, if there's any major change won't you. How's Max holding up? Have you seen her?"

"Yeah, she popped in for lunch on her way back. She's tired but seems to be coping alright. Worried of course and she'll miss not having the dogs around. Talking of which I'd better go and get them in from the garden."

"Sure, see you soon," and Sasha rang off.

Once the dogs were in, Charlotte mixed the pasta with some pesto, threw a salad together and ate at the kitchen table whilst checking the agenda for the evening's meeting. She was conscious that she hadn't had a moment to herself all day and hoped she could get through the meeting quickly, but that would be a little unpredictable, depending on the pastoral issues the visitors would bring. Patch laid his head-on Charlottes lap and Stitch settled down across her feet. "Poor things, you must be wondering what's going on too. Well I'm sorry, but I've got work to do." Charlotte stood up which provoked general tail wagging. Early evening was probably another walkies time, but they'd have to settle for the garden again later.

Later that evening Charlotte collapsed in her favourite soft armchair in the lounge with both dogs at her feet, although Patch had tried to impersonate a cat by trying to climb up on her lap. The volunteer pastoral visitors meeting had finished at 9.30pm. There were no new people to put on the list. The greatest concern had been for an elderly lady who used to play the organ at St Swithen. She still lived in the village in her small cottage, but had been seen late at night or early in the morning wandering around her small garden in her nightdress, which at this time of the year was a little worrying. Charlotte thought about own her early morning jaunts in her pyjamas taking out the rubbish on a Monday morning and hoped nobody had noticed. However, this was a very real concern so Derek agreed to visit poor old Muriel with one of the volunteers as well as having a discreet word around the village and the local GP. They had three people in the benefice in hospital including one who was about to be transferred to Bristol for cardiac surgery. Charlotte nearly said she would visit when she was up there, but stopped herself. Now she regretted her decision, partly because she regretted having to cover up her personal life, but also for not thinking a bit quicker and simply saying she had a family friend in hospital in the area. It would be an excellent reason for visiting. She also knew how much it would mean to George to receive a visit from home and she could have taken his wife. She might employ the family friend idea later which, after all, was not far from the truth. Mike was a friend, although there was the added complication of David.

"Too many things to think about," she said out loud, which induced more tail wagging, on otherwise sleepy dogs. How a dog could stretch itself out to their full length, appear to be fast asleep, but still wag its tail vigorously enough to disturb the sheets of newspaper that Charlotte had discarded on the rug, she had no idea.

She picked up the phone to ring Max when she heard what sounded like a motorbike roar up her driveway followed by a loud knock at her door, throwing the dogs into frenzied barking, which far from reassuring Charlotte made her jump out of her skin. With unusual nervousness, she answered the front door, keeping hold of Patch and with Stitch close behind.

"Hiya Auntie," said a leather clad figure as he pulled off his black crash helmet to reveal a shaggy mop of blond hair. "Are you busy?"

James was a high-spirited youth of seventeen who from time to time, from the age of fifteen, took it into his head to turn up on his aunt's doorstep unannounced. Up until last year this would coincide with the only bus that crossed the northern part of the moor and therefore his visits would be at a reasonable hour, but since he had his motorbike it could be at any time of day or night. Whatever time he arrived, the reason was usually the same, he had fallen out with his mother or had had another argument with his father.

"James!" Charlotte made no attempt to hide her resentment. In that one word, she managed to convey annoyance, tiredness, boredom as well as a great fondness for her sister's son. However, on this occasion she felt as if this might just be the last straw, on what had been two extremely long and emotionally draining days. She wasn't sure she could cope with either her nephew's excitable recollections of the latest family drama, or the call she would shortly make to her sister reassuring her that her wayward son was safe and would probably be staying the night and yes, she would ensure he got up early enough to make it back to Plymouth in time for his morning classes. By now it was gone ten and all Charlotte really wanted to do was to ring and have a very long chat with Max.

The phone went.

She wondered if it was Erica, her sister, or even her ex-brother-in-law, if James had been due to stay the night at his fathers.

Charlotte let her nephew in. "Come on in then, take your boots off in the hall, whilst I answer the phone. Don't mind the dogs and go and make yourself a hot drink."

"Haven't you got a beer?"

"Not if you're driving back tonight."

She heard the answer phone kick in and all Charlotte could think of was that if it was another pastoral emergency, she would resign on the spot, cut up her collar and run around her own garden naked just to attract a little of the support that she hoped old Muriel would soon be getting. James was taking his boots off but was still looking at his aunt with a lost soul look that could twist her around his little finger and she knew he was there for the night.

"Yes, alright, in the fridge, but only one, you're underage remember?"

"Thanks Auntie."

"And don't call me Auntie," she called after him as he scampered off to the kitchen closely followed by both dogs. Charlotte couldn't work out if they had also fallen in love with the scruffy teenager who always melted her heart, or whether they were in fact simply keeping guard. But as soon as James bent down to pat them both, their tails wagged and it was obvious they too, like everyone else had been caught by his charm. Everyone that is apart from his parents who seemed to spend most of their time either arguing with James, or arguing about him, hence James' escape route to Auntie Charlie.

Charlotte went to her study to listen to the message. It was from Sam who simply asked her to ring him. Charlotte contemplated the naked garden option, but thought it might scar her unsuspecting nephew for life, so quickly rang Sam back.

"Sam, Charlotte here, what is it?"

"Sorry to ring so late, but I had a message from the family about the funeral on Friday. They want to see me again tomorrow. Do you mind if I'm a few minutes late for supervision? It's just that I know you have St Nicholas school in the morning, so I might not have got you before you left. I can ring the family in the morning and see them on my way." Sam was as earnest as ever.

"That's fine Sam, but try and get here by 11am. I've got a funeral at Sheepsgate at two and I'll need a bit of lunch before then. Are you okay? Are the family being difficult?" It was a family Charlotte had had dealings with before and they had a tendency to want to discuss every detail and demand written notes in triplicate.

"No, they're okay, they just wanted to run over the talk with me they were a bit concerned that I had all the dates correct."

91

"Hmmm," murmured Charlotte, "sounds like them."

"Sorry, I didn't catch that," said Sam, a little louder down the phone as if there was a problem on the line.

"Oh nothing, just be as firm as you can, telling them you have another appointment to get to or they'll keep you there all morning." At this rate, thought Charlotte as she put the phone down, it would be morning before she got to bed. She looked at her watch. Nearly quarter to eleven. She wondered why Max hadn't phoned, and then remembered she had turned her mobile to silent during the pastoral meeting. Sure enough, on the screen was a missed call sign. This was not the peaceful country vicar's life she had once craved. She phoned Max.

After asking how Mike was doing, which turned out to be reasonable news, she gave a report on how the dogs were doing. Charlotte then relayed how the rest of her day had been including the recent arrival of James. Like Charlotte, Max was very fond of James, although also found his unannounced arrivals a little exasperating so she had a lot of sympathy for Charlotte.

"But you are exhausted Babe, don't let him keep you up half the night. What's wrong this time?"

"Who says there's something wrong?"

"There always is!" said Max, but with a lightness to her voice which revealed the way she found the nature of James' visits and the easy-going relationship he enjoyed with his aunt rather appealing.

News of James arrival seemed to relieve the tension in Max's voice.

"Shall I come and join the fun?" joked Max, knowing that James' reports of his latest exploits and the resulting row with either his mum or dad, or both on the rare occasions they were seen together, were always worth listening too. In fact, she suspected the reason he descended on his auntie was because she could always see the funny side. That particular gift would be difficult to muster when Charlette was so tired. "Any idea what it might be about?"

"I've hardly said two words to him since he arrived" admitted Charlotte. "I've let him loose on my beer in the kitchen, with the dogs for company. I suspect it may have something to do with the fact that he appears to have turned blond since we last saw him."

"Yep, you could be on to something there!" giggled Max.

James was also the only member of the family who had fully accepted Charlotte and Max as a committed couple as if it was the most natural thing in the world, which for them of course, it was.

"I'd better let you go and find out, and any way, I need my sleep. Don't forget I spent last night in a hospital chair."

"Oh, I'm sorry sweetheart, you really must be exhausted." Charlotte suddenly regretted having kept her loved one on the phone for so long.

"Hey, it helped. I'll sleep better now. Night night. I'll give you an update on Michael tomorrow. Just don't let James keep you up too long. You're shattered too," and with that Max rang off leaving Charlotte to ring her sister to let her know where her son would be staying the night, before returning to share a beer and a chat into the early hours with her nephew.

93

Chapter 8

Charlotte was glad that the dogs didn't wake her till seven in the morning to be let out. She had finally got to bed just after one o clock, having thrown a sleeping bag at James telling him to find his own way to the spare room.

The latest Carter family catastrophe had indeed been about the sudden change of hair colour. Apparently, Erica had given James £60 for a new pair of trousers, a shirt and a jumper for school, in addition to the £50 his father had given him for shoes. James had managed to find shoes in the sale of a cheap shoe shop, buying a pair unlikely to last through the winter, but saving him £40 in the process. He had then managed the same entrepreneurial trick with the clothes saving another £30 giving him £70 to splash out on his new image. What James had found almost comical was that his parents had actually agreed that he had deceived them both, and agreement was not something that came easily to Erica and William. So, James was feeling rather pleased with himself and his new haircut.

His father, William, was furious about being taken for a ride by his teenage son, something that dented his pride, which was far more serious than denting his wallet.

Having been confronted earlier in the evening by both mother and father, at the same time, in the same house and saying more or less the same thing, James had felt somewhat bewildered and rather than wait for the unusual unity to break down into the rather more familiar slanging match had managed to escape by faking contrition and going to his room like a sulky teenager. He had then sneaked out of his window, lowered himself onto the driveway, slipped through the side entrance to the garage, donned his leathers and crash helmet and was half way to Langford before either his father or mother had even realised he was missing.

In her fatigued state whilst her defences were down Charlotte had found herself agreeing with James that he had shown sound stewardship with his parents' money making it go much further than it would have done otherwise, although she had asked if he thought he would show such careful thriftiness if he was buying a pair of jeans to look good on a date.

"Get real!" was the only reply she had received to that question.

The problem was that Charlotte honestly liked her nephew's new look and was rather pleased he had shown such cunning to obtain the money he needed. There was a time before her sister and her husband finally divorced that the young James would barely speak, afraid that anything he said would be used in evidence against one parent or the other, which was why Aunty Charlotte became a bolt hole for him.

That was the conversation into the small hours. Now it was now time to drag James out of bed and persuade him to get back to Plymouth for his first lecture at 10.00am. Charlotte hadn't told him about Michael.

Charlotte thought about saying something over breakfast, if she ever got him that far. By now it was nearly eight. Charlotte had taken the dogs for a brief run across the field almost as soon as they had woken her up, although she had decided against the idea of simply pulling a coat over her night clothes, for fear of being labelled another Muriel. She'd then fed them, showered and dressed herself in the casual brown trouser suit she preferred for school and was now banging on the door of the spare room.

"James, I'm sure you don't have p-jays with you and equally sure you don't want me to see your boxer shorts, or whatever you men wear these days."

"Yeah, yeah I know. I'm on my way. You got any coffee?"

"It's already on. Toast or cereal?"

"Fried egg?" James had a habit of pushing the boundaries, even if it only over a breakfast option.

"Only if you make it yourself."

"Toast please."

Charlotte smiled to herself. She had almost offered to have him to stay on a long-term basis when the divorce had got really messy, but in the end decided that a very busy, homosexual female country vicar would probably do more harm than good to a fourteen-year-old vulnerable teenager, if not to his personality, then certainly his street cred! In the end, he had stayed for occasional holidays and had gradually regained his confidence so that by sixteen he was a normal stroppy teenager, a fact demonstrated by his latest escapade.

James lumbered down the stairs and into the kitchen dressed in his black school trousers and new shirt.

"You didn't have those on last night." Charlotte pointed out.

"Didn't you see the rucksack Auntie Charlotte?"

"Don't tell me you'd actually had the forethought to pack a bag?"

"Even got my stuff for school in my top box," James said smugly.

"In that case, next time, have the forethought to give me a ring before you leave, or at least stop on the way somewhere to give me some warning. You frightened me and the dogs out of our skin."

"That reminds me, I didn't ask you last night. They're Max's dogs, aren't they?"

"Uh huh." Charlotte was not all that forthcoming. She had no problem telling James the full story, but time was already a bit tight for him to get back in time for classes and for Charlotte to run through her notes before she too was due at school to lead the morning assembly.

"Charlie is everything okay?" For all his new-found strength of character and laddish behaviour James was still, deep down, a very sensitive individual.

With a deep sigh, Charlotte conceded. "Max's brother was involved in that pile up on the M5."

"Oh, my God...." Charlotte shot James a disapproving look, "... sorry, but he is alright, isn't he? I mean he's not dead or anything?"

"He's been badly injured...." and she told James all she knew, which she realised was still not a huge amount. She didn't tell James all the complexity of the situation and he hadn't made any connection with what he might or might not have heard on the news about the Bishop's involvement. When Charlotte had finished relaying all she could, James got up from his chair, brushed off the toast crumbs from his shirt and went over to his aunt. Without saying a word, he put a pair of strong young arms around his aunt's shoulders and held her tight, at which point Charlotte broke down and wept into his shoulder, leaving a damp mark on his clean new shirt.

"Oh, James I am sorry. What a wimp." Charlotte regained control as quickly as she had lost it, but realised that all the emotion was only just below the surface. She'd need to be careful today. She couldn't let down her professional mask at the funeral that afternoon.

"You're no wimp," said James, "and you know it. I'm just sorry I turned up last night and let me ramble on so much. Why didn't you say anything? I'd have gone away again."

"That's probably exactly why I didn't tell you last night. I'll be fine, thanks. Sorry about your shirt."

"It'll soon dry and any way my nice new, eight quid jumper will cover that up!" he smiled.

"Come on, we've both got school to get to and you've got an hour's journey on that machine of yours, so get moving." And with that she gave her nephew a playful punch in the chest, to which he responded by pretending to stumble backwards which managed to confuse the dogs who joined in with a mixture of barking, jumping and tail wagging until Charlotte let them out for a final 'pee' in the garden.

James left shortly after, churning another groove in the gravel of the rectory driveway whilst drawing attention to the fact that the vicar had entertained a mysterious overnight visitor.

"That'll get the tongues wagging," Charlotte chuckled to herself.

She rather enjoyed hearing rumours about male guests knowing they were as far from the truth as they could be, and such gossip tended to stop other tongues wagging for a bit.

She had precious little time left for wild thoughts before she too had to leave for the local primary school. She loaded the dishwasher, finished off her essential coffee and mentally checked that she had left sufficient instruction for Linda who would let herself in a little later. She might even catch Linda at school when she was dropping off her own children. Unfortunately, yet again, Charlotte was aware that she had squeezed out the prayerful start to the day that she craved. At least she had enjoyed the brief, revitalising early morning walk with Patch and Stitch, which helped clear her head.

She let the dogs back in from the garden and settled them in the kitchen. She left the coffee out for Linda to help herself and went to the study to collect her notes and the hand puppets she needed for the morning story. Her mobile beeped in her pocket. It was a text from Max reporting no news on Mike and hoping the evening had gone well. Charlotte tapped a reply to say that all was well added a few kisses and returned her thoughts to the day ahead. Her mobile announced a caller.

"Hi," said Charlotte as she picked up the phone adopting the cheery informal method of answer reserved for the few friends and family who knew the number.

"Has he left?" came the curt reply.

"Hello Erica," Charlotte sighed, "Yes he left about half an hour a go. He's heading straight for school."

"What about his books and school clothes."

"He's organised your lad, had everything with him."

"What, the little...... you were in this together."

Erica had an unfortunate tendency towards paranoia thinking that others were often plotting against her. Understandable given that William had done just that in the five years leading up to their divorce.

"Erica, please don't start that. I had no idea he was coming until he roared up my driveway and fr..." Charlotte was about to add, '.... and frightened the dogs' but stopped herself, definitely not wanting to open that particular can of worms. Thankfully Erica was too wrapped up in herself to notice the abrupt end to the sentence and Charlotte added quickly. "He's fine, just needed a bit of a moan and a bit of space. He'll be home after school, I'm sure, but go easy on him. Shouting matches won't help."

"Oh, Miss no-it-all, now are we? Shame you've never had kids, then you'd know how it really is."

"Erica, I'm sorry, I really don't have time for this."

"No, you never have time. Miss High and *Al*mighty," and with that put the phone down.

All Charlotte could do, was take a deep breath as she firmly laid both hands on her desk controlling the scream that was threatening to escape. She exhaled slowly and stood back up, before picking up her bag and headed off for St Nicholas Church of England Primary School, where, in twenty minutes' time she would stand in front of 180 children and tell the story of Noah with the help of a panda glove puppet, a stuffed penguin and very odd looking giraffe whose neck had a tendency to bend over due to the compacted stuffing. Willing volunteers would play Noah, his wife and sons and Charlotte predicted chaos and excitement as each class became gorillas, lions, birds, elephants, kangaroos and camels with big humps. The children would love it, and unless Charlotte managed to regain control and quiet at the end, the teachers would spend the rest of the morning gunning for her resignation as they tried to quieten down the excitable youngsters. But she was well liked and usually managed to pull it off, so wasn't unduly concerned.

Chapter 9

David dropped Lizzie, Joshua and Catrin off at Frenchay Hospital before doing further battle with the commuter traffic on the M32 heading towards Bristol City Centre which eventually delivered him to 'Explore-at-Bristol.' To increase a sense of anticipation for Heather they had arranged to meet Vince and Maureen at the ultra-modern coffee shop in the entrance foyer. It had worked and Heather had been more than happy to stay with her granddad knowing that she would soon see Grandpa Vince and Granny Mo.

David and the rest of the family had left Exeter just after 8.00am. David had left a few instructions for Sally, the most important of which was to encourage her to leave early and take back some of the extra time she had worked the previous day. Their faithful and trusted cleaner was also due in at 10.00am and Catrin had left an explanatory note about the children's toys in the bathroom and the nappies hanging from the radiators. Not that it would bother Brenda; she always took what she found at face value, never questioned, and as far as David and Catrin could work out, had never gossiped about what she had found. They could pretty much rely on that assumption ever since poor Brenda had walked into John's room early one summer's morning not realising he was home on holiday from university. She found him naked in bed with Wendy, long before they were husband and wife. Brenda nodded a simple, "Morning John," adding "Miss," in the direction of Wendy, as she had never met the young woman before and of course didn't know her name. She turned around and quietly closed the door, ignoring the stifled giggles coming from the bedroom as she walked down the hall.

For weeks John nervously awaited Brenda's weekly visits, expecting her to have mentioned something to someone about his early morning visitor, but never a word was said. John recalled the story eventually telling his parents sometime after he and Wendy were married and it transpired that as far as anyone could tell Brenda had mentioned it to no-one. Brenda was a very trusted member of the household staff.

David parked easily in the underground car park although it would cost him a fortune. Heather excitedly jumped around beside her grandfather, who was now less formally dressed in brown corduroy trousers an open necked shirt and a cream coloured V-neck jumper over which he wore a wax jacket against the January drizzle. He had replaced his normal black leather shoes with casual dark brown slip-ons and over his shoulder he carried a small rucksack with the essential things a grandfather would need for a day out with his four-year-old granddaughter: juice, wet wipes, favourite cuddly toy, emergency biscuits and a spare pair of knickers and trousers in case of excitable accidents.

Vince and Maureen were waiting patiently in the entrance area and were delighted to see their granddaughter. The plan was to spend the morning with David and Heather, have lunch with Lizzie and Joshua, visit their son in the afternoon and then go on back to their own home in Plymstock for a few days where they were going to look after Max's dogs so she and hopefully, Charlotte could visit Max. After the weekend, Lizzie would take the children home. She would find some sort of routine of visiting Mike from Gloucester with grandparents juggling the child care. David could only offer limited support as his own diocesan duties still needed his attention. But for today, his attention could be on his family and he was content to be pulled around by a four-year-old, rather than pushed round by church bureaucracy.

As a bishop, he once thought he would have power to change things. The sad truth was that he was seen to have authority, but in reality, held very little real power. With little Heather, he wanted neither to exercise power or authority, but simply to have fun.

Heather had now persuaded three grown adults, all of whom had children of their own and should have known better, that a little girl needed a second breakfast of large chocolate cookies, covered in smarties, washed down with a strawberry milkshake. Her grandparents decided coffee was more palatable, but had still been persuaded to eat a colourful cookie each. David found himself wondering at the persuasive powers of his granddaughter, until he thought about his wife and daughter earlier that morning ganging up against him when it came to wearing a tie or not. They won, and he was feeling the cold chill on his rarely exposed neck.   With three doting grandparents in tow Heather would have the time of her life.

At the hospital, Catrin on the other hand was struggling. Joshua had been sick, twice, all down her lamb's wool cardigan, which on reflection had been an unfortunate choice of attire. She might even text David and ask him to pick up a cheap sweatshirt somewhere, but she was worried he would come back from the popular attraction with a brightly coloured hoody and 'I'm a Bristol Explorer' or something similar emblazoned on the front.

Lizzie was with Mike and the Orthopaedic Consultant whilst Catrin had sole charge of her tiny grandson, wishing at that moment that she had agreed when Maureen had said the previous evening that she would stay at the hospital. But Catrin knew how much she would enjoy the trip with her granddaughter and had been sure she could cope with Joshua. After all she had had four of her own, but little Joshua wouldn't settle, probably sensitive to this constant change to his routine. It was possible he could sense the anxiety in his mother, even though he was barely a month old. After a few minutes, Lizzie thankfully came back to find her mother.

"Lamb's wool and baby sick don't really combine well Mum. Here….." Lizzie handed over a piece of muslin fabric, "…..didn't you use the nappy liner?"

"It slipped off," said Catrin raising her eyebrows with a shrug making out she wasn't at all bothered. "I'm more interested in what the Consultant had to say."

"Pretty good news really. He's still poorly of course but things are looking good. Not sure how long he'll be in hospital yet, but he's going to be in that external frame contraption for a couple of months. And of course, he won't be able to use crutches because of the shoulder, so he's not going to be very mobile. The neurologist was there too, which was a miracle. He's pleased with Mike's improvement overnight. He's breathing by himself, moving the bits that aren't broken and responding to pain. In fact, he swore at the junior doctor doing the test. They asked if that might have been out of character."

"What did you say?"

"Oh, Mum I was so embarrassed. I wanted to say yes, but only last week he dropped a book on his toe and hopped about like mad repeating……., well you know it began with S and ended in T. I was laughing so much at the time he looked ridiculous holding onto his foot hopping on the other before he sprawled on the sofa. That seems a lifetime away now. Still, I had to agree his choice of vocabulary was nothing to do with a possible brain injury changing his personality. Lovable gentle bloke that he is, he can still swear as good as any other man when in pain. Just as well they don't give birth, delivery suites would have to be X rated!"

Lizzie was trying to stay as positive as she could, her mum knew that. They enjoyed the joke at the expense of the men in their life, before Catrin continued.

"Well, you'd better brace yourself if you think that might have been embarrassing. We'll have a lot more to cope with before we get the old Mike back. It's hard to imagine him immobilised in that thing."

Catrin was still holding Joshua who had miraculously settled and was sleeping in her arms. But thought she should ask, "Are we going to take Joshua in so his daddy can see him?"

"Let's wait till Mike's on the main ward and away from so many tubes and machines. At least it will be on an orthopaedic ward and not a neurology unit. They are now pretty certain there's no brain damage. The scan was clear. His body just shut down because of all the other injuries, apparently."

"That is such a relief. I tell you what, let's go and get a coffee. Let Mike sleep for a bit." Catrin was also relieved that her tiny grandson could be kept away from the wards a bit longer. She was so concerned about germs, knowing how vulnerable a tiny baby was.

"Let's find a quiet corner so I can feed him properly." Lizzie had got up before dawn to plug herself into the rubber pads in an attempt to suck out a feed so that Joshua could stay with his grandparents. But the only bodily fluids Lizzie had expressed were distressed tears. So, after twenty minutes she had given up, crying out that she was not a prize dairy cow and was unwilling to have her teats sucked by anything other than her own child. Then she threw the machine against her bedroom wall just as her father was passing, and just like she did when she was little, launched herself at her dad, and cried all over his clean shirt.

Mike was aware that he had lost a couple of days. He knew he was in hospital. He knew he was seriously hurt. He still had various tubes coming out of veins and orifices and what felt like the cut off bottom half of a fizzy drinks bottle stuck on his face, which he realised was probably an oxygen mask. A nurse was administering something into what looked like a washing up liquid stopper sticking out of his arm. He had a vague memory of some spotty teenager sticking needles into his leg, but other than that, his world was still hazy. He thought Lizzie was there and was sure his mum and dad had been to see him, but he couldn't be certain. He slept.

Later on that morning, Mike was transferred to a side room on the orthopaedic ward. Once he was comfortable, Lizzie brought Joshua in and laid him on the bed next to his daddy. Mike was awake but not fully alert. He had been given large doses of pain killers before he was moved and whilst the frame around his leg was readjusted. Catrin had gone off the ward to phone Mike's parents so that they would know where to find him. They would be allowed in outside normal visiting time whilst Mike was still off the main ward. The whole family decided to meet for a late lunch and then go to see Mike in the afternoon.

Max received a call from her father giving her the positive news. She was out visiting one of the local farms at the time. A dairy farmer was worried about two of his cows, who seemed very uncomfortable when attached to the milking machine. Max stood outside the milking shed in her manure covered wellingtons as the Dartmoor drizzle trickled down her back listening to her father recalling the events of the morning and how David seemed such a good father and grandfather. It was quite evident that young Heather had twisted all three grandparents round her little finger. Max was glad to hear her father sounding so relaxed, but really wanted to hear more about her brother. She thought it was a good plan for her parents to come on back that evening and an even better plan for them to look after the dogs over the weekend, meaning she and Charlotte could visit Mike together the following day.

Max found the conversation slightly strained. Her parents still hadn't made any connection between David and Charlotte. To them David was simply their son's father in law and the grandpa of Heather and Joshua. They had had a wonderful morning and would all see Michael in the afternoon before heading back to the West Country. David had even relayed his concern to Vince and Maureen about Lizzie and the problems she had with the milk machine, which to Max's surprise her father relayed to her. She didn't have the heart to tell him where she was at that particular moment and wasn't quite sure how she would then go back to continue the examination of the problematic udders with the image of poor Lizzie attempting to attach her own human equivalent. She was slightly concerned about the way everyone was keeping so positive. Mike was doing well, but he was going to be in hospital for weeks and off work for months. Had anyone asked the question about his long-term prognosis? Even as a vet, she knew how difficult it was to give pet owners the full story when things looked bleak. She vowed that between them, she and Charlotte would get a few more answers the following day. She just hoped that their united presence wouldn't bring too many difficulties. They really didn't want to run into Bishop David just yet. She had visions of Charlie diving behind hospital screens or hastily donning a surgical mask to avoid detection, but stopped herself slipping into a fantasy world best kept for more intimate locations. She would ring Charlotte later. It was no good trying her now, she had a busy day ahead of her. Max kept her mind on the undercarriage of two large and rather tetchy cows.

Despite the numerous copies of the e-mails sent earlier that week, Charlotte had forgotten to take her guitar to school, so the children sang unaccompanied. Sure enough, all one hundred and eighty, bar a few off sick with coughs and colds, had joined in wholeheartedly, pretending to be various animals. One Year 6 kangaroo had threatened to bounce on a year two camel-with-a-big-hump but the young camel was saved by a swift thinking lion tamer, otherwise known as Mr Fell the Year 4 teacher. Miraculously Charlotte had even managed to do a very good impersonation of a wild life ranger at the end and had resumed the sense of calm. She had come across a CD of animal sounds in the staff room just before she went into the hall and as she put pictures of lush green landscapes on the screen, gave the cue to one of the Year 6 pupils to start the CD. With a little encouragement, every child was soon spellbound by the sounds of distant lions, cockatiels, the haunting sound of wolves and the screeching of owls as the bright images came up on the screen. Considering it had been a hastily thrown together talk, Charlotte was extremely pleased. Not at all like the end of the previous term when the quiet moment at the end had been annihilated by an unfortunate Year 5 pupil, who without warning, projectile vomited over an extremely distressed Year 3 pupil sitting just in front. It had been put down to the excitement of the approaching Christmas holidays, which was why Charlotte was a little concerned about another excitable assembly.

She enjoyed a coffee with the Head-teacher after the service as they discussed the arrangements for a series of visits to the church the following week. Combined Year groups were due to visit in one hour intervals looking at various aspects of church architecture according to their curriculum. Combining the visits on the one morning meant reduced heating costs for the church, more effective use of time for Charlotte, less administration for the school, and more parents willing to give up one morning to help with supervision. The down side was an anxious few days ensuring that everything would fall into place.

Charlotte was back in her study by 10.30am and glad to have half an hour with Linda before Sam was due to arrive for his supervision session. She suddenly felt exhausted, which was hardly surprising.

She remembered the journey through the morning moorland mist and the care with which she had chosen her outfit. She remembered watching the light dance through the old medieval stained glass in the Bishop's study. She thought about his wife hovering outside the study. She remembered how the Bishop had actively controlled his anger when Charlotte had broken her news and wondered how he would react when he discovered, as he would do at some point, probably within the next few days, that they would both be visiting the same hospital bed, and the loose family connection neither of them had known about.

She thought about James and had a fleeting uncharacteristic pang of fear as she hoped and prayed he was now safely seated at his desk, even if it was only to yawn through his 'A' level history lecture. She thought about Max and the future she hoped they would have together. She thought about Erica and William and the messy divorce that had nearly cost them their son. Her thoughts were clambering over each other and that was without all her parish responsibilities that were constantly vying for her attention. As if on cue Linda's voice broke through her thoughts.

"Charlotte, you're miles away. I might as well be speaking to myself." Linda had been photocopying sheets for the Sunday services, chattering away to Charlotte about the PCC that evening. Linda acted as secretary to the main benefice PCC, although each church management sub-group had their own chair and secretary.

"You look more than ready for your day off tomorrow. Any plans? Off out with the dogs on a nice long walk I bet. I hear the pub at South Bridge do good lunches and they don't mind dogs." Linda was a very chatty individual and Charlotte loved her for it, especially on days when she seemed to run from one meeting to the next. A little light chatter was good for the soul.

Linda had been known to make sandwiches for Charlotte as she sprinted in and out at lunchtime, or to turn up for work with a casserole under her arm for Charlotte's supper that evening. But to Linda's concern even her light-hearted approach seemed to be lost on Charlotte that morning.

"You need a break love," she added.

Charlotte had been sat at her desk staring into nothingness with all her thoughts swimming around in her mind, and had, for a moment even forgotten Linda was there and was certainly not aware that she had been trying to have a conversation.

Charlotte rubbed her forehead trying to bring herself back to reality.

"Just a few things on my mind. I'll be fine."

One of the things that concerned Charlotte most was that if she resigned, Linda may well be out of a job. The benefice had been reluctant to fund the two days Linda worked and were certainly not keen to give her a decent wage at first. But with combining it as a Deanery post and finding a small grant to set up a decent office, she was now an official payee. Charlotte hadn't thought it wise to disclose her plans to Linda, until after the meetings with the Bishop were complete and a definite decision had been made. Not that she thought Linda would spread any rumours, but if her job was on the line it would be understandable if she let something slip. Charlotte then thought of Sasha needing to find different lodgings.

Linda's voice once again broke through her thoughts.

"Come on Boss, can't have you cracking up, Sam is due in twenty minutes and you've got old Moll's funeral over at Sheepsgate this afternoon. Why don't you get a breath of fresh air, take the dogs out in the field for ten minutes? I'll give Sam a coffee when he arrives."

"He'll probably be a little late. I'm not really expecting him much before 11.30. I'm okay. Now what were you saying about the PCC?"

and Charlotte dragged herself back from the brink of insanity to re-engage with the daily task of running eight parishes.

It was 11.45am when twenty-nine-year-old Rev Samuel McDonald finally made it to the Rectory for his supervision session. It had given Linda and Charlotte time to catch up on a lot of business, but left only just over an hour before Charlotte had to leave for the funeral. Linda turned her hand to making a few sandwiches for her boss and the trainee, ensuring they would at least eat something. The sessions were more than simply checking what Sam was doing. It was an opportunity for Sam to learn from Charlotte as she also shared some aspects of her week. On this occasion, they used the example of the young couple who came to see her the previous evening. They also talked about the funeral Sam was taking on Friday as well as going through both their diaries, partly so that they knew when they would actually see each other, which was often a problem across such a spread-out area and eight churches, and partly to ensure they hadn't been asked to do the same thing and partly for Charlotte to have oversight of Sam's time management.

It was the latter that was difficult. Charlotte could pack in a huge amount into her day which might be threatening to somebody straight out of college. She often reminded Sam that she had over fifteen years of sermons to draw on if necessary; she could often negotiate her way around a quick home visit in just twenty minutes and as she had the status of Rector people were simply grateful she had dropped by, but if Sam attempted such a fleeting visit, tongues would start wagging and he would be criticised for not paying enough attention. However, Sam was always trying to cram too much into his day and often, she sensed, felt a bit overwhelmed. All she could do was pass on a few tricks, like

112

the value of having a pressing engagement after about forty minutes into a visit, which was quite long enough for most situations, or the use of the answer phone when desperately trying to finish off a sermon, or in Sam's case sometimes an essay. She often reminded Sam of the danger of agreeing to do something without having a diary in your hand or forgetting to mark in time for administration, which even a second-year curate had to do on occasions.

Linda brought in sandwiches and tea, and dutifully reminded Charlotte of her own pressing engagement at 2pm, just as her palm top gave the thirty-minute warning. So, having given relative justice to Linda's efforts, she invited Sam to stay and finish off the rest and to talk to Linda about the PCC that evening and the timings for his presentation on Healing Services that he was keen to try. Charlotte picked up her robes, books and notes for the funeral and headed off to St Hilda's, three miles into the next small hamlet of Sheepsgate.

She also shot a brief arrow prayer giving thanks that Michael was still alive.

Maureen, Vince, Lizzie, David, Catrin, Heather and baby Joshua all squeezed into Mike's room at 2pm. But it was obvious this was far too much for poor Mike, especially when Heather knocked against the cumbersome frame around his leg, making her father stifle a cry of pain.

Heather wanted to stay with her mummy and daddy, so the grandparents took Joshua to the day room. It was good for the four of them to have some time together. There was only so much you could say about operations and hospitals, so in between passing the young chap round like a parcel they chatted about their respective families.

"What does Mike's sister do for a living?" Catrin asked. "It wasn't really the time to chat on Tuesday night."

"She's a vet round the villages just outside Plymouth," chipped in Vince. "Keeps her busy. She was made a partner last year. They're in the process of buying up a practice in Okehampton, and she might move across to run the place."

"Sounds positive," said David. "Where does she live now?"

"Victorian terraced cottage in Tavistock," said Maureen, "It's quite small but it's got a good-sized garden at the back for the dogs, completely surrounded by a six-foot-high brick wall. It's funny, it's almost like a miniature version of Lizzie and Mike's place."

Maureen was proud of both her children. They had done well in their careers and both owned their own homes.

"Couldn't she commute to Okehampton?" asked Catrin.

"I think she's hoping to buy a second property with her partner and they might rent out the terrace in Tavistock," said Vince.

"Ah, do I hear wedding bells?" Catrin's face lit up, "Perhaps David could do you a discount!" She chuckled. David shot a slightly annoyed glance in her direction to which she replied "Only joking dear. Come on Maureen, what's his name?"

Maureen looked over to her husband for inspiration, or guidance, or support, or perhaps a life jacket she wasn't sure, but Vince had clammed up realising he had let something slip that perhaps Max would rather have kept from her brother's in-laws. He'd almost forgotten that the crazy man chasing Heather around the wide-open spaces of the science and nature exploratory was a bishop. But now was reminded that David may not be all that sympathetic to his daughter's chosen lifestyle.

"Charlie," Maureen blurted out. She didn't want to lie and suddenly realised she didn't need to, well not too much. But she also wanted to change the subject as quickly as she could before they got drawn into a complex string of half-truths that would be sure to trip them up.

But before she could work out a U turn, Catrin handed Joshua over to her saying "Charles. Sounds like a good strong name. What does he do for a living?"

Vince seemed to wake from his momentary lapse of conscious thought.

"Oh, we're not absolutely sure," which was sort of true.

They knew what Charlotte did by name only, but had no real understanding of what her day to day life really entailed. He wasn't sure why he was being so cautious with David and Catrin, but there was a nagging feeling in his mind about David's 'kingdom' or whatever the churchy areas were called. Whatever it was, he certainly didn't want to make things difficult for Charlotte, "something to do with the community."

"Social Worker?" offered Catrin.

Maureen frowned at her husband, but thankfully cottoned on to his train of thought so nodded in agreement. "Yes, something on those lines. Now then young man," as she lifted Joshua up to her nose and sniffed his bottom, "I think you might need a nappy change."

David had been thoughtful for the last few minutes. He remembered the time he had told a girl on a first date that he was training to be a community worker, rather than let on he was actually training for the priesthood. Their relationship didn't last.

"I'll do it Maureen," said David. "Why don't you and Vince pop back in and see Michael? You'll want to make a move soon if you are going to avoid the worst of the traffic. We don't need to leave till this evening. Heather can sleep on the way home."

He took Joshua in his arms and laid him on the floor as Catrin collected the changing bag from the bottom of the children's buggy, one that would convert from the present setting making it similar to a pram, right through to a toddlers' push chair. It even had an attachment for Heather to stand on at the back.

Maureen passed Joshua back to David, as she did.

"Be good for your Grampy," said Maureen, giving Joshua a peck on his forehead, and she and Vince left the day room to spend a little more time with their son.

"Was it my imagination or did they seemed guarded?" quizzed Catrin.

David didn't answer directly, but instead replied with his own caution. "If Maxine wants to keep her private life a secret it's none of our business."

"Alright, no need to be tetchy. Perhaps I should sort out Joshua. Why don't you go and have a walk around outside, get some fresh air?" After thirty-five years of marriage Catrin thought she knew when her husband needed a break and was one of the few people close enough to tell him, but she didn't always get it right.

"Catrin, I'm fine. Vince and Maureen didn't want to discuss Max, and I respect that, especially in parents, no matter how old or young the children are."

Ignoring the caution, Catrin persisted, "So you think they were keeping something back?"

"It's really none of our business, love, let it go." David was still calm, but firm.

"Can you take that purple pious shirt off for just a moment and have a good old gossip, there's no-one else here."

Catrin was a very good Bishop's wife. She was extremely supportive and rarely complained about the limitations her husband's job placed on their private life. Not only that but she was very good at bringing David back to earth, dragging him away from the risk of overstating his religious values and was never overawed by the importance of his position. She knew every single one of his vices, and such knowledge gave her equal power. David had already got out a clean nappy and was in the process of removing Joshua's Babygro.

"Phew stinky man, you've performed well. You know love, it never ceases to amaze me, how green their poo is at this age."

"Okay, you win, no more questions," said Catrin, backing down as she crouched down on the floor next to her husband and beloved grandson, "but I still think there's something about Charles that sounds a bit sinister. Why else would they be so hesitant? You could do with a bath little one. Where are those wet-wipes? Do you remember days before tubs of wipes David?"

"No, thank goodness!" said David grabbing three from the pot in an extravagant gesture and resisted the temptation of spouting off his favourite comment about those in the third world content with a rag to wash through, as he pulled an environmentally unfriendly disposable from the plastic packet of nappies for new-borns.

Lizzie walked back in with Heather attached to her hip.

"Phew, that's a stinky one," she commented unknowingly mimicking her father's words. "I've let Vince and Maureen spend a few minutes alone with Mike. He's getting tired though. He keeps on about wanting to see his sister. I didn't realise they were that close. Oh Dad, I thought you were good at nappies, you've got it the wrong way around."

She unhooked Heather and placed her on the floor so she too could crouch down next to her gran and grampy and join the family effort to change one nappy on one small child. Much to Heather's delight she was allowed to clamber on top of her granddads back and he immediately responded by playing 'horsey'. Soon laughter came from the largely unused day room, which was a welcome reprieve from the sobriety of the last forty-eight hours.

As David, Catrin and Lizzie enjoyed a few moments of light hearted childish play with Heather, Maureen and Vince were keeping vigil in Mike's room. They looked anxiously on as their son seemed to battle through a haze of sedation. "Max......" Mike seemed to call for his sister. Maureen looked questioningly over to her husband, but he shrugged. Neither could understand why Mike was so eager to see his sister.

"Ssshh love, we're going home now. Max will come soon. We're going to look after the dogs for a few days." Maureen was desperately worried about her son and was struggling to hold back her tears. He seemed like a child again; vulnerable, dependent and defenceless.

"Dad?" Many things were going through Mike's mind. When he closed his eyes, he relived the first few minutes of the accident. He remembered pushing his way out of the car and then nothing. He was still confused about his injuries. He couldn't understand why so much seemed to be wrong, when he had walked away from the accident. No-one had thought to tell him that he had in fact survived two accidents on that winter's afternoon. All he knew was that he had been involved in a serious car accident.

Mike spoke again, his voice a little stronger, "Is Max here?" He had a vague recollection of his sister on that first night, but his memory was playing tricks.

"Max will get here soon love," and turning to her husband Maureen whispered, "I don't understand why he's so concerned about Max, they hardly ever see each other?"

"May be that's why. They were close when they were little." They turned back to look at their son, but he looked as if he was asleep again.

"Come on sweetheart," Vince put an arm around his wife's shoulder, "let's leave him to rest. It's already gone four and we promised Charlie we'd pick the dogs up by six."

Mike seemed to suddenly rally and even appeared to attempt to sit up using his one good arm without much success.

"Hey come on son, steady on, you can't do that, I'll get a nurse." His father was concerned.

"No....., I'm okay" spluttered Mike through a sudden searing pain at his shoulder. "The dogs....with Charlie."

"Yes, they're fine. There's nothing for you to worry about. We're going to get them now on our way home. I think Max is going over later tonight and hopefully they can see you tomorrow." Maureen was puzzled by Mike's anxiety.

"David..... don't tell him."

119

"Don't tell him what son? I'm sorry I don't understand. You have to concentrate on getting better. Come on settle down. Are you in pain? I'll get the nurse to give you something." Vince used the voice he once used for both his children when they refused to sleep at night. Mike gave up and shut his eyes only to be transported back to a fretful sleep of hazy terrors and confusion.

Maureen and Vince gently kissed their son goodbye, but he didn't stir. They left, briefly pausing at the day room to say goodbye and give Heather a final hug.

The remaining adults took the children to the hospital restaurant, giving themselves a break and allowing Mike to sleep for a while.

Chapter 10

The drizzle and mist from earlier in the day had persisted long into the afternoon, making an extra mournful backdrop for the burial after the funeral. Molly Edith Sidcup had been known in the small hamlet as Old Moll ever since she had been widowed during the second world war at just twenty-eight years of age. The shock and stress had turned her hair white over-night. She had no children and had never remarried, but had taught at the Sunday School until she was eighty-two so was well known and respected, although not always well liked. She had a tendency to speak her mind and often did. She had certainly not held back when Charlotte was appointed Rector to the benefice. She had written to the Bishop to explain to him that he had no business sending a young woman to do a man's job.

At the age of ninety-one she had persuaded an eminent orthopaedic surgeon that she was quite fit enough for a hip replacement. There were some who thought Old Moll had known the successful man when he was a young boy attending her Sunday School, but the rumours were never confirmed. Two years later she somehow managed to persuade the same surgeon to perform a minor exploratory operation on her knee but sadly, although not unexpectedly, had suffered a stroke on the table. She survived, but never returned home, ending her battle three months later, on a hospital ward in Exeter.

Charlotte had the task of drawing the story of Old Moll's long and somewhat turbulent life to an end. It emerged that Moll had in fact had several affairs over the years, but Charlotte chose discretion over the stories she included in the formal tribute, knowing that the more colourful aspects of Moll's life would be shared later in the Red Lion, where several villagers would gather for the traditional wake.

After the short service in church the mourners made their way to the rather bleak graveside. The wintery Dartmoor wind whipped around the tomb stones and sent a chill through those who shivered waiting for old Moll to be lowered into the red tinged, sandy damp soil. Out of respect, all those who had attended the service now gathered for the final words of committal. There were a handful of villagers, joined by a couple of support staff from the hospital ward along with the surgeon, who Moll had so efficiently manipulated, laying weight to the Sunday School claims.

The only surviving family had made the trip from Kent; a distant nephew and his wife. The nephew had made the funeral arrangements over the phone. Charlotte had struggled to connect in any meaningful way with the family. They didn't seem to know very much at all about their aunt.

For the tribute, Charlotte padded out what she already knew by talking to one or two older parishioners. The nephew seemed more concerned about keeping the cost down, rather than what might be included in the service itself. He started off by suggesting they didn't need an organist as he didn't want to sing any hymns. Charlotte had persuaded him otherwise. The nephew's real interest seemed to rest with Old Moll's cottage. He had even asked Charlotte if she knew when the cottage could be cleared out so they could renovate the place and turn it into (yet another) village holiday let. Charlotte had been very restrained in her response, adopting an extremely professional manner. She couldn't believe it when the couple had held each other close and sobbed all the way through the service. As far as anyone could tell, they hadn't seen their aunt in over ten years, since their own father had passed away in the neighbouring village of Upton. Charlotte tried not to linger too long over her thoughts of hypocritical relatives.

Old Moll was safely interred and handfuls of earth thrown down onto the coffin. One or two people threw rose petals, which Charlotte thought was a nice touch. For all her eccentric and annoying ways, Moll had held a soft spot in many people's hearts. If you kept on the right side of old Moll she would remain a loyal friend, as long as she was allowed to talk straight without you taking offence. Her loyalty had soon extended to the new vicar, ever since Charlotte had made several round trips to the Exeter hospital. Old Moll's long standing and very outspoken views of female priests had quite changed, and she had made those enlightened views quite clear to a certain Philip Dixon, the Lay Reader who refused to accept communion from Charlotte. Philip mysteriously stopped visiting Moll and hadn't turned up to the funeral.

Charlotte decided not to join the wake but returned home by 3.30pm, just missing Linda who had left to pick up her children from school.

It was then that Charlotte realised she had chance of the first bit of space in nearly three days. She glanced through her study door and noticed a couple of messages from Linda but would deal with those and attack her e-mails after a cup of tea and a walk with the dogs.

She was expecting Vince and Mo to call between six and seven. Any later and they would have to wait till Max arrived with the key sometime after nine. Charlotte felt her whole life was a constant merry go round of organising and prioritising. It always was. There were never enough hours in the day or days in the week, but tomorrow was her day off. She would at least spend it with the woman she loved, albeit around Mike's bedside. Just the small matter of the main benefice council meeting that evening when the annual budget would be discussed, in addition to the planned improvements to St Nicholas. She would survive only in the knowledge that at the end of the day she could at long last collapse into Max's arms with a large glass of Merlot.

She was so tired. She would need to dig down deep to gain the energy to chair the meeting whilst remaining calm, keeping her irritations about certain people in check. They were the ones who could always be relied on to complain about something truly trivial, or always took forever to point out a potential problem that would probably never happen, or always reminded the council about previous mistakes.

Although the moor had remained misty all day, the late afternoon had at last brought some dry weather. Charlotte gulped down her tea and put collars and leads on two excited dogs. She could hear the work phone in the background but whoever it was would have to wait, she needed some fresh air.

"I don't think she's in." Vince tried to ring Charlotte to tell her they were about to leave.

"Leave a message," said Maureen.

"Er, hello. Hello Charlie. This is Vince. Just to say we're leaving Bristol. Hope to be with you about six. Er, bye. Over."

"You're not in the army now, you silly old bugger." Maureen was a down to earth Devonian born and bred.

"I know, but I still don't like leaving messages on those things."

"Well you'd better press the off button on your mobile then, you're still connected and Charlie's tape will be full."

"Oh," and added in a louder voice. "Sorry Charlie," before doing as Maureen directed.

They started up the engine and headed off to Langford.

Patch and Stitch were delighted to be out. Charlotte took them down the lane towards Combe Cross, past the cottage where Moll's brother used to live, where she noticed a new looking Audi sitting outside with a German number plate. 'Another letting,' she thought to herself. 'No wonder the nephew wants his hands on Moll's cottage.'

It was a very popular area for holidays, not far from the sea but still on the edge of the moor and not far from the bustling towns of Exeter and Plymouth. They walked up and through St Agnes graveyard. Charlotte let her thoughts wander and found herself contemplating just how much of her time in any one week she spent dealing with death; there was usually at least one funeral each week in the benefice, always a bereaved family to follow up and quite often an issue lurking about a headstone in ill repair.

Once through the church grounds and into the open space behind, she took the dogs off the lead and they bounded off running the full breadth of the field in huge circles, chasing each other, sniffing out the hedges, always returning to Charlie every few minutes, either as a reminder they were still there, or as a reminder to themselves that Charlotte hadn't gone too far. They were brilliant dogs and she was definitely a second mum.

Back in the small terraced house in Tavistock, Max had returned home for a shower before the evening surgery. The delightful dairy cows had taken a dislike to so much attention being paid to their undercarriage and had managed to push an off-guard Maxine backwards onto the cattle shed floor. 'At least it wasn't in the manure covered yard' she thought, as she picked bits of straw out of her hair. Only once had she returned home with cowpat in her hair, but that was when she and Charlie had been out rambling with the dogs and Max was showing off on top of a stile only to slip off onto a soft but rather smelly landing.

Max had been out on rounds all day and hadn't even stopped for lunch, although friendly farmer's wives had kept her going with coffee and the occasional biscuit. She would have to be at the practice by five, so only had an hour to shower, eat something and get back. She packed an overnight bag to take to Langford, although practically everything she needed was already there. She'd go straight from the surgery and hoped to be at the Rectory by the time Charlie got back from the PCC. They'd both need a drink by then and Max would cook them supper.

In the shower, she found herself thinking of their plans to buy a house in Okehampton. In a strange sort of way, she hoped it would still be years before they could live together. She really didn't want Charlie to stop being a priest. But Charlie often got so upset about being forced to lead this double life that she knew something would have to change. She couldn't help the nagging feeling that it would be their relationship that would end and not Charlotte's career, but she pushed those thoughts to the back of her mind. They would find a way. 'If only the church could see sense, everyone would be happy,' she mused.

Back at the hospital Mike was awake as Lizzie walked into the side room. The sleep had done him good and he tolerated being propped up slightly supported by several pillows.

"Where's Heather?" he asked, much brighter than he had been all day.

"In the day room with Mum and Dad," Lizzie answered adding, "you seem brighter."

She reached over and gave her husband a peck on the cheek. Mike responded by reaching up with his good arm and stroking her cheek.

"I feel it," he said, using the same arm to adjust his position slightly, but grimacing as he did so. "Are your mum and dad still here?"

"Hmm," frowned Lizzie, "maybe not as bright as you thought. I've just said they're in the day room......"

"Oh sorry. Yes of course. In the day room with Heather, and Josh hopefully."

"Josh-ua!" When they named their little boy Joshua they vowed not to shorten it. That promise lasted about three days, before Mike adopted 'Josh'. 'It's more manly' he had said, to which Lizzie replied. 'A three-day old baby is not supposed to be manly!' But coming from a family tradition of shortening names in was inevitable. At least 'Heather' couldn't really be shortened.

"Yes, they're all there." Lizzie assured her husband, "I'll go and get them. Heather really wants to see you."

"No wait a minute." Mike put his arm on Lizzie's. "I need to ask you about what's happened. It's so confused. I know I got out of the car and I was fine. But now look at me, I'm a mess. Max was here. At least I think she was..... yes, I know she was.... I can't really remember. What

127

happened to the others? In the accident, …… it was horrible. Screaming…… and the next thing I remember, was trying to wake up, but everything was just grey." As he spoke Mike got more and more agitated. He was still attached to a pulse monitor and Lizzie noticed the number rising steadily.

"There's plenty of time for all that. Calm down this isn't doing you any good," and with that a nurse walked into the room

"Mr Tannin, what are you doing?" She busied herself checking Mike's blood pressure. She shone a light into his eyes, squeezed the drip that was still attached to his arm and manually took his pulse.

"Try and keep him calm Mrs Tannin. He's still in shock." The nurse left before Mike or Lizzie could say a word.

"Mike, please don't get worked up like that." Lizzie rested her hand on his arm again and sat down on the chair resting her head close to his. This seemed to calm him again as he found himself closing his eyes.

"Was I hit by something?" he asked through half closed eyes. Lizzie glanced again at the monitor. It seemed back to normal.

"They think you got out of the car, but then got hit by a truck. That's when you sustained most of the injuries, but you'll mend, you just need time and lots of loving care, and I've got lots of love to give."

"Like Max." It was an odd comment thought Lizzie. But before she could ask Mike what he meant she realised that he had once again dropped off to sleep. Those brief moments of wakefulness were obviously going to be very brief for a while. She stayed where she was, her head still resting close to his and without realising it, she too nodded off to sleep for a few minutes.

Joshua was getting hungry and needed his mummy, Heather was getting bored and wanted to see her daddy, so David went off to see if it was okay to bring the children in to Mike's room. The single room was situated just behind the Nurses' station and as he approached, the nurse put her finger on her lips and beckoned him over. She whispered to David to look into the room where he saw his daughter bent over the bed, both of them sleeping. But, just as if she could feel their eyes on her, she awoke and sat up suddenly making Mike moan in a somewhat more drugged induced sleep. She turned and saw her father and the nurse and mouthed 'sorry'. But there was no need, both were smiling. She got up slowly and walked over.

"He's sleeping again, but he's so worried about what has happened. I think we need to tell him a bit more." She directed her comment to the nurse.

"If he's asking, then tell him, but go gently. He will switch off when he's heard enough. Don't push it too hard. He's been through a lot." The nurse turned back to her station and busied herself with her prescription charts.

"That's what he did just now, Dad, just seemed to drift off to sleep when he'd had enough. He's still asking about his sister. I think I should ring her, and ask her if she can come up again."

"Are they close?" asked her father.

"Well that's just it, I don't think they are, not really. They do see each other I suppose. Mike sometimes pops in on a Friday night if he's been working down that way. The firm have got show rooms in Plymouth and Exeter. But she never comes up to see us. There's about eight years between them, so no, I didn't think they were that close."

129

"She was with you Tuesday night. Dropped everything, no hesitation. Not all sisters would do that."

"True. I must admit, part of me thought that was just for Maureen and Vince's sake. Oh well, sisterly and brotherly love. It's a strange thing eh Dad?"

Lizzie was thinking about her own siblings and the fights they used to have and the distant relationship they now enjoyed, but she knew that they would always be there for each other and was already looking forward to John and Wendy visiting over the weekend.

"What time is it?" She asked her dad.

They were still by Michael's door so David spoke quietly so as not to wake him. "Just before five. Joshua was getting fractious, probably needs a feed and Heather is getting bored and desperate to see her dad."

"We'd better go back to the day room for a bit, let Mike rest a little longer. I'll feed Josh and we can bring the children back in later."

They heard a quiet distant voice coming from Mike's direction, it sounded like "UA!" but Mike's eyes were closed. Lizzie looked over to him, he briefly opened his eyes and mouthed "Josh-ua," smiled and closed them again.

"He'll be fine dad, I know he will." Lizzie smiled and gave her dad a great big hug.

Charlotte had been out with the dogs for nearly an hour, longer than she had planned, but it was such a very welcome end to the afternoon.

It was dark by the time she got home, although it was still only 4.30pm. Coming through the back door she pulled off her wellies and managed to grab both dogs before they bounded inside with muddy paws. Using the now very soiled towel set aside for the task, she wiped eight paws, two muddy tails and two tummies. Then she released them both to chase each other to their water bowls. She decided to feed them early so the food would settle before the car journey back to Plymstock. All her domestic chores complete she left the dogs to chomp down their food, which wouldn't take long and skidded along to the hall to her study to see how many messages had been left in her absence.

The first must have been just as she was going out the door. It was from Vince and she chuckled at his old army style of communicating. It was however effective and she knew she had just over an hour before they were likely to arrive. A couple of people had left a message to give their apologies for the meeting that evening. One person had been honest enough to simply say they were too tired. 'If only I could say that,' she thought, but censored her thoughts reminding herself that she had just been able to take an hour off to go on a walk and actually got paid for chairing such meetings, unlike the rest of the members who did it in their free time, after work, and often before dinner. There was also a message from Sash.

"Where the fuck are you Vic? Ooops hope Linda's not listening. Sorry Linda. I've tried your mobile Charlie, but it's switched off, or your battery's run out. Just wondering about..... Oh, well. You know. Look give me a ring, will you?"

It was obvious that Sasha was trying to ask about Michael but had suddenly realised that Linda might indeed still be picking up messages, hence the disjointed prose. Charlotte checked her phone. It was off and when she tried to switch it back on, it was indeed out of battery.

"Damn," she said out loud, as an inquisitive Patch popped his head around the door of the study, his whole rear end wagging to and fro, excited that he had found his adopted mum.

"Come on you, go and lie down in the lounge with your sister while I find the charger for this phone." More tail wagging as Charlotte led him back down the hall on her way upstairs to retrieve the charger from her bed side table. Sash had a habit of knowing things, thought Charlotte. It was uncanny. Whilst she was upstairs she changed into a light grey trouser suit and cream clerical shirt ready for the evening meeting.

Back in the study she plugged in her mobile and texted Sasha to reassure her that Mike was still alive, doing well and she and Max would see him tomorrow. She then collected her file and notes for the meeting which would be held in St Nicholas Church, so that the gathered minds could relate architectural plans for the new development to the actual building. Then she remembered she had to turn on the heating, so abandoned her preparations, picked up the large church key from the wall cupboard, slipped on her trainers that lived by the front door and took a brisk four-hundred-yard walk to the church. It was five thirty.

Vince and Maureen had made excellent time, having left Frenchay on the outskirts of Bristol just after 3.30pm. There were no hold ups on the motorway and they had got to Exeter in record time. Rather than stop they decided to take advantage of the clear road and made their way down the A38 before heading cross country to arrive at Charlotte's Rectory shortly after 5.30pm.

No answer.

Or rather the only answer was the sound of two excited dogs, pretending to sound like good guard dogs and failing.

"Try her mobile," suggested Maureen.

Vince found the contact list and rung Charlotte's number – they heard her land line through the rectory door.

"Ring off a minute," said Maureen, as she listened with her ear against the door. The phone stopped. "Silly old fool, give it yer." Maureen peered at the phone. "Oh bother, I need my reading glasses," and gave the phone back to a patient Vince, who tried the next number down. Maureen again listened carefully at the door. She heard a strange noise that sounded like a flock of sheep, interspersed with more barking. Then Vince spoke into his phone.

"Charlotte love we're at the Rectory. We'll wait in the car. Sorry we're early. Can you let us know when you'll be home?"

"In about two seconds," came the reply from behind, "as soon as Mo has removed her ear from my door! Hello both." Charlotte gave them each a hug. "Come on inside, it's too cold to stand on the door step. Watch the dogs though, they're running loose!"

It was an apt warning as both Patch and Stitch slid around on the wooden hallway floor, rear ends wagging, jumping up, turning circles and barking. Charlotte trying to sound authoritative kept saying, "Down! Down both of you. Down!" which in the excited melee did not seem to have a great effect.

"DOWN." Vince used a voice that the women hardly ever heard. It made them both jump but to Charlotte's quiet pride didn't do much to quieten the dogs. Admitting defeat Charlotte grabbed their collars and led them both out into the garden to run off the excess energy.

"Phew, now then you two," Charlotte turned her attention to her 'nearly-in-laws'. "I'm sure you could do with a cup of tea."

"That would be lovely," said Vince.

"But don't let us interrupt your work," added Maureen.

"I'm okay for a bit. Sorry I was out when you arrived, I had to pop down to church. I couldn't have been gone more than ten minutes." Charlotte led them towards the kitchen.

"Dogs are a bit boisterous tonight," Vince said anxiously.

"Excitement! Don't worry, they've been really well behaved. No unwanted messages which is good. They've been for a walk this afternoon and I've already fed them, so all they'll need is a short walk tonight.

"Charlie, love, you are good." Maureen was genuinely fond of her 'second daughter' as she often called her.

Charlotte smiled but then her face dropped, "Oh bum, I've not told Sasha, you're taking them. I'll text her in a minute! Come on, first I'd like to know how Michael is. Max phoned earlier and said he was conscious and seemed to be making good progress. You know we're hoping to go up tomorrow?"

"Yes. We're pleased. He keeps on asking for Max..........." said Vince and with Maureen's help continued to give Charlotte an update as they sat in the kitchen whilst Charlotte made tea.

"Mike's parents seem nice," said Maureen as the medical update began to wane. "We met them at the wedding and at Heather's baptism of course, but that's all. It's the first time we've really spent any time with them alone."

Charlotte wasn't sure if Mo and Vince had made the connection between her and David. She didn't want to start quizzing them. As Charlotte was pondering these thoughts, Maureen was struggling with her conscience. She didn't know whether or not to confess to Charlotte that she had somehow let David and Catrin think that Max was about to settle down with somebody called Charles. She caught Vince's eye. He seemed to know what was going through his wife's mind and discretely shook his head.

"Well time's getting on love, we'd best make tracks." Vince got up and helped his wife to her feet. "Let's get those dogs sorted, if we ever manage to drag them in from that that paddock of yours."

It was true Charlotte's back garden was huge, but when she opened the door, both were lying down waiting patiently, their tails twitching just enough to show their pleasure at being shown some attention, but this time they stayed calm, apparently having got the message that over-excited dogs would not be tolerated at the Rectory. Vince and Charlotte loaded them into the back seat of the Mondeo whilst Maureen 'powdered her nose', as she liked to describe it.

It was six thirty. Charlotte waved them off and hurried back to her study to finish getting her papers ready for the meeting, grabbing an apple and a banana from the fruit bowl to keep her going till she and Max enjoyed a late supper.

Chapter 11

Liz was trying to persuade her daughter to say goodbye.

"Heather, kiss Daddy goodbye. We have to go home now."

David and Catrin had left Lizzie and the children alone with Michael for a few minutes.

"I want to stay with Daddy. I can sleep in his bed." Heather had been extremely quiet in Michael's room and had sat most of the time on her grandpa's lap. Now she was on the other side of the bed holding her daddy's good hand.

"You have to look after Mummy for Daddy." Mike was feeling weak, but managed to ruffle his daughter's hair. "Mummy will need your help with Joshua."

"Grampy can do that. I can look after you."

Mike felt a tear trying to escape.

"Time to go Heather, no arguments. Daddy has lots of people to look after him. You've got a special day with Grandma tomorrow. She's taking you swimming." Lizzie put on her most positive encouraging voice, partly to convince Heather that arguments were pointless and having spotted Mike's distress, to distract her attention from her daddy for a moment, giving him time to compose himself.

"Ready?" David's head appeared at the door.

"Nearly. Heather go with Grampy. Can you take Josh Dad? I'll be there in a minute."

"We'll be in the main corridor," said David, lifting Joshua gently against his shoulder.

"I'll come by myself tomorrow Mike. Except I'll probably have Joshua with me though. I can't leave him all day. At least I can't go all day with him feeding. I'll burst, unless I can get that stupid machine to work."

"Be careful, I'm worried about all the driving. Why don't you have a day off. Max is coming, isn't she?"

"Yes, and I'd like to see her. I hardly know your sister, and any way, I hear she's got a new man."

"What?" Mike tried to sit up, without success and groaned in pain.

"Steady on. Mike!" Lizzie was taken aback by Mike's obvious surprise and immediately regretted bringing it up when she was about to leave. "I'm sorry, I assumed you knew. Our parents have been on a fact-finding tour. She and Charles are hoping to buy a house in Okehampton."

Mike's reaction was an even bigger surprise. "Charles?" He laughed, although it hurt to do so. "You mean Charlie?"

"Charlie, Charles. What's the difference?" Lizzie was puzzled and couldn't work out what was so funny.

"Is Charles coming tomorrow?" asked Mike his voice still quavering partly from the knowledge of Charlie's confused gender and partly through weakness, as he struggled to stay awake.

"No idea. I wouldn't have thought so. What's so funny Mike?" Lizzie was confused.

"Oh nothing. Really it's not funny." But he was still chuckling, "It's not funny at all. It's tragic. It's so trag......" But Mike had drifted off to sleep. Lizzie kissed her husband, stroked his hair and laid her hand briefly on his chest before turning away and heading off to find the rest of her family.

As she left the room Mike opened his eyes again and mouthed "I love you," but it was inaudible.

By the end of a busy animal surgery, Max had played host to three cats, four dogs, a rabbit, a budgie and a pair of guinea pigs. The guinea pigs had been brought in by their young owner because they wouldn't stop 'fighting'. Having checked the sex of the little creatures, Max had explained to the owner that the only course of action was to keep them separate, but turned to their young owner's mum and quietly explained a rather more amorous reason behind their encounters. Max decided it was best left to Mum to explain in as much or as little detail as she felt appropriate for a six-year-old.

It was nearly seven by the time surgery was finished. She had a quick chat with the receptionist whilst they went through the rota for the weekend. Max then checked the three in-patients, leaving them in the very capable hands of the on-site nurse for the evening, before she left leaving the receptionist to divert the emergency calls to the on-call vet and to lock up the main surgery.

Twelve hours after her shift had started Max was officially off duty. She would be at the Rectory in very good time. She decided to ring her parents.

"We're home. The dogs are fine." Vince adopted his radio voice as he replied to Max on his mobile. "Why don't you ring on the proper phone?"

"Dad, I'll pop round on my way to Charlie's. She won't be home till about ten. Be there in about half an hour."

"Alright. Over." The phone went dead.

Max had rung for an update on Mike not the dogs, but that was her dad. She scrambled into her Land rover and took the back lanes to Plymstock.

"You going to tell her?" Maureen was in her apron cooking scrambled eggs on toast for a light supper when she heard Vince on the phone assuming correctly that it was her daughter.

"Tell her what?" asked Vince.

"About us changing Charlie into a bloke!"

"We didn't. They did."

"Hmm and we didn't correct them." Maureen bent down to place the bread on the grill.

"It's not our place. It's their business."

"But why doesn't Lizzie know? She must know. Mike must have told her."

"What does it matter?" Vince tried not to sound too concerned.

"It matters because we've deceived them and they're nice people."

"We didn't really mean to. It was awkward. They'll forget about it. They'll be more concerned about their daughter than what their daughter's sister-in-law gets up to in bed."

"Vince don't be so vulgar!" Maureen had been stirring the scrambled egg and now she turned and wagged the wooden spoon at her husband.

"I'm not. I don't see what all the fuss is about. Just drop it love and watch those eggs. I think they've caught."

"Oh bloody Nora, that's my best milk saucepan."

"Don't let Charles hear you using language like that," Vince grinned,

"Very funny. Poor thing will be Charles forever now! We'll have to tell Max though. She'll be here in a minute."

Vince glanced at his watch, "We might not get chance to say much tonight. She won't have many minutes to spare. By the time the dogs have half licked her to death she'll have to be on her way to Langford."

"I feel sorry for them." Maureen was scrapping the eggs into the bin, "I'll have to soak this pan. It might come clean."

"Sorry for who?" asked Vince, "Lizzie and Mike or the eggs?"

Maureen threw a tea towel in Vince's direction which he caught in one hand.

"Max and Charlie actually. All they want to do is live their life and here we are worried to even admit to good people that they have a relationship."

"Their choice." Vince looked away.

"You don't really approve do you."

Vince sighed and scratched his neck. "Any more eggs, or do I need to go and get some?"

"Don't change the subject."

"Look, love. What I truly think doesn't matter. I like Charlotte as a person. I wish my daughter had found a nice young man and had had babies. But if she's happy that's all that really matters. But at the moment I think our main concern should be for Mike. Let's just drop it. Now do we need more eggs?"

"No, there's a new half dozen in the fridge." Maureen knew the subject was closed, for the time being.

Bishop David Graham, wife, daughter, granddaughter and grandson arrived home via the fish and chip shop at 7.30pm. Heather had enjoyed a bag of crisps in the car but had refused the sandwich and apple they had bought at the hospital.

Although it was late, the four-year-old greedily tucked into her small portion of fish and a few chips sat on the kitchen floor eating out of the paper whilst her mother ran her bath. Joshua was asleep in his baby carrier.

"I can't believe we did all that today." David was sitting with a glass of beer at the kitchen table.

"So much for a day of rest, Bishop!" Catrin was busy dividing the rest of the fish and chips onto three plates as she looked over to her husband. She softened her voice adding "I'm sorry you've had all the driving today. You must be tired. Will you be okay tomorrow?"

"Of course, plenty of life in the old boy yet," replied David as he patted his ample stomach.

"You should go easy on the beer and chips, you know what the doctor said about your cholesterol."

"Yep. He said to go easy on the beer and chips and I do I am most kind to them once a week and I give them a loving home in here!" once again pointing to his stomach.

Lizzie could be heard calling down the stairs. "Has Heather finished? Her bath is ready."

"Nearly, shall I put your supper in the oven for a bit?" Catrin answered.

"Please. Is Joshua still asleep?"

"Like a baby!" Catrin called back up.

"Send Heather up when she's finished." Lizzie went back to sorting out the bedroom while she waited for her daughter.

"Come along poppit, quick splash and into bed. You must be tired too," said David as he stooped down to pick up the discarded fish wrappings.

"Night Grampy" and Heather kissed her grandfather's cheek.

"Do I get one too?" Catrin asked her granddaughter, "and your brother, but gently he's asleep."

Heather crawled across the floor to kiss her brother on the forehead and held up her arms to her grandmother, who picked her up in a bear hug, gave her a kiss and carried her to the bottom of the stairs. "Incoming child," she called up to her daughter.

"Right you are. Come on Heather climb up those stairs. Give your grandparents some peace and quiet for five minutes." And in answer to her mother's voice Heather obediently clambered up the stairs under Catrin's watchful eye.

"She's growing up already," said Catrin back in the kitchen putting all three plates back in the oven to keep warm.

"She's too tired to make a fuss you mean," replied her husband.

"Cynic!"

"Realist more like. No, she's great. I really enjoyed today. Hope Vince and Maureen got back okay."

"Ring them," suggested Catrin.

"Do we have their number?"

"Not sure, it'll be in the address book if we do, under Tannin."

"Funny that!" David was used to the clear instruction he often received from his wife.

"Sorry," Catrin joined her husband sat at the kitchen table, "I'm tired too. Don't bother them tonight, they must be shattered poor things. Didn't they say they were picking up Max's dogs from someone?"

"Oh yes. I wonder why this new man Charles couldn't look after them?"

"Too busy maybe."

"Maybe." A brief companionable silence descended between them. David broke the spell, "I think I'll go and help Lizzie. Keep an eye on Josh."

"Joshua!"

"Hmm. Whatever you say."

Max arrived at her parent's home just before 8pm. It wasn't exactly on her way, but she wanted to see the dogs and get a proper update on her brother. Her mother greeted her at the door with the usual, "Are you hungry love?" before planting a kiss on her cheek.

"Hi Mum. No, I'll eat later with Charlie, thanks. Where are the dogs?"

"Your father's just taking them round the block."

"I would have done that Mum."

"Yes, I know, that's why he's taken them, otherwise we'd never get chance to talk before you'd have to go again. He'll be back in a minute."

"You know me too well. You got the kettle on?"

"Already brewing. It's under the cosy."

Max went into the kitchen, leaving her mum in the lounge. She poured a mug of strong steaming tea for them both and poured milk into a third mug ready for her father. She took the mugs into the lounge and handed one to her mother.

"You must both be tired. Are you sure about looking after the dogs tonight?" Max sipped her tea holding the mug between her hands.

"Bit late now love. Of course we're sure. When do you want to pick them up?"

"Slightly depends on Charlie," said Max taking a sip of her tea, "either tomorrow evening or Saturday morning if you can cope with them for that long. I'm on call again from 6pm on Saturday."

"Leave it till Saturday then, they'll be fine. Will you stay at Charlie's tomorrow night?"

"Like I said it depends on Charlie, but hopefully."

Maureen reached for the biscuit barrel on the side table and passed them across to her daughter.

"Maybe just one," Max said as she reached in for a chocolate covered digestive. "You need to go easy on the biscuits Mum," she said as she watched her rather over-weight mother take two ginger nuts.

"At my age, dear, I don't mind if I wear elasticated waist bands."

Max dropped the subject of her mother's weight, although it worried her.

They heard the back door open and the sound of Vince trying to control the dogs long enough to perform the near impossible task of wiping their paws. He gave in and two dogs bounded in through the kitchen to land wet paws on their mistress.

"Oh Patch, that was a clean jumper. Get down Stitch. Yes, I'm pleased to see you too," said Max as she wrestled the dogs from her lap who were both attempting to outdo each other by showing their affection.

"Sorry Max, I couldn't stop them," said Vince as he followed the dogs in through the kitchen having poured himself his mug of tea on the way.

Max had managed to get them off her lap. "You wouldn't believe they had been to obedience classes and agility training would you. Now get down. Go on LIE DOWN," and she gave a firm command by pointing to the ground, which seemed to do the trick.

"They're just pleased to see you. You should be flattered," said Maureen, although she was a little concerned for her soft leather sofa, thinking she would find a couple of old blankets to lay across her furniture as soon as Max was gone, if not sooner.

"Flattened, more like" said Max, having finally regained control. "Sorry Mum. No damage done."

"Hi Dad." And she got up to give her father a hug. "You okay?"

"Bearing up. How long have we got them for? We'd like to go back up to Bristol on Sunday and maybe stay again for a couple of days. Then I think the plan is to go up to Gloucester, isn't it love?" he said turning to his wife.

"Something like that. We've still to work things out with Catrin and David."

"I've just said to Mum I'll pick them up on Saturday, is that OK?" Her dad nodded his agreement.

"How did you get on with them? Lizzie's parents I mean." asked Max The dogs were now lying quietly as Max rubbed their backs with her feet.

"They're very nice," said Maureen handing the biscuits to her husband, who to Max's surprise refused.

Noticing her reaction, he said "Watching my weight. Trying to set your mother a good example. I'm not doing very well though!"

His wife shot him a quick glare but ignored him and carried on. "We got to know them quite well."

"Good," said Max, wondering whether or not to pursue just how well, but chose to steer the conversation back towards her brother. Having received the update, she wanted, she glanced at her watch. It was just before 9.00pm and she was anxious to get to Langford before Charlotte got home, but couldn't resist a little probing about Mike's in-laws before she went, so said cautiously, "I'm surprised David could get time off work."

"It was his day off, and any way in his position I think he controls his own diary love," said Maureen

"I don't think so Mo, he'll have secretaries to do that for him," said Vince.

"You know what I mean. If anyone is their own boss it must be a Bishop!"

"You know he's a Bishop then!" Max said, realising she had slipped forward to the edge of the sofa with her hands clasped tightly in front of her. She sat back making a determined effort to appear more relaxed, but changed her mind and bent over to make more fuss of the dogs.

"Of course we do," said Maureen, "but it didn't matter to us. We just treated him like any other bloke and he's great with the kids, thinks nothing of rolling up his sleeves and changing a dirty nappy, more than your dad did when you were little."

"Yes I did!" said a rather hurt Vince.

"Not often."

"Well I was away a lot. Somebody had to protect the country."

"I know dear, and I'm very glad you no longer need to," and just as Vince thought she was going to add something about being proud of him she added, "gives you more time to catch up on the delights of dirty nappies and snotty noses now you are a granddad."

Max decided to drop the interrogation about David. "I'd better be going. Thanks again for looking after the dogs. I hope they'll be no trouble. I'll pick them up Saturday morning. Oh, did Charlie give you some dog food?"

"All here love, and their beds, bowls, toys, leads, biscuits and chewy bones," said Vince.

"How organised, I don't know how she does it."

"Same way as you do love, energy and determination." Vince was very proud of his daughter. Then as an afterthought he added, "Max, there's something we ought to mention." He spoke carefully but still his wife frowned at him as if to warn him to stop. He ignored the look and continued.

"We may have said something we shouldn't to David and Catrin."

"What do you mean?" Max already had her jacket on, which had stimulated more tail wagging but sat down again, which calmed the dogs.

147

"We may have somehow implied that you had a partner," said Vince, looking not in Max's direction but glancing over to his wife.

"You did what? Oh Dad, you didn't tell them about Charlie, did you?" Max had a slight edge to her voice, more from anxiety than anger, but she remained calm.

"Sort of," he still looked at his wife, but she had her mouth firmly shut. He was the one who had mentioned Max's partner in the first place.

"Dad, what do you mean sort of?" Max was already wondering just how she was going to tell Charlotte that her parents had somehow managed to spill the beans, but just how much?

Vince took a deep breath and said, "Your mum mentioned Charlie, but Catrin assumed that was short for Charles."

There was the briefest of pauses whilst Max took in what her father had said. Then she smiled.

"So, I'm going out with a bloke called Charles?" Max sat back down in the chair and let out a loud chortle which made poor Stitch jump. But Max's laughter was short lived, as she quickly realised the implications of a string of lies and asked in a sarcastic tone. "And what does this Charles fella do for a living?"

"We're not sure," said Maureen finally deciding to join in the conversation, "we thought he might do something in the community. Sorry love, we didn't mean to deny Charlie, it just didn't seem the right time to put the record straight, if you know what I mean."

Max started to laugh again and shook her head at the same time, demonstrating the mix of emotions going through her mind, but she didn't want to upset her parents, they had enough to worry about. "You two are incredible. Don't worry about it, probably for the best in the circumstances."

"What do you mean?" asked Maureen.

Max came straight to the same point she had intended to avoid. "David is Charlotte's boss."

"Oh my Lord in heaven! I never thought. But he lives in Exeter. We wondered, but never thought he might be. Oh goodness, does it really matter?" Maureen was flustered, thinking they may have made an even bigger mistake.

"Don't worry. Nothing happened. But do us a favour and avoid any further details, will you?" Max stood up, hugging her mum and then her dad as she continued. "I really do need to go, it will be nearly ten before I get to 'Charles,'" she smiled. The momentary sharpness in her voice was gone.

"Sorry," said Vince again.

"Stop saying sorry, no harm done. It must have been difficult working out what to say. Thanks for not letting on. Not yet any way. I'm just so sorry things have to be like this. It's not fair that you two should be made to feel so uncomfortable." The dogs had stood up again expecting a drive back to their own home and were surprised by the firm command to 'Stay' that came from their mistress.

Max left her mum and dad waving at the door and felt rather emotional as she spotted the tails of both dogs slowly droop as she manoeuvred her ungainly vehicle out of the drive way.

Max was left alone with some confused thoughts on the forty-minute drive to Langford. She was relieved that Bishop David and Charlie had not been forced into a potential corner by her parents but somewhat disappointed that they had felt the need to deny the truth. She also wondered what, if anything, to say to Charlie. She didn't want to spoil the evening, what little there would be left of it, so concluded she may not mention it till the drive up to Bristol the following day.

By the time she pulled into the gravelled drive at Langford Rectory, Max was nearly ready to drop. She looked up and spotted an upstairs light was on. Charlie's car was parked at the side and Max wondered if she was already home. She drove the Land rover round the back out of sight of the front gate, in case of prying eyes. The kitchen light was also on. She tried the back door, but it was locked, so Max used her own key to let herself in. There was a note on the kitchen table in Charlie's handwriting. It read

Steak in the fridge, I thought we could have boiled potatoes and salad with it, unless you want chips, there are some in the freezer. Red wine on the side – don't drink it all, save some for me. I should be home between 9.30 and 10. C xxx

It was nearly ten o clock already. Max turned on the oven for chips, then took her bag upstairs. She looked into the spare room. James had left the sleeping bag on top of the bed. She moved it but left the used towel in the corner of the room. She turned down the bed and ruffled up the sheets. It was a routine that would be difficult to break once they were able to live together, pretending to be just good friends, booking twin bedded rooms on holiday but only using one, jumping on the other to make it looked slept in. The routine of Max having 'her' room, was to keep up some sort of pretence if questioned and still keeping to a half truth. She left her bag on the bed and went back downstairs to open the wine.

Back in the kitchen Max put the radio on. She liked the peace and quiet of the country, but she missed the company of the dogs and the Rectory seemed very large and empty being there on her own. She didn't know how Charlie coped with it. She understood perfectly why she had invited Sasha to lodge with her. At first Max had resented Sasha's presence, annoyed that she was under the same roof as Charlotte, when Max, her life partner had to book a convenient time to visit. It was shortly after that Charlie had given Max her own key. Max would still check that it was okay to call. She didn't want to turn up in the middle of an important parish meeting, but having complete access to the house demonstrated trust on both sides. That act convinced Max, that Charlie and Sasha had nothing to hide. That rocky period was well in the past. Sasha and Max had become good friends.

Max put the chips in the oven and chopped the salad into a bowl and made a dressing. She laid the kitchen table and poured herself some of the wine.

"Mmm, that's good," she said out loud. She glanced at her watch again, just gone ten. She went into the lounge in search of some gentle romantic music to put on whilst they were having their late supper. She may have a brother seriously ill in hospital, but she would still make the most of the rare evening she could spend alone with Charlie. Tomorrow would be stressful enough.

Charlie often made the trip to Max on a Thursday night and would drive back very early on the Saturday morning, but it wasn't always possible. It was not unknown for Charlie to dash back for a parish function on a Friday evening. It annoyed Max, especially when the so-called function was seen by most of the parishioners as a nice social occasion for Charlie to get to know people. "What about me? I want to get to know you even better," she would say. "In the biblical sense, I mean," adopting a hurt little pouting attitude which would usually result in Charlie tickling her into submission whilst at the same time promising all sorts of treats the following Friday, much to Max's delight.

She heard the front door open and slam shut.

"The stupid, bloody, arrogant, hypocrite!" Charlie was declaring to no-one in particular. "Who the bloody hell does he think he is?" She stormed into the study and pressed the button of the answer phone.

"You have three messages," spoke the digital voice.

"Then deal with them your bloody self. Leave me alone, I've had enough." Charlie threw her briefcase down and collapsed into her study chair.

Charlie had either not realised that Max was there, or genuinely didn't care. Max knew Charlie had a tendency to keep things bottled up and would just explode on occasions, but it would take a lot. She was also annoyed that the remnants of a short evening were now disappearing rapidly and what should have been a romantic welcome and a relieved falling into each other's arms after the strains and stresses of the last few days was in danger of disintegrating into a tearful end before it had even started.

Max poured a glass of wine and crept down to the study, pushing the door open and for a moment standing in the door way.

"I'm home sweetheart," she said, coming into the room and placing the wine in front of Charlie who lifted her head from her arms. She'd already been crying.

"Max, I'm sorry I didn't think you were here. Did you hear all that?"

"Yep. What happened?"

"What hasn't happened these last few days? We'd got through the agenda, including all the stuff about St Nicholas. Actually, that bit went really well. We managed to agree the budget without too much difficulty and there I was thinking we'd be finished by nine, when Philip bloody Dixon...."

"Isn't he the difficult Reader?"

"The very one," said Charlie taking a large gulp of wine. "Hmm nice," she said taking another. "He stands up, as if he owns the place. 'Point of order madam chairwoman' and you know how that riles me to start off with. Then he tries to suggest that we've 'misrepresented' the accounts, failing to declare in full, the projected cost of the development therefore 'jeopardising future mission opportunities'."

"What does he mean by that?"

"No idea, but he's got this notion that if we spend all that money on one church, it would somehow detract from the other communities and went on and on about how we needed to treat each parish as equal partners, suggesting that we needed to fund loos in every bloody church in the benefice."

"Where's all that come from?" Max had moved some of the papers on the desk and was sitting on the edge sharing Charlie's glass of wine, having left her own in the kitchen.

"He's just trying to make life difficult, as he has done right from the beginning. To think I persuaded the PCC to recommend we retain his licence despite the complaints we were having. I didn't want to make an enemy of the man, but whatever I do, he tries to block it. We've come all this way, spent about £3,500 already on surveys and plans and he manages to delay the whole project until a small working party comes up with a benefice review of all the building work that may be carried out over the next ten years. Do you know what bloody annoys me the most?"

"No, my darling, what is that?" Max was living a little dangerously with just a hint of sarcasm in her voice, but she was starving and wanted to get back to her own glass of wine and the steak.

"He's bloody right. I had to agree with him, because I had said the very same thing to the buildings and finance group two years ago, when we first started thinking about St Nicholas. I sat in that meeting suggesting that before we made a major decision on one church we carry out an audit of need on all eight churches. Philip was on the committee and managed to persuade the other members that it was not necessary and that we should start with the main church first. And now he's taken a complete bloody U turn managing to delay the whole project by about six months if not longer, which means reapplying for the heritage grant if we don't get started on the actual build by the end of the year."

"Well maybe he's beginning to realise that you are right after all," suggested Max.

"Hah! That's a good one. But that's not all. After that additional fifteen-minute discussion, under 'Any Other Business' he had the audacity to mention that he had received a complaint about young hooligans driving their motorbikes around the Rectory Grounds late at night and asked if the Rector would care to cast any light on the situation. No concern for my safety. For all he knew I may have been in real danger, but then of course he knew that wasn't the case. He knew it was James. He met him once and looked at him as if he was something that crawled out the sewer, just because he had long hair and leathers. So, I had to explain to the whole PCC that there was no need for concern, it was a member of the family. It just feels I can't breathe without someone knowing about it. Then I asked Philip Dixon if he would care to disclose the name of the complainant, in private if necessary so that I could make a personal apology for any disturbance caused. He declined of course, but he had such a smug look on his face, I really think I could have hit him."

"But you didn't." Max shot a startled look at Max.

"Of course not. I'm a lady!"

Max was relieved that Charlotte already seemed to be calming down.

"Well then Lady Charles, may I escort you to the kitchen where our chips are awaiting the company of two succulent steaks?"

Charlotte frowned. "Lady Charles? Where did that come from?"

"Ah, yes, that. I'll tell you later. Come on, I'm starving" said Max jumping down from the desk and pulling Charlie up from her desk chair kissing her on the lips as she did so, whilst at the same time slowly removing her white clerical collar from the tunnel of fabric at the top of her shirt and released the top two buttons allowing her finger to linger momentarily in the small indentation at the base of her throat.

"I thought you said you were hungry," said Charlie clasping Max's hand.

"Ravenous," she replied with a glint in her eye.

"Then let's eat, and I'd like some more of the delicious wine. You've drank half of my glass."

Max was relieved that Charlie had put aside the stresses of the PCC, at least for the time being. Philip was banished from the conversation and for the next twenty-four hours or maybe a little longer. Max and Charlie could be a couple, enjoying each other's company, sharing in family life, even though that in its self, meant a long drive up and back to a Bristol hospital.

Chapter 12

It was early on Friday morning, just three days since Michael Tannin's miraculous escape from the motorway crash involving several vehicles including a laden car transporter and oil tanker.

The enquiry had already begun into the cause of the accident that had seen the deaths of four people and serious injuries to many others. It was a miracle that there were not more fatalities. Unconfirmed reports suggested that the driver of the car transporter had been using a mobile phone when he lost control in a sudden gust of wind, causing him to swerve into the middle lane of the carriageway right into the path of the coach. Three cars had been hit by the coach as the driver struggled to regain control. The coach had over turned and slid down an embankment. The transporter ended up across all three lanes and, although many cars, including Mike, managed to brake and avoided ploughing into the transporter, the ensuing chaos caused a number of other accidents. The oil tanker was simply too heavy to stop in time. The driver had, with huge skill and presence of mind, managed to squeeze his tanker through the tiny gap left between the carnage on the main carriageway and the hard shoulder and pushed past the transporter. Mike received a near fatal blow from the tanker just as he stumbled away from his car. This bowled him down the embankment near to the final resting place of the coach. As the tanker then ploughed into Mike's car the impact ruptured one of the main feeder pipes on the tanker and a spark from scraping metal had been enough to set off a minor explosion engulfing the main tank. The driver managed to scramble clear from his protected cab, but sadly the more vulnerable occupants of a nearby car were not so fortunate.

The driver of the transporter had survived the accident and clambered out of the cab before the tanker struck. In a state of shock, he had apparently put himself at great risk in a vain attempt to save some of those trapped. He received severe burns and his life still hung in the balance. The press, however, had quickly dropped the hero worship when it transpired that the driver may have caused the accident. One of the tabloids ran the cruel headline "Fallen Angel may meet his Maker."

The police were still trying to piece together the evidence and were hoping to speak to Mike and the other casualties as soon as possible.

Mike had been very distressed in the night, as nightmares plagued any sleep he tried to get. Images were thankfully blurred, but the noises were all too clear. When he was conscious all he remembered was the sound of screaming in the distance. He was almost afraid to ask what had happened, and beginning to understand that although he had received severe injuries, he had been very fortunate to have survived.

He lay cocooned in what to him looked like his old meccano set.

He found himself praying for the first time since his childhood. He simply thanked God for allowing him to still be with his children and with Lizzie and promised to do the best for them. He didn't promise to start going to church. He didn't promise to do amazing charity work. He simply promised to bring up his children knowing about the possibility of the existence of God. But others had lost their life, which was difficult to accept. He decided to keep his options open and allow his atheism to be challenged. In the early hours of fretful sleep, he decided to embrace a positive agnostic stance until more evidence could prove to him one way or the other.

'Mind you,' he thought to himself 'with a Bishop as a father-in-law and his nearly sister-in-law, a priest, he might have to give in to the possibility and see where the journey took him.' He then found himself wondering if David and Charlie had already met around his bedside, but recalling the strange conversation about his big sister shacking up with a bloke called Charles, it was safe to assume the Graham family had not yet met his sister's long term partner.

He had managed to keep her existence from his father-in-law for years, instinctively knowing that things could get awkward for them both if they knew about their family connection. He had nearly let his sister in on his secret before the wedding. She was being as stubborn as a mule about wanting an invitation for Charlie. Mike really wanted to invite them both. He nearly took Charlie to one side to explain, but it had been rough for Charlie and his sister just before hand and he was worried that Charlie might walk out on his sister again if she knew about David. Thankfully Max had backed down from her high horse at the last minute agreeing to go without Charlie, so he had stayed quiet.

He wasn't really sure why he had kept the charade going, deciding to be the one to keep the parties separate. It seemed the right thing at first when he had found out that David was in fact the Bishop of Exeter and Charlotte was one of his priests. As time went on he just fell into the role of protector and deceiver, so much so that it became a habit. It was a habit that would probably now need breaking and he hoped he could speak to Max in order to explain before it got Charlie into trouble.

The morning ward routine was beginning. He could now manage to drink tea from a special beaker, the problem of output was still taken care of by a catheter and other motions didn't seem to present an imminent problem, although he had begun to eat a little food the night before, so it would be something he would need to tackle within the next day or so. He thought of his little boy, so vulnerable and helpless, dependent for everything and reflected that he too for the moment was as dependent as Joshua, although at least he could still speak and didn't have to rely on a mum interpreting his cry.

Two nurses came in to help him wash. It was a welcome break from the monotony of staring at the walls of his tiny cubicle. They chatted away about the weather and the ward routine. Mike wasn't sure if they were talking to him or around him, unless it was to ask him specific questions about discomfort. It didn't matter.

There was television, radio and phone on an arm attached to the bed, but he needed a prepaid card to use any of the devices, so he would have to wait until a member of his family came to visit. He had already asked if he could be transferred to Gloucester, but it sounded as if he was to stay in Bristol for the time being, until surgeons could be sure the frame was doing what it should do, and he was warned that could take several days. He wondered how Lizzie would cope, but he was sure her mum would find a solution.

The morning wash over, he was again left with his own thoughts. Hoping a visitor might turn up soon, but he drifted back to restless sleep for another two hours.

Charlie dragged Max out of bed at 7.00am. Max was not a morning person, more of a night owl. She had kept Charlie up the previous night till after midnight. They found solace in every soothing mouthful of delectable red wine and in the embracing warmth of each other's arms, the stresses and strains of the last few days gradually ebbed way. They talked of their future and, without reference to the immediate difficulties, allowed themselves to dream of a stable life together, and revelled in the hope that even the tiniest details of domestic life would one day be shared. So, after just six hours' sleep Charlie staggered down the stairs to entice her drowsy partner to full consciousness with a fresh pot of steaming strong coffee.

She looked around the kitchen at the discarded frying pan and greasy chip tray noting that 'tiny details of domestic life,' would include an equal share in the most mundane matters of shared living.

"Just remind me why we have to be up so early, when we could so easily still be lying in bed." A bleary-eyed Max had made it down the stairs and was propping up the kitchen door frame adorned in a sloppy t-shirt that doubled as night attire. Charlie had pulled on an old pair of track suits bottoms, but she too had a loose t-shirt on beneath an even looser sweatshirt.

"Your little brother is lying in a hospital bed, wondering why his big sister and her amazing partner haven't been to see him, that's why," answered Charlie. "Did we open a second bottle last night?"

"Not sure, why?"

"There's one here half finished with the cork rammed down its neck. I'm sure we drunk more than that."

"Must have, my head says at least a bottle and that's just me."

161

"Mine too." Charlotte looked around the kitchen and spotting something under the table bent down to pick up another bottle. She turned it round in her hands as if trying to remember something about the previous evening. "Oh, I remember now. We are definitely getting too old for things like that."

"Speak for yourself old timer, I'm not as old as you remember?!"

"You will be in a couple of months. What do you want for breakfast?" Charlie asked holding up a loaf of bread in one hand and a cereal pack in the other.

"Full English!"

"How about toast?"

"How about eggy bread?"

"If you do it."

"Deal."

And so, the day began.

At the Bishop's palace, Joshua had been fractious most of the night and a very bleary eyed Lizzie stumbled into the kitchen at 7.30am. Her father had already begun his day. He had a huge amount to catch up on from the previous few days but was to spend the morning engaged with what the business world would call performance reviews, but in the world of church jargon and pastoral sensitivity were known as a 'reviews of ministry'. Bishop David had devoted the morning to conduct three such reviews. They would be an opportunity to discuss matters of ministry in some detail, but unlike the secular world, the Bishop as manager had little or no authority to insist on any course of action and it would have absolutely no bearing on what the priest would be paid.

These were the thoughts Bishop David had grappled with earlier that morning when he sat in his small private prayer room as the dawn chorus heralded the beginning of a new day. Once again, he was acutely aware of his impotence. He had considerable influence and that was often enough to give the impression of power, but he was tied down by church bureaucracy. In business speak he was a managing director of four sub-companies, in his world known as Archdeaconries, which were split into twenty-five smaller management units called deaneries, each of those with around twenty parishes. Very few of the parishes had their own priest, but nevertheless there were two hundred and seventy-five priests, plus all the volunteers. Then of course there were all the staff in the church schools, all the support workers in the church office, it really was quite a set-up. Yet he could not move any of the staff around the diocese without a formal appointment procedure. He had next to no power to dismiss any priest and if he did, he would have to live with the knowledge that his action had also made them and their family homeless.

Early that January morning, shivering slightly as he commenced his morning devotion, he found himself pondering the possibility of retirement. He thought about Vince and Maureen and the uncomplicated life they seemed to lead, now that they were into their retirement years. He prayed for his own family each with their own lives to lead as teachers, lawyers and for his youngest Ruth, in her final year at medical school. He prayed, of course for Mike and Lizzie, regretting that his role would now be limited as the pressures of his own job would once again take over.

He also found himself praying for one of his priests, Reverend Charlotte Northam, whom he had spent time with earlier that week. He hoped she would see sense and continue in the calling God had set on her heart.

But his praying felt empty. He knew his family life was distracting him.

In the privacy of that small simple room he felt the tears running down his cheeks. He loved his children, he loved his grandchildren and he loved his wife but they had so often come second to his ordination. Second to the numerous evening and weekend meetings when most fathers would decorate a child's bedroom, or take them to a football match, or whisk their family off for weekends at a holiday park. Even now when his daughter needed him most, he would spend the whole weekend travelling across his diocese attending 'important' church events. It would be left to his wife, who would juggle the children and the visiting, to support their daughter.

For a moment, he questioned the point of church, if all it did was distract from family life, sink money into ancient buildings and exclude those who didn't fit the norm. He allowed the tears to run down his cheeks. He must have spent nearly an hour in that small room.

As darkness gradually turned to the weak fresh light of a new day, he rose from his devotions and reluctantly dragged himself to his study to go through the notes and letters left for him by the trustworthy Sally from the previous day. She would be in later to act as secretary, receptionist and confidant. David was conscious that she knew as much, if not more, about his diocese and certainly more about him and his family than any of his priests or diocesan officers.

By 7.30am, having been up for nearly three hours with just a cup of tea and his own thoughts for company, he left the offices of the Palace and joined his daughter in the kitchen for cereal, toast and a strong cup of coffee. They enjoyed a rare few minutes alone before their peace was broken first by little Heather charging into her grandfather's lap, closely followed by Catrin with her hair wrapped in a towel.

Half an hour later David reluctantly excused himself from the family scene of shared domesticity to return to the less inviting scene of diocesan husbandry. An hour after that, Lizzie, having finally mastered the skill of expressing her lactating breasts, left to make the journey back up to Bristol. Catrin was to stay at home to look after Joshua and Heather.

Chapter 13

Parking was unpredictable on the hospital grounds and expensive if visitors intended staying for the whole day so Max and Charlie had parked about half a mile away in a fairly deserted lane. They both felt slightly guilty as they were used to inconsiderate tourists parking in awkward places in the villages where they both worked, but guilt gave way to necessity. It was a pleasant morning and they enjoyed the walk back to the hospital. It was about 10.30am when they arrived. They checked with the reception desk that Mike was still on the same ward. The receptionist insisted on ringing the ward to check about the open visiting policy, which irritated Max.

"We've not left at the crack of dawn and driven two hours only to be told we have to wait until 2.00pm to see our brother."

"I'm sorry madam, I'm sure they will let you go up, but we are strict about patient's rest periods." The receptionist was very polite and very firm. Charlie was quietly impressed.

Thankfully Mike was still in a side room and the sister was happy to let them up.

On the ward a young woman in uniform from behind the nurses' station greeted them and directed them to Mike's room, reminding them to wash their hands and apply the gel before going in.

"He's not contracted some sort of infection, has he?" asked Max.

"No, that's exactly what we wish to avoid." The young nurse spoke with a slight accent which neither Max nor Charlie could pin down. "He is in a vulnerable place because of the insertions into his legs and we wish that he is kept from any risks of virus." She smiled and started back to the station, but then called back. "I am so sorry, I should check that you are family."

"Yes," said Max

The nurse looked towards Charlie.

"Yes, ….." Charlotte hesitated for a moment, but added, "we're both family."

"It's just that we have had a little trouble with a local journalist. They want to speak to the accident victims, so you will understand if I ask how you are related. I have met his wife and his parents."

"I'm his sister, Max. Max Tannin."

"And you?"

"I'm…. a close friend," said Charlie, looking at Max.

"Oh, well I'm not sure…….." the nurse began her sentence but was interrupted by Max.

"She's my partner, Mike's sister-in-law, well nearly. I hope that's okay with you." Max made a statement rather than a question and was almost aggressive in her approach with the young foreign nurse which Charlie found uncomfortable. She was also taken aback with how quickly Max had jumped in to explain their relationship, which she didn't think was necessary.

"I am sure it is no problem. Let me see if Mr Tannin is awake." The nurse appeared slightly more cautious, choosing now to take them, rather than simply pointing them in the right direction.

Out of earshot Charlie asked Max, "What's got into you? You were really short with her. She's only doing her job."

"I know. It's lots of things. I don't like hospitals for a start."

"What? But you're a vet, you're used to medical things."

"Hmm, animals and doting owners or livestock and scrupulous farmers. I'm not exactly very good with ill humans." Max gripped Charlotte's hand for the briefest of moments, making sure the nurse wasn't looking.

"That's why I wanted you with us Tuesday night. I feel so uncomfortable in these places." She let go as the nurse glanced back in their direction.

"It wasn't so bad when I had to be strong for Mum and Dad."

Charlotte looked questioningly at Max.

"I'm okay." Max said.

"That's debatable. Try and ease off a little, you're making me feel uneasy too. And why go telling our life story? She would have let me in."

Charlie, noticing the nurse disappear into a side room, reached down and took Max's hand again to reassure her that she wasn't annoyed with her, just surprised.

"Come on let's go and see Mike. We can talk about your hospital phobia later."

"It's not a phobia, I just don't like them."

"I know, I know, just like I'm not that keen on spiders, mice and rats."

"Yes, my sweet but that is definitely phobic."

"Exactly! Now come on concentrate on Mike." Charlie let go of Max's hand again when the young nurse emerged from the side room and beckoned them forward.

"He's awake, please go in." And this time she went back to her station to continue with her report writing.

"It's my big sister! What took you so long? And Charlie, do I get a hug? But make it gentle."

"Hi Mike," Charlotte was the first to go over to Mike and gently kissed him on the cheek. "It's good to see you."

She rested her hand on his shoulder for a moment longer than a friend might. It was one of those small acts that might make a stranger jump to the wrong conclusion. For Mike and Charlie, it was no more than family affection. They had become close over the years, following in the steps of the close relationship between Mike and Max, which few people really knew about, including their own family. Years of a shared secret had cemented a bond despite the eight years' difference in age.

Charlotte stood aside and went around to the other side of the bed to give Max some space.

"Hiya kiddo!" Max sniffed. "Good to see you awake this time. You slept through my last visit," and then much to the surprise of both Mike and Charlie, burst into tears as she stretched herself across her brother.

"Hey come on sis." Mike's voice was stifled by his sister's hug. "You're the strong one in this relationship. I'm okay, I've still got two arms and two legs, actually there's more to me now than there was before: they've added a few bits here and there."

He moved her slightly with his one good arm, so he could breathe easier. "Go steady I'm a bit like a jigsaw before it's been stuck together and varnished. Charlie?" Mike looked over to Charlotte to intervene. She came across and took Max in her arms.

Just as the young nurse got back to her station another visitor arrived for Mr Michael Tannin.

Lizzie asked if was alright to go on in.

"Yes of course. His sister has just arrived with her partner. They've just gone in."

"Oh good. Thank you."

'Mmm' thought Lizzie, 'I get to meet this unknown handsome stranger. I wonder what he's like?' And she wandered down into Mike's room.

"Hi love......" Lizzie's cheery welcome trailed off as she took in the scene. It was perhaps not the best moment to meet Max's unknown partner for the first time.

"Lizzie!" exclaimed Mike.

Charlotte looked up to finally meet the woman she had only ever seen in photographs. Max immediately regained control, keeping her face turned away from Lizzie for a moment in order to wipe her tear stained face. She turned to face Lizzie.

"Hi Lizzie," said Max……….. "Meet Charlie, Charlotte!"

"Charley?" Lizzie appeared puzzled and frowned momentarily but it only took a second for the penny to drop.

"Charlie!" She held out her hand to Charlotte. "Er, nice to meet you. I take it you are a friend of Max?" She looked over to Max and then glanced over to Mike and asked a hundred questions by repeating "Charlie?"

Mike nodded at his wife. "Charlie!"

She smiled, put down her hand and instead reached out both arms.

"More than just a friend then Charlie?" And much to the surprise of Mike and Max, gave Charlotte a hug.

170

"I'm not sure who's welcoming who to the family, I take it you've been part of our family for some time?"

"About ten years," said Charlotte simply.

"It's good to meet you at last but what with all the tears?"

"I've got a sensitive side Liz," said Max "it's just you don't get to see it very often," and she too gave Lizzie a hug.

"Hey, ladies. I hate to break up this women's fellowship, but when do I get a look in?" Mike was intrigued by the scene of feminine solidarity he appeared to be observing. He had assumed Lizzie would be appalled to know about his sister's chosen lifestyle. Lizzie had grown up in a strict Christian household and her father had to uphold the church's teaching on such issues. Her show of affection and welcome was exactly the opposite of what he had expected.

"You can wait for a moment my love. It's not as if you are going very far," said Lizzie, but immediately came over to the bed and kissed her husband firmly on the lips.

"Steady on, you're embarrassing me," said Mike when he was allowed up for air, but hoped for a second display of such affection. He wasn't disappointed.

"Should we leave you two for a moment?" Charlie was still reeling from what had just occurred. She had just been outed by her partner to her Bishop's daughter round the hospital bed of her Bishop's son-in-law who in actual fact was still poorly enough to be in a side room under regular observation. She needed a moment alone with Max.

"No, please don't go," said Lizzie "You've only just arrived. Let's all stay for a bit and then we could go and grab a coffee somewhere, I

171

want to know all about you." Lizzie was animated and seemed almost excited.

Charlotte pressed her lips together in a smile, but melted into the background against the wall at the foot of the bed, lost in her thoughts about how much to tell Lizzie. She was glad that, what might have been a devastating moment when Lizzie first walked in, had turned out to be one of relief, but Max having a female partner was only half the story. Charlotte wondered just how much she could or should hold back from Lizzie. David already knew she was gay and in a partnership and that she was ready to leave the priesthood, so what was she worried about? All through her ministry she had worked hard to remain true to herself, and at the same time, avoid scandal. But what would happen if the press was to hear about her family connection with the Bishop? However tenuous, it would draw journalists like bees to a honey pot. David would have to dismiss her. He'd no longer have the choice of keeping it hidden, as he had wanted her to do.

As Max and Lizzie talked to Mike about his treatment, the food, the nurses and the children, Charlotte was caught up in her own thoughts as she leant against that white stark hospital wall, looking as if she was joining in, but in actual fact her mind in a different world. A world without PCC meetings, without the laughter of children during raucous collective worship, without young women desperate to marry before their fiancé risks life and limb in a bloody war, without mercenary relatives shedding crocodile tears before spending their inheritance, without the dear unsung heroes who tirelessly gave so much of their time, cleaning the churches, running the Sunday School, supporting their neighbours and providing a listening ear to those who need it. She tried to imagine a world with free weekends when she would no longer don her robes and lead dedicated members of her villages in worship. She imagined evenings in front of the television rather than working late into the night pouring over architects' plans, or sweating over sermons.

"I said are you coming for a coffee?" Max had stood up and had turned to face Charlotte. "You are miles away and have hardly said a word."

"Sorry, just a bit tired. You know what I'm like on Fridays."

"What's so special about Fridays?" asked Lizzie. "I love them. They are the start of the nice relaxing weekend, or they used to be before kids. Still I guess we'll be having a few more quiet days before you are back on your feet again, won't we love!" She held Mike's hand.

Charlotte mentally kicked herself for inadvertently giving more reason to fuel Lizzie's inquisitive mind, but was glad it had passed without further comment. "Coffee sounds good. What about you Mike? Anything we can get you?"

"A whisky?!"

"Other than that," smiled Charlotte.

"There is something. This TV and phone needs some sort of pay card to get it to work. Could you get one for me?"

"Of course we will," said Lizzie. Now you have a rest whilst we're gone. It's already quarter to twelve so we might as well have an early lunch. Yours will be here soon. We'll be back about 1.30pm how does that sound?

"Fine by me, have a good chat, you've quite a bit to catch up on. Sorry I've kept it from you so long."

"Kept what from me for so long?" asked Lizzie, her voice light.

173

Max was standing beside Charlotte and surreptitiously took her hand. She half expected to have it snatched away. Charlotte was obviously struggling with a mix of emotions. Max, on the other hand, although concerned about Charlotte was relieved that she could finally be herself with Lizzie and Mike and was delighted that it had been so easy.

Rather than snatch her hand away, Charlotte held on to Max in a tight grip. She was annoyed by the way the revelation about their relationship had overshadowed the support she wanted to give Mike and her annoyance was threatening to spill over in tears, so she kept a grip on herself by keeping a firm grip on Max's hand.

Mike answered quietly. "I'm sorry I kept you in the dark about Max and Charlie."

"You knew?" Lizzie's voice rose by two or three tones and she frowned as she sat back down again on the chair nearest her husband.

"But why didn't you tell me? Why didn't you all tell me? What did you think I'd do? Out you? What difference does it make? We live in the twenty first century. It's only the church that's behind the times. Believe me Dad and I have had this discussion. Even he struggles with it. Oh, sorry Charlie, I should have mentioned that Dad is a Bishop of all things, but maybe you knew that already, it sounds as if I'm the only one left out of the loop. Honestly Mike, you know I'm no prude. Just how long have you kept this from me?"

"I'm sorry love, it's a bit complicated. I'm sorry, really sorry, but I think Max and Charlie better explain, I'm feeling really tired again," and as if following a cue line the same young nurse as before came back into the room.

"Mr Tannin you seem to be getting a little excited again. No wonder with three beautiful women at your bedside. I need to give you some medication before your lunch. Maybe your wife, she stay, but maybe the others go for a little while."

"No, really, we were just going to get a coffee ourselves. You rest for a bit Mike. I'm sorry to upset you." Lizzie gave her husband a peck on the cheek and pushed back his hair with her hand, then added another light kiss on his forehead.

"See you in a bit Mike. Get some rest," Max added. Charlotte waved her fingers and smiled. Next to James, Mike was probably her favourite male companion.

They left Mike to the mercy of the young but obviously very capable nurse.

Max, Lizzie and Charlotte found the hospital restaurant and ordered three adequate coffees to have with some sandwiches. It had only just turned twelve and the restaurant was still fairly quiet and they easily found a secluded table in the corner.

Charlotte was the first to speak as they sat down. "Lizzie I'm sorry. Today is about Mike. We're all here for one reason and that is to try and support you, your husband and the kids as much as we can. But I'm glad you now know about me and Max and I hope we can help."

"Thanks, but what would really help me now, is to satisfy my curiosity and tell me all about yourself Charlie. You've obviously been part of Mike and Max's family for some time. Have you met Heather? I know you haven't met Joshua yet. In fact, neither have you Max. We hardly ever see you. I suppose I'm beginning to understand now. But listen, I don't have a problem with you – both of you. I mean it, but I do feel a bit hurt that you couldn't trust me. Like I said we don't live in the dark ages anymore. So, come on tell me about yourself." Lizzie finally paused for a breath and a sip of coffee.

Charlotte looked over to Max for moral support. Max took it as a cue to start off the story, which left Charlotte feeling anxious about how much Max would disclose. She was still hoping she could avoid explaining to Lizzie what she did for a living, but her hope was waning.

"Well," Max began "we met on a walking holiday about ten years ago."

"Ten years!" exclaimed Lizzie. "That's longer than I've known Mike. You've been together all that time?"

"More or less," said Max. "We did have a sticky patch about five years ago, but we got over that." She noticed Charlotte throw her a warning glance.

"So, have you done this civil partnership thing?" asked Lizzie. Charlotte noticed she looked across to Max's hand as she asked. 'Looking for a ring' she thought to herself, 'one day'. She felt Max's eyes on her and she looked up to see both Max and Lizzie looking at her for an answer.

"Oh, sorry you're asking me... well we.. no, not yet." Charlotte felt flustered again and was annoyed at not being her usual cool calm self.

"Neither of you popped the question?" Lizzie was obviously enjoying herself, but all Charlotte could think of was the way that as soon as a straight person learned that a friend was gay they felt it gave them the right to interrogate them, however friendly it seemed. There was no malice in what Lizzie was asking, far from it. It was friendly and warm, but Charlotte hated the questions and the delving into a life that she and Max worked so hard at keeping very private. She wasn't used to it. She had never flaunted her sexuality, it was just the way she was. It was just the way Max and her lived: together, but separate, catching the odd night together every so often. A relationship conducted on the phone and by e-mail mostly. Perhaps the questions simply highlighted how inadequate it all was. The thoughts that sped through Charlotte's mind clamoured for attention, but she kept her concentration and dug deeper to regain the control in her voice and her emotions. She had wanted to meet Lizzie for some time. Mike had talked about his wife and little Heather, although of course had never let on what Lizzie's dad did for a living.

"I think we've both popped the question on many occasions, some more romantic than others," Charlotte gradually regained her confidence, "but we won't bore you with the details, so yes we will one day, when the time is right. It's just not practical at the moment."

"So, you don't live together?"

"No," Max joined in, "not at the moment."

"Oh, hold on, didn't Mum and Dad mention you two buying a house in Okehampton?"

Charlotte shot a glance at Max as she wondered just how much Maureen and Vince had let on.

"Umm, maybe, as an investment perhaps." Max was cautious.

"Listen to me, I'm asking far too many questions. I'm sorry. Max, can I just check, when your mum and dad were talking to my mum and dad about you having a partner called Charles, they actually meant

Charlotte and do they know that Charles is a Charlotte, and that you and Charlie are an item?"

"Yes, yes and er yes," said Max answering all three questions.

"And are your mum and dad okay about it? What about your family, Charlotte?" Despite apologising for asking too many, Lizzie still persisted with the questioning.

"My mum and dad are fine," answered Max. "I'm sure ideally they would have preferred a Charles....."

"Thanks," quipped Charlotte.

"You know what I mean sweetheart..." said Max, resting her hand on Charlotte's arm, "but they love Charlotte like a daughter." It was strange to hear Max say 'Charlotte' she had obviously momentarily picked up on Lizzie's approach.

"And your parents?" asked Lizzie in Charlotte's direction.

"I never told them. Both Mum and Dad died a few years ago. Mum had a stroke. She was Dad's main carer. He had cancer, but he also died not long after."

"Oh, I am sorry," but still the questions kept coming. "Any brothers and sisters?"

"One sister, Erica, divorced. One son, James, who likes to think he's a rebel, but he's a big sensitive softy, and knows all about Max and me and thinks it's great."

"One son? You mean ...."

"No no.... Erica's son. Not mine, goodness my life is complicated enough without that." Charlotte answered quickly.

"So, what do you do for a living?" asked Lizzie in an offhand manner with no idea that this was the big question Charlotte had dreaded.

"Charles was some sort of community worker I believe. Is that true of Charlie?"

"Would anyone like another coffee?" asked Max scraping back the chair as she stood up in a botched attempt to change the topic. It only served to raise Lizzie's curiosity even more. "Or something for pudding maybe? Yoghurt? I saw some cake. Or maybe we should be getting back to Mike? It's gone 1pm."

"Sit down Max." Charlotte pulled her partners sleeve in an attempt to make her sit down again. "She's Mike's wife and anyway it's got to come out some time, might as well be now."

Charlotte felt the same as she did when she was sitting in Bishop David's study just four days previously, when her connection with her Bishop was purely professional, when she was regarded as one of the most respected priests in the diocese and when her future appeared to be mapped out. Unknown to her, she had already been earmarked by David as a future Bishop when the Church of England scrambled its way into the gender equality of the twenty first century, but she had self-condemned that reputation by simply being honest, deciding that her integrity was more important than promotion and prestige. By bringing him into her world she had placed her Bishop in an impossible position of compromised values and virtue.

She once again felt the surge of apprehension but just as determined she simply said, "I'm a priest, your dad is my boss."

Max expected a dramatic pause. She was disappointed. Lizzie let out a huge laugh which turned quite a few heads in their direction.

"You're a priest! In Exeter?" Lizzie obviously found it amusing, which simply bemused both Max and Charlotte.

179

"No, not in Exeter, on the edge of Dartmoor, in a group of villages that would be horrified if they knew the full facts about me." Charlotte gave a hint of warning in her voice mixed with a plea if Lizzie was astute enough to hear it.

"And my dad doesn't know about you two?"

"Not exactly, although as of Tuesday, he does know about my sexuality," confessed Charlotte.

"Charlotte, I know who you are." Lizzie was suddenly serious.

"Eh? What do you mean?"

"Dad's talked about you once or twice, well quite a bit really. He thinks you do a really good job. Haven't you applied for the Archdeacon position?"

Charlotte was visibly shocked. She was very surprised that David had mentioned such things to his family.

"Ah, that's a bit tricky. I was asked to, but it's a bit complicated." Charlotte felt very uncomfortable talking about church matters with the Bishop's daughter. She obviously knew a bit about what was going on in the Diocese which was unexpected.

"Why is it tricky? Because of you and Max?" Lizzie seemed to have forgotten that her husband was lying in a hospital bed just a few hundred yards away, and probably beginning to wonder where they had got to and where his phone card was.

Max tried to break up the intense questioning, sensing Charlotte was getting more uncomfortable, "Perhaps we should continue this later and get back to Mike."

"Yes, of course," agreed Liz, but also seemed to dismiss the suggestion by continuing her questioning. "But Charlotte has Dad made life difficult for you?"

"No, he hasn't. It's me really. He's asked me to think about the role."

"But it would be great, keep it in the family."

"Er yes, it…." Charlotte was feeling a little staggered by Lizzie's enthusiasm, but regained her composure, "Your dad didn't even know I was in a relationship before Tuesday. He thought I was going to accept his invitation to stand for Archdeacon, but instead I told him I wanted to resign my orders."

"Wow!" Interrupted Lizzie,

"He didn't accept," Charlotte continued, "and asked me to go away and think about it a bit more. Now it's even more complicated. I only found out on Wednesday that Max was related to you by marriage."

"Which almost makes you and Dad related. This is great, real 'News of the World' stuff." Max and Charlotte gave each other a worried look, noticed by Lizzie.

"Oh look, I'm so sorry I didn't mean it. It's my warped sense of humour. Now I'm embarrassed. Me and my big mouth! And my boobs are going to burst soon." She added only to cause more concerned looks between her two new friends. "Oh, bloody hell I've done it again. You've never had kids and experienced the delights of breast feeding. I feel like a dairy cow. I've got to express some milk. Won't be long, you two must have things to talk about, I'll be back in a few minutes, as long as I can get this stupid machine to attach itself properly," and she disappeared without noticing the stifled giggles coming from Max.

"She is not what I expected. What's wrong with you? You think it's funny talking about spilling the beans to the 'News of the World' or the 'Sun'?" Charlotte couldn't quite work out whether to be annoyed, deeply worried, or to join in the mirth.

"It's her reference to dairy cows. Dad told me on the phone about the problems she was having with her milk when I was in the middle of a cattle yard, having just examined the udders of two prize Friesians. Poor Lizzie would be horrified if she knew." Max was really giggling now.

"Well I'm the only one who seems to think that we're in trouble here. It would be a field day for the popular press if they found out." Charlotte was genuinely concerned about both herself and David. It would be a one day wonder, but she hated the thought of dragging her church through the gutter press. Max just laughed even more.

"For goodness sake Max, you know how serious this is."

Max continued to giggle whilst she said "I know it is, but all I can think of is the press finding out about the Bishop's daughter in a milk shed."

"Oh for goodness sake, pull yourself together woman. Get a grip. We've got some serious thinking to do. The Bishop will have to accept my resignation now, which means huge changes for us. How do you fancy a lodger, because that's what it will be, when I lose my home within the next three months?" Charlotte had become very serious and continued with her firm talking. "Had you forgotten that we're actually here to spend time with your brother, who only a few days ago, was fighting for his life and we still don't know the full extent of his injuries? What happened to all your talk about getting straight answers whilst you were here?"

Charlotte's tirade had the desired affect and sobered Max into a more serious state of mind.

"Well first off," said Max, in a very controlled and calm way, demonstrating once again her normal commanding approach to life that Charlotte admired so much, "you need to calm down."

"Calm down? You were the one having a giggling fit." Charlotte talked in a forced whisper.

"What I mean is, it's no use getting worked up, it doesn't change anything. So what if Lizzie knows."

"She's my boss's daughter – and you are her husband's sister!"

"And?"

"And…….. you know the…..well…."

"That phobia, paranoia thing," stated Max.

"What are you talking about?"

"Fear, that's what. You are petrified about your name being splattered over the press. It won't happen, the whole gay issue, it's not news anymore. Now if you were sleeping with a fifteen year old….."

"Max, how dare you….."

"I'm not saying – oh this is stupid. The press are not interested in some country vicar."

"But David…."

"Oh, come on, there's no connection here, not really. Will you stop worrying. Nothing has changed. You've told the Bishop. You said yourself the decision is made. It's just a waiting game. My darling, I love you and want us to have a normal life. Now I know your mind is made up, I can't wait to get a ring on your finger and for us to live together."

183

Charlotte started to protest but before she could get a word in Max continued "I know the Bishop asked you to sleep on it and I know he and you had no idea about the added connection between the two of you, but let's face it, it isn't as if you are going out with his own daughter, now that would be newsworthy."

"Don't mock!"

"Sorry! But the whole gay issue is old news."

"But it's not, is it? Not when church is concerned. Just think how much it's been in the news lately with the Lambeth conference last year. Bishops were banned just because they were in support of the ordination of gay priests. There's a quiet witch hunt going on."

Max just shook her head. She was fighting a losing battle. She was thankful to see her sister-in-law return.

"Lizzie's coming back and now I need the loo. Just remember I love you and want to spend the rest of my life with you. My job is safe, we'll survive and if this wasn't a public place I'd kiss you right now." Max slipped out following Liz's directions to the ladies.

"Everything okay Charlie?" Lizzie had calmed down.

"Yes fine, thanks. What about you and the er... you know, extraction." Charlotte wasn't usually embarrassed by such things. She had once had a bride in a similar position when she was nearly an hour late for her wedding because the car had broken down. Her breasts were so swollen she had used the vestry to feed her baby overlooked by Charlie who was desperately trying to calm her down. Funnily enough bride gowns were not made for discreet breast feeding.

"Oh, that was fine," lied Liz, "the only thing is I need somewhere to keep the milk cool so I can use it later but the cool box is still in the car. I'll have to go back. Shall I see you on the ward?"

"Why don't we wait for Max, she can go on up to the ward and I'll walk back with you. Is it far?" A brief chat alone with Lizzie, might be a good idea, she thought.

"It's not too far, I'll be fine," said Lizzie. On the other hand, she had heard quite a bit about this 'young' priest from her father and had often hoped she would have an opportunity to meet her at some point. She never expected it to be quite like this though: in a hospital, her husband rammed by an oil tanker leaving the surgeons to put the bits back together as best they could. The anxiety about how she was going to cope with two small children and a potentially disabled husband had returned whilst she was alone sitting on the loo expressing the liquid needed to keep her son alive. The two most important men in her life dependent on her like no other.

"Lizzie, you've gone a bit pale, are you sure you're okay?"

"Just feeling a bit tired. There's so much to think about." Lizzie sat back on the chair.

"About Mike you mean and the children." Charlotte checked, knowing that was what Liz had meant. Knowing that any concerns about herself and Max would wait.

"Mike, the children, my business, Mum, Dad, Mike's job, the mortgage, the other loans to be paid, all the bills and," she paused briefly, "I like you and Max. Charlie I'm so sorry to ask you all those questions. I was crass and insensitive." Liz felt a tear escape and she wiped it away before it glistened on her cheek.

185

"Oh Liz, you've nothing to apologise for. I'm sorry it all came out today, here of all places. But like I said before, we are here for you and Mike and the children. We want to help in any way we can." Charlotte wanted to reassure Liz but hesitated.

"I could do with a hug," said Liz, which was enough for Charlotte. She pulled her chair next to Lizzie's and gently laid a firm and comforting arm around her Bishop's daughter, very much the way a mother would comfort an older child and thought again how appropriate it was that priests were often called 'Father'.

She said nothing, ignoring the quizzical looks from others in the restaurant, as Lizzie sobbed into Charlotte's shoulder. Charlie found a clean tissue in her bag and handed it to Lizzie. Charlotte spotted Max coming back and put a finger to her lips indicating to her to say nothing.

After a few minutes, Lizzie looked up and simply said, "Pray for me."

So, in the middle of a, by now, crowded dining room, both Charlotte and Max rested their hands across Lizzie's shoulders and asked for God's strength to uphold mother and wife, God's peace to calm the anxieties that threatened to overwhelm and for God's love to embrace the whole family. Charlotte didn't pray for healing for Mike but rather for God's power to flood through his body and his spirit to be lifted to renewed hope.

After a moment of silence in which it felt as if the world had stood still, Lizzie again lifted her head. "You are both Christians aren't you!" It was more of a statement than a question. "Charlotte, Dad was right, you are a brilliant priest. Don't throw it away without a fight. I'm on your side. I've never felt like that before. As you prayed, both of you, it was like something warm flowed threw me. No wonder you're a good vet Max. You must have God on your side!"

Charlotte broke that moment with reminding Liz about the practical need to get the baby milk to the cool box. "Will you come too Max? I need you both at the moment."

Max felt slightly overwhelmed by what had just happened. She knew Charlotte had a good reputation for coming alongside people in their moment of greatest need, but had never been part of it before and had never prayed for someone like that in the middle of a public place.

"I'd like to spend a few minutes with my brother, if that's okay with you. Would you mind if I went on back to the ward? He'll be wondering where we are. I'll get the TV card on the way. He can watch 'Top Gear' later when we've gone." Max was trying to lighten the mood slightly.

"Of course. He's been asking about you a lot these last couple of days. You two are obviously closer than I realised. You go on." Lizzie too was regaining her composure.

"Come on then," said Charlotte, back in practical mode, "let's get little Josh's milk in the cool."

"JOSH-UA" said Max and Lizzie together and they all laughed.

Max walked steadily back up to the ward collecting a TV and phone card on the way. She was trying to work out exactly what she was feeling. She was worried about Mike of course. She hated seeing her little brother so vulnerable but the conversation with Liz had produced so many more unexpected emotions. If she was honest, part of her felt excited. She was excited about what had happened in the busy restaurant. She was excited by Lizzie's relaxed acceptance of her and

Charlotte. Max allowed herself to believe that she and Charlotte would actually get married and have a proper home together. But as always, the excitement was tinged with regret about how much Charlotte would have to give up and how much other people would lose out because of it. With mixed emotion, she entered her brother's room to find it occupied by a middle-aged woman sitting next to an elderly gentleman attached to several monitors.

"Oh I'm sorry. I must have the wrong room." Max stumbled her way out again as a nurse passed by. "Can you tell me where I might find Michael Tannin?"

"He's no longer with us," said the nurse.

"What?" Max did not hold back her shock.

"My dear I don't mean... he's been moved to another ward that's all. They are better equipped to assist people in a frame like Mr Tannin. We are more head injuries here. It's just down the corridor." The nurse didn't apologise for giving Max such a fright, but whisked herself off to continue with whatever important errand she was on.

'Damn,' thought Max to herself. 'Do I stay here and wait for Charlie and Liz or do I go off and assure my little brother we haven't totally abandoned him?' She chose the latter and turned up on the ward to find Mike in a long old Victorian Ward looking slightly dishevelled and not very happy.

"Hello Little Brother, still trying to run away from me?" She kept her manner bright.

"There you are. You've been gone ages. Where are the others?"

But before Max could answer an older nurse had come up to the bed and was addressing Max.

188

"Excuse me, are you visiting?"

"I am yes, he's an inmate." Max said, pointing at Mike, still keeping a lightness in her voice.

"Visiting time is from 2.30pm. Can you come back in half an hour?"

"What? Is this the dark ages? I've driven up from Plymouth to spend time with my brother and just chased around the hospital trying to find him," Max was quick to take offence.

"I appreciate that madam, but we do insist on our patients having their rest period and you might disturb the other patients, so I have to request that you come back in a few minutes. Why don't you go and get a coffee in the restaurant, it's just across the grounds." The nurse was pleasant but gave the distinct impression it was no use arguing.

"Fine, yes of course. I'll be back in half an hour." The nurse walked away but Max noticed she kept an eye on her to ensure that she would actually go. Max turned back to Mike "Charlie's gone with Liz to take something to the car." A little coy about saying it was breast milk.

"I'll go back to the old ward and meet them there. We didn't know you were being moved."

"Nor did I. I was just about to have my lunch but that seems to have got lost somewhere. Can you get me a sandwich or something?"

"Course," said Max, "but I'll try and find out why you haven't been given anything, that's disgraceful."

"Don't upset them Sis. They're really busy."

"I won't, I'll just ask, nicely." Max spotted the nurse looking up from the desk. "I'm being watched, I'll be back soon. Oh, and here's that card for the phone."

"Thanks, we can sort it out when you get back."

Max arrived back on the first ward just as Liz and Charlie got to the door.

"Max! What are you doing out here?" asked Charlotte

"Mike's been transferred onto another ward," said Max. "They moved him when we were having lunch. He's not had anything."

"Is that good, that they've moved him I mean?" Liz was concerned.

"Probably means he's not so critical. He's on a main ward, but for some strange reason that means stricter visiting, so we've got to lose ourselves for another twenty minutes or so. I said I'd get him a sandwich."

"Don't they realise we have to come from some distance?" Liz was annoyed.

"I told them," said Max "but it's not long to wait. I looked on the door visiting is ten till noon, two thirty till four-thirty and again from six till eight."

"Oh well," said Charlotte, "we don't have to feel guilty about being away for so long. Let's walk over to the hospital shop and find something for Mike."

A short time later they were heading back towards the ward having spent most of the last minutes talking about the children. Max was wondering when she might see her new little nephew.

"Why don't you call in on your way back to Plymouth? You know where the Palace is Charlotte," suggested Liz, without really thinking it through.

"Good idea, it wouldn't be too far off our route would it love?" Max too had forgotten the implications.

"I'm not sure that would go down too well," said Charlotte pointedly. "I could drop you off Max and pick you up later."

They were back outside the ward.

"Think about it," said Lizzie still seemingly oblivious to the connotations of Charlotte turning up at her parents' house with Max in tow. "We can decide later."

The next two hours passed by with working out how Mike would operate the TV and phone whilst still semi prone. They helped him drink tea out of a cup, as the ward had run out of beakers, but that was resolved by Charlotte visiting three other wards and eventually tracking down a replacement. They disappeared for a short while, when Mike felt the need to use a bed pan, but apparently, nothing came of the urge.

"Too much info little bruv," said Max.

Max also managed to track down a Registrar who came over to the bed and gave them all an update.

They were pleased with Mike's progress, had no more concerns about inflammation around the brain, and everything had settled down nicely which was why he had been transferred to a main Orthopaedic ward. They asked again about transferring him to Gloucester, but that seemed to be problematic, until the frame had been fully set which may not be for several days. At which point Mike groaned.

"She seemed nice," said Charlotte once the Registrar was out of ear shot.

"I thought that too," said Mike, at which point Liz gently thumped her husband and Max, slightly less gently, thumped Charlotte, which caused more laughter from their bed area. The older nurse who had first greeted Max, just happened to be passing at the time, and raised the eyebrows at the foursome as if they were troublesome children.

"You'll get us chucked out," said Charlotte.

"Now that would be scandalous headlines 'Gay priest kicked out of hospital ward'" joked Max

"Don't mock," said Charlotte, "and be careful what you're saying, you never know who's listening."

"Ah, the paranoia strikes again." Max had often teased Charlotte about being overly cautious, especially when they had been away from the parish on holiday, far away from prying eyes. But nonetheless she respected her concern.

"I'll need to be going soon love," Lizzie said to Mike. "I've suggested Max and Charlie pop in to meet little Joshua."

"You are joking, right?" Mike attempted to pull himself further up the bed.

"No, it's on their way and they haven't met him yet. Charlotte hasn't even seen Heather and she's already four years old. It's easier than a three-hour trip up to Gloucester.

"And how will you explain to your dad how we know Charlotte and why we haven't mentioned this before?"

"Oh, I'll hover round town for a bit, I don't mind."

"Charlotte," said Max. She rarely used 'Charlotte', apart from when she was trying to sound very serious or if she was annoyed with her partner. She spoke quietly but firmly, "David knows you are gay. He knows you are in a relationship. You have already offered your resignation. He might as well know the full story." She was matter of fact and to the point. It was almost convincing, but Charlotte was uneasy.

"There's too much going on for everyone. The bishop, …er, your dad," said Charlotte looking over at Lizzie, "doesn't need any extra complications, and I certainly don't want to be the cause of any unpleasantness between you. It would be an intrusion. He thinks Max had fallen in love with some sort of male social worker, not one of his female priests, the one he wants to promote to Archdeacon. You know it's almost comical...."

".......if it wasn't so tragic." Mike finished off Charlotte's sentence for her.

"You know what, I think you *should* call in. I'm fed up with the secrets too." He pulled himself up a little, cringing a little at the effort but continued.

"It's not just you that's affected you know. Me, Mum, Dad, Max we all have to walk on egg shells afraid we might let something slip. David knows nearly the full story, might as well make it a hat-trick."

Charlotte was taken aback at Mike's forthright disclosure. She looked across at Max.

"Is it really like that?"

Max gave a weak nod, but still trying to indicate support rather than criticism.

"I've not been very fair to you, have I?" said Charlotte, "I always thought I was the one in the difficult position, but I've dragged you in too." She touched Mike's arm, "all of you. What does that make me?" But before they could answer she looked down saying, "Selfish, I guess, I'm sorry. No more lies. Promise."

The sounds of the busy ward continued in the background. Visitors, paramedics and nurses bustled up and down, but there was a stillness around Mike's bed as three people looked over at Charlotte. Her resolve for integrity and honesty suddenly deepened even more.

But Charlotte was still not keen to visit the Bishop's Palace that evening. It was too soon.

"I've got a meeting with your father at the end of the month. I'll tell him the whole story then," offered Charlotte as a compromise. "Max, why don't you go on back with Liz. I can stay with Mike a bit longer and meet you somewhere in Exeter later."

"And just how do I explain arriving with Liz if I'm asked?" Max stared at Charlotte holding her gaze as firmly as if she had her head in a strong grip.

"What am I supposed to do?" cried Charlotte. "I can't just turn up on Bishop David's door step and tell him, 'by the way your grandchildren will one day, by law, get to call me auntie, so I might as well meet them now' can I?"

"Why not?" said Max, "I want to see Joshua."

"I'm not stopping you."

"And I'd like you to come with me. This is family, Charlotte. Family life and quite frankly you are not all that good at it."

"What? Oh come on, this isn't fair. I'm trying to do what's right here." Charlotte was annoyed and hurt at the onslaught.

"We're going to upset Mike, you two go on. I'll ring you on your mobile when I get to Exeter. How long do you need?"

"I could ring Mum, I'm sure she'd like you to stay for supper. It will be way after six when we get back, which reminds me I could probably

194

do with the use of the day room if it's quiet. It's milking time again!" Her light-hearted reference to her lactating breasts served to lift the oppressive sombre mood. "I'll see you in a few minutes." She escaped, before she received an answer about the offer for supper.

The day room was in the middle of the ward but down a short corridor. There was no-one else in the room so she managed to attach the pump and successfully drew off a few millilitres from each breast. She then took out her mobile, checked for signs about usage. There weren't any so she made a swift call to her mother.

"I was expecting you to ring long ago, how are things?"

Her mum sounded concerned and slightly put out that her daughter had not rung, but launched into a whole series of questions and suggestions before Lizzie could draw breath. "When do you expect to be back? Naomi's coming home for the weekend. She thought she'd come via the hospital and arrive home about nine, so we could have a late supper. John and Wendy said they could meet you up in Bristol tomorrow. I thought we could take the children as there'd be enough of us to look after them. Ruth isn't going to make it home though. She's got a deadline to meet for her dissertation. She's only just gone back after Christmas, so it is a bit difficult." Finally, her mum paused for breath. "So how is it going?"

Rather than answer her mum's question Lizzie asked, "Mum, can you cope with one or two extra for supper?"

"One or two? Sounds like the request of a teenager who turns up with about six. I remember those days, so who is it?" Catrin was intrigued.

"Max is here with.... with Charles." She knew she was playing chicken. "They're on their way back to Plymouth. She hasn't met Joshua

195

so I thought they could pop in and wondered if you could throw in some extra veg."

"I'm doing a big stew; your father won't be home till nearer ten, so a stew can just keep simmering till he's back. He's got a confirmation service. Actually, he nearly forgot about it, which would have been embarrassing. He'll have the usual bun fight after the service of course, so he won't starve."

"So, it's okay, if they pop in? I'm not sure they'll want to stay till nine though." Lizzie knew in her heart of hearts she was playing with fire, but she was rather enjoying the adrenaline boost born out of mischievousness, rather than the stress of the last few days.

"No problem." Catrin had no idea what she was agreeing to. "Naomi won't mind if we eat before she gets here. It'll keep. Heather will need something anyway. Now tell me how's Mike getting on?" Liz gave a brief account of the day, the fact that he had been moved to a main ward and that he seemed to be doing really well.

"And what's Charles like?" asked her mum out of the blue.

Liz had been wondering if her mum had actually heard her mention 'Charles', but not a lot slipped past Catrin.

"Well," said Lizzie, "er, nice. We got on well," and taking a big breath added. "You'll like her."

"I'm sure I will. There are not many people I don't like. I'm looking forward to meeting ......" she paused. "Did you just say 'her'?"

"Yes."

"Oh!" Catrin wasn't quite sure she understood. "That was ....unexpected. I thought Vince and Maureen had met him... er her."

196

"They have, but," Liz hesitated "….they were a bit uncertain about letting on to you and Dad that Charlie was actually Charlotte and not Charles."

Lizzie was choosing her words carefully. She wasn't quite sure how much to say on the phone, but she was also preparing the ground to avoid too many shocks. Charlotte was right about one thing, there was a lot going on.

"Well, everyone to their own. They're not, you know all dressed in pink or anything? This Charlotte - she's not got rings in her nose and red hair. I don't want bad influences on our Heather. You need to be careful love, don't get too friendly."

"Mum, I'm shocked. No, she's nothing like that at all. She's lovely. Don't jump to conclusions. You'll be surprised when you meet her," very surprised thought Lizzie. "She's really nice. She's been a huge support. They are both Christians you know."

"Hmm, I'm not sure about that. Just as well your father will be out."

"Mum, I had no idea you were so anti…..."

"I'm not." Catrin quickly interrupted her daughter. "I just don't understand why women have to do that sort of thing." She seemed to think for a moment. "But as long as they act properly, I'm sure it will be alright. Just make sure you don't leave Heather with them."

"Mum, I don't believe you. Just listen to yourself. You have just uttered every prejudice in the book. Wait till you meet them. They are good normal people. Now are you sure you'll cope?"

"Yes, of course. I'll cope. I'm a Bishop's wife, nothing is supposed to phase me, I'll welcome them with open arms. What time do you expect to be here?"

"It's just before five now, so about 6.30pm probably. Oh, and Mum, how are the kids?"

"Yes, I wondered if you'd ask. Well Sally's been helping out a bit. She took Heather out to play on the green at lunchtime. Joshua's been okay. A little bit crotchety at times, obviously missing his mother's breast. Did you manage with the pump?"

"Yes fine, I've saved it in the cool-box. Thanks mum, see you later," and with that she rang off.

She sat for a few moments thinking about the brief conversation with her mum. She realised they had never really discussed people like Max and Charlie. She knew the church's teaching, but she always assumed her mum and dad were quite open-minded. After all, her sister Naomi, was divorced and living with a man several younger. John had been found in bed with his girlfriend by their cleaner, who had never breathed a word outside of the family. Only Lizzie seemed to play things by the book. Ruth just seemed to work all the time.

So she had been a little shocked by her mum's reaction and apparent prejudice. At least she had ascertained that her dad would not be around. They all knew he would have to be told at some point, unless they all wanted to continue with this facade and quite frankly she didn't want Heather and Joshua brought up with lies. She was keen for them to know their aunty and was more than happy to include Charlotte as part of that family. Perhaps she was going to be the one to force the issue. Her life had already been turned upside down, so what was just a little more upheaval. 'Get it all over and done with, in one go,' she thought to herself.

With renewed determination, she went back to Mike's bedside. To find them laughing about something a nurse had said that morning.

"I've just spoken to Mum," she said, "and she is more than happy for you both to call in for supper. It's stew as we're all expected at different times. Hope that's okay." She sat down and waited for the response.

"You mean you and Max," said Charlotte.

"No all of us. I told mum that Max had brought 'Charlie' to see you Mike." Lizzie felt a little sheepish, but she was not going to back down. She waited for the further protests from Charlotte. They didn't come. There was silence.

Mike was the one to break the trance.

"You know, I wish I wasn't stuck in this hospital bed, I'd love to be a fly on the wall," Mike grinned.

"You've helped keep this secret for so long, I'm surprised you find it so funny," said Max

"Yeah, well near death experiences make you see things differently. Life is for living, not hiding away from." Mike turned philosophical. "I'm serious. I spent the first few hours of consciousness wondering if Charlotte had already turned up with you around my bedside, and the next couple of days wondering why she hadn't. Then the more I thought about it the crazier this secret seemed to be. Why waste years apart when you two could be much happier living a normal life?"

"You know why, I'd be out of a job and a home," reminded Charlotte.

"You have a home with my sister and her two dogs. You can get another job if you have to. Anyway, what's the problem? You've already told my father-in-law by the sounds of it."

"Yes, and all he wanted me to do, was to keep the secret and pretend I'd never even mentioned it," retorted Charlie.

"He asked you to do that?" Liz was visibly shocked. "He asked you to be dishonest? He who drummed it into to us to never to tell lies."

"I'm afraid so, but that's just the way it is. It's probably what keeps the church going in some places. There are some good priests out there, whose vocation has been tested and proven and yet they, like me, are forced into hiding a major part of their lives, and then of course when it all comes to light, it is dubbed some sort of horrendous scandal." Charlotte looked around, worried about who was listening. When no one seemed to be taking any notice she continued. "The scandal is the lies in the first place. Shove things under the carpet and pretend they aren't happening. I'm sorry Liz, it sounds like I'm getting at your Dad. I'm not. He's a good bloke. He was only trying to do what he thought was best."

"By asking you to lie?" Lizzie was still annoyed at her father and was still reeling from the conversation with her mother. "They are just living in the dark ages. Look Charlie, Mum doesn't know who you really are. All she knows is that Charles is in fact Charlotte, but she won't have put two and two together, not yet any way. And Dad isn't there tonight. He won't be back till late, and you'll be gone by then. Come on back and meet the kids. Meet Mum properly. Will she recognise you?"

"Probably. We have met a couple of times before." Charlotte felt her resolve to steer clear of the Palace that night beginning to wane. The others were right. It was going to come out sometime, so it might as well be sooner rather than later. She had already pretty much decided that she had to leave the priesthood. 'Honesty and integrity.' She reminded herself of her new resolve, 'so what's the use of backing down now?' she thought.

"Okay, I'll come in, but if your mum is uncomfortable, we'll go. The last thing I want is to cause any more stress for you all. I'm sorry it's all come out like this."

"I'm not!" said Mike.

"You're not?" questioned Max .

"No, if something good comes out of this, it's the chance to stop all this stupid deception."

"We'll see, Mike. Don't build your hopes up," said Charlotte, "Max and I may need to leave the country!"

"PARANOID!" Chorused the others, just as the older nurse was coming around the beds reminding visitors that visiting time had in fact ended five minutes ago.

They said their goodbyes. Liz explained the plans for the next day and Max and Charlie promised to visit the following week as long as Max could persuade her business partner to cover the Friday surgery again. As the women said goodbye at the hospital entrance they agreed that they would give Lizzie a head start and try to arrive about 7.30pm, after all they needed half an hour to go and track down their car again.

Chapter 14

Lizzie had been back in Exeter for just over half an hour. She and her mother had talked briefly about Mike. The real revelation of the day for Liz had been the discovery of the big secret that her husband had kept from her all these years, but she hadn't discussed that. Liz was still hurt that Mike hadn't felt able to trust her, but they would sort that out when he was a little stronger. Whilst Liz was feeding Joshua, her mother had bathed Heather. Then, the conversation had revolved around the children. Heather had wanted to tell her mum all about helping granny bake bread and cakes and about Sally and the park. She delighted in telling Lizzie that Joshua had pee-peed over Grandpa's pink shirt at lunch time when he was changing his nappy.

Just after 7.30pm Max, Charlotte at her side, rang the bell next to the huge, old, oak door.

Back in the kitchen it appeared that Catrin had forgotten about Lizzie's invitation to Max and partner. When the doorbell went. "That can't be Naomi surely," she said, "it's not even eight." She was flustered.

"It'll be Mike's sister," said Liz hurrying to the door scooping up Joshua and leaving her mother with Heather and a story book.

On the doorstep, Max and Charlotte waited for the door to be answered.

"So, this is where you come for your business meetings. It's a bit imposing," mused Max.

"I don't really think about it anymore. Somebody's coming," and the huge door opened to reveal Liz holding a small baby in her arms.

"I thought it must be you." She held Joshua out in front of her. "Joshua, meet your Auntie Max and Auntie Charlie. Come on in," she said, clutching Joshua back close again.

"Mum's in the kitchen with Heather. Do you know the way Charlie?" Lizzie wasn't going to pretend that Charlotte was a stranger to the Palace, there was no point.

"Afraid not, I've only ever been that way," said Charlotte pointing in the direction of the offices.

"I suppose you have. Well it's down there to the right. Brr! It's cold out there. Are you hungry? Mum has cooked up a huge stew. Heather's already had hers but we waited till you arrived. Look, I haven't said anything else. We've been too busy with the kids. Dad's not here by the way. He's already gone to the confirmation service. He won't be back for ages."

As she followed on behind Max and Charlotte, she reminded them that her sister Naomi would be arriving later. "She works up in London, in a law firm. She's quite a character, knows her own mind and can be a bit fiery."

Apart from the wedding Max had never met any members of the family, giving the impression that she was not close to her brother. Now of course Liz understood that was not the case.

"Is she a lawyer?" asked Max.

"No, she's a legal secretary, but she seems to more or less run the firm. Go in through the door on your right, Mum's in there with Heather."

Lizzie disguised her nervousness. She hadn't had the chance to talk to her mum any more about Max and Charlie. They really had been too busy with the children and she was a little anxious about the reception they would get.

Her nervousness was nothing compared to what Charlotte was feeling, who was by now regretting having even gone up to the hospital. She had David's voice in her mind from the conversation three days previously, 'Don't rub it in – please, I'm trying to be fair.' She was hardly being fair now. This had been a stupid decision. She had allowed herself to be pushed into something she knew was a bad move. Only Max seemed at ease, she turned around to Liz and reached out towards Joshua, who was content in his mother's arms.

"And I guess this is my little nephew. Hello Joshua, we've heard a lot about you."

"Would you like to hold him?" asked Liz. And without waiting for an answer handed him over to Max, "Here you go."

"Oh no, Charlie's the expert when it comes to babies. Just don't let her dip him in water like she usually does to the poor little blighters." It was perhaps Max's way of trying to put Charlotte at ease. She could feel she was tense and she too suddenly wondered if this had been such a good idea, but they were here now and would make the best of it. Before Charlotte had time to protest, she had a four-week-old baby thrust into her arms. He didn't complain, much to her relief.

Lizzie squeezed past and opened the kitchen door. Charlotte nodded at Max to go in first. She had no idea if Catrin would recognise her and she hadn't worked out what to do if she did or indeed what to do if she didn't. She was glad David wasn't there, although she did feel a bit guilty that it would probably be left to his wife to tell him.

"Come on in," said Liz. Rather than introducing the adults to her mother she bent down to her daughter. "Do you remember Auntie Max?" Lizzie took Heather's hand and encouraged her towards her auntie.

"Heather say hello to Auntie Max and...." she beckoned Charlie to come in, who was still hovering in the door way, "Auntie Charlie."

Heather started to walk over to Max, who had also crouched down but the little girl quickly turned her attention to Charlotte who still had careful hold of Joshua.

"You've got my brother. Are you a boy? Charlie is a boy's name."

Charlotte was still out of visual range of Catrin. Max and Lizzie stood back up and watched as Charlie stooped down to Heather's level still carefully holding little Joshua. She ignored Heather's question about her gender but asked, "So this is your brother? He is a lovely brother. Does he cry a lot?"

"Mmm sometimes. He did a pee-pee on Grandpa today."

Trust children to come straight to the interesting stories thought Charlotte. "Oh my, I bet that was funny," she said, holding the youngster's attention.

"Yeah, it was. Grandpa had to put a clean top on. Are you going to stay? Can you read me a story?" Heather had obviously decided Charlotte was a friend. Max looked on with a strange pride. This was the second time today she had been reminded of why Charlotte was a priest. First the way she responded to Liz in the middle of the restaurant and now how she had managed to put a little four-year-old completely at her ease whilst the other adults looked on mesmerised.

"Well, maybe I can, but I think I had better say hello to your grandmother first," said Charlotte getting up from her crouching position and handing a sleepy Joshua back to Lizzie.

"That's Granny," said Heather pointing to Catrin.

"It's rude to point, Heather," said Lizzie.

Heather continued chatting without responding to her mother. "You my Auntie too?" she asked Charlie, still seemingly ignoring Max.

"Er, yes I suppose I am," replied Charlotte looking over to Max for encouragement, who just shrugged her shoulders and held out her hands, as if to say, 'go with the flow'.

"Like Auntie Max?"

"Yes."

Catrin took over. "Come along Heather let the nice lady into the kitchen and close the door. There's a draught blowing down that corridor."

She made a huge effort to be as welcoming as possible. She was still apprehensive about welcome this strange couple into her home, but, like always, she would be the perfect hostess. She held her hand out to Max

"Max, it is good to see you again, in slightly better circumstances. We are so relieved that Mike is making good progress, a way to go yet though we fear." As Max rather formally shook her hand, Catrin took both of Max's in her own to shake them warmly. Her manner was warm.

Charlotte, still standing slightly out of sight thought about the number of times she too had been made to welcome slightly unexpected and at times rather unwanted guests. She found herself marvelling at Catrin's skill and demure.

"I don't think we got any sleep on Tuesday night," continued Catrin. "How are your mother and father? At least we have had the opportunity to get to know them a little better, if that doesn't sound too insensitive."

"No of course not, Mum and Dad felt the same way. They are fine, thank you. I saw them yesterday evening. I think they will go back up to Bristol after the weekend, perhaps stay again for a couple of days. It's too far for Dad to drive up and down in one day. And thank you for inviting us for supper, there was no need, really. It was very kind of Lizzie to invite us to see little Joshua." Max was interrupted by Heather.

"And me too, you can see me. I don't think you are my Auntie. I don't remember you. Auntie Naomi is coming too, because Daddy is poorly. He got runned over." It seemed that Mother, daughter and granddaughter all had the same tendency to talk 'nineteen to the dozen'.

Charlotte was now visible but it seemed that Catrin had not yet registered her presence. She was happy to hover in the background and wondered if Catrin wouldn't recognise her after all. They had only met a couple of times, and although they were in the kitchen of the Bishop's Palace this was completely out of the normal context in which the Bishop's wife would seek an audience with her husband's priests.

Max spoke again, first to Heather. "Don't you remember when Daddy brought you to see me and we took the dogs up on the moor and flew your kite? Look I've got a photo." She took out her wallet from her coat and opened it up to reveal a very windswept Heather running along with Patch and Stitch, her daddy running behind pulling a colourful kite.

"Is that me?" asked Heather, "Where's Mummy and Joshua?"

207

"It was before Joshua was born. Daddy brought you down to see your other grandma and grandpa so that Mummy could catch up on some work I think." She looked up inquisitively at Lizzie.

"Oh, I remember that weekend, it wasn't that long ago. In November I think," said Lizzie, "we've got the same photo somewhere. Yes, I must have been eight months pregnant at the time and glad of a bit of time to myself. Don't you remember Heather?"

"I think so. Where's Auntie Charlie?" she asked still looking at the photo.

"Aunty Charlie wasn't with us. I don't think you've met Auntie Charlie before." Max was intrigued at how Heather was obviously trying to work things out in her little mind.

"Oh." And with that she seemed to lose interest and went back to some Lego bricks in the corner of the room.

"How rude of me, Charlie, or is it Charlotte? I think we've established it isn't Charles." Catrin was obviously trying to make light of the recent confusion. "Do come on in you are still half in the dark over there." Catrin held out her hand to Charlotte as she stepped from the shadows into the full light of the kitchen.

"Hello Mrs Graham."

"Charlotte!"

It felt as if time in the Palace kitchen had momentarily stood still as both Max and Lizzie realised that Catrin had indeed recognised the Reverend Charlotte Northam, Rector of the East Dartmoor Benefice of eight rural parishes in the diocese of Exeter. Charlotte wished Joshua would start crying, or for Heather to demand attention, but infants don't perform to command, especially not by telepathy. When that hope failed, she adopted Catrin's approach and simply held out her hand but as she did Catrin unexpectedly turned away to face Lizzie.

"Is this your idea of a joke? Do you know who this is? Charlotte, do come and sit down. I think there has been some terrible mistake." Catrin was flushed. Charlotte could only imagine what was speeding through Catrin's mind; the muddled thoughts, trying to make sense out of the dislocated scene. Completely separate parts of her life had suddenly clashed in the heart of her private home to the cacophony of emotion that she was struggling to control.

Catrin could not bring herself to believe the logical conclusion that was mushrooming in her mind. There had to be a different explanation. She was trying to bustle Charlotte over to a kitchen chair.

"Mrs Graham, I'm sorry," said Charlotte. "Lizzie has told you the truth, there's no mistake."

"No no. You don't know what she told me, she tried to make out... well it doesn't matter. Now can I make you a cup of tea? I take it you are a friend of Max, what a strange coincidence. How nice of you to take her to see her brother, my husband always said you are a good person. Did you have other visits to do in Bristol?"

"Oh bother!" said Charlotte, to the surprise of everyone present. "Actually, yes I did. I forgot. I'm useless!"

"That's not what my husband says. He is hoping you are going to be our next Archdeacon, isn't he? I'm sure your parishioner wouldn't have expected you to go all the way up to Bristol. Was he or she expecting you?"

"No, thankfully, it would have been a surprise," Charlotte was feeling the moment slipping away and didn't want Catrin to manipulate

209

the truth, not now they had come this far. She decided in that moment to make it clear that Lizzie was right about her facts and to avoid any more deception. "Mrs Graham..."

"Do call me Catrin...."

"Catrin, Lizzie was right, is right. I'm Max's partner and have been for about ten years."

Catrin simply didn't react, but very coolly spoke to her daughter, using her full name.

"Elizabeth, can I have a word in private. Heather come along it's bed time." Catrin's voice was so firm that Heather didn't dare to argue, she just looked back and waved to Max and Charlie. "Come along Heather, now please."

Max and Charlotte were left alone in the kitchen. Max sat down at the kitchen table with Charlotte.

"We could just go," suggested Max after a moment's silence.

"And just make things worse? If that were possible. I told you this was a stupid idea. And I'm an idiot for agreeing to it. I should have waited and told the Bishop at the end of the month. Why am I so easily misled?"

A heavy silence fell between them, neither one knowing what to say, both lost in their own thoughts. Charlotte looked around at the homely scene. The stew was simmering on the old Aga. It felt as if this room usually beat to the rhythm of family life, as if this was where the real decisions were made. Charlotte felt as if she had violated that space somehow, that she had invaded the privacy of her Bishop and his family. And because he knew nothing of the revelation, she felt like a thief, stealing something precious from the person she respected, which made her want to run away just as Max had suggested, but she wasn't going to. She would stay and face her crime.

"It's their problem you know, not ours." Max spoke into the silence, stirring Charlotte from the dark thoughts that were pressing down on her. "Did you see how quickly she whisked off little Heather? She could just about cope when she was dealing with strangers, but when it was someone she knew, she couldn't. She obviously likes you, that's the problem. So, her judgment is under question."

Max wasn't looking at Charlotte as she spoke. She was staring at the window ledge with its small vase of flowers, a small china windmill and a cardboard charity box with 'Church Urban Fund' written on the front in large purple letters. She caught sight of a family photo hanging near a notice board. It had obviously been taken several years previously when Catrin and David's children were still either teenagers or in early adulthood.

"It's not her fault, we shouldn't have come." Charlotte had gone headlong into self-blame. It was something she was very good at and very practiced.

"We didn't invite ourselves you know. We haven't even had a cup of tea yet." Max was the opposite, and would only admit guilt when all else had proven insufficient.

"I'm sorry sweetheart," said Charlotte. "I think Catrin was okay with you. She was making a huge effort to accept you it was only when she realised that the stranger she knew as Charlie, was in fact the respected priest she knew as Charlotte. It must have been a shock for her." Charlotte would now make excuses for other people's behaviour.

211

"I don't see what the big deal is. David already knows you're gay. There are more important things to worry about than what two people get up to in their private life." Max was getting more animated.

"Keep your voice down, they'll be back in a minute" Charlotte was desperately trying to stay in control of her emotions and wanted to be anywhere but the private kitchen of her employer.

In actual fact, it would be several minutes before Catrin and Lizzie reappeared. They ignored Heather's pleas for a story from the 'nice lady'. They didn't seem to hear when she asked again and again for her 'blankey' that she had left downstairs and when she started to sniffle she was told to be quiet. Instead they talked over her whilst they supervised her cleaning her teeth. Lizzie changed Joshua's nappy and told Heather to go away when she tried to help, all the time listening to her mother berate her for not 'warning' her.

"But Mum I didn't have chance to tell you more." Lizzie was mystified and hurt by her mother's ardent response. "I don't understand. Max and Charlie are really lovely people. You know how much Dad respects Charlotte. Heather really took to her too."

By now Heather had unceremoniously been put to bed without her usual story and a very swift goodnight kiss from her grandmother. By a miracle both she and Joshua had settled quickly despite the charged atmosphere.

Mother and daughter continued their conversation in the hall. They kept their voices low so as not to disturb the children even further, but they kept up with the recriminations. One annoyed for not being given the full story in advance, the other angry because of a perceived

212

overreaction. Lizzie realised she had over stepped the mark when she accused her own mother of being immoral.

"I'm immoral? How dare you talk to me like that." Catrin forgot about her sleeping grandchildren and put the full force of her emotion into her voice.

"You may be a mother yourself young lady, but you are still my daughter and you do not question my morals when yours are so obviously skewed."

Lizzie was visibly shocked by her mother's outburst, Catrin had not raised her voice to her daughter for several years. Catrin immediately regretted her outburst.

"I'm sorry," she said in a resolute voice as she lent her back heavily against the wall. "Why are we arguing?"

"We're not, not really, we just don't understand how we can have such different points of view. Now, there are two people in your kitchen who are wondering where we've got to. I can either go downstairs, apologise to my sister-in-law and politely ask her and her partner, who up until thirty minutes ago, was someone you respected, to leave, or we can both go down and apologise for being so long and at least offer the poor women a cup of tea. You do realise that Charlotte didn't want to come, but I insisted so I do feel responsible."

Lizzie was leaning against the banisters with her elbows propped up on the rail looking surprisingly relaxed but feeling far from confident. "We will not agree Mother, so let's stop trying. But I do regret suddenly dropping this on you in this way. It was perhaps not the best thing to have done - so for that I am truly sorry."

Catrin seemed to think for a moment before saying with some resolve, "You go on down. I'll be there in a moment. Offer them some stew if they'd like some." Catrin turned towards the bathroom. Lizzie stepped forward and placed her hand on her mother's shoulder.

"Thanks Mum."

"You have nothing to thank me for," said Catrin without turning around. "I haven't changed my opinion," and she walked on down the hallway.

Lizzie felt snubbed, but rather than attempt to heal the current rift made her way back to the kitchen.

The doorbell rang before Lizzie got as far as the kitchen. Thinking it may be her sister she answered it and was stunned to see her father standing in the door way.

"You look as if you've seen a ghost! In the rush, I forgot my key. Brr! It is cold out there tonight. When did you get back?" David asked his daughter before planting a kiss on her cheek. "How's Michael?"

"Dad!" She spoke loudly, perhaps hoping that Charlotte and Max would hear, but what good it would do remained a puzzle. They could hardly hide in the broom cupboard. Internally Lizzie was now kicking herself, wondering why she had not listened to the older wiser Charlie, rather than bamboozling them into paying a visit. It had turned out that the whole reason for 'popping in' had been very short lived as the children has been whisked off to bed before Max had even got to hold Joshua.

"Dad, you're back early." Liz stumbled slightly over her words.

"Lizzie, is everything alright? Michael is okay, isn't he? Well I mean, as well as can be expected." David put his large bag and the thin case

214

containing his Bishop's crook down on the floor and placed his hands on his daughter's shoulders.

Lizzie roused herself into reality. "Yes, Mike is fine. He's been moved to the main ward and he'll be able to watch TV tonight."

"Oh, well that's great, love." David assumed his daughter was simply weary, but wondered what was so special about TV. He didn't ask. "I'll just put my things in the study. Are you all in the kitchen?"

"Er yes, we're all in the kitchen." Lizzie looked over her shoulder towards the kitchen door.

"Is Naomi here yet?" David was taking off his heavy woollen coat and hanging it up on the wooden hooks which must have been nearly two hundred years old, but still strong after several generations of Bishops had placed their cloaks and scarves upon them.

"Naomi, oh I'd forgotten about her." Lizzie was talking to herself, but obviously loud enough for her father to overhear.

"That's a nice thing to say, when your sister has driven all the way from London to see you." David was his usual light hearted self, his comment had no bite to it more of a tease, but Lizzie was feeling overly sensitive after the head to head with her mother.

"Oh, I didn't mean it like that," Lizzie was swift to correct herself. "It's great that she can come down, but no she's not here yet, but," she hesitated, looking at her watch, "it won't be long. It's already nine o clock," and as she said it, she realised she and her mother had left Charlotte and Max in the kitchen for about forty-five minutes. "You're home early," she repeated herself.

"I only had to go as far as the Cathedral love. I stayed for the photos, but then made my excuses. Everyone was very understanding. The

215

media has sort of done us a favour with that unsolicited announcement. So here I am. I'll be in, in a minute. Get the kettle on, I could do with a nice cup of tea."

'Mmm' Lizzie thought to herself. You could do with more than that in a minute'.

And before she could mention their dinner guests he had bustled down the hall to his study. She slipped into the kitchen to find Max and Charlotte still sat at the kitchen table. Charlotte was looking distinctly uncomfortable. Max had her hand on Charlotte's, but quickly took it away when Lizzie entered the room.

"Dad's here!" was all Lizzie said.

Charlotte reacted by closing her eyes, and covered her face with her hands. She kept them there for a moment in a strange sort of praying pose. As she took them away she simply said "Great!" conveying in that one word, annoyance, submission and dread.

Max wanted to say something, but remained silent. The focus had shifted from the main connection being between herself as Mike's sister and Lizzie's sister-in-law, to the professional relationship between Charlotte and David. It was always going to be that way. This had always overshadowed their relationship. 'Not for much longer though,' she thought to herself and regretted the slight smugness that accompanied the thought.

The door opened and in walked David. "Max, there's a surprise, on your way back to Plymouth?"

"Yes," Max was reluctant to say too much but added, "Lizzie invited us in to meet Joshua."

Charlotte had her back to David and hesitated for a moment before turning around.

"Hello Bishop," she said.

"Charlotte, what are you doing here? Is something wrong? You've obviously met Lizzie and I imagine you've been introduced to my son-in-law's sister, Maxine." David was blissfully unaware of the complexity he had walked into. It was almost comical the way he tried to assert his command on the situation drawing completely the wrong conclusion.

"Lizzie, you've heard me talk about Reverend Northam. Maxine I wonder if you'll excuse us, I imagine there is something of some urgency you wish to discuss with me Charlotte. I must say this is highly irregular."

David felt annoyed at this intrusion on his family life, even if it was from somebody he happened to like and respect, but turning up unannounced late on a Friday evening was quite unacceptable and he was deeply troubled by Charlotte's actions.

"Dad, Charlie is a guest." Lizzie emphasised 'Charlie', throwing an apologetic glance towards Charlotte, who felt she was in a scene from some corny soap opera or a bad dream and half expected to wake up.

"Yes love, she is. But I'm sure she hasn't just popped in for supper," and turning his attention to Charlotte asked. "Have you been waiting long? My wife should be here. I expect she's putting the grandchildren to bed. Has my daughter been looking after you? You could have waited in my study."

The last comment was more of a command than an offer, he did not make a habit of inviting his priests into the family kitchen.

217

He continued, but addressed his next comment to Lizzie, "and Elizabeth, I'm sure Reverend Northam would prefer 'Charlotte', I don't think we know her as 'Charlie'" and chortled in a jovial manner.

"Bishop, it's fine. I am known as Charlie, and actually I have simply popped in, I'm afraid. It's not a business visit so to speak, more social really."

Charlotte chose her words carefully articulating each one, keeping her speech very slow and steady trying not to convey her nervousness. In the next two or three minutes, she would have signed the death certificate of her twenty-year career as an Anglican priest. It had already been written out four days previously. She found it difficult to breathe. Her heart was pounding. She wanted to reach out and take Max's hand, giving all the explanation needed in that one simple act, but it would be too dramatic and she didn't want this moment to be insulting in any way. She simply wanted to remain true to her own self. 'No more lies' she reminded herself, but she didn't pause too long, she didn't want Max or Lizzie to say anything, she wanted to say this herself, in the right way.

"Bishop I'm so sorry for this intrusion. It was wrong of us to come." She emphasised the word 'us', hoping to give a clue before she had to spell it out.

For the second time that evening there was stillness in the kitchen. David held Charlotte's gaze for two or three seconds, which felt like a lifetime before slowly turning towards Max. Charlotte opened her mouth to speak again, but David interrupted her.

"I wonder if you and I could have a quiet chat in my study?" It was a question but there would be only one answer as Charlotte followed

David back through the open door of the kitchen towards the business end of the Palace. They bumped into Catrin in the hall.

"David, I thought I heard your voice.....oh." She stopped as she saw Charlotte behind. She stood aside to let them pass, as if David was leading a solemn procession.

"Maxine and Elizabeth are in the kitchen" was all he said, the use of their full names carrying great meaning.

Once they were in the study with the familiar soft leather sofas and the smouldering ashes of an open fire, David spoke again. "Charlie," the use of her nickname caught Charlotte off balance and she looked puzzled. "Have you any idea what is going through my mind?" he asked.

"I may be able to guess, Bishop."

"You might as well call me Dave!" he said

"Sorry?" questioned Charlotte.

"The one thing I asked for was discretion. I explained to you that we could work this out. I had been impressed by your honesty and respected your integrity. I was convinced we could find a way through this. I asked you to arrange time away from the parish to think this through. But you have done none of this....."

"Bishop, it's only been a few days, there's been a lot........."

"Yes, a lot going on. I know. It seems we have both been struggling under the pressures of family tragedy."

Charlotte suddenly realised that the Bishop, far from being angry, seemed upset.

"You know why I said call me Dave?" Bishop David had sat down on one of the sofas, Charlotte was still standing.

"No,"

"When you call me Bishop, it demonstrates respect. Nobody ever calls me Dave, unless they are trying to be funny, or, on occasions, if they have purposefully tried to undermine my authority, tried to belittle me or even embarrass me. I think you have attempted all those things this evening."

The Bishop unclipped his white clerical collar and laid it on the coffee table. He unbuttoned his top shirt button and leant back against the sofa cushions. He still sounded hurt rather than angry. It made Charlotte feel uneasy.

"Come and sit down Charlotte," David had reverted to his usual name for her. "Do you have any respect for me?"

"Of course I do Bishop. I'm sorry. It was not my intention to embarrass you, or belittle you. I didn't even want to come." Charlotte was defensive, she felt like a teenager trying to explain herself to a father.

"I'm not sorry you came." His voice was now strangely soft. "I'm hurt because you didn't tell me the full story. You said you were in a relationship. You didn't say you knew my daughter."

"I don't.... I didn't. I met her for the first time today." Charlotte was still standing.

"You expect me to believe that? How long have you two known each other? How long have you dragged my daughter and my son-in-law into your lies?" David looked very tired.

"Bishop. I'm telling you the truth. I met Elizabeth for the very first time today, around Mike's bedside." Charlotte was vehemently defending her honesty.

"But you've known Michael for some time?"

"Yes. Max and I have been together for about ten years. I've known Mike and his parents pretty much all that time." Charlotte eventually sat down on the edge of the other sofa. She thought about the smart suit she had worn when she was last in the room and she now looked down at her jeans and trainers.

"But you are trying to tell me you had never met Elizabeth."

"I hadn't, no. Max has and little Heather, but Mike was really funny about me meeting any of his wife's family. It caused quite a tension between him and Max. She nearly boycotted the wedding because of it, but he was simply trying to prevent....... prevent.... prevent this," she said waving her arms around the room. "Bishop I didn't even know about the connection until after the accident. It wasn't until then that Max and I put all the fragments together. I'm sorry, I know it all sounds far-fetched but it's the truth."

"And what is the 'this', that we are preventing?" asked David.

"Well, this......," she struggled to find the right word, "altercation".

"Charlotte. I'm not in dispute with you. Surely I explained my position on Tuesday."

"Yes, you wanted me to keep it hidden." Charlotte rediscovered a little of her confidence.

"Yes, I thought that was an option. I could have accepted your resignation, but I was trying to prevent you giving up something that is important." David's voice was firm but gentle.

"My life is important. My relationship is important."

"And your career is important," added David, expecting a response from Charlotte. His comment was met with silence. "Isn't it?" he demanded.

"But at what cost? Even this evening, look at what Max and I have managed to do. We overheard Lizzie and Catrin arguing, we've upset you. Mike has been drawn into secrecy with his wife and his in-laws for years, all because I have to be discrete, which quite frankly is just another word for dishonest."

"The more people who know, the more difficult it becomes to keep your discretion," stated Bishop David.

"And the fewer people who know, the more difficult it is to have a normal healthy social life. I love Max. She is a fantastic person. How many times do we preach about love being most effective when it is multiplied? We have a lot of love and a lot to give away. It's what keeps me going in my ministry. Could you have achieved what you have without Catrin?" She knew she was being hostile.

"I know."

Charlotte expected a different response from her Bishop. After a moment's pause he continued. "I know you love Max and I know that strong support is vital in ministry. I know that you probably have no choice in the way you are. I know the church is blinkered. I know I can't ignore what you have told me, and I know that you are a superb priest. I know you would make a brilliant Archdeacon….."

Charlotte interrupted. "If I wasn't gay."

"That's not what I said. You would make a brilliant Archdeacon just as you are. Your sexuality doesn't change your ability as a priest. In actual fact, it probably makes you more understanding and more tolerant of people. I could be wrong."

Again, there was a heavy pause. Charlotte heard the doorbell in the background, but it was ignored by David.

Charlotte spoke again into the silence, "Catrin seems to have quite a different opinion."

"Yes, I'm aware of my wife's difficulty with this issue. She's been strangely sheltered all her life and isn't even aware of the number of people she knows who are gay. She would be rather taken aback. You're not the only priest in this diocese in your situation."

"I'm aware of that, but it's not always easy to seek each other out. There's a lot of anxiety involved." Charlotte was still unsure of herself and didn't quite know which direction the conversation was going.

"Can I be quite clear about something?" asked David

"Of course."

"You are in a monogamous, stable relationship with Max."

"Yes."

"And have you made it legal?"

"No."

"Will you?"

"Yes, but not whilst I'm still in holy orders."

"Hmm." David was thoughtful. "When you do..... make it legal, will I be invited?"

Charlotte was completely taken unawares. "I er.... I don't know. Yes, maybe. I'd need to talk to Max........ Would you really want to come?"

"I'd be honoured. I'm not sure about Catrin. Like I said we don't always agree on everything. You do know I will have to accept your resignation."

David was matter of fact as he added this last sentence. It hit Charlotte as hard as if he had hit her full force in the stomach. She closed her eyes to regain her composure. She felt as if David had given her a brief but obviously false security and then battered it against jagged rocks tearing her new-found hope to shreds before she had chance to embrace it.

David continued his discourse, "You leave me with no choice. You have brought your partner to my home, introduced her to my family. I cannot pretend I know nothing about it. You offered your resignation. I accept it. I will speak to the registrar about your pension and we may be able to evoke a resettlement payment. I'm afraid we may simply have to pay you off. That's the best we can hope for, but you have my personal support." David appeared to be completely unaware of the irony and hypocrisy of his final statement.

Charlotte's emotions were all over the place. His initial response was totally unexpected, only to be followed by any hope of support completely shattered. She felt confused. This was somebody who could stand up for her, who appeared to be on her side and yet was still willing to let her go. However, she remained in control.

"How long do I have Bishop?" It sounded like she was a patient asking for a prognosis. That's what it felt like. One life was about to end, she only hoped another would begin.

"We shall discuss the details at the end of the month. I'll need to make some enquiries. You have made an appointment with Sally, haven't you?" David was suddenly business-like and Charlotte wondered if the request for an invitation to the civil partnership ceremony was simply an underhanded way of gaining information about the true nature of her relationship with Max.

"Can I ask you something Bishop?"

"You might as well call me David."

"David. Can I ask you something?" Charlotte was still very cautious.

"Of course."

"If I was to break it off with Max, would I still have to leave the priesthood?"

"Oh, I wasn't expecting that. Well, you know the rules. If you assured me that you were not in a practising homosexual relationship, then there would be no grounds for dismissal." David was straightforward in his answer but added as an afterthought. "Is that likely?"

"No," said Charlotte without hesitation.

"I didn't think so. I had hoped that giving you time to think through your options would persuade you to see sense and continue with your calling, rather than choose to continue with this friendship that is going to cost you so dear, but turning up on my doorstep with your lover in tow convinced me that it was not going to happen. So, what's the point of pretending you will see sense? I can see now that your mind is made up. If I'm honest I knew it on Tuesday."

Charlotte was confused by Bishop David. On the one hand, he appeared supportive, on the other almost aggressive. She was however not going to let this moment go, without taking the opportunity for some further clear talking. "It isn't a choice I should be forced to make."

"I know. But it is where we are. We cannot afford to take the chance. The rules are clear. We don't deny that some people appear to be attracted to the same sex. It is simply not acceptable behaviour in the priesthood."

"We don't excommunicate gays from our churches. We re-marry divorcees."

"Charlotte please it is late. You know the rules as well as I do. I don't make them. Remember, authority, no power. I cannot change the rules to suit my own beliefs. Lay people we tolerate, we don't in the priesthood. Simple as that."

"It's wrong!" said Charlotte simply.

"It may be, but we are not going to change it, and you, my dear, have said enough to get yourself the sack, but I do not wish to use the disciplinary measure, so I accept your resignation. Go home. Get things in order in your parish as best you can. Don't say anything yet and we'll discuss it again in a couple of weeks' time. Hopefully we can keep this whole mess out of the press, for both......all... our sakes. Now I need a cup of tea, and I suspect that was my other daughter arriving. Would you care to join me in the kitchen?"

The conversation was over and so was her career. It came as no surprise, but rather than feeling great sadness Charlotte was both angry and puzzled. She was angry at the hypocrisy, angry at the rules which disempowered educated men and women. Yet she was puzzled by her Bishop's apparent underlying support. She was angry at herself for being so easily persuaded into visiting the Palace that evening and putting David into a difficult position and dragging his family into what should have been a professional conversation between the two of them.

She also found herself angry at the Bishop. Angry for the way he so casually reminded her that resignation was now the only option. She knew it already. She had told him the same fact just three days previously. Now it felt like a command from David rather than an offer on her part and it stung. He had the upper hand and she felt she had lost his respect, yet he had still invited her back into the family home which also puzzled her. Anger and puzzlement invaded her thoughts as she followed David back into the warmth of the kitchen, where the stew continued to simmer on the Aga and nappies dried off on the drying rack, where his family were gathered around the huge kitchen table and where her partner sat alongside. On the one hand, she felt like an imposter, invading this family scene but on the other she felt strangely close to David. She had no intention of exposing her anger that evening.

Lizzie, Max and Catrin all immediately turned to look towards David and Charlotte as the kitchen door swung open. The other woman, whom Charlotte assumed to be Naomi, continued talking for a few moments, until she realised she no longer held the attention of those seated around the table.

Max had been putting in a huge effort to make small talk with Catrin and Naomi. Lizzie was obviously doing her best to keep her mind and the conversation focused on Michael and the children, actively ignoring the temptation to continue any discussion with Max about what might have been occurring in her father's study. There was a marked tension between her and her mother, which Max had seemed to pick up on, but Naomi seemed blissfully unaware. In fact, it seemed as if Naomi had been doing most of the talking, reinforcing the idea that verbal exuberance must be a genetic trait passed through the female gene.

It was Naomi who broke the brief question laden silence, probably because she had no idea why there seemed to be such an immediate tension in the room. She got up from the table and went over to her father who was still standing in the door way of the kitchen, unintentionally ignoring Charlotte who had just slid onto the bench next to Max.

"My dear Bishop," said Naomi in a very upper class voice, "how delightful to make your acquaintance!" and then she flung her arms around her father's neck to embrace him in an enormous hug and planted a kiss on his cheek.

"I've been here ages Dad, what have you been doing?"

At that point she suddenly seemed to realise that somebody else had slipped into the kitchen. Turning quickly to face Charlotte she appeared momentarily flustered

"Oh, hello. I'm most terribly sorry. I was too busy swamping my old man! I'm Naomi, Catrin and David's daughter, Lizzie's sister and everything."

"Charlotte, or Charlie if you like. I'm a friend of Maxine, er Lizzie's, Elizabeth's sister in law, er Mike's.... Michael's sister." Charlotte struggled slightly to construct a sensible sentence, she too was still feeling on edge following her conversation with the Bishop.

"Mike's sister?" Naomi was confused.

Max came to the rescue. "I'm Mike's sister...."

"Yes, I know that. And this is your sister too?" Naomi frowned as she surreptitiously looked between Charlotte and her father.

"No," Charlotte had regained some sense of equilibrium. "I'm a friend of Max. I've been up with her to visit Mike."

"Oh, I see that was nice of you, and how do you know Dad?"

Although Naomi hadn't appeared to notice Charlotte when she first walked in, she had obviously realised that she and her father had indeed walked in together from the Bishop's offices.

"Professionally!" interjected David, trying to avoid a lengthy and detailed conversation, "Now is there any stew for a poor hard working Bishop? I'm famished!"

His attempt at steering the inquisitive Naomi away from Charlotte didn't succeed.

"Professionally? Not a fellow woman in a man's world by any chance?" Naomi's interest would not be swayed.

"I don't follow," said Charlotte. As David gave in and helped himself to a helping of stew.

"I work in the legal profession. I'm a clerk to a law firm, administrator and trouble shooter really. We have six male and one female lawyers, two other female secretaries and me. I'm the one who attempts to keep everything in place. It's a man's world."

Charlotte got the feeling this was a speech that Naomi was used to making. She waited for the inevitable question. It came next.

"So, I wondered," continued Naomi, "if you were one of Dad's female priests?"

"You make it sound like I've got a harem," taunted David.

"I've heard worse," added Charlotte.

"So?"

"Er, well yes....yes I am." Charlotte had a slight cautionary tone in her voice as she answered the Bishop's eldest daughter. She also

229

managed to shoot a quick glance in David's direction, but it was Catrin who interrupted the inquisitive Naomi.

"I expect Mike's sister and her friend would like to get on back to Plymouth. It's already getting late. Charlotte, my dear would you like to take a little stew with you for later, I have a spare plastic container, it will save you cooking."

"Mother!" Lizzie gently reprimanded her mother, "Surely Charlotte has time to eat first."

Charlotte picked up on Catrin's dis-ease. "No, I think you mother is right. Max, is it okay if we leave now?" and as an afterthought she added, "Have you had chance to catch up on all you needed with Lizzie?" as if to emphasise that it was for Max's benefit they had made the detour to the palace that evening.

"Er, yes, that's fine. It is getting rather late." Max was trying to keep up with the non-verbal cues her partner was giving her. She was desperate to hear about the discussion that had taken place between Charlotte and the Bishop, but Naomi had a parting question whilst Catrin insisted on providing Charlotte with a take away stew.

"Have you far to go?" she asked. It was an innocent question.

It was Max who answered. "Not too far. I live in Tavistock, but I'm staying with Charlotte tonight," and quickly added, "to save the extra journey." She didn't have to add that detail. There was nothing to explain. It was quite legitimate for Charlotte to have a friend to stay the night, after all there was plenty of room in the Rectory.

"And where's your parish, Charlotte, here in Exeter?" Naomi persisted with her questions, which seemed unnecessary, perhaps it was time spent with so many lawyers. Charlotte took it in her stride.

Questions about her parish were on more solid ground, or it would be for a little while longer. Discussing parish life would soon be a thing of the past, but she ignored that thought.

"About fifty minutes from here, on the edge of Dartmoor. A little place called Langford Well that's where I live. I've got eight villages altogether."

"Langford? There's a strange coincidence. Do you know any other Charlotte's in Langford?"

"Er, no not as far as I'm aware. I know most people in the village. Comes with the job." Charlotte was intrigued. She had no idea who this person was, other than she was the Bishop's daughter, yet was there some other strange connection to be made just to put the icing on a remarkable evening?

"I don't suppose for one moment you have a lodger answering to the name of Sasha?"

"Actually, yes I do, part-time that is." Charlotte once again glanced over at David and as she did, noticed Catrin standing by the door with a plastic container of stew staring at her eldest daughter. She looked flushed.

"I thought it was you!" Naomi broke into a grin.

"We have a mutual friend; your lodger, Sasha. Well I assume you are the Charlie she talks about."

"Sasha Paynter?" asked Charlotte.

"The very one! She edits our company magazine. She's excellent. She often talks about her country residence. She hates living in London. I must admit I wondered if she meant you two were... you know. Goodness me, but I know now how very wrong that was of me. She

231

didn't actually mention you were the local vicar. How very exciting. Dad is this 'The' Charlotte you've mentioned before?"

David was stirred from his task of finishing a second helping of stew, but before he could answer Naomi was off again. "I've heard Dad speak very highly of you, one of his stars as far as I can make out. Make sure you hold on to this one eh Dad?!"

Catrin could hold back no longer. "Naomi, please will you stop this tirade of questions, I don't know what poor Charlotte will think of us." And as if she had read Charlotte's mind added "Charlotte my dear, we don't gossip about the affairs of the diocese, but it is true my husband does mention one or two people from time to time and he did think very highly of you."

That short little word felt like a sword piercing her heart. 'Did.' Strangely enough Charlotte was reminded of a biblical quote, '*For the word of God is living and active, sharper than a two-edged sword, piercing to the division of soul and spirit, of joints and marrow, and discerning the thoughts and intentions of the heart.*[1]' Had Catrin really intended to strike such a blow or had it been a slip of the tongue. Did she feel that any admiration the Bishop had once held for Charlotte had now evaporated?

It was Max that broke into Charlotte's thoughts, and on this occasion, was quick enough to prevent further questions from Naomi, or further comment from Catrin. Charlotte couldn't work out if Max had caught

---

[1] *Quote from the Revised Standard Version of the Bible from Paul's letter to the Hebrews Chapter 4 verse 12.*

Catrin's use of the past tense or not but when her partner spoke Charlotte heard a discernible prickliness in her voice.

"Mrs Graham thank you very much for your kind hospitality." Max stood up, and in the same movement gently nudged Charlotte who slid off the bench and also stood, "but I really think Charlotte and I should take our leave. It was lovely to meet my little nephew just such a shame time was so short. Heather is a delight. Lizzie, we'll be in touch, and remember what we said about helping out, anything at all. Mike is my brother. Nice to see you again Naomi. We'll tell Sash we've met. She'll be..." she paused, "surprised, and Mr Graham, thank you for all your support. Come on Charlie, let's go."

"I'll see you out." Lizzie had remained very quiet for the past moments, following her father's example but was determined to snatch a few moments alone with her sister-in-law before she departed. She followed Max and Charlotte to the side entrance they had used just an hour before.

"Well that went well!" was all Charlotte could say when they were out of earshot away from the kitchen.

"I hope Dad didn't give you a hard time." Lizzie's voice wasn't eager for details it was full of genuine concern.

"Lizzie, we shouldn't have come." Charlotte turned to face Lizzie. Lizzie thought she noticed a tear escaping from Charlotte's eye and automatically went to give her new friend a hug.

"I am so sorry Charlotte."

Charlotte avoided the hug by grasping Lizzie's hands in her own. "You have nothing to be sorry for, absolutely nothing. I should have insisted I stayed away. This is all so stupid. All I want to do is support you and Mike, and Max, all the family." She let go of one of Lizzie's hands and reached out for Max. "All I've done is added another complication and that thing with Sash to cap it all!"

"Hmm that was a strange coincidence," added Max slipping her free arm around Charlotte's waist, "but this can wait for another day, I really do think we should get home."

"You two are good together. I won't forget today." Lizzie was still holding on to Charlotte's hand.

"The day of great revelation, no I don't think I'll forget it in a hurry." Charlotte squeezed Lizzie's hand to assure her she wasn't angry with her.

"No, actually I didn't mean that." Lizzie seemed a little embarrassed but she went on. "I mean the way you both prayed with me, in the restaurant. I've never known such peace. It was so strange. Charlie whatever happens, you must never turn your back on God. He needs people like you – and Charlie needs you Max. You really are a special couple," and with that she scooped them both into a hug.

They hadn't heard David creep out of the kitchen hoping to catch one last word with Charlotte, but he had heard every word. His own eyes had already misted over.

Chapter 15

They were already in the car heading back towards Langford when Charlotte announced that she couldn't face going back to the Rectory.

"Then let's go home," said Max.

"To Tavistock?"

"Where else?"

"Anywhere but back to the parish."

Max didn't need to ask why.

They travelled in silence. Max was driving Charlotte's car having left the cumbersome Land Rover at the Rectory. They would drive back the following day to reacquaint driver with owner. It was a conversation they didn't need to have.

Max interrupted the reflective silence. "You didn't pick up the stew."

"Took you long enough to notice."

"I'm glad."

"That I didn't pick up the stew?"

"Actually no, it smelt lovely. We could have frozen it! No I was talking about tonight, everything that has happened."

"I didn't want her stew." Was all Charlotte could say. In the darkness, Max couldn't see the channels created by the tears rolling down Charlotte's face.

"I know." There was so much Max wanted to say, to ask, to discuss, but it could all wait until she could hold Charlie in her arms. It would wait until she could reassure her, not only with well-meaning words, but by holding her close, by looking with absolute honesty into her eyes and by patient listening. Max still had no idea what had gone on in the privacy of the Bishop's study, but she could hazard a guess. Her guess would not be far wrong. She changed the subject from stew to Saturday.

"Are you busy tomorrow?"

"Wedding at 2pm, and just the usual preparation for Sunday, you?"

"Not really, I'm on call from 7pm through to Monday morning."

"How far can you be away if you are on call?" It was a question that in ten years Charlotte had never asked. It was assumed that if Max was on call she would be in her own home, after all that was always the case for Charlotte, who was on call most of the time.

"We've never made a ruling as such, but none of us live much more than twenty minutes from the surgery. We could get called out anywhere in our catchment of course."

"I guess Langford is a bit too far."

Max knew this was what Charlotte was meaning with the first question. She had had time to think it through. "You know how much I'd like to stay with you this weekend."

"Yes. I do. No need to add the 'but'. We'll soon have every weekend together." Charlotte let the statement hang in the air before adding, "It's over Max."

Max gripped the steering wheel but said nothing. She then spotted a lay by and pulled in. They were twenty minutes from home.

"I want us to have this conversation at home. We can open some wine. I'll get out the cheese and biscuits. We can talk till the early hours and I'll make sure you are back at the Rectory in ample time for that wedding, but not now, not here in a dark lay by at 11pm. I want to know every detail of your conversation with the Bishop. I am furious at the way his wife spoke to you and am stunned by Naomi and her constant barrage of questions, to say nothing of her assumption about you and Sash! One good thing has come out of this, I am closer to my sister-in-law than I ever felt possible. It is not over, whatever you may mean by that, it is not over."

Max could just about see Charlotte in the gloomy light. She waited for perhaps just a second, possibly two, before pulling out again into the main carriageway. Charlotte said nothing.

They pulled up outside Max's Victorian home. Charlotte was still quiet which Max found unnerving. Max opened the front door. It seemed very quiet without the dogs. The whole street was quiet and the night was very still. It was as if just for a moment the world held its breath.

Still in silence, as if on some obscure retreat, they went into the kitchen. Max opened the cupboard, took out two wine glasses and opening another door took out a bottle of wine. Charlotte broke the silence.

"It really is over Max!"

"You said that in the car, you're scaring me. What exactly did the Bishop say to you?"

Max held the two glasses in one hand and the bottle in the other. She carefully placed them on the table but instead of opening the wine, went over to Charlotte and knelt down beside her, looking up to her, gently placing one hand on her knee and the other on the back of the chair. Max was cautious, she was unsure if she would receive rejection. She was disconcerted by the way Charlotte was holding such composure and yet the words 'it's over' spun around her. With great courage, reminding herself of the promise Charlotte had made of weekends to come, she managed to ask her partner cautiously, slowly, carefully, "What is over?"

"My life." replied Charlotte without hesitation. "Everything. My home, my work," she paused briefly before adding, "my calling, my reason for being, wiped out."

Max wrestled for the right words, "Is that what he said?" was all she could manage. So much was running through her mind. She felt an enormous burden bearing down on her. The person she loved so much, the person she admired and looked up to was so empty. There was no light behind her eyes. She was drawn, with sallow grey looking skin and for the first time ever was the image of a middle-aged woman Max had never seen before.

"He asked me if I was in a stable monogamous relationship with you."

"And you said?"

"Yes!"

"That's a relief! And you don't want that to change?"

Charlotte was startled. "What? No of course not. It's the one thing I've got left."

"Oh."

"You didn't think..... oh Max, you idiot. This isn't over, everything else might be, but not this..... is it?"

"No!"

"It won't be easy though. I've not got a clue what happens next, not a clue...." Charlotte's voice trailed off.

"Wine?" Max seemed to be getting good at using just one word.

Charlotte followed suit. "No."

"Bed?"

Charlotte frowned at Max and in a somewhat irritated tone declared "No."

She continued this time. "He asked if we were going to make it legal."

"Interesting!"

"And asked if he could come."

"What?" The one word replies continued to slip from Max's lips, but she did venture to open the wine at the same time, poured herself a glass and absentmindedly poured a second for Charlotte.

Charlotte seemed to forget her abstinence wish and took the wine.

"I said I'd ask you."

"But that's a good sign, isn't it? Surely, if he was serious, he's on your side... our side." Max had propped herself against the breakfast bar.

"That's the hypocrisy of it all. I truly believe he is – but in the very next breath he goes on to say he now has no option but to accept my resignation. For one very brief moment I thought I wouldn't need to, one brief joyous moment I thought he would decide to accept my honesty and my ministry. In the next second it all crashed down, shattered into tiny little pieces all over his study floor, surrounded by his bloody books, his systematic study of God, his tomes on the lives of the saints, his essays on reconciliation, his theology of liberation, anti-racism, anti-ageism, even anti-soddin' sexism."

Charlotte could swear, but not often. "And then he says he has no choice. Of course he has a choice, he has a choice to speak out against this ridiculous discrimination, he has a choice to make a stand if he really wanted to, yes with me dangling on the end of his string, his little puppet that he could use for the purpose, I'd do it you know Max, I really would, I'd be willing to be paraded round as an example. I could do that."

"And what's the other option?"

"What do you mean 'What's the other option?' He gave me no option; just told me he would have to accept my resignation." Charlotte sipped some more of her wine. Just a little of her pent-up frustration had been released, but she was still angry.

"What if you withdrew the resignation? If it wasn't for me, you wouldn't have to resign." Charlotte looked straight at Max. It wasn't a challenge, it wasn't a test, she knew exactly what she was saying.

"You're serious."

"It is an option."

"No. It isn't, not any more. It never has been, not now, not five years ago, we've been through this. It is not an option." She stopped, thinking carefully whether or not to include the next bit of testimony. She would.

"I asked him, you know..... I asked him what the consequence would be if I was no longer in a relationship." Charlotte watched Max take a gulp of wine. Max said nothing, just waited. "He asked if it was an option...." Charlotte was drawing out the account, not to make Max feel uncomfortable, but because she was still reliving every emotion of the moments of the dialogue. Max watched Charlotte turn the wine glass in her hands. "I didn't really need to answer, he knew there was no way I'd give up on you. Maybe he still hoped I wouldn't give up on the priesthood."

"You shouldn't have to."

240

"No." Charlotte finished her wine in one final swig. "It's late. Let's go to bed."

"You sure? There must be so much swimming around in your mind, I know there is in mine."

"Uh uh…, the future, Mike, little Heather and Joshua, David, what Catrin will have to say, to say nothing of the shock in store for Sasha when she gets back, the parish, Linda, Sam.... yes, there is a huge amount floating around, but in the meantime, somehow, I have to get through the next few days, so do you my sweet, so let's call it a night. Tomorrow is another day – another life!"

As they got into bed they found themselves thinking what might be happening in the Bishop's Palace. It was nearly midnight.

As soon as Charlotte and Max had left the Palace and after the initial annoyance that Charlotte had left the stew behind, the conversation immediately turned back to Mike. No more mention was made of the revelations made in the last half an hour and David had chance to catch up with the day. Naomi was blissfully unaware of the argument between her mother and sister and completely in the dark about Max and Charlotte.

Eventually as the old Grandfather clock chimed eleven o clock, and young Joshua could be heard stirring on the baby monitor. Lizzie decided to head off to bed. Naomi busied herself loading the dishwasher, but was shooed away by her mother, so she followed her sister upstairs.

"You alright sis?" Naomi intercepted her as she was coming out of the bathroom.

"My husband's in hospital, my son has just filled his nappy, I'm exhausted, yeah I'm fine."

"Sorry stupid question. Shall I sort out Joshua?"

"You? You wouldn't know which end!" Lizzie dug her sister in the ribs with the tub of wet wipes.

"I'll have to soon," added Naomi.

"Hmm well you'd better get a move on, Mimi, you're not getting any younger you know. How's Tom?" asked Lizzie.

"Oh, great thanks." The two sisters went into the big double room where Joshua was getting fractious. Lizzie changed him whilst Naomi looked on. "Sorry about tonight."

"What do you mean?"

"Oh, I don't know, taking over the conversation, giving Max's friend a hard time, well not a hard time, just... oh I can be a bit like a dog with a bone sometimes, you know getting hold of something, not letting it go. I mean we're all here 'cos of Mike aren't we. Funny coincidence though, her and Sasha Paynter, and then, well I just wanted to know more about her, about them if I'm honest. Don't you think there was something a bit strange? And Mum seemed really on edge. She couldn't wait to get rid of them, but then you must all be exhausted. Oh, I'm sorry there I go again."

Lizzie had finished changing the nappy and had settled Joshua back in his cot. "There is nothing strange about them, but you were right about Mum being edgy. They're an item that's all." Lizzie sat down on the bed and indicated to her sister to sit down next to her.

Naomi widened her eyes, "Mike's sister and Dad's clerical blue-eyed girl? Bloody hell, sis, that's a bit of a bolt out of the blue. I'm speechless."

"No you're not," her sister grinned.

"No, not really. I knew there was something, and I blurted out about Sasha. Whoops. How long have you known about it? Does Dad know?"

"You really do like to interrogate people don't you. As it happens we all only found out today!"

"Today?" Exclaimed Naomi, "tell me more." And Lizzie did her best to recount the events of the day.

Meanwhile downstairs Mr and Mrs Graham cleared the kitchen without further conversation. Only once did David break into the heavy silence with the words. "I hope they got back safely."

"Who?" asked his wife.

"Max and Charlotte."

"Oh," was the only reply he got until Catrin added, "you should be more concerned about your daughter than rebellious feminists."

"I'm concerned about all of them, and Charlotte is not rebellious, just......." David wrung the tea towel he was holding around one hand, "..........just misunderstood."

"That's what you might say about a naughty child." Catrin either ignored or chose not to see the sadness in David's eyes. Instead she reverted back to her usual role of organiser and curator of the house. "Let's not get into this now. I'd like to say it's none of my business, but when it involves my daughter and grandchildren it is my business."

David picked up on her first comment. "Like you said, let's not get into it now. Time for bed I believe. Tomorrow is another day."

They made their way upstairs and heard hushed voices coming from the large double room that Lizzie was sharing with Joshua.

"The girls have a lot to catch up on," murmured Catrin so as not to wake Heather.

David agreed with a nod and a low grunt. He wondered just what stories they were catching up on, but wouldn't share his curiosity with his wife.

Chapter 16

Philip Dixon called in at the Rectory early that Saturday morning, as the church clock struck on the quarter hour before nine. He assumed the Rector would be back from morning prayer at St Nicholas.

As a Reader, of course, he had intended to join Sam, Charlotte, Roger and Derek for the weekly time of prayer for the parish, but his wife had not been all that keen for her husband to sit in a cold church at eight o clock in the morning. He had not argued, but had another slice of toast before heading off to discuss, in person, a convenient time to arrange a meeting of the newly formed Church Review Group. He had, in his mind, already adopted the position of chair, and would easily convince others that it was to relieve some of the burden from the Rector. He would of course confirm this with her when they met. He had thought of phoning first, but he knew how fond the Rector was of using her answer phone and he needed an answer in order to get on with the details. He did like things done properly 'and if a job is worth doing, it is worth doing by oneself and doing well,' he thought to himself in all sincerity as he rang the doorbell.

There was no answer. He rang again and rapped the large brass door knocker. Still no answer. He huffed to himself and walked around to the church, assuming Charlotte was still talking to Sam or one of the other assistant priests.

Before he got as far as the church he saw the other ministers walking together down the church path and called out. "Is the Rector still inside?"

"She's not back yet," answered Sam.

"Not back?" Mr Dixon frowned. "Not back from where? She's not due to be away."

Sam could have kicked himself as soon as he had opened his mouth. Charlotte had mentioned to him, quietly, at the end of the PCC that she was going to be away for the day and might have got back late on the Friday evening so would be grateful if he could open up and lead the weekly team prayers. It didn't happen often, but was not uncommon. It was the likes of Mr Dixon who held that the Rector should never be away from the parish unless it had been discussed well in advance.

"I mean she may not be up....." Sam was not making things any better.

Roger and Derek had gone on ahead deciding to leave the curate to deal with Mr Dixon. 'Nice of them' Sam thought to himself. He had one last stab at diverting Philip away from any criticism he may dream up against a long-suffering Charlotte. She and Sam had had many a professional discussion about dealing with the Mr Dixons of parish life.

He decided on honesty. "She was visiting friends yesterday and didn't think she'd get back till late, that's all," and as an afterthought added, "Can I help you, Philip?"

One thing Philip was not keen on, was younger people calling him by his first name, but he let it go, after all, this youngster was a licensed male parish priest in the Church of England.

"I don't think so young man. It is a matter I wish to discuss with the Rector in person."

By this time both men had reached the lych-gate.

"I take it Morning Prayer was without mishap in the Rector's absence?"

246

Sam swallowed back his irritation. "Yes, thank you... er... Philip."

Like Charlotte, he had learned to tolerate Mr Dixon, was always very polite but in truth never wished to engage him in a lengthy conversation. 'Without mishap' he thought to himself. 'What does the old codger think would happen? We might topple the odd pew with our fervent and earnest prayer or set the church alight with the candles!'

He couldn't resist a slight dig at the self-righteous ignoramus. "We missed you of course, Mr Dixon."

"Ah, yes, couldn't be helped, Sonny, family matters you see. My first vocation is to my dear ailing wife. Something perhaps you'll learn at some point, eh lad?! I think I'll go back to the Rectory and see if I can rouse our rector," and with that he left Sam seething at the put down.

Mr Dixon once again banged loudly on the front door of the Rectory. He then decided to try his luck at the back door. He immediately noticed the battered old Land Rover at the side of the Rectory, but it didn't occur to him that the Rector's VW Golf was nowhere to be seen. After another five minutes of banging and peering through the windows of the kitchen he gave up, went home and left a curt message on Charlotte's answer phone. It was ten o clock.

David had woken early that morning at 5.30am with a headache. It didn't help to have had a doubly disturbed night, first being unable to get to sleep until two, the conversation with Charlotte and the troubles facing his middle daughter swirling around his mind, and then being awoken again by his young grandson demanding the attention of his mother's breast. Catrin appeared to sleep through the searing cries. He

247

guessed after four children and a break of several years she had become immune to such invasions to her sleep pattern. He was not so fortunate.

And so, at 5.45am he rose, took a couple of painkillers and plodded down to make an early pot of tea. He would take a cup up to his sleeping wife at a more civil time.

He was surprised to see that somebody else was already sitting in the gloom. It was Naomi hunched over a mug of something steaming. "Morning Dad, couldn't sleep? Or just being religiously early?"

"The former."

"Our youngest family member can certainly make himself heard!" yawned a sleepy Naomi.

"Hmmm, I know someone else who was like that when she was little, and doesn't seem to have grown out of it!" David topped up and re-boiled the kettle to make the tea.

"I take it you mean your loving eldest daughter?"

"Who else my love?" David was glad his daughter was up. On the whole he got on well with all his children. He and Ruth didn't always see eye to eye, but he recalled similar problems with all of them whilst they were still students. He and John could have a good argument, but it all seemed part of good male bonding and usually ended with agreement to disagree, very much like his discussions with Catrin on certain issues.

"Penny for them?" the kettle had boiled and Naomi was pouring water into the tea pot when she roused David from his thoughts.

"Oh nothing, much, I was thinking about you four as kids."

"Steady on it's a bit early for reminiscing Dad. Is the tea for you or Mum?"

"Just me at the moment, your mother seems to have forgotten what it is to be woken up by hungry babies. We could see if Lizzie wants one."

"I'll take one up. I'll let it stew a bit for you though."

"Thanks love." David liked a strong cup and his family were well aware of his needs.

Naomi was only gone a few minutes before she re-joined her father in the family kitchen.

"Lizzie was grateful for the tea. She couldn't understand why we were up so early!"

"You didn't say anything about Joshua?"

"Course not."

"You two were chatting into the night."

"Sorry, did we disturb you?" Naomi poured herself and her father two stronger cups from the brewing pot.

"No, not at all, I heard you finally go to bed about one, that's all. I was awake anyway. I was a bit concerned about Lizzie though, I thought she was tired."

"She just needed to talk things through a bit. I'll drive her to Bristol today, and don't worry, four hours sleep is enough for me once in a while, I'll be careful." She could see the concern in her father's eyes before he needed to voice it. "Doesn't sound as if you got much sleep either, things on your mind?"

"As always."

"Not just Mike, I suspect." Naomi cupped her mug of tea in her hands, blowing across the top, but keeping her eyes firmly fixed on her father.

"Not just Mike, more worried about Lizzie and the children, wondering how we'll cope over the next few months." David glanced at his watch; still only 6.15am. There was a group of newly confirmed young adults coming to the cathedral that day and he was due to speak to them later in the morning, but the rest of the day was more or less his own. He had some preparation to do for the following day but he was intending to help out with the children as much as possible. Naomi sensed there was more on her father's mind.

"Lizzie told me about Mike's sister," she said.

"Does it bother you?"

"Not that she's gay no. Why should it? It's her life. They seem really good together, the bit I saw anyway, but I did put my big foot in it, didn't I, with that stupid comment about the lodger. Quite a coincidence though, you have to agree." Naomi wasn't quite sure how her father had expected her to react. She continued talking. "I've never met Charlie before Dad. It really was just one of those weird coincidences. Will it change anything?"

David glanced at his daughter, with a slight puzzled look.

"Liz filled me in on Max and Charlotte."

Naomi waited for a moment whilst her father seemed to form an answer in his mind, until he said simply.

"I can't discuss it with you, you know that." David was still in his dressing gown, sitting at his kitchen table across from his eldest daughter with whom he had had many a heart to heart over the past few years.

For a moment, Naomi allowed her father's answer to hang in the air. She had hoped for a different response but she wasn't all that surprised at the one he had given.

After a short interlude, she said simply, "Dad, this isn't just work, this is about Max, Mike's sister. Mike's done his best to keep the peace over the years. He understood better than most how difficult it would be. You'll have to face him, at the very least."

"Of course I'll face him. I've got nothing to hide."

"Meaning?"

"Meaning......... meaning nothing. Like I said I can't discuss it. Not yet anyway. I'm sorry." He stopped abruptly and lowered his head into his hands, "I'm just so sorry it's turned out like this."

"What's there to be sorry about? It's just another of those weird coincidences, isn't it?" Naomi was confused, taken aback by her father's reaction.

"Power," was all he said. "Power to change nothing and too much of a coward to even try."

"What on earth are you talking about?"

"You would have thought I, of all people, could make a choice."

"I suppose so." Naomi remained confused.

"But I don't. I don't make the rules you see. Oh, I can try and shape them, if I want to. I might even manage to bend them from time to time, but I can't actually break them. Not when it's black and white. It's OK when it's grey and murky. I can do something with grey and murky, I can cope when it's not quite out in the open, but not like this, not laid out for all to see. And," he paused, "I don't want my family dragged in."

David seemed to have forgotten he was talking to his daughter, but just stared into nothingness, talking to no-one in particular. He continued speaking in a thoughtful way that was almost inaudible. Naomi watched, her lips firmly closed, as her father struggled with some inner burden. "I suppose she could just carry on as before, so long as we all just keep quiet about it... but no, that can't be. If the press got hold of it, it would be just scandalous. No, it has to stop. There's no choice, no choice at all."

"Dad what on earth are you talking about?" Naomi finally broke her silence.

"What? Oh, Naomi!" He appeared almost startled as if he'd forgotten she was there. "What's the time? I'd better take a fresh tea up to your mother. Put the kettle on will you love. I'll be back in a moment." David disappeared to his small private chapel, still in his dressing gown, leaving Naomi somewhat perplexed and none the wiser. She made the fresh tea as asked and, after her father failed to return after a few minutes, took a cup up to her mother who was just stirring.

Mike too had woken early after a fitful night. The only thing on his mind was the pain in his leg. He had called the nurse several times but there was nothing she could do and in the end a young bleary eyed doctor was called who had prescribed a much stronger drug that had knocked Michael out for a couple of hours around two that morning. By five o clock, the pain had woken him once more. The drugs he had been given were still sloshing around his system and he felt himself drift in and out of consciousness. Each time he became aware of his surroundings the only thought on his mind was pain. His personal battle was far from over.

After five hours of sleep Charlotte opened her eyes onto a new day. She was surprised she had slept that long. Max remained in a deep sleep, gently snoring beside her. Charlotte looked at her and under her breath whispered "I hope you're worth it."

Max stirred slightly turned over and continued breathing deeply.

Charlotte looked at the bedside clock. Just before six. She thought about trying to snatch another hour's sleep, but quickly found her mind darting between the events of yesterday, the wedding later that day and the realisation that Sam would indeed need to make excuses for her if she was not back in time for Team Prayers.

She was about to rouse her slumbering partner and then stopped herself.

"What does it matter now?" she thought, "so I don't make the Prayer. Sam can open up. He'll soon need to be doing a whole lot more than that."

She tried to place the emotion she was feeling. There was certainly a mediocrity of guilt, but that was not the overwhelming feeling, sadness? No, that wasn't it, not this morning. She didn't even sense any of the anger lingering from the previous night much to her astonishment. As she was running through these various possibilities she began to realise that what she felt was a sense of relief. She had made the decision to leave ministry long before she had the interview with Bishop David. She had been annoyed that he had thwarted her determination at that point. It had taken her many months if not years to come to that decision. But now, finally, it was done, and she was relieved. She was sure the feeling wouldn't persist for long. There would be many anxious days ahead as the process of leaving the parish and resigning her orders was put into place, but for now, in that moment, she savoured the respite.

Trying not to disturb Max, she slipped out of bed and went down to make some tea. The kitchen was cold. She wrapped herself in the fleece throw that was hanging over one of the chairs as she waited for the kettle to boil.

Her mind wandered to Mike and she hoped he had had a good night. She also thought about David and Catrin. She assumed they would be too caught up in family matters to give her situation much thought, but stopped herself. The situation was part family now. Her sense of relief had already started to fade. She felt the familiar heaviness of burden upon her back. 'Too many people are involved,' she thought, and again the guilt crept back in.

She poured the boiling water into the first mug and then moved the bag to the second. 'Lizzie and Mike should be our concern, not this,' she thought. She added the milk and took both mugs back to the bedroom.

Max was awake but still rubbing her eyes. Radio Two was crooning in the background.

"I could get used to this," Max said.

"You'll have to," Charlotte's burden shifted and eased a little.

"So how are you feeling this morning my darling? Did you sleep okay?" Max glanced at the bedside clock. "Ugh, it's still early sweetheart," but sat up and sipped her tea.

"A bit mixed up," said Charlotte, in answer to Max's question, "relieved in one way; it's all out in the open now, well not quite, but you know what I mean, but annoyed it happened the way it did."

"Annoyed at who? Me? Lizzie?" Max wasn't unduly concerned if her partner did feel annoyed at her, she too felt relief more than anything. She didn't necessarily want it to happen for Charlotte's sake, but now it had, she was secretly pleased. They could start building a proper life together. In her mind, she was already planning the honeymoon!

"Not at any one especially, annoyed at the timing. It would have worked out like this in any case, but it was all a bit forced. David knows I would have resigned, but in the end, there really wasn't a choice."

Max put her mug down. "Come back to bed for a moment." Charlotte sat back down and Max drew her closer. With her arm around her she said, "you wouldn't you know."

"Wouldn't what?"

"Wouldn't have resigned."

"Of course........." Charlotte let her voice trail off.

"You wouldn't, would you? We've been here before."

"But I went to see him this time."

"Yes, I know, I couldn't believe it when you said you had actually told him."

"You underestimate me my darling," said Charlotte jabbing Max in the ribs with her elbow.

"Ouch!" Max pretended to wince in pain. "I know you thought the Bishop was hypocritical when he told you to keep your mouth shut and just get on with the job, but if he could live with that couldn't you? At least you had been honest with him."

"I'd tried that, but just think back to last night, how awkward it was as little bits of the truth seeped out. The tension in that kitchen was palpable. You're not sorry, are you?"

Charlotte glanced at the clock as she spoke, she was conscious of her commitments back at the parish and would soon need to persuade Max that they needed to get up, but neither did she want to cut this conversation short.

Max noticed her glance, "no need to rush is there?"

"No, but nosy parkers will soon notice your car and wonder where mine is. Better not give them more fuel for the fire just yet. That will all come soon enough, if the real reason for my imminent departure gets out." Charlotte repeated her question, "So, are you sorry or not?"

"Yes and no. I'm not sorry that we can finally be a proper couple. I am sorry that you are going to lose your job because of it. I am sorry that it all came to a head in the way it did last night. I am not sorry that we get on so well with Lizzie, but I am really sorry that it took Mike's accident for it all to happen."

"Me too. That's the worst bit, but maybe we can help Liz more now than we could have done."

"Not quite sure how, but yes, I hope we can. Now who's first in the shower?"

Max suddenly leaped out of bed and made a rush for the bathroom but wasn't quick enough and went back to listening to Radio Two for ten minutes whilst Charlotte delved into Max's vast supply of shampoos, conditioners and body scrubs.

Chapter 17

Lizzie and Naomi arrived on Mike's Ward just after ten thirty. Naomi carried a sleeping Joshua still tucked snugly in his car chair. Lizzie looked down the ward. The curtains had been drawn around two of the beds so they couldn't see Mike at first. "Which bed's he in?" whispered Naomi.

"You don't need to whisper Mimi." Lizzie smiled at her sister. She knew of Naomi's distinct dislike of hospitals and illness and was touched that she had given up a weekend to show her support.

"You go on, I'll take Joshua for a little bit of fresh air." Naomi offered.

Lizzie chuckled this time. "You're not going to get out of it that easily. Joshua is fine, he's sound asleep and any way it's raining. You can take him to the nearest coffee outlet when he wakes up, but first you might as well see how Mike is, you've made it this far."

"Humph!" snorted Naomi. "I thought I was here to help you with Joshua."

"You are and he will need you in a little while, and when he needs me, you may just have to keep Mike company."

"Okay, I know. I'm here to do my bit, let's delve in and see what they've done to him."

Lizzie made her way to the Nurses station in the middle of the ward to check that Mike could receive visitors. Naomi hovered by the door.

"Can I help you?" A young nurse approached Naomi.

"Oh, it's okay thanks. My sister's here to see her husband, I'm just looking after the baby."

"And who is your sister's husband?"

"Mike, er Mr Michael Tannin."

"Oh, I see, just a moment. Can you wait here please?" and the young nurse went into a small side room near to where Naomi was standing.

'That's exactly what I was doing,' Naomi thought to herself. "Hospitals," she said under her breath raising her eyes heavenward towards nothing in particular. Then she noticed her sister coming towards her with an older nurse.

"He's not well Mim. Some sort of infection."

"We don't think it's a good idea to bring the baby in, Mrs Tannin. He's being barrier nursed."

"What do you mean?" asked Naomi.

"Visitors will need to wear a gown, gloves and a mask. In here Mrs Tannin."

Naomi was left outside whilst the older nurse led Lizzie into the small side room where the young nurse had just disappeared. This time she heard the sound of plastic gowns and gloves being pulled on and ripped off and another door swinging open. Then the younger nurse came back out.

"What's going on?" demanded Naomi.

"I'm just a student. You'll need to speak to Staff Nurse."

"The one that has just gone in with my sister?"

"Yes. I can get you a chair if you like. He's a lovely baby. Is he yours?" enquired the student, trying, but failing to put Naomi at her ease.

"No I just picked him up from the maternity ward at a knock down price." Naomi had a strange habit of trying to make very bad jokes when she was nervous. It was a habit that irritated the partners in the practice and had often got her into trouble when she was younger.

"Sorry?" exclaimed the young nurse.

"Don't fret, he's my sisters.... well and Mike's, er sorry, Mr Tannin's little boy. Look, he is alright isn't he, I mean he's not you know, about to die or anything? He was doing so well yesterday."

The young nurse looked around as if hoping somebody else would pop out of a door ready to answer Naomi's candid question. No one came to her rescue. She tried to hide behind her position. "I'm not really qualified to say........ he's not dead though."

"Ok, well that's a start, but he is quite ill?" Naomi was trying to be sensitive to the poor girl's inadequacies.

"He's got a nasty infection in his leg. I'm not sure how bad it is, but we are concerned. I really do think you should speak to a senior nurse. Sorry, I'd better go," and before Naomi had chance to ask another of her questions, the student had scampered off presumably to answer the buzzer that had been resonating around the ward for the past few minutes.

Naomi looked down at Joshua who was amazingly still asleep.

"Not sure I like you on this ward little man, not with these infections about." Naomi was blissfully unaware she was sounding like her mother. She would have been mortified at the thought. "We'd better wait for your mummy though."

She watched her nephew as he unclenched his fist, opened his eyes just a little, but was soon back in his own little dream world. She found a chair nearby and waited.

259

Max and Charlotte returned to the Rectory in Langford at ten thirty. Charlotte pulled up round the side of the house, next to Max's Land Rover. They went in through the back door, into the kitchen.

"Shall I get the coffee going?" asked Max

"Good idea, I'll need a caffeine overdose if I'm going to get through today. I'd better check the messages.

As Max found the strongest coffee and started the machine Charlotte went through to her study. She was still in her off duty jeans and sweatshirt. She sat down at her desk. Only three messages she thought to herself, not too bad at all. She clicked the play button.

The first one was from the mother of the bride asking about when to drop off the order of service, but there was no need to answer, the ushers had already been instructed to arrive at St Agnes by one o clock, complete with service sheets. But she would ring the bride's home quickly to remind them of the arrangements.

The second one was from Linda, reminding Charlotte that she had put the wedding registers back in the safe at St Nicholas, and not to forget to give herself time to collect them before she went over to St Agnes. Again, Charlotte wondered just what sort of reaction she would get from her faithful supporters such as Linda, and even more importantly what would happen to Linda's job.

The third one was from the delightful Mr Dixon.

"Charlotte, my dear."

'What does he want now?' she thought.

"I called earlier today...."

'Shit!'

260

"Fortunately, Sam explained that you were away from the parish. I wasn't aware you had any leave coming up."

'Cheeky so and so'.

"I am rather anxious to arrange the meeting of the Church Building Review Group."

'Is he now?'

"I was rather hoping we could discuss possible dates, however in your absence I have contacted one or two others and we feel Thursday week is best. Of course, if you can't make it I'm sure we can manage without you. I take it you are back for services tomorrow, I was not aware of any alternative arrangements. I'm sure we can discuss this on your return."

There was a moment's pause and then Philip Dixon's distinctive voice chimed in once more. "This is Philip Dixon. 897654 ringing on Saturday morning at 10.15am."

Charlotte listened to the automated voice repeating 'You were called, today at... 10.15am. Telephone number 01432 897654. To use ring back.....' She pressed the button to stop the mechanical command.

"Coffee's ready," she heard Max call from the kitchen.

"Coming," she called back. 'Of all people,' she thought. 'Why on earth did he have to call round the Rectory before ten on a Saturday morning? Arrogant so in so, bloody annoying..........' No appropriate word came to mind. 'After prayers,' she thought, 'and why this morning of all mornings. He never goes to prayers, well only about twice a year, always using some lame excuse about his wife. He's the sort of person who looks down on poor 'unfortunate' unmarried men and women. His wife probably wishes she was still single,' she mused. 'Probably put Sam in a difficult position too.'

"Just going to make a quick phone call," she shouted back in the general direction of the kitchen. 'Ha,' Charlotte's thoughts were still on the troublesome Dixon, as she dialled the number for Mrs Wicks, the bride's mother, 'I'll not be single for much longer though, what will he think of that?!'

"Mrs Wicks?... Charlotte here from St Agnes. Sorry not to get back to you before, it was my day off yesterday..... thank you, yes, a very pleasant day. No need to worry about the service shee...... oh, you've spoken to them...... Yes, the church will be open by 1pm, the verger will be there..... No, I'll be a little later about half past. How's Becky?....... Is she?...... Oh, I'm sure it's just nerves. I'd better let you go, not long now."

She put the phone down. 'Poor Becky' thought Charlotte and wondered when she and her new husband would actually get around to telling their parents that she was two months pregnant already. 'Nerves? More like morning sickness. At least she'll be fine by 2pm.'

Mr Dixon could wait. 'No need for me to be there!' He knows where he can put that thought! On the other hand, he could be right. That's one character I won't miss.' Charlotte wandered back to the kitchen where a cup of steaming coffee awaited her return.

David was already at the Cathedral with the newly confirmed, discussing his recent trip to St Georges Church, Bagdad in Iraq, when Catrin received the call from Naomi to say that Mike had taken a turn for the worst.

"He's not in any immediate danger," she reassured her, "but it is not looking good." Catrin was all for bundling Heather into the car and speeding up to Bristol to be with her daughter.

"There really is no need Mum. You wouldn't be able to see him and it would only upset Heather."

"But what about Joshua? He mustn't be in contact with an infection like that." Heather had found her Granny and was tugging at her skirt. "It's alright Poppit, Grandma is just on the phone with Auntie Naomi.

"Can I speak to Daddy?"

"Not just now, Auntie Naomi isn't with Daddy at the moment."

Naomi could hear Heather in the background. "Let me speak to her Mum."

"Why, what are you going to say to her?" there was anxiety in her voice.

"Nothing much, don't worry." Catrin handed the phone to an eager Heather, who immediately clammed up.

"Hello Heather. Mummy and Daddy say hello. Do you want to say hello to your brother, he's here with me?" Heather nodded her head and shook her hand.

"She's waving at you," said Catrin.

"That's lovely Heather. Can I talk to Grandma again now?" Heather nodded, handed the phone back to her Grandmother and ran off back to her drawing.

"How's Lizzie?" asked her mum.

"Worried of course." It was said with sincerity not sarcasm. "She's just gone back in with him. He's conscious apparently, but feeling really rough. They don't really want me to go in but at least I can look after Joshua."

"Will you manage?" Catrin's opinion of how Naomi would cope with a new born was not great.

"I've not had to change his nappy yet, if that's what you mean, but yes I'll manage." Naomi was only too aware of her inadequacy and didn't need her mother to remind her.

"Any idea how long you'll stay?" Catrin was in usual organising mode.

"Certainly until Mike's parents get here. I think they are going to stay for a few days. It just depends on the next few hours with Mike. Lizzie might decide to stay overnight. I can always come home, get some things for Lizzie and drop them off on my way back to London tomorrow, as long as you are okay with Heather." Naomi hadn't really had chance to discuss much with Lizzie so she too was thinking on her feet.

"Do Maureen and Vince know what's happened?" Catrin was as concerned for them, as she was her own daughter.

"Who?" Naomi asked.

"Mike's parents."

"No, not yet. Lizzie tried to ring them, but there was no answer, probably on their way."

"Ring me later. I'll let your father know."

"I assumed you would. Isn't there some sort of prayer circle or something he can tap into?"

"There's strange coming from you." It was understandable that Catrin sounded surprised, Naomi was not known for her regular attendance at church.

"It's still there, Mum, just not so obvious these days and any way Mike needs all the help he can get. Lizzie was going to ring Charlie too, might as well get all the family priests involved."

As soon as she said it Naomi wished she hadn't, she could hear her mother's sharp intake of breath and almost felt the scowl she imagined had etched itself across the usually composed appearance. Naomi waited for her mother's response. It didn't come. So she continued.

"I'll ring later to give you an update."

"Yes, that would be helpful. Goodbye dear," and she put the phone down.

Naomi looked at the phone for a second, before ensuring it was turned off. She was heading back to the ward when Joshua decided it was time to put his auntie to the test. She could smell him even before his lungs let out the first squeal. 'How can such a little thing make so much noise?' she thought. A few minutes later she discovered how effective such a little thing was of making something else too.

Max had originally planned to pick the dogs up at eleven that morning giving her parents plenty of time to get up to Bristol, have some lunch and still be in good time for afternoon visiting. She phoned them from the Rectory at quarter to, very apologetic saying she would be there in half an hour. With all the excitement of the previous day she had actually forgotten that they were going up to Bristol to stay for a few days. Thankfully they were understanding. Max didn't go into any detail about the previous evening. She would think about what to say, if anything on the drive over.

Having said a fairly emotional goodbye to Charlotte, she manoeuvred the Land Rover from the side of the house and out into the Devon lanes.

It was a good hour later that Charlotte had a call from Lizzie.

"I am so sorry," said Charlotte, "of course I'll pray," she said in answer to Lizzie's request. Is there anything else we can do to help? Have you spoken to Max?"

"No, there's no answer on her mobile, and I can't get in touch with Mike's parents either." Lizzie was holding back her tears, Charlotte could hear it in her voice.

"I expect they are on their way to Bristol. Max will have picked up the dogs and probably be on her way back home. Try ringing her in an hour or so, or I could if you like. I don't need to go out till one o clock."

Charlotte had never felt so involved with Max's family. She had a hunch the dogs would be coming back to Langford very soon but almost in the same thought she realised there was no reason why she shouldn't be with Max in Bristol if things got really bad. She tried to put such thoughts out of her mind. "Who's with you at the moment?"

"I've got Naomi here. She's having a crash course in baby management. I didn't want to leave Joshua behind, but, of course, they don't want him anywhere near Mike."

"I'm not surprised. That's for the baby's benefit, I guess." Charlotte was glad to keep Lizzie talking for a few minutes; it would be stressful keeping some sort of vigil by her husband's bedside, watching him struggle.

"They don't even want Naomi to go in. I hope they'll let Maureen and Vince go in though. Do you think they will be at risk too?" Lizzie and Naomi had taken Joshua to a small coffee shop not all that far from the ward. Naomi was overhearing the conversation and nodded as Lizzie asked the question, mouthing it's their son.

Charlotte was equally as sure. "I don't think his parents would be too concerned about any risk. I'm sure they are tough enough to cope. Do you want me to try and ring them too? They might have their mobile on.

"It might be best to leave it till they get here. I don't want them being worried and rushing. He is very ill, but the nurses and doctors don't seem too concerned. They keep on saying about it not getting into his blood stream."

"I'll just try Max later."

"That will be good. Tell her not to worry too much. She can always ring the ward." Making sure Charlotte had the hospital number. "Hold on, Naomi wants to speak to you."

"Charlie, I just wanted to say I'm sorry for putting my foot in it last night."

Charlotte couldn't think what she meant, but before she could say anything Naomi went on. "I hadn't realised that you and Max were together, and I jumped to the conclusion about vicars not being... well you know, when I said about you and Sasha and then correcting myself because you were a priest and then... well I feel a bit stupid that's all, and it's okay with me, I'm not anti or anything, not like Mum and...... well, actually Dad is okay too, or he would be if he could, but well you know......, oh there I go again, I always open my big mouth. Look I just

267

hope we can get to know you. Sasha is great, and as I said, she has mentioned you, so any friend of Sasha and all that, but I'm so sorry it has been like this, with Mike so ill. Well any way, perhaps when things have quietened down we could get together some time. I don't mean – oh sh.... no I shouldn't say that, should I? I'll hand you back to Lizzie," and with that she'd gone.

Compared to Naomi, Lizzie sounded remarkably calm but Charlotte could sense the very understandable strain in her voice. "I'll speak to you again soon," she said, and went on, "sorry about Naomi. If it's any consolation she is now a lovely shade of pink." Charlotte could hear Naomi snort most indignantly in the background. It made her smile.

"Tell Mike I'm thinking about him, if you can, and don't forget, if I can help, I will."

"Thanks," and with that Lizzie rang off.

Charlotte went back to her last-minute adjustments to the wedding talk, but she suspected her mind would only be half on the wedding that afternoon. The other would be firmly up in Bristol. She would try Max just before she went across to St Agnes.

Chapter 18

For over a week Michael Tannin: mechanical engineer, husband, father, son, brother, fought the infection that ravaged his body. With the strictest precautions possible, he was taken back to theatre no less than three times. Metal plates and screws that had been inserted to stabilise his shattered pelvis had been removed and replaced. Each time Lizzie, Maureen and Vince were told the risk was greater and warned to be prepared for the worse. Still Michael fought on.

Police officers turned up from time to time expecting to obtain the obligatory statement from the accident victim. Each time they were sent away by hospital staff. When they became more persistent, the full extent of Michael's injuries and prognosis were explained. They stopped badgering.

Lizzie knew nothing of this.

Naomi had been a willing weekend taxi and courier service. She had driven back to Exeter late on the Saturday night to collect essential items for both her sister and her nephew whilst they booked into a Travelodge with Maureen and Vince. She drove back to Bristol on the Sunday morning, taking Catrin and Heather with her. On Sunday afternoon Naomi drove her mother and her puzzled little niece back to Exeter.

It was decided that it was better for Heather to remain in the care of her grandmother and the ever faithful and adaptable Sally.

Naomi joined the weekly commuters returning to London early on the Monday morning. Although part of her felt she was in some way abandoning her family when they needed her, she had to admit that returning to the high pressurised atmosphere of the law firm would be a lot less emotionally draining than the events of the weekend. She promised to stay in close contact with Lizzie.

Once firmly plugged into the M4 her thoughts had meandered back to the conversations of the Friday evening. She found herself hoping that Sasha would be in contact. As the cold January sun began to break through and light up the capital's sky, Naomi found herself composing a few subtle questions that might just prise from Sasha, little snippets of information about her holy landlady. She knew it was a worthless activity. Sasha would remain loyal and faithful, but Naomi had to admit her intrigue about Charlie and Max was insatiable.

John and Wendy had driven straight to the hospital on Sunday from their home in Birmingham. As with Naomi, hospital staff were very reluctant to allow them to visit Mike. Far from feeling frustrated, John suggested they all take a break to visit the burger bar they had noticed on their way to the hospital. This suggestion came shortly after Heather had thrown an impressive tantrum when told she was not allowed to colour in the squares on the paper hanging at the end of one of the beds on the ward.

Catrin opted to stay with Maureen and Vince. She whispered to John it was to be there for them in case anything was 'to happen'. Wendy whispered to Lizzie that perhaps Catrin needed a breather from her disgruntled granddaughter.

Lizzie found it hard to drag herself away from Mike's side, but had to admit that an hour concentrating on being a mum to her children rather than her unaccustomed role of victim's wife would be a break in itself.

Only Ruth was absent. Weekend leave was simply not an option for a final year medical student from Queen's College, Nottingham. She hadn't even enquired. John suspected she took after his father when it came to a sense of calling and duty. Ruth had just pursued it in a different direction.

David carried out his weekend duties as planned. Many people had heard about the accident and offered polite support.

He felt detached.

In between each engagement, he tried ringing Catrin but only ever got through to her voice mail. Even before his family had returned that Sunday evening he was on his way to York at attend the meeting of an incredibly important committee about the Church's Response to Global Warming. He knew where he would rather be, but couldn't bring himself to abandon what he considered his duty and calling.

His daughter tried very hard to understand.

Later in the week, he did manage to call in to the hospital on his way back from York on the Tuesday evening, just as his son-in-law was returned to the ward from his second operation. Michael was enveloped in some sort of plastic tent. It looked like a scene from a thriller about chemical warfare rather than the delicate balance of a man's life.

After a short time with his daughter, her in laws and his grandson he returned to relieve his wife from the torments of a very upset and confused little four-year-old, who was by now missing her mummy and daddy terribly.

Max managed to get up to the hospital just before Michael's first operation on the Monday morning. Charlotte could at least have the dogs again and offered to keep them with her whilst things were so

271

uncertain, so that Max could dash up to Bristol at more or less a moment's notice, if she felt it was necessary.

Charlotte for the time being had her duty to the parish to consider. She struggled with each task, knowing that her time as a priest was fast drawing to a close. Linda became increasingly worried about her, noticing how often she just seemed so far away. Charlotte had explained that a friend was seriously ill in hospital, which she hoped would be enough information to prevent Linda's naturally enquiring mind conjuring up too many other possibilities and inadvertently starting alternative rumours around the villages, which was all too easy to do. There would be plenty of gossip before too long, but for now she would try and contain it.

James was the surprise package. Late on the Thursday evening around ten o clock, he once again sent gravel flying on Charlotte's driveway. She had only just returned from a joint meeting of Church wardens and sides-persons from each church. She was tired. She still had to sort the dogs out. She was fed up with treading on egg shells and annoyed that she was getting drawn into petty arguments about who should take up the collection to the altar rail, whilst all she was really worried about was her partner, once again travelling alone up to Bristol early the next day after being on call all night. Charlotte had thought about asking Linda to look in on the dogs so that she could travel up with Max, but it was just asking for trouble. Her secretary was curious enough about the presence of the dogs, but thankfully had not connected all the small fragments of information. It was a shame Sasha had needed to spend the whole week up in her London flat, she would have been a huge help with the dogs. Charlotte and Sasha hadn't even had chance to talk about another mutual friend. Naomi had obviously got caught up in work and as there was no magazine due, couldn't really find an excuse to contact Sasha, so for now, nothing more had been said. So as Thursday evening arrived, rather than preparing for a trip up to Bristol the village vicar looked at the pile of paper work she would begin sorting through the next day and the scores of files that would need leaving in good order in the not too distant future. Not a good way to spend a day off, which added to her feeling of despair that evening. The last thing she needed was another burst of youthful hot-headedness from her fervent nephew.

When James arrived however, the surprise was, that far from any crisis between her nephew and either his father or mother, all was apparently quite calm on that front. His parents just hadn't spoken all week and had decided to take the strategy of ignoring his latest 'attention seeking blond haired behaviour!' So, he had spent the week non-verbally making his stand simply by keeping his new look in tiptop condition by adopting stringent personal hygiene, including styling and gelling, whilst deciding to shock his mother by new found responsibility over his college work.

That evening he had announced that his aunt had invited him for the weekend. "But I hadn't!" Charlotte had protested when he had told her.

"No, but you need help with the dogs and I bet you'd rather be with Max tomorrow than cooped up here, so crack of dawn tomorrow off you go!"

James had a self-assured grin about him. How could his aunt possibly refuse?

"It would have been nice if you had actually asked before organising my life for me," was her initial response.

"I thought about it, but you would have refused my help, insisting that I could not possibly be left with the dogs alone for a whole day, or more to the point, your precious vicarage, so I took the chance. It's more difficult to send me packing now, isn't it? And before you ask, I don't have college tomorrow because the lecturers have some sort of training session, so it's all sorted. All you have to do is get to Bristol. That is what you want to do isn't it?"

Charlotte was lost for words. She didn't know whether to wrap her arms round him and give him a great big hug, or to hit him for being so presumptuous. Instead she said, "Okay, you win, do you fancy a beer?"

"Thought you'd never ask Auntie Charlie!"

Charlotte rang Max, who had already been called out to a very sick dog and later that night would probably have to perform a caesarean on a cow. Charlotte therefore insisted on driving to Tavistock to pick Max up early the following day and drive them both to Bristol. She then joined her nephew in a beer as they chatted about college, family and dogs, grateful to have his company and for his initiative that would allow her to spend time with Max the next day. She gave him a big hug before she went up to bed, leaving him to enjoy the benefits of a large detached house with a good music system.

Life was to remain very complicated for all concerned for many weeks and months to come. Lives that would twist and turn around the others; sometimes supporting and complementing, sometimes crashing into the others battling a path through the quagmire created by brokenness, anxiety, frustration, misunderstanding, grief, change and

274

reclamation. Relationships would be tested to breaking point. There would be surprises along the way. There would be disappointments. At times, each hour seemed crucial, each minute to be treasured; at others participants in the drama would be anxious to see the weeks and months long past and for the future to take hold.

Chapter 19

A week later, Rev Charlotte Northam; Rector of the East Dartmoor Group of parishes consisting of the villages of Langford, Winstone, Sheepsgate, Easton, Mutton, South Bridge, Upton and Coombe Cross, waited silently for Bishop David. The meeting was scheduled for noon. Given that Mike was once again due to go into theatre, Charlotte had suggested postponing. Her Bishop had decided that, despite the circumstances, they would proceed as planned.

At twenty minutes past midday, Sally showed Charlotte into the Bishop's study. Charlotte was a little surprised to see a plate of sandwiches and a pot of coffee already standing on the large central table. She was even more surprised to discover that the Bishop was not in his study. Sally invited Charlotte to pour herself some coffee, explaining that the Bishop would not be too long.

Charlotte desperately tried to read Sally's face for any hint of the knowing look that would suggest she knew the gist of Charlotte's last conversation with the Bishop, both the formal and the rather more informal one. Sally either did not know, which Charlotte found surprising, or she was very good at concealing her private opinions. Charlotte assumed that Sally would be fully aware of Mike's crucial operation scheduled for that morning and therefore David's preoccupations that day. However, unless Sally was fully acquainted with all the facts, she would never guess that the exact same events were also invading Charlotte's mind.

Charlotte poured some coffee and waited.

Ten minutes later, half an hour after their scheduled appointment, the Bishop walked through to his study. Charlotte was once again rather surprised. Bishop David had discarded his usual mauve shirt and clerical collar. Instead he was dressed in dark green corduroy trousers, a checked shirt and fawn jumper. Charlotte immediately felt over dressed in her grey trouser suit and black clerical shirt.

"I suppose I could have asked Sally to let you into the kitchen," he said.

Charlotte immediately felt very uncomfortable, at the rather barbed remark so obviously referring to the last time they had seen each other. The Bishop sensed her tension. He hadn't really intended to cause her even greater anxiety so he tried to explain.

"I've been trying to get Heather to eat some lunch. I heard you had made quite an impression in those few minutes you spent with her, you might have some success with lunch. Dorothy, one of the vergers, has very kindly stepped in to look after the children, but my granddaughter decided to have a strop so I've just been trying to calm her down a bit. Actually, I hadn't realised the time. It's all a bit unreal at the moment isn't it."

"Have you heard anything?" Charlotte tread carefully. She was sitting in front of him, as one of his priests, about to hear how they would go about managing the parish, and possibly the media, once her resignation from the priesthood was announced, yet he was behaving very much the grandfather of her partner's niece and nephew.

"I spoke to Catrin about fifteen minutes ago, he's still in theatre."

Both knew the enormity of what Michael was about to face. They both knew the other was fully aware of what was going on. There was no need to explain to the other what was on their minds. It was ironic that the operation had been scheduled for that very same day.

David felt the coffee pot. "I'll get some fresh. Do help yourself to a sandwich," he said as he walked back out of the study and, Charlotte assumed, back in the direction of the kitchen.

Once again, she waited. There was a brief rap on the other door and Sally popped her head around the corner. "I just wondered..... oh, where's the bishop?"

"Gone to get fresh coffee."

"That's what I was going to offer to get. Oh well. Umm are you two alright? Is it going okay?"

"We haven't really started yet," Charlotte said. "The Bishop was rather detained by his granddaughter."

"Oh, I am sorry. I told him I would go in. Poor little mite......." Sally seemed to suddenly clam up as if she stopped herself saying anything more. "I'll speak to you later."

Charlotte knew there would be various papers to sign, which is probably what Sally had meant.

David came back in with the coffee.

"Well I suppose we had better try and concentrate on the matter in hand," he said as he poured himself a cup and offered some fresh to Charlotte. "What will you do?"

Charlotte was somewhat thrown by his question and his rather abrupt launch into the conversation. She had expected some discussion on how she felt the parish would take the news of her departure and thought he would try to ascertain the current picture. She assumed there would be an explanation of the process and be told legally what needed to happen.

She knew they would need to discuss how they would actually make the announcement in the parish, what would be the official story and how to handle the subsequent questions. She had more or less expected David to explain to her what would happen. By his question the Bishop seemed to be putting it into her court. Charlotte wasn't sure how to answer, so was blunt.

"I was rather hoping you would tell me Bishop."

"Tell you what to do? Why on earth would you expect me to do that? What you do with your life after this is up to you. There will be some ongoing pastoral support of course, but surely you must have some idea? Have you thought about teaching? Could you go back to your old career? Is that an option?"

"You mean when this is all over!" Charlotte finally understood David's question.

"Of course, what did you think I meant?" David appeared a little perplexed and slightly exasperated. For a moment, Charlotte reminded herself that they were both facing a difficult day, both professionally and personally.

Charlotte did her best to answer, part of her wanted to yell out 'It's none of your bloody business' but she resisted the temptation. Her boss was trying to be supportive before they needed to face the hard facts.

She and Max had discussed various options, but given all that was going on with Mike, their plans were far from concrete. In reality Charlotte was very unclear about her future, except that Max would not see her destitute, but how could she say that to David, so the only thing that came out was, "Nothing is finalised yet."

David was feeling just as awkward. In the past two weeks, his waking hours had revolved around supporting his daughter, although not all that effectively, reassuring his wife, equally rather ineffectively, distracting his granddaughter, at which he had been moderately successful, attending various committees that he found he had no interest in and in between, agonising over his decision about what to do about Charlotte, a process, he realised would never find a satisfactory conclusion.

"Charlie," he used the nickname deliberately but not sarcastically, "can we talk just as equals for a moment?" He didn't wait for her to answer. "We both know how difficult this is. Part of me still wants to find a way to keep you. I don't want you to give up this life. You are a good priest. My daughter has reminded me of that a lot these past two weeks, and I want to thank you for all the support you've given her....."

Charlotte started to protest saying she had hardly done anything, but David very subtly raised his index finger to stop any interruptions.

"But we live with hypocrisy. I don't like it any more than you do. It will seem an empty promise at the moment, but I assure you there will come a time very soon, when I will do what I can to fight your cause. I'll need to placate Catrin, of course. She is rather old fashioned when it comes to these things........"

Charlotte managed to interrupt his flow. "I don't want you to compromise your own integrity, any more than I will my own. This is my decision. It's taken me a long time. Perhaps my discernment was flawed when I first felt called to the priesthood..."

"Never......" interrupted David, but Charlotte ignored him.

"But I don't think I could have done what I have if it was. Sorry if that sounds big headed, but it's what I believe." Although Charlotte

280

paused, David chose not to interrupt this time. "It's been at a cost," she said, "and now I'm putting family first, my family, and ironically your family." Again, she paused briefly wondering if that might have irritated David, but he didn't respond. "Nothing has changed since I saw you two weeks ago. No, that's a stupid thing to say. A huge amount has changed, but my decision is the same. I'm resigning my orders. My loose connection with your family is merely secondary, so please don't feel guilty and feel you have to make all sorts of promises for the future. Let's just sort out what needs to happen."

Charlotte wondered if she had taken the Bishop too much to his word about talking as equals.

David sat back further into the old sofa where he had settled when he came back in with the coffee. He folded his hands behind his head and let out a sigh.

"That's why I wanted you as an Archdeacon; you can talk to me plainly. I am disappointed, sorry and angry that things have worked out this way, truly I am. Yes, there is some regret, not guilt, and the promise was not an empty one. I'm just not sure what it means yet, so do you really have no idea about your next step?"

Charlotte decided David was genuinely interested and decided to share with him some of her discussions with Max about the veterinary surgery in Okehampton, the house they were hoping to buy and the possibility of Charlotte working part time as an administrator for the practice if the hopes to extend really took off. It would take a while to sort out, so in the meantime they would live in Max's house in Tavistock.

David watched Charlotte as she did her best to fill David in on her plans. She often said "nothing is finalised of course," before continuing with the next part of her story. David resisted the urge to question Charlotte more deeply about some of her plans. Charlotte sensed his reticence. Money would be tight, but they would survive, and yes, at the right time they would enter into civil partnership.

"Money," said David, finally finding his voice. "That brings us on to some of the legal things we'll need to discuss. I've been talking to the Registrar......"

David then went on to explain how they had found a way to freeze Charlotte's pension but in a way that interest would still be paid. She could then draw down on it at the age of 65, so she would not lose quite as much. There would then be a percentage of the lump sum and the monthly payment.

The Bishop chose not to divulge the intense arguments he had suffered with both the Registrar and the Church Commissioners as he had first prevented them writing off the pension completely by persuading them that this was not in any way the result of disciplinary action and neither would it be. He had then attempted to release the lump sum in advance of retirement age to give Charlotte at least a little capital to help with a deposit on some property or perhaps even re-training. This suggestion fell on firmly closed ears, so he had settled for the freeze rather than loss.

He then went on to say that it had however been agreed that after she had physically left the parish she would officially, but very quietly, be on a period of sabbatical leave so that she would still receive her stipend for a further three months. This he had secured by reminding the Board of Finance about their pastoral responsibilities to clergy and the fact that Charlotte had never requested any sabbatical leave, a nifty little move that he also decided not to burden Charlotte with. Only after those three months would she then have formally left the ministry.

If Charlotte had been honest she would have admitted she was disappointed not to receive the percentage of the lump sum that would eventually have been owed to her. It would have been money that would have gone towards refurbishing the house they were hoping to buy. All of her current savings, and all of Max's, would go towards the deposit they needed. They could now, only obtain a mortgage on Max's earnings. She was however grateful for the extra three months' pay.

David had also managed to persuade the Registrar that there was no need to rush the process as the parish would need time to adapt. So, if Charlotte was in agreement she could stay for up to six months, as long as she remained very discreet during the whole of that time.

Charlotte was not so keen on this, expecting it to be a maximum of three months, if not sooner. She knew it would be very difficult to stop the rumours flying around the villages.

She would try her best.

She did suggest that she could try and take a few weeks' holiday during that period to give her some time to make arrangements and, she added, to help in whatever way she could with the other events that concerned both her and David.

"I know Lizzie would be grateful," admitted David. "I'm not so sure Catrin would approve and of course, I still need you to act with the outmost discretion. Everyone I've talked to is so touchy about the media getting hold of something and making a mountain out of a mole hill, if you know what I mean." He paused and glanced at his watch. "I wonder if there's any news?"

"I'm sure Catrin would ring. Do you need to check on the children?" Charlotte was also suddenly brought back to the reality of Michael's situation, probably still on the operating table.

"I'm sure I would be called if I was needed. Dorothy will cope. She's really very good with them. Comes with having five her own and a growing number of grandchildren I suppose. We need to discuss some dates, but we need Sally for that. I'll call her. Please do have a sandwich."

"To be honest I'm not all that hungry."

"No nor me. I do wonder what's happening up there." Charlotte knew David was referring to Bristol.

Max was sitting in her Land Rover about three miles from Mutton, one of Charlotte's villages and at the northernmost end of the vet's practice. She had been visiting the owner of a small holding who kept pygmy sheep, more as a hobby than for any profit.

She looked at her watch it was after midday. She wasn't needed back at the main practice until two, so at long last allowed the huge significance of this day to flood her mind.

It was a bitterly cold January day, but the winter sun did its best to cast out the darkness that lay heavily on Max. She could have gone up to Bristol to be with Mike, or at least the family as they waited. Instead she had stayed the previous night with Charlotte and bundled the dogs into the Land Rover that morning to take them with her on her rounds.

Although close to the parish, they wouldn't go back till later that evening.

Despite all the good intentions Max and Charlotte would be together that night. Discretion was all well and good, and they would be discreet, but that did not mean staying apart, especially on this day. They just weren't sure where they would be that evening – Tavistock, Langford, Bristol.

Patch poked his head through the headrests and cocked it to one side, perhaps questioning his mistress what was on her mind.

"Not sure where you'll be tonight either. Funny old day, to put it mildly," and she ruffled his head, which obviously made Stitch a little jealous, so she managed to clamber over the top of the passenger seat.

"If Charlie saw you do that, she'd skin me alive and insist you have your harness on, but I'll not let on if you don't. Now back you both go," and once she'd given Stitch a hug she managed to push them both back onto the back seat.

She got out her mobile, tempted to send a text. But wasn't sure who to? She could text Charlie, but she'd still be with the Bishop. How they could sit in the same room and concentrate on parish matters she didn't know, although she'd managed to trim the hoofs of twelve pygmy sheep that morning and made sure their new owner was now competent in the delicate act. Her parents would be at the hospital with Lizzie and Catrin. As she stared at her phone it suddenly sprung into life. It was a text from Sasha.

Will b bk 2nite. Can b there 4 dogs. Any News.

"Well that solves one problem I suppose." Although Max liked Sasha, part of her was not sorry that in a few months, she would no longer be living under the same roof as Charlotte.

Sasha had been surprised when Charlotte had broken the news that she would soon no longer be living at the Rectory and accepted that she would have to move out within the next few weeks. It wasn't a big problem, she would just spend more time in London until she managed to get her own place somewhere rural between her London clients and those she was developing in Exeter, Plymouth and Bristol. What she was even more surprised to learn was Naomi's connection in the unravelling saga.

Bishop David jumped up to assist Sally as she pushed open the door of the Bishop's study armed with diary and what appeared to be a number of documents. A mere split second later she was nearly bowled over as Heather tore into the room with a sock on her hand.

"Look Grandpa, 'Dorthy' made me a sheep," and she made baa like noises whilst opening and closing her hand inside the white sock, which Charlotte suspected may have been an old football sock before it's reincarnation to a woolly sheep, or was it just returning to its original state?

"That's lovely darling but......." David showed great interest in the woolly sock whilst putting his hand firmly behind her back and began steering her back out the door in the general direction of the amazing sheep making Dorothy. He wasn't quite quick enough.

"Oh...." exclaimed the little puppeteer as she caught sight of Charlotte, "Is Auntie Max here too? Can I show her my sheep?"

"No darling, you have to go back to look after Joshua and Dorothy" interjected her Grandfather, rather surprised that his granddaughter remembered Charlotte.

"Where's Auntie Max?" Heather walked over to Charlie as bold as anything and climbed up onto the sofa next to her. "Do you like my sheep?" and with hardly a breath reached out and pointed to the clerical collar around Charlotte's neck. "Grandpa's got one of those, because he's a bishop. Are you a bishop?"

"Come on Heather, Grandpa is working. You need to go back to Dorothy." David bent over to pick up Heather but she quickly climbed onto Charlotte's lap.

"But I want to see Auntie Max."

"Auntie Max is working too, with the animals, I'm just here to see your Grandpa today." Charlotte was a little taken aback but rather chuffed by the way this small child had already made the connection between her and Max.

"Why you seeing Grandpa?"

"I work with your Grandpa at the moment."

"That's nice. I like you..." and she put her arms around Charlotte's neck gave her a brief hug and then clambered back off the sofa saying, "bye Auntie Charlie," and ran back out of the study 'baaing' and waving her white sock as she went.

"She's like a little whirlwind that one," said Sally pretending to ignore the glances that were being exchanged between her boss and his priest.

"I have the forms for Charlotte to sign Bishop."

287

"Thank you Sally. We'll need to work out some dates as well. Can you put the forms on the coffee table?" He paused for a moment and then as if he had suddenly made up his mind he decided to continue, "I'm sorry about Heather, you must be wondering..."

"Bishop, it's none of my business," she interrupted as she moved towards the door.

"Sally, the dates. We could do with your assistance on that one," said David. Sally turned back. She had indeed been puzzled by the actions of the Bishop's granddaughter and distracted by the thoughts running through her mind.

It was decided that Charlotte's last Sunday in her benefice would be the last Sunday in July. Formal announcements would be made after Easter.

It would be extremely difficult to keep silent about her news until then, but breaking the news publicly too soon would be even more disruptive. This way there would be time to quietly organise certain things in the parish before it was widely known.

Despite Charlotte's intention for a quiet departure, she agreed to David's suggestion to arrange a joint service within the benefice that day and surprised by his offer to either preach or preside whichever Charlotte would prefer. It was not only rare for a Bishop to attend a leaving service, but given the circumstances Charlotte assumed David would rather keep his distance.

These thoughts however, Charlotte kept to herself not wishing to bring them up in front of Sally. Charlotte would officially cease to be a Clerk in Holy Orders on the 31st October. The appropriate legal documents would be drawn up from the information on the completed forms that lay on the coffee table.

There had been some discussion between David and Charlotte about the reason given for Charlotte's request to leave the ministry and even more discussion about what would be said in the parish. During this discussion, Sally, as discreet as ever, had offered to make more coffee. It was evident to Charlotte that Sally knew the reasons for her decision to leave but perhaps not the family connection that had emerged between herself and the Bishop, even if young Heather had unwittingly done her best to supply the information.

Then Sally left them again, picking up the left-over coffee and sandwiches.

"Bishop.......er David," said Charlotte as soon as Sally had left the room. "What does Sally actually know? I felt I was having to talk in riddles a couple of times, I'd rather she knew, well about me any way."

"I wouldn't worry about the riddles, Sally is the most astute woman I know, including Catrin. She knows of course you are leaving ministry, not just the parish. She hasn't asked why. She's obviously left us to sort out the official story. She'll see the documents of course, before they go to the Registrar. She'll have picked up on Heather's little display, but I think she would have had to make a huge leap to have made any sense of it. How much do you want her to know?"

Charlotte thought for a moment before answering, "I would want the parish to know the real reason why I am leaving ministry, at the appropriate time. I know the press might decide it's newsworthy"

"So, Sally.......?"

"I can't tell you what to tell your staff. Personally, I would prefer her to know the full story, perhaps leaving out your family."

"We'll tell Sally today what we eventually tell the parish, tell her the official line."

"Which is.....?" Charlotte glanced down at the papers in front of her, sighed and read out the sentence. "Rev Northam has given many years of dedicated service to the ordained ministry. For personal reasons, having left the East Dartmoor Benefice she will resign her orders to follow a different path."

Charlotte and David hadn't heard Sally come back into the room. "That's the sort of statement that will only irritate parishioners and incite the local press, if I may be so bold. It is nowhere near the full story, is it? Rumours are far more dangerous in my experience."

"What would you say, Sally?" asked the bishop.

Sally hardly took a breath, "The Church of England does not allow practicing homosexual priests to exercise an ordained ministry. Rev Northam has therefore taken the decision to resign Holy Orders in order to pursue a different path with her life partner." She paused for a moment, "who I assume is Auntie Max, but that last bit of information is probably best kept out of the public domain if possible. The press, like secretaries are quite good at making connections. From what Heather has just been saying, I'm guessing Max is her father's sister."

David and Charlotte stared at Sally.

"I'm sorry," she said, "but it's not difficult to put two and two together. When a perfectly good priest suddenly announces she's leaving, there has to be a very good reason. I thought you were terminally ill or something Charlotte, tied myself up in knots for days

290

until I plucked up courage to ask David if that was the reason, and was mightily relieved when he assured me it wasn't, I can tell you. I think you are making a mistake mind. Can't you just go on as before? It's worked for years.... Oh." Sally stopped abruptly. "I am so sorry, I am talking completely out of turn, it's not my place to......"

"It's alright Sally," Bishop David beckoned her forward, "in a way you are right, about being honest anyway."

"Charlotte, I was rude, I'm sorry." Sally sat down on the far end of the sofa.

"You weren't rude," reassured Charlotte.

"What we write on the official papers will be brief. No more than a sentence that states it is Charlotte's personal decision to resign her orders. That way no disciplinary reasons are brought into question, and it will be clear that it is not because of illness, or some mental disorder, purely a personal life choice." David sat back looking rather pleased with his decisive answer.

Charlotte on the other hand felt irritation rise from her stomach. She didn't want to challenge the Bishop on his line of thought, there was enough to think about on that particular day. He was right. She was not ill, she was not mentally unfit. It was her choice to enter into a relationship, but that's where the choice ended. She didn't want to leave ministry, the choice she made had been forced upon her; truthfulness or dishonesty. As a Christian, let alone a priest, she had chosen honesty.

Her life would be turned upside down because she was being honest with herself and with those around her. Even Max didn't want her to stop being a priest, no matter how difficult it was to share her with so many people. It was a decision, not a choice, defining it as merely a personal choice diluted it. It sounded no more important than where to go on holiday.

Legal documents were one thing. She could live with such a statement, but explaining her decision to her parish was another. She and Max would still be living in the area. It was where Max had built up her practice and they were not prepared to move away. People would soon get to know they were a couple.

After so many years of secrets, Charlotte wanted this to be as open as possible and to squash any chance of rather more sordid rumours before they took hold. But as always, she swallowed her intense feelings and just nodded. Sally of course noticed her clenched jaw and glanced down as Charlotte released the edge of the cushion that she had grasped in her fist. She also said nothing.

The phone rang.

Chapter 20

Catrin and Lizzie were standing together outside the hospital wing. It was cold. Catrin held the phone with one hand holding the other around the shoulders of her shivering daughter.

Sally had answered the call but passed it immediately to David when she heard Catrin's voice.

"How is he?" was all David said.

"David, it's not good news. They couldn't save the leg. They amputated above the knee."

"Oh no....... oh no, poor Michael. How's Lizzie?"

"She's here."

"Dad? They couldn't do it. He's lost his leg Dad." Lizzie sounded more stunned than upset, speaking as if she couldn't believe it herself.

Charlotte could hear just one side of the conversation, but enough to know their fears had come true. She quietly took out her mobile to see if Max had been trying to contact her. Charlotte had switched the phone to silent when she arrived at the Palace for her meeting with David. There was no message. Max probably didn't know. Sally was still in the room, she looked across at Charlotte and mouthed silently "I'm sorry."

Lizzie handed the phone back to her mother. Catrin and David had a brief conversation, but were too stunned to discuss very much, they simply went over the practical arrangements for that evening. Catrin was about to ring off when Lizzie gestured that she wanted the phone again.

"Dad, is Charlie still with you?"

"Er well, yes she is."

293

"Can I speak to her please?"

David walked over to Charlotte and handed her the phone, "It's Lizzie," he said and looked across at Sally. She thought he looked almost embarrassed, or apologetic.

"Lizzie, I'm so sorry." Charlotte felt very self-conscious, talking to Lizzie in front of David and Sally.

"Don't be, but be strong for us. We need you. Me, Mike, the kids. Maureen and Vince are so upset." Lizzie sounded very earnest, not at all what Charlotte had expected.

"I'll do whatever I can Lizzie."

"First, can you speak to Max and make sure Dad rings Naomi and John, and Ruth I suppose?"

"Of course. Is Mike conscious yet?"

"No, not yet. When can you and Max get up here? None of us thought he would have to wake up to this. I think he'd like to see Max, and Charlie I really want to see you. I need your strength." Charlotte was taken aback. She was glad that David was obviously trying to fill Sally in and was largely ignoring the conversation going on between her and his daughter. "Of course I can. I'll speak to Max and we'll make it up as soon as we can. Liz, when do you think Mike will be aware of what's happened?" She took a gulp of breath before adding, "he is …..stable, isn't he?"

"Yes, oh yes, thank God. They are almost certain they've removed all the infected bone. He is still really poorly, but he'll recover now. That's what we have to hold onto. It's just the shock, it will be huge. I'm really worried for him. Speak to Max. Do what you can Charlie, please. I'd better go. I'll speak to you later."

She rang off leaving Charlotte staring at the phone, a number of things going through her mind. She realised she was alone in the room, guessing David had gone to speak to Dorothy and to say something to Heather, although she hoped David wouldn't try and explain too much to his little granddaughter too soon. Still sitting in her Bishop's study, she rang her partner.

The mobile went straight to voice mail. No way would she leave a message. She couldn't believe it was already quarter past two. Max would be in the middle of surgery. She thought for a moment and then rang the practice number. She asked the receptionist to ask Max to ring her as soon as possible, even between clients. The kindly receptionist started to explain that it was not possible for Max to do that unless it was urgent.

"Max knows I wouldn't ask her to ring unless it was of vital importance. Please just pass on the message," and rang off before the receptionist could protest some more.

Charlotte started to pick up the papers, taking the copies that belonged to her and piling up the rest for Sally to deal with. She looked at the documents that would eventually seal her demise as a priest. 'All this was complicated enough,' she thought to herself. 'Am I making a mistake? Timing...... If the press get hold of this..... David, what will he do? No, this is nothing to do with David's family, it's a loose connection, no journalist would be interested. I don't need to make a stand..... Why am I doing this? Perhaps we could move away....... run away? No way....' "Oh, bloody hell!" she cried as she thumped her fist onto the table in her frustration.

She hadn't heard David come back into the room and probably didn't realise her last phrase was audible. The frustration was genuine and uncontrolled. Before David could say anything, Charlotte's phone rang. It was Max.

"I'm sorry, but I do need to speak to Max," she said turning to the bishop. "I'll take it outside."

"Of course," was all David said.

Charlotte stepped out of the study into the dark wood lined corridor, "Max?"

"It's Mike isn't it, you've heard something.... he's not, oh God Charlie, don't tell me that."

"No, Max, he's come through the op. He's okay......" Charlotte hadn't finished but Max interrupted.

"Oh, thank God, so they didn't have to amputate after all. Oh, I'm so relieved thank you..... thank you for good news for once."

Charlotte grasped a handful of hair as she nearly shouted down the phone, "Max please, just listen." Charlotte knew she wasn't handling this well. "Max, please, just sit down and listen, get away from main reception." Charlotte could hear the sounds of anxious animals and owners in the background and the murmur of the reception desk continuing with the ordinary business of the afternoon. There was a pause as the sounds faded further in the background.

"Ok, I'm in the back room, but he's okay, you said he was alright."

"Max, they couldn't save his leg." How Charlotte wished she was with Max in person, rather than standing in the dark corridor of the Palace. "I'm sorry, sweetheart. They tried, but the bone was too infected."

"How far?" Max's response sounded clipped, as if she was struggling, holding back the tidal wave of emotion threatening to flood her heart and soul.

Charlotte's eyes were rimmed with red, but she dare not let her emotions go, not yet, not now. She just kept to what she knew. "Above the knee. I'm not sure exactly. Lizzie's desperate for us to get up there. She's really worried about how Mike will react. She wants you to be there."

"Oh, I see. Both of us?"

"That's what she said."

"Good, then we should go. Did she mean today? Could you do that?"

"Not a lot to lose now I suppose. I'll postpone tonight's meeting and get Sam to do communion in the morning." Charlotte switched to management mode. "We can't take the dogs. Can anyone over there look after them? Or I guess Linda might pop in. I don't want to drag James over..."

"Slow down, didn't Sasha text you as well? She's coming back tonight. She said she can look after the dogs."

"Oh right, so that's settled, we'll go up this evening."

"It seems crazy you driving all the way back home only to go all the way up the motorway again. Can't I meet you in Exeter?"

"No, don't do that. Meet me at the Rectory. You'll have to drop off the dogs and I've got a couple of things to sort out. What time will you be there?" They worked out the details hoping to be up in Bristol by 7pm. Charlotte texted their ETA to Lizzie before going back into the Bishop's study to collect her belongings.

Heather was with her grandfather. She ran up to Charlotte again and gave her a big hug. "Come on Poppit," said David gently pulling her away from Charlotte, "let Auntie Charlie get her things. She's got to go home."

"Can't you read me a story?" Heather shrugged off her Grandfather and directed her plea to Charlotte.

Charlotte crouched down to Heather's level. "Not today sweetheart. I'm going home to Auntie Max."

"And Daddy?"

"Daddy's in hospital my love," said David, looking quizzically at Charlotte and the ease with which she spoke to Heather about 'home' and 'Auntie Max'. He was accepting of her decision and her lifestyle, but not quite so comfortable, he realised, when it might influence his granddaughter.

"I know," said Heather, "Daddy's got a poorly leg and I've got to look after Joshy."

Charlotte smiled at Heather's name for her brother and could just imagine the conversation earlier that day when her mother undoubtedly had difficulty persuading Heather to stay with her grandfather. Charlotte wanted to scoop her up again in a hug as if to protect a vulnerable little girl from the responsibility she felt for her brother, and the road that lay ahead, as her father faced months of readjustment. Instead Charlotte played the 'professional' role and waited whilst Bishop David pointed Heather back in the direction of the patient Dorothy.

"We'll speak about the parish again within the next few weeks," said David, adding, "I imagine our paths will cross before then. It's a sad business but we'll cope."

298

It was odd the way they had to constantly switch roles: most of the conversation had been professional, but interspersed with the news from Bristol, Charlotte becoming Aunty Charlie, David being Dad and Grandpa. For all his support Charlotte noticed how her Bishop demonstrated a lingering reticence over her relationship with his granddaughter's aunt. If it hadn't been so close to home, would he have been so willing to offer discreet support? It would be a question that would be left unspoken.

David then looked at Charlotte making sure he had her full attention, "Don't do anything reckless. The press can be very harsh."

Charlotte said nothing but nodded and shook the hand David offered her.

The conversation had ended. She left the study and made her way back to the main entrance.

Sally met her at the door and looked Charlotte straight in the eye. "I'm sorry about what's happened with you. Just try and keep the Bishop's family out of the story. They have enough on their plate as it is. Drive carefully." Sally nearly pushed a stunned Charlotte out the door. Sally had spoken in such a kindly manner and yet the words were so very barbed.

Chapter 21

Charlotte returned home mid-afternoon. It took her just over an hour to deal with the various messages that had been left, both on the answer phone and hand written by Linda. She didn't dare look at e-mails, they would have to wait.

She phoned Sam and made sure he was available to take the midweek communion service at St Nicholas. He sounded rather pleased there was a 'crisis' that needed his help and made the right noises when Charlotte explained it was a 'family emergency.' He assured her that he would remember the family in the prayers and pushed her for details but Charlotte said just a little too firmly that it would not be necessary. Sam was disappointed not to offer more of a shoulder for his boss but put the rebuke down to the stress she was under. He made a mental note to mention his concerns to Roger or Derek or maybe Linda, she might have a womanly touch.

Charlotte also rang Linda to warn her that she would need to let herself in and the two dogs may well greet her, that Sasha would be around, but that she herself would not. Linda was also puzzled by a family crisis being so significant that it pulled Charlotte away from the parish at short notice.

When Linda asked Charlotte what she should do about Mrs Harlow who was due to discuss the refurbishment of ST Nicholas the following afternoon she was sure she heard a sort of stifled scream coming from Charlotte.

Charlotte had in fact over looked the appointment and at that moment really didn't care about what would happen to the old church buildings, they would soon not be her responsibility, a thought she didn't share with her secretary. She assured Linda that if she was not back in time the churchwarden would be able to discuss the project, although she had deep reservations about leaving such an important discussion to just Mrs Harlow and the warden. She would ring Roger and see if he was available, but in her heart of hearts knew that she would make sure she was back in time.

By the time Charlotte had rung Roger, the warden and Mrs Harlow to explain to them that she was very sorry but there was a chance she may not make it to the meeting because of a family crisis, she was really beginning to wish she had either given some other excuse, or had got Sasha to lie through her teeth and claim Charlotte had been struck down by a debilitating migraine and must not be disturbed. She was still berating herself for always wanting to be 'honest' when she heard Max pull up. She couldn't believe it was already five o clock. Max had done well to get off so early.

They settled the dogs, managed to speak to Sasha on her mobile, who again reassured them that she would be back by seven thirty at the latest and would be more than happy to dog sit, dog walk, dog play and, if necessary, perform the ultimate sacrifice which was to dog poop scoop if little accidents had occurred. Patch and Stitch would remain in the kitchen, just in case Sasha got delayed and got home to discover that she did indeed need to perform the ultimate sacrifice!

By half past five they were heading up to Bristol.

Chapter 22

Lizzie moved to one side as the nurse checked the various machines that monitored Mike's heart rate, pulse and oxygen saturation. She checked his temperature and the flow of the drip administrating a steady dose of broad spectrum anti-biotic and the one keeping Mike hydrated during this crucial period of recovery. She took down the second blood transfusion and noted the amount of fluid that had been collected via a tube coming from the stump. The nurse seemed satisfied with her findings, but only nodded and smiled at Lizzie as she left the room, offering no further reassurance or explanation of what she had just done, not that Lizzie needed explanation. She was beginning to think she could do the job herself. She had seen it done often enough over the past few days.

Mike was still very drowsy under the influence of strong tranquilising pain killers. Lizzie took his hand gently in her own, being careful to avoid the tubes, and dug deep for the courage to keep up her vigil.

She jumped slightly when the nurse returned. She may even have dropped off to sleep for a brief moment as she sat there resting her head next to Mike's hand.

"Two more people have arrived Mrs Tannin, and I think I saw your mother with Mr Tannin's parents in the waiting room," said the young nurse.

"What's the time?"

"Just after seven. It's alright you can have somebody with you for a little while, but not more than one and we'll ask you to go by about

8pm." She was young and very soft spoken, but the nurse was firm and good at setting the boundaries.

"I'll come out. I hope it's Mike's sister, and do call me Lizzie, and it's Mike," said Lizzie, pointing towards her husband. She bent down close to Mike, kissed him on the cheek and said, "see you in a moment darling." She touched his hand and left the four bedded Intensive Care Unit for the first time in over two hours.

In the waiting area, decorated in calming pastoral colours and kitted out with soft furnishings and a small kitchenette, Catrin was doing her best to fill Max and Charlotte in on the events of the afternoon.

Maureen and Vince sat at the table on kitchen chairs clasping mugs of tea in their hands, as if they were a precious gift.

Catrin, it appeared, had appointed herself as coordinator of operations and appeared almost invigorated by the crisis in which she found herself.

As soon as Lizzie walked in, her mother bustled around, making tea. Both Max and Charlotte felt uncomfortable. Maureen and Vince seemed very overwhelmed and as Charlotte glanced over at them, she noticed how drawn, grey and old they looked. Her heart went out to them, but it was Lizzie who seemed to take in the scene. After a few moments of submitting to her mother's overbearing enthusiasm, she calmly but firmly took back the control from her mother.

"I want to talk to Max and Charlotte," she said. "Mo, Vince, I'm sure you'd like to sit with Mike for a bit. He's still not really awake, but he'll know you're there."

"We'll go on in then," said Vince as he helped Mo out of the kitchen chair.

"Are you alright, Dad?" Max had also seen how exhausted her parents seemed. It had been a harrowing couple of weeks as their son battled with infection after infection, fighting to save his life, failing in the end to save his leg.

"We're glad you're both here love," was all Vince managed to say as he and his wife summoned the energy needed, to once again sit at their son's bedside.

"Mum," continued Liz, as Maureen and Vince left, "Can you give me a ring when you get back to Exeter? I'll be back at the lodge by then."

"But I can stay." She protested.

"I'd prefer it, if you were to go home, please. Dad needs you to help with the kids. Tell Heather I'll see her tomorrow."

Lizzie's tone was gentle enough, but still firm and it did not sit comfortably with Catrin.

"Well if you're quite sure you'll be alright up here alone." She said.

"I'm hardly alone Mother, am I."

"No, no, of course not, but you know what I mean.... I'm your mother."

"And I really need my mother to be a fantastic grandma to my two lovely children and to help my poor father. I'll be home tomorrow, but if anything happens I'll ring you immediately, I promise." She gave her mother a hug.

"Good bye then. Bye Max, Charlotte." Catrin looked as if she was about to give Max a hug as well, but then appeared to side step away and simply touched her arm adding, "I'm sure Mike will come through this."

Charlotte felt as if she should say something, but was struggling to think of the right words.

"Have a safe journey back Mrs Graham, the roads are not too bad and the traffic should have calmed down now, getting out of Bristol." Ever practical Max had stepped in to fill an awkward silence.

Charlotte still struggled to find the appropriate pastoral response. "Er, yes..." she stumbled "....yes, have a good journey."

As soon as Catrin had left the small waiting room Lizzie flopped down on one of the soft, rather clinical looking chairs. "I can't stand it any longer."

"It's been an exhausting day Lizzie. You're bound to feel worn out." Charlotte seemed to regain her pastoral heart, or at least she thought she had as she sat down opposite Lizzie.

"No, I don't mean Mike, well I do, of course I do. It's so awful, I'm desperate for him. I don't know how we'll cope. I don't know how he'll react, after all he's been through, trying so hard to fight against losing his leg and still it's come to this. I'm so glad you're here, I really am. I'm not sure if he'll be aware of it tonight or not. Max, can you and I go in soon? Charlotte, would you mind staying with Maureen and Vincent? They might appreciate having somebody to talk to and I'm sure they won't mind....., oh I'm so stupid, I keep on forgetting they've known about you two for ages."

Lizzie seemed to pause for breath, she wasn't really making much sense, but before either Max or Charlotte could speak she continued. "What I can't stand is the way we need to 'be careful not to upset Mother'. I mean it's none of her business."

305

"But its fully understandable she's upset, she worried about you, Mike, the future." Charlotte had adopted the pastoral stance, leaning slightly forward in her chair, but not too much so as to invade Lizzie's personal space.

"Charlie, I think you are a brilliant priest, but just at the moment, you are not helping, and quite frankly you are being rather obtuse."

Charlotte sat back in her chair as Max moved over towards her as if to shield her from Lizzie's apparently chided comments. Unexpectedly Lizzie began to laugh. "And you are so much a couple. It's lovely to see."

"Lizzie you're not making any sense. What on earth are you getting at?" Max once again came straight to the point.

"Just now, Mum was so obviously walking on egg shells around you two. You were standing at either side of the room, quite unconsciously trying not to offend her in any way. She quite naturally wanted to give you a hug Max, but then got cold feet. Perhaps she thought it would rub off or something. She's petrified about you two being a 'bad influence' on Heather, but in the same breath she likes you both. She is struggling like mad with you Charlie. She really respected you and was quite willing to accept you were a good priest, even though you were a woman, but gay as well, that's really made her question her ability to discern good character. She used to think she was good at that, you see, but now she's not so sure. Oh, but what gets me, is that she is so obviously wrong – and no-one will actually tell her. No-one is ever going to say to a homophobic Bishop's wife, 'You are wrong'!"

Whether it was the strain of the whole day, they didn't know, but Lizzie had raised her voice and seemed slightly hysterical.

"Mrs Tannin," the young nurse interrupted them, "excuse me, but Mr Tannin appears to be conscious and is asking for you."

"Really?" Liz quickly regained her composure, "Max, can you come too? Charlie, like I said, perhaps you could look after Mo and Vince."

"Of course," they both said together, which even in the circumstances, made all three smile recalling Lizzie's comment about 'so obviously a couple.'

Max and Liz waited patiently whilst a second nurse completed the regular observations. Mo and Vince had gone back to the waiting room. Mike was opening and closing his eyes as if waking up from a very deep sleep, struggling to get his bearings. Max noticed how little the nurse spoke to Mike, which surprised her. Once the nurse had finished she simply gestured that they could come in, but still said nothing.

"Not very talkative," said Max.

"Didn't you spot her name?" asked Lizzie, "Spowcoski, or something like that. She probably doesn't speak English very well, which is a bit worrying."

"Don't be prejudiced. As long as she can do her job, and I guess when most of your patients are unconscious the language barrier isn't really a problem."

"You have a point I guess. Hello darling, how you doing?" Lizzie returned to her position next to her husband. After blinking a few times, he finally managed to open his eyes.

"Bit .... thirsty." Mike's voice sounded very dry and gravelly.

"I wonder if he can have a drink, there's water here, but I'll go and check." Max realised she was glad of the excuse to leave the ward, even though she had only just arrived.

She was really not good at human illness, much better with the animals who couldn't tell her how much it hurt, or question her judgement and strangely enough the owners didn't seem to all that often either. She made a quick exit to find the nurse and regain her composure, before being the supportive big sister that Mike needed her to be.

"It's gone..... isn't it." Mike struggled to speak, reaching up pushing his oxygen mask away from his mouth.

"She's gone to see if you can have some water, she'll be back in a minute." Lizzie touched Mike's cheek.

"My leg, it's gone." The fogginess was clearing from Mike's eyes. He was fully conscious, although still groggy.

"Yes." Lizzie was honest. "They had no choice Mike. They saved your life. I still have you. Heather and Joshua still have a daddy"

"And I still have a little brother," Max walked back into the unit with the polish nurse in tow.

"Misser Tann, you can 'ave water now." She filled a beaker with a small amount of water, put in a straw and expertly helped Mike take a small sip by lifting his head, avoiding the numerous tubes and cables that appeared to be attached to every part of his body.

The nurse spoke to Lizzie and Max, "Ee can 'ave water, but only little, please. Like this," showing them the small amount they should give him. "You can put water on ees mouth too." She showed them how to moisten Mike's lips with a small pink sponge stuck on the end of a thin plastic stick. Once again, she checked the tube coming from Mike's stump. She briefly lifted the covers from the metal cradle that lay over the bed and visually checked the bandages over the wound.

"Is everything alright?" asked Max.

"Yes, is all good. No worry, please." She left Mike's bedside to attend to another patient on the unit.

"Is not all good," said Mike, even in his groggy state trying to mimic the nurse. "Is all bad, very bad." His voice was matter of fact. His attempt at humour by copying the nurse's accent was typical of her brother, but it was Max who saw the tear escape and trickle down his cheek. The two women sat either side of his bed. "Where's Mum and Dad?"

"Out in the waiting room with Charlotte," answered Lizzie.

"Charlie, good. Thank You." Mike closed his eyes again and appeared to drift off back to sleep.

Max wiped a second tear from her brother's cheek. "Not sure what to say to you little brother, but we'll be here for you. Charlie and me, and we're here for Lizzie and the kids, and just so's you know, you ain't sitting on your back side and being waited on left, right and centre." Lizzie looked a little shocked by Max's words but didn't see the squeeze Mike gave his sister's hand, and just the smallest hint of a smile in the corner of Mike's mouth.

The women stayed for a few minutes more, before going back to join Maureen, Vince and Charlotte.

Back in their room in the Travelodge a few hours later Max was feeling guilty.

"I'm not sure why I said that. He'd only just woken up. It was just minutes after he'd realised he was left with only one leg and I started going on about him not sitting around all day. How callous is that?"

"And tell me again what he said."

"Nothing."

"And what did he do?"

"Just squeezed my hand."

"And smiled!"

"Sort of."

"We'll see him in the morning and get going with the support you promised him." Charlotte handed Max a hot chocolate made from the sachet of instant powder left in the room.

"And that was pretty stupid too. Ow, that's hot." She put the chocolate down on the bedside table.

"What do you mean?" Charlotte climbed onto the bed next to Max.

"What support can we possibly give Mike? We've got enough going on ourselves, let alone Catrin controlling the whole situation and making sure we don't get a look in."

"Now that is a bit harsh."

"It's true. Lizzie's obviously getting fed up with her, but needs her to help with the children. Whatever she says, she needs her mum and dad and our presence causes problems."

"We'll still do our bit. What's brought this on? You were fine over supper. Your mum didn't eat much though."

"I noticed that too. Mind you, pasta isn't really her thing."

"It was the only place open nearby, either that or a burger."

"I know, it was fine, but she looked so old tonight."

"You're worried about them, aren't you? Worried about them, worried about Mike, worried about Lizzie, worried about us."

"I'm worried about you."

"We'll be okay. It's going to be tough, but we'll be fine. Let's get into bed."

"In a minute." Max took Charlotte's hand stopping her moving away, "I am worried about you. I mean all this with my family, but you are facing the most difficult decision of your whole life. You are throwing everything away because of me. What if it doesn't work out? What if we don't make it? Then there's the business. I can't expect you to support me all the time. You need your own life."

"Whoa, slow down. What's got into you? We're in this together. All the way. Yes, I admit I wish everything was not happening all at once. On the stress scale – well I don't think there's a scale big enough, but you're acting as if it is your fault. We've had this conversation numerous times. It's taken seven years of these conversations, before I finally plucked up the courage to take a stand."

"But you shouldn't have to. I'm frightened Charlie."

"Frightened? For Mike?"

"No for you and me."

"We'll cope. We'll do what we can for Mike, I'll sort out the parish and we'll be together. Together in all of this."

"I'm frightened you'll change, and if you change, we'll change. I love you. I don't want you to change Charlie." Max, completely out of character started to cry. Not big sobs, but heavy tears welling up in her eyes and quickly spilling over down both cheeks. She sat on the bed, making no attempt to wipe away the tears. "You can't just support me and my family, you can't just support me and the business, you certainly can't be just my wife, looking after the home and having my meals ready."

"I've no intention of just being.........."

"You need to do what you do. It's who you are. You care for people, you teach people, you marry them, baptise them and bury them. You get things done. You mend broken relationships..."

"Not always."

"Shut up. You annoy the pants off colleagues who dare to undermine your authority. You get loos fitted in old church buildings that are about to close down, get rid of the mouldy old pews and start up a Toddler Group."

"I've only done that once."

"And you could have helped a load of other parishes to do the same. You are an idiot."

"Thanks for your support."

"Charlie." Max was kneeling up on the bed facing Charlotte who was lying perched against the head board. "I don't think you should give it all up. I really don't. The more I think about it, the more I can't let you do it. Not for me – and not for us. You won't be the person I fell in love with."

"You fell in love with me, not the role."

"But it's part and parcel of who you are. You are a priest. You just happen to be a gay one." Max sucked in the tears that still poured down her face.

Charlotte leaned forward and dragged Max into a hug. "And I'm in love with you. And because of that I can't be a priest."

"You can," Max sniffed. "We just carry on like before."

"No longer an option." Charlotte attempted to brush away the tears from Max's face, but Max moved back, and simply looked at her partner through reddening eyes.

"Then we move abroad, where you can. I've been thinking. We could move to the States, or Canada one of those liberal churches. We could move to San Francisco or somewhere."

"Max, we're in Bristol because your baby brother has just lost his leg. We are here to support your family. Let's just get back to reality. Now I don't know about you, but I have had one helluva day. I need to go to bed and get some sleep."

"Nothing is signed yet though. The papers are not finalised. You could say you've changed your mind, go back to how it was before."

"Max, you are being ridiculous. You are tired. We've had a huge shock today. You are worried about Mike, but we need to stop this crazy conversation. We've been through all this. I know what I'm doing."

"No, we haven't, and no you don't."

"What do you mean? We've talked and talked about this."

"And every time, I've told you I don't want you to give up the priesthood."

"But you are just being supportive. In the end, I decided there was no choice."

"Exactly – *you* decided. You are proud of me – because I'm a vet, because I do a good job, because I'm successful, because I've got plans to expand the business." Max wasn't crying any more, and once again she knelt up on the bed.

"Of course I'm proud of you, you idiot. I don't understand. What are you driving at?"

"I'm proud of you too, so proud of who you are. Have you any idea how proud I was when you prayed with Lizzie in the restaurant? or when little Heather just took to you, trusted you, like she knew there was something special...."

"Don't be silly. Like I said you are just tired........"

"I'm not being silly. God gave you gifts. He called you, it was tested, proven and you do a fantastic job. I don't want you to give it up......" Charlotte's mobile rang.

"Ignore it," said Max.

"It's Sasha."

"She can leave a message."

"She's at home, in the Rectory, alone, with your dogs, I'm answering it," insisted Charlotte. "Hello? Sasha hi, is everything alright? .... Oh, I am so sorry, of course we should have......... no, it's not good news........... Naomi? ....I see yes....... Yes, I'm sorry we should have told you, ... yes, I can imagine.......... Of course not, you're a friend........... she is Lizzie's sister so of course........ thank you, Sash....... yes we do, we really do............ Oh, yes, I'm sorry........ yes, I know it affects you, ... I guess it was in the rush....... no I know I really am sorry.... okay, I won't, thank you...... oh yes, not till July....... yes, it is longer than I thought. The Bishop has done well..........I forgot to ask.......... yes............... I will, but look we'll see you tomorrow evening........ that would be lovely, I'll ask Max." Charlotte put her

314

hand over the phone. Sasha has offered to cook us a meal tomorrow evening. Is that okay with you? Max just nodded. "Yes, that's fine, thank you Sash, and I am really sorry for not ringing you earlier and I promise I'll speak to the property department as soon as I can........ no, I won't.... alright, see you tomorrow night. Have fun with the dogs. Bye"

"What was all that about?" Max appeared to have calmed down and was getting undressed.

"We didn't ring her and tell her about Mike. All she knew was he had had his operation and we both wanted to go up. Naomi had to ring her about something and told her. She said she felt just like a lodger and merely a dog sitter, rather than a friend, having to hear it from a client like that. Then she asked how I'd got on today and when I might have to move out of the Rectory and what was the response about her staying on for a bit until they had decided what to do with the building, but of course I'd forgotten to ask, so she was a bit upset about that too. But the dogs are fine and she's fine really, still offered to cook us a meal tomorrow."

"She might try and poison us!" laughed Max. "Come here." Max was by now undressed. "I'm sorry. I meant everything I said, but not the way I said it. I am worried about us though. What we have is so good, I don't want us to change and with everything else changing, yes I'm worried."

"I know, and I'm sorry that I'm still determined to stick with my principles."

"Honesty and integrity."

"That's them!"

"Ironic though, two of the best qualities anyone would want to have in a priest and because of them you're not going to be one anymore."

"You've accepted it again."

"Accepted. Yes, I know when you've made up your mind and deep down I know I won't change it, but every so often I need you to know that I don't like it. Time will tell, about this decision changing us, for the better or for the worse. No matter what you say, it will change us."

"Max, my darling, you are standing in front of me stark naked. You will get cold. I'm feeling rather over dressed, so let me get out of these clothes and we'll carry on this conversation in bed."

"Hmm, good idea."

Charlotte ignored the glint in her partner's eye. She got up from the bed taking the used cups into the small en suite.

Max got into bed.

Charlotte was getting undressed when she said to Max, "It's not like you to get so upset."

"Like I said, I'm worried, but as long as I have you, we'll be okay. I can support Mike and Lizzie and even tolerate Catrin if I have to, with you beside me."

"Oh, that's so sweet." Charlotte collected the cups from the sink and put them back onto the dresser before climbing in next to Max.

"So, Reverend Northam, will you marry me?"

"Of course I will Dr Tannin." Charlie hugged Max close to her. It was a light-hearted exchange they had shared numerous times and was something of a tradition between them.

"No, I mean it. I'm being serious this time. If you do go through with ditching the priesthood, you'll be free and available, so Charlotte

Veronica Northam, will you stay with me for the rest of our lives? Will you allow me to love and support you in sickness and in health, for richer, for poorer, for better, for worse till death do us part?"

"Are you actually proposing to me Dr Tannin?"

"Yes."

"Seriously?"

"Yes."

"My darling, you know the answer, but just for the record, yes, I will, but when we start making real plans let's choose a slightly more romantic setting than a Travelodge in the middle of Bristol with your parents just the other side of that wall and your sister-in-law on the other side of that one!"

"San Francisco?"

"Don't start that again...... but I suppose we could always go there for our honeymoon!"

Chapter 23

The polish nurse was busy removing all but one of the cannulas from Mike's body. The drain on the stump remained. Mike was about to be transferred back to the main orthopaedic ward. Desperate to get back to her children and ready them for a trip to see their father the following day, Lizzie had left at lunchtime having reassured herself that Mike was in good hands. Maureen and Vince had decided to stay on for another few days until Mike was finally transferred to Gloucester, but had taken a break whilst Max and Charlotte helped to settle Mike back onto the ward, before they too journeyed back to Devon to face a disgruntled Sasha.

Max was bravely chatting to her brother as he tried not to squirm too much as electrodes were ripped from his skin and tubes were pulled from his veins. Charlotte sat close but made sure she was not in the way. Mike had made an incredible recovery from the operation the previous day. He appeared very positive and enjoyed several jokes with his sister. He was obviously in a lot of pain and it was easy to tell when he needed a dose of morphine which he was able to provide for himself through the small pump still inserted into his stomach. It would be sometime before he was free of painkillers.

Charlotte had managed to speak to Linda and Sasha that morning and was pleased that everything appeared under control back in the parish. Linda had not asked too many questions which was a relief, but apparently had quizzed Sasha about the dogs. She would get more of the story later that evening.

Max was growing more confident around the hospital and seemed to provide her brother with the strength he needed. In fact, her outburst the previous evening appeared to have cleared the air for her. She had been nervous and on edge before. She had woken that morning feeling positive about the future, although nothing had changed and her brother was still, at that stage, critically ill in Intensive Care. Six hours had made a big difference and now they were moving back to the main ward, it was four in the afternoon.

They were soon trundling down the corridors of Frenchay Hospital. The Polish nurse was accompanying them, along with two porters. Both Max and Charlotte were carrying various bags belonging to Mike. Mike winced every time the porters pushed him over a bump in the flooring, or over a door threshold. Frenchay Hospital is made up of a series of old buildings joined together by bricked in corridors which snake through the grounds, disorientating even some of the permanent staff let alone patients in a morphine induced haze or visitors battling to juggle bags, coats and a newly acquired Zimmer frame, left by a well-meaning physiotherapist moments before the party left for the new ward. Unfortunately, the physio was called to another patient with chest problems before he could explain why he had brought a Zimmer frame to somebody who until that moment had not even been allowed to sit upright.

Once on the ward, Mike was subjected to a series of medications directly into the remaining cannula. He was given a bottle to relieve himself, the catheter having been removed and asked if he wanted a bed pan or if he thought he could use a commode.

He looked across at his sister. "And if you mention potty training, I'll somehow hop over there and give you a piece of mind."

"I'd do nothing of the sort, I'm just pleased you don't have to sit on those nappies any longer."

"I warned you," Mike laughed as he tried to haul himself up using the bar above his bed, but quickly slumped back with a huge groan as pain once again shot through his stump and into his body.

"Steady superman, less than twenty-four hours ago, you had only just come out of major surgery." Max reached over and rearranged her brother's pillows.

Thank you for coming up. I'm not sure how you both managed to be here, but I'm so grateful. Lizzie would have stayed longer if you hadn't been here."

"Oh Mike, I'm sorry, we would have gone..." Charlotte started to apologise.

"No, no I mean it's a good thing. She needs to get back to the children. I don't like her being away from Joshua, nor does she, and Heather needs her mummy. Once I'm back in Gloucester it should be easier for her. All this travelling and being away from home it's a nightmare for her. You two being here meant she felt confident to leave me, that's what I mean. So really - thank you."

"Will you cope with Mum and Dad being around?" asked Max.

"Yeah, they're okay. They are quite amazing really. How do you think they are coping? Charlie, what do you think? You seem miles away, in a dream world."

"Hmm, what? Oh sorry, I was just thinking about something back in Langford. Your mum and dad? Looking a bit tired I guess, but they are made of strong stock, they'll manage. They will enjoy seeing the children tomorrow. They're going to take Heather to the zoo, aren't they?"

"Something like that. I suppose Catrin will come too."

"Mike don't be like that," chastised Max.

"Can't believe she hasn't got on your nerves yet."

"Well, if I'm honest..."

"See!"

"Listen you two, I hate to break up this sisterly, brotherly mutual support business but Max I think you and I should make a move soon." Charlotte was pleased that Mike seemed so much more positive and hated to drag Max away, but two dogs and a lodger with a meal awaited their return. She was also feeling a little guilty about missing the meeting with the architect, but kept it to herself.

"Back to life in the fast lane," Mike said with a heavy sarcasm.

"Not for much longer." Charlotte spoke under her breath not so much in response to Mike but from her thoughts in an unchartered land she had not yet visited. Mike misunderstood and assumed she was talking about his own predicament.

"Might be a while though Charlie." Mike sounded very positive and almost excited, "The physio was saying it would be a few weeks before the wound is strong enough for me to put any weight through the stump."

"We were here, when she told you Mike. Remember? It's great to hear you so positive, but take it easy bruv, one step at a time.... doh! I'm sorry, that was a bit insensitive."

In an innate response to her indiscretion she made to slap her own head, but Mike started laughing which broke a tense moment for all three of them, Charlotte included, who was also quietly berating herself for the reference to her own situation which Mike had thankfully misconstrued.

At that moment, Maureen and Vince walked back onto the ward and for the first time in days were mightily relieved to see their son in such good spirits.

The road to recovery for Mike would not be without its crisis points. There would be times when he would swear at his physiotherapists completely out of character. He found himself still battling to accept what had happened and would face long days of depression. He had to face more questioning from police and give evidence in court at the inquest about the accident. He also found it hard to be cocooned in illness and disability whilst his sister's life was turned upside down by circumstances beyond her control. He was trapped by his own limitations for many months before he had the strength and the ingenuity to repay Max and Charlotte by offering his own support in their crisis moments.

Chapter 24

For a few weeks, it was as if nothing had changed or was about to change in the East Dartmoor Group of Parishes. The frosts lost their hold on the Devon moorland much faster than they did in the Gloucester countryside that now took up much of Max's precious spare time.

For three weeks Charlotte concentrated fully on her work, her staff, her wardens, the projects that needed her attention. Occasionally Linda mentioned that Charlotte looked a little preoccupied about something, but Charlotte only spoke of the friend in Bristol who was ill. Patch and Stitch stayed a little more often, but without attracting much comment from parishioners. She didn't travel to Bristol in that time, only when Mike was finally transferred back up to Gloucester did she make the trip with Max and finally get to see Lizzie in her own home, much to the delight of an excitable little Heather who insisted on showing Charlotte her room and all her dolls.

It was Sasha who exhibited the greatest degree of stress during those first few weeks of apparent calm. In a momentary lapse, she let slip to Linda that she supposed she would soon have to start looking for somewhere else to live. Linda was immediately concerned and asking if there had been a disagreement between Charlotte and Sasha and started quizzing Sasha asking if that was the reason Charlotte had appeared so distant on occasions. Sasha made a rapid recovery and explained that her consultative work was taking off in Bristol to such an extent that she may have to relocate. It appeared to satisfy Linda but alerted Charlotte to the thin ground they were treading when Sasha confessed her *faux pas*.

Whether or not that small indiscretion had been the trigger for the events that followed will remain a mystery. Charlotte will maintain that such an insignificant exchange would never have sparked a major parish outcry, but the real culprit remained allusive and may never have realised their part in the ensuing trauma that plagued Charlotte's last months as an ordained minister in the Church of England.

It had been decided to make the announcement to the parish at one of the few times when all parishes would be represented. Once a year the benefice held an annual meeting. At this meeting reports would be given from each benefice working group and each individual church. The shared accounts would be received and the budget for the coming year announced. It was an opportunity to discuss with the benefice as a whole any major building work that needed doing in a particular church or a particular project that would be tackled over the coming year.

It would come as a shock and overshadow the meeting but having discussed the alternatives with Clive King, the Archdeacon, the Bishop had agreed with Charlotte that making the announcement at the joint meeting was by far the best solution and would give the benefice just over three months to get used to the idea before Charlotte actually left. His only insistence was that the Archdeacon would be present at the meeting and deal with any questions about the eventual vacancy and the process involved in replacing Charlotte as Rector of the benefice.

It was a good plan. Charlotte would make her statement about deciding to take a break from parish ministry to follow a different career path. She had reluctantly agreed not to give the full story at that stage.

She would not even declare that she was leaving ministry completely, in fact there was still some disagreement about the difference in resigning her orders and simply leaving full-time stipendiary ministry on a long-term basis. The Bishop had made a U-turn and was still keen for her to remain in Holy Orders. It was still in the hands of the registrar.

Charlotte felt like a pawn in some complicated game of politics, power and pride between the Bishop, the Church Commissioners who held her pension and the Chancellor who interpreted Church Law. It was ironic that as the wrangling continued Charlotte's resolve to resign grew stronger, whereas it was her Bishop and her lover who wanted her to keep her options open. Without realizing it they were in total agreement, although they had not met since the evening in the palace kitchen several weeks earlier.

Mike was sat in his wheelchair in the day room of the rehabilitation ward in Gloucester Hospital finishing his toast and contemplating the day when the ward volunteer wandered in offering him a selection of newspapers. He chose a cheap tabloid, deciding it was all he felt up to on that particular morning. Flicking through the gossip about Prince Harry's latest girlfriend and another footballer's affair, his eye caught the headline to a small article on the fourth page.

Secret Sex in Devon Vicarage

Sources close to a rural church community in the heart of the Devon countryside have alleged that their vicar is engaged in a secret love affair with her live-in female lodger. The Vicar; Rev Charlotte Northam of the East Dartmoor Group of Parishes was unavailable for comment but has apparently evicted her long-term lover from the Vicarage to avoid losing her job as rector of the church she now works. This is just the latest in a long line of sordid affairs and sex frolics that have plagued the Church of England in recent years. A parish spokesman commented that news of the affair will come as a blow to the close-knit community. Other sources suggest that concerns have already been raised with reports of loud music coming from the vicarage until the early hours, underage drinking and roaring motorbikes on the driveway disturbing the peace and tranquillity of the pretty village of Langford. Rev Northam's own future still hangs in the balance.

Mike was shocked. He couldn't believe what he had just read. He looked again at all the names, but there was no doubt. He read the article again, three times, in stunned silence, before retrieving his mobile phone from his track suit trousers and making the phone call to his sister. It was early she would still be at home.

The answer phone in the rectory study took the third call of the day. Charlotte hadn't heard the phone from the shower it was not yet 6.30am.

Sasha was in London and still asleep when her mobile buzzed into action at just 6.45am.

"Mike, what's wrong it's not even seven in the morning." Max was out walking Patch and Stitch when Mike called.

"Have you seen Charlie recently?"

"Of course I have, we visited you only last week Mike." Max's voice was full of concern, Mike often had lapses of memory but a call this early with another apparent confusion really worried her.

"Is everything alright between you?"

"Well, yes, of course. Can't say life is simple with everything going on, but we're ok. What's this all about? Can't I ring you back? I'm out walking the dogs."

"Then perhaps you should get yourself a copy of 'The Sun' newspaper."

"Oh, sorry Mike is there something about the accident?"

"No, it's Charlotte, the press has got hold of something, page four, bottom right hand corner."

"About her leaving? How did they get hold of that? It hasn't even been announced yet, and any way it's hardly news worthy stuff."

"It's worse, something about her and Sasha. I'm really sorry sis, it's not very nice. Ring me when you get home, I'll stay in the day room I can use the phone in here."

Mike rang off leaving Max confused. She left the dogs tied up outside the newsagent on the corner and brought the newspaper. Outside the shop, she opened up to the page Mike had said. Her eye called the headline straight away, but she closed the paper quickly, knowing it was the article but not wanting to believe it.

But a moment later, once she had composed herself, still outside the shop with two impatient dogs baying for her attention, she opened it up again and read the article.

In her coat pocket, she gripped her mobile, not knowing whether to ring Charlotte immediately, to ring back her brother or perhaps to call Sasha in London. She was angry, she was shocked, she was upset, she felt all eyes were looking at her, even though the street was deserted. She cut the walk very short and hurried back to the cottage.

Charlotte heard her answer phone beeping at her as she reached the bottom of the stairs. She checked the hall clock, thinking that perhaps she had overslept, but no, it was still before seven. She pushed open the study door saw the machine beeping away. 'Oh, good grief, I'll deal with you in a minute, I need a cup of tea first.' The phone rang again. Rather than answer it she decided to let the answer phone screen the call. If it was pastoral emergency it would give her a couple of moments to get her head together before responding. She listened.

"Reverend Northam, my name is Paul Granger from the Times newspaper. I'm sorry to call you so early but I wanted to give you an opportunity to respond to today's shocking story. I'm sure you would want our readers to learn the truth..........."

Charlotte picked up the phone.

"This is Charlotte Northam."

"Oh, good morning. How are you today?"

"I'm fine thank you, can I ask you what this is all about?"

"The story in The Sun Mrs Northam."

"It's Ms Northam, or I prefer Charlotte. I'm sorry I really don't know what you are talking about."

"Have you any comment, er Charlotte?"

"Comment about what?"

"About the article, about your affair."

"What article? I've already said I don't know of any article." She heard a newspaper being pushed through her door, which surprised her as she didn't have a paper delivered. Still with the phone to her ear, she opened the study curtain to see an older man not a young newspaper deliverer walk back through the rectory gateway.

Paul Granger continued talking as Charlotte went to the door with the phone in her hand and bent down to pick up a copy of The Sun.

"I just want to get the facts straight Ms Northam. It's a rather disturbing account of your lifestyle."

"I have no idea what you are talking about......" She took the newspaper back to her desk and started flicking through the pages, but before she got to the article a piece of advice from a journalist friend suddenly came back to her.

"Mr Granger, I would be only too willing to give you a full statement, can I take your telephone number and I will certainly ring you back within the hour."

"Well, it will only take a moment to clarify the situation Ms Northam, if I can just ask you a couple of questions."

"I'm very sorry Mr Granger, I am willing to answer your questions but you will need to give me a phone number. I also need to ensure I am talking to the most appropriate person. I am certain you understand Mr Granger, a journalist of your high calibre."

"Yes, of course Reverend. I will expect clarification on this matter within the hour." She had by now spotted the headline and had to ask twice for the number to be repeated as she struggled to keep her concentration. Having made sure Charlotte had the correct mobile number the journalist rang off.

Sasha was startled when her phone rang early that morning.

"Naomi! You are up and about early but could I possibly ring you back after eight when I'm at my desk?" Sasha was used to Naomi's eagerness when it came to deadlines for work, but ringing at 6.45am was a bit much.

"It's not work Sasha, I wanted to know if you were alright."

Naomi had folded back The Sun newspaper at page four and made a little square so she could hold the article in one hand and the phone in the other.

"Well, to be honest....."

"I knew it, it can't be true. I don't believe it. She always seemed so nice. I knew you liked her but she and Max seemed so close." Naomi was either excited or anxious, Sasha could not quite work out which.

"Unless of course, it's both..... no, no way."

"Naomi, I'm fine. It's just a bit early. But I haven't understood a word you've said."

"You need to get hold of a copy of The Sun newspaper, page four. No wait, let me read it out to you." And she did.

There was silence.

"Sasha, are you still there?............ Sasha?" Naomi's voice was suddenly almost frightened and full of concern.

"Yes....... I'm still here...........that is the biggest load of crap I have ever heard. Where on earth did you read it?"

Sasha knew she had turned pale, she felt physically sick and in fact thought she would need to make a dash to the bathroom any second.

"It's not true then?"

"No, it's not bloody true. Who the hell do you think I am? And Charlotte, oh my God, this will destroy her. Underage drinking? Hidden sex orgies? It's rubbish."

"It didn't say orgy."

"Bloody hell Naomi, you know what people are like."

Sasha suddenly remembered she was talking to a respected client.

"Oh God, I'm sorry Naomi. Look thank you for warning me, I doubt Charlie would have seen it. I'd better warn her before she's caught off guard. Can I speak to you later?"

"Please do. But there's absolutely no truth in it?" Naomi sounded very earnest.

"No, of course not." Although in the back of her mind, Sasha was thinking about the sneaky beer James would consume when he stayed with his aunt and the late hour he sometimes roared up the drive. "Er, which paper did you say?"

Naomi gave Sasha the details again before ringing off. Then she agonised for the next ten minutes before deciding to ring her sister, but decided against ringing her father she would discuss that little dilemma with Lizzie.

Charlotte heard her mobile ringing from the front room, where she had left it the night before.

She missed the call.

It was Max. Picking it up she started to ring the number. But then rang off. Max didn't read any newspapers unless she was on holiday with time to kill. There was no way she would have heard about the article yet. She knew she would need to ring her, but needed a mug of steaming coffee in her hand. The main landline rang again. Charlotte remembered the other messages on the answer phone and was brought back to reality wondering if there really was a pastoral emergency demanding her attention. Once again, she picked up the phone.

"Reverend Northam?"

This time it was a female voice, speaking before Charlotte had chance to give the usual 'Langford Rectory', greeting.

"Er yes, this is Charlotte Northam, can I ask who's speaking?"

"Reverend Northam, glad to get through to you, sorry it's a little early in the day, I'm following up on a news item in today's newspaper. Isabel Sweet, researcher from the BBC, Radio Four. Your story has caused quite a stir."

"Er, Miss Sweet, I'm terribly sorry, but I've only just discovered the story myself, I've not really read the article.........." Charlotte suddenly stopped.

"Reverend? Are you still on line Ms Northam?"

"I'm not on air am I?" whispered Charlotte.

"Goodness gracious, no Reverend Northam. We would never do that, but we would be most interested in taking a response from you to play after the eight o'clock news."

"This evening?"

"This morning."

Charlotte took a sharp intake of breath.

"I'm sorry, this is all such a shock, it's just not true, I've no idea where it's come from.... I'm sorry I need to speak to the Diocese.... I'm sorry I can't talk to you at the moment, but .... er yes," Charlotte regained a small amount of composure, slowed down her breathing and once again was back in control.... "I would be only too willing to speak to you Isabel but not just at the moment, can I ring you back in an hour or so?"

"That's cutting it a bit fine Miss Northam, we want this on air at 8.10am."

"I'll do my best."

And Charlotte made a note of Miss Sweet's phone number with a promise to ring within the hour. She then listened to the other three messages, one was from the Telegraph left the previous evening at 11.00pm, which Charlotte had not heard and was very annoyed about, she couldn't help but wonder if she had answered that call this mess could have been stopped before it had really started. The second was from a local independent radio station left at 6.30am that morning, the third claimed to be somebody 'on her side' who only wanted the truth, she assumed that was the call she had heard as she got out of the shower. There was no name only a mobile number, which she decided to ignore. It was just before seven, she put on the local radio and prayed she was not one of the features.

Max got home just in time to switch on the radio. She was sure this was just a small article that would be ignored by any self-respecting journalist, regarded as tabloid gossip only fit for the rubbish bin.

Bishop David often listened to the local radio station after his morning prayers and before spending an hour at his desk. He liked to be aware of local news as well as national headlines.

'A rather disturbing headline has hit a national newspaper today about local priest Reverend Charlotte Northam. Reported in 'The Sun' this morning, it appears that all is far from well in the sleepy Dartmoor village. The newspaper reports scenes of drunken sex and loud music eroding the peace of this quiet little village. So far Reverend Northam has been unavailable for comment, your local radio station will bring you up to date with events as soon as more details become available. But for now, back to Matt and a travel update........'

In Langford Charlotte turned off the radio and sat in silence at the large wooden kitchen table allowing her coffee to go cold. She heard the landline ring again and again, rightly or wrongly she ignored it. Her mobile vibrated and buzzed next to her, she ignored that too.

In Tavistock, Max allowed the travel report to merge into the music but she didn't hear it. She tried to call Charlotte, there was no answer.

In Exeter, Bishop David was already calling his press officer.

In London Sasha had read the article for herself in a small coffee shop around the corner from where she lived. She wondered just how soon it would be before the press would evade the gravel path of the Rectory and how long it would be before she could ever return. She also tried to ring Charlotte again and again, but got no answer.

It was not long before there was loud banging at the Rectory Door. The vultures had landed. Eager for their own pickings from a story of such human interest wondering how long they could keep it alive and fresh for the public to chew over. It had all the right ingredients, sex, religion, scandal, fallen morality, even the gay issue, it was all there.

Charlotte remained still and shocked. She read the short insignificant article for the hundredth time. It was full of lies, but even more worrying was the slight echo of truth that permeated the story. She had no idea who could have sold such a story to the tabloid press. She assumed somebody somewhere had done it for money. She couldn't get the thought out of her mind that somebody in the parish had decided to make her existence unbearable and was trying to force her resignation. "If only, if only, if only............" She said out loud.

There was a loud bang on the back door and a sharp rap on the window. Charlotte jumped. Had they heard her? She stayed still, like a wild animal caught in the headlights of an on-coming car.

"We just want to hear your side of the story Reverend Northam. We're sure it's not true, perhaps if you just speak to us we can get this all cleared up." The loud male voice was coming from behind the back door.

Charlotte felt very frightened. She decided to ring the police.

Having assured her they would send a patrol car she then rang Max.

"I don't know what to do," her voice tense. "What will they think of me? The curtains are still drawn. I promised to ring back, it's already half past seven. The phone is going incessantly, but I'm scared to move. I'm under siege."

"I'll come over....."

"NO!" Charlotte shouted, then dropped her voice again to a horse whisper.

"No, don't do that, they'll be all over you," She pleaded. "I just need to put the story straight, but I'm afraid of making things worse. I mean, there have been complaints about James and his motorbike so that's true. And I've allowed him to drink beer on the premises ever since he was fifteen for goodness sake. And it's true that Sasha has to find somewhere else to live."

"Yeah, but you're not evicting her are you."

"No, but its close enough."

"Not because of some sordid love affair gone wrong."

Silence

"Charlie......"

"No of course not."

"You're sure on that, you went rather quiet."

"Of course I'm sure..... Max this is not how it was supposed to be. This was supposed to be about us, about honesty, about me acting out of integrity, if I leave now it will look as if I'm running away. Why couldn't

I have just told the parish when I wanted to, none of this would have happened. Who on earth could have done this?"

"I could hazard a guess."

"Who?"

"Philip Dixon."

"He wouldn't. Surely he's not that conniving or mean." Another loud rap at the back door.

"And you've rung the police?" Charlotte could hear the fear in Max's voice.

"Yes, but they're miles away and I doubt my life is actually in danger, just my reputation and career, well that doesn't matter anyway. I bet the Bishop will stop trying to keep me on after all this. Oh, David! I should ring him, or the Archdeacon. No I have to ring the press officer, but I'll need to go to the study, Maybe I should just get this over with."

"Calm down sweetheart, please. Ring this press officer first. He's probably been trying to ring you himself."

"*She* might have done; the phone's being going non-stop."

"Sorry, 'she'. Then ring her."

"Yes, I will. Thanks. I'll ring you later. Be careful though, the press may somehow drag you into this."

"I'll be very careful, for your sake and ours. By the way have you rung Sasha?"

"Oh, no I haven't."

"I'll ring her, at least she's in London and not in the Rectory."

Charlotte spoke to the press officer, explaining what was going on outside with around three journalists eager for her attention, or blood. At

337

which Annette insisted that Charlotte remain very calm and cool headed. She explained that if Charlotte felt strong enough it would be better to speak them. Hiding would only arouse further suspicion. Annette then took down the numbers that Charlotte had already obtained for the local radio station, Radio Four and the Telegraph. The confident press officer suggested she would ring on Charlotte's, behalf and with the agreement of the Bishop express their support for a well-respected priest. She also explained that the Diocese would have to protect themselves and would add that a full investigation would be carried out into the allegations and if there was any truth in the story full disciplinary action would be taken.

Charlotte was rather taken aback at how forthright Annette was being, but had to agree it was the only way forward. Annette also assured Charlotte that she was fully versed with the real story of Charlotte's imminent departure and they would have to think carefully how and when to release a formal press statement in the light of current developments. Again, Charlotte was a little shocked that Annette had been briefed on her situation. It was almost as if the diocese had been expecting something like this to happen. But she didn't question it.

All that was left was how to deal with the press actually standing on Charlotte's doorstep. Annette quickly dictated a statement that Charlotte could read to the gathered elite of the local and tabloid press once Charlotte had invited them inside into the kitchen and offered coffee and tea.

"In other words, get them on your side, enough time has lapsed already, you need to act quickly. I know it is distressing to have them banging on your door, but you have to get the upper hand, be calm, be confident, do not look fearful or guilty. Don't answer too many questions. Whatever you do, don't get into a long and complicated debate. Read them the statement, give them each a copy and stick to your story. Let the diocese investigate not the press. Are you looking smart?"

"Ur, yes I suppose so."

"Make up? Collar on? Smart skirt."

"Well Yes, I've got a funeral this morning, I've actually got black trousers on, is that a problem?"

"Are they smart? Is it a smart suit? Shame it's black though, you might look a bit austere. But you've no time now, throw a coloured scarf on, take away the starkness a bit, but not a red one, that really would be the death nail."

"This is stupid, it's not happening to me."

"Yes, it's hard, and yes it's happening. I'm sorry Charlotte but you have to deal with it. Just tell me one thing is there any truth in this ridiculous story?"

Pause

"Charlotte? Tell me this is not true, please." Annette's voice was anxious.

"It's not the truth, by a long way, but I can see where certain elements have arisen, but no, it is not true and certainly not the bit about sex with my lodger."

"Good, that's alright then, we'll talk later. Now good luck." She rang off.

Charlotte sat on the bottom stair just in front of the large Rectory front door to put on her shoes. Standing up she checked her clothing, put her hand through her hair to give it some volume and gripped the door handle firmly.

339

Opening the door, she found two journalists still on the step, one female, one male. They were talking to each other like old friends. Perhaps they were. She saw two more people in a car at the end of the driveway. Talking to them was a familiar figure. Philip had indeed made himself available for comment it seemed.

He glanced up and walked boldly towards her. She watched him, as the two journalists on the door step started to ask her questions. The voice inside her told her to stay calm, to react courteously towards the Mr Dixon, to not give the journalists any more of a story than they already had. She turned her attention to the journalists.

"Good morning, I'm so sorry for the delay, this has all come as a bit of a shock. Would you care to step inside for some coffee? And I will be than happy to answer your questions."

"That's very kind of you Ms Northam, thank you. We are from The Daily Mail," and the male reporter showed Charlotte his press card. His female colleague had a camera.

"Do you mind if we take a picture reverend?" She asked.

"Not at all, but please, can we do this inside. I believe one of my parishioners would like a word with me." Charlotte hurried them inside, but remained outside to greet her rather excited looking Reader.

"Rector. I came straight over when I heard the news. Dreadful business. Pack of lies of course. That's what I've just been telling those people." He waved in the direction of the car. The two people still sat inside appeared to be taking great interest in the conversation on the Rectory step.

"Yes Philip, it is a dreadful business." She kept very calm. "I wonder, would you mind perhaps coming back later on, I think I should speak to the press and get this matter cleared up and I have a funeral over in St Winnoc's at eleven."

"Well I thought perhaps I could help." Mr Dixon peered past her into the Rectory obviously trying to get a glimpse of the two reporters who were hovering just inside, probably wondering if there was a story to be had from the keen parishioner on the door step.

"I'm sure you been more then helpful Philip, if you wouldn't mind." Charlotte started to close the door, she spotted the occupants of the car getting out, as a police patrol car pulled up outside the rectory gates.

'This day could get no worse', she thought to herself. 'Why did I call the police? How stupid can I get?'

The policeman intercepted the two men in the car, whilst the policewoman made her way towards Charlotte and Philip. Charlotte was very aware of the reporters behind her in the hall lapping up all the detail.

"We received a call about harassment madam, is everything alright?" The police officer took out her Identification and flashed it in front of Charlotte, looking at Philip.

"Yes, I'm sorry. I panicked earlier."

"The report says you 'thought you were under siege', Reverend Northam." The officer was joined by her colleague who in turn was followed by the two people in the other car.

'I still feel I'm under siege,' Charlotte thought to herself.

"There was a lot of banging and shouting, but it turns out these people were just anxious to speak to me."

"So, there's nothing wrong then Reverend Northam?" the male officer spoke.

"No, I am so terribly sorry to have called and wasted your time." Charlotte bit her lip, she could just imagine the next newspaper article. 'Sex crazed vicar wastes valuable police time.'

"Well, we'll leave it there on this occasion. Perhaps a little less hasty in the future, Reverend. But we are here to help, remember that." The officer turned to go but addressed Philip as he went

"Sir".

Mr Dixon followed the police officers across the gravel path. Charlotte could hear the phone ringing in the background, but ignored it. She welcomed the other two reporters in, who claimed to be from another local paper.

In the kitchen, sat around the familiar wooden table, having stalled the questions by serving coffee and biscuits Charlotte suggested she read out her side of the story.

This morning I was shocked to discover that an unfounded article about my private life had found its way into a national newspaper. I am appalled by the content of the article, none of which is true, and I expect a full apology from the newspaper concerned.

"But your Lodger is looking for an alternative place to live Reverend Northam, we have it on good authority," stated one of the reporters from the car.

"That is true, but not for the reason reported in the article."

"Can I ask you, for our readers, to confirm the reason?"

"She has decided to move on. Lodgers do have a right to do that."

Charlotte reminded herself not to get defensive just remain calm and keep to the facts, don't offer any opinion. She was careful not to use Sasha's name.

"And the motorbike episodes? There have been complaints made, have there not?" The local reporter seemed very well versed in the background to the story.

"I have a nephew who often rides his motorbike over here."

"Late at night I understand."

"He has been known to arrive after 10pm on occasions yes."

"It seems a little late to be visiting an auntie."

"He knows he can come here anytime."

"Problems at home?" this question came from the male reporter from the Daily Mail.

"No more than any teenager. Look," Charlotte knew she was beginning to sound a little exasperated, "I'm really sorry you've had a wasted journey. As you can see there really is no story here. I don't know where this came from."

"Just a picture then Reverend, and we'll be on our way." This time the female photographer was asking the questions.

"Yes, if you must," Charlotte winced as she heard her the edge in her own voice, she recovered her composure "Yes, of course, that will be fine, Where?"

"Just here will be fine. In the kitchen, in the heart of the home, nice and relaxed." And the photographer started clicking away taking several photos before apparently finding one that satisfied her.

Charlotte stood and was preparing to show the gathered press towards the front door.

343

"I am sorry for this intrusion so early reverend, but we really did want to know your side of the story. Just one more question if I may..." the Daily Mail was being persistent. "Are you in a committed relationship?"

Charlotte felt what little colour she had drain from her face. She held on to the door frame as she felt her legs turn to jelly and wondered how much of the reaction had been noted.

She steadied herself.

This was the reason she was leaving and she had wanted it to be out in the open. She had nothing to lose by being honest. Everything was in place. The bishop knew, her family knew, there was nothing to stop her being truthful. Yet this was not the way she wanted her parishes to find out. Not only that, she feared for Max who might also be tracked down and hounded.

"Reverend Northam?" badgered the journalist.

The flash of the camera momentarily blinded her, but seemed to snap her out of the trance like state she had fallen into.

"Please," Charlotte said. "You have your photographs and your statement. I'm afraid I have my duties to attend to."

"Will you answer my colleague's question?" The journalist from the local paper wanted to know.

"Isn't it rather unusual for journalists from different papers to question people at the same time?" Charlotte was almost unconsciously evading the question as she felt an enormous pressure and an almost burning sensation deep inside.

"Not at all, we find collaboration very effective Ms Northam." The photographer raised the camera again, only to be restrained gently by her co-reporter.

"I think we have enough photos now Kate, and enough material for our follow up."

"Come on Doug..." the photographer whispered under her breath towards her colleague. "Look at her. Guilt written all over her face. Priceless!"

"No, this is too invasive, we've got a response."

"What! Are you serious? Doug, don't you dare go soft......" but Kate was cut off as Doug scraped back the kitchen chair and gestured to Charlotte to show them out. They heard the phone ringing in the background.

The two local reporters also stood up, but didn't move at first.

"Gentlemen, let me show you out." Charlotte's voice had regained its strength.

"A word of advice Ms Northam," said one of them "by avoiding our questions you have already admitted your guilt. Do not be taken in by this gentlemen's apparent concern."

Kate and her colleague shot a glance towards the local reporter. Charlotte was standing between them looking at each in turn, her mind still in turmoil, trying to work out the games being played, still trying to find the right response. She had names rushing through her mind, Max, Lizzie, David, Sasha, Catrin, Mike, Maureen, Vince, James who had also dragged into this with his wretched motorbike and boyish persuasion convincing his aunt that the occasional lager in the safety of home would not hurt anyone. Names were real people, real people who would be hurt now, whatever she said. Linda, Derek, Sam. Who had managed to leak the story? She thought of Sally at the Palace whose day would likely to be littered with phone calls from the press. And she thought of Linda, about to walk into chaos.

After a momentary hesitation, Charlotte said "Sit down, I've had enough of this."

She took a copy of the Sun, opened it out to page four and slowly read the article out loud.

"Let me tell what is true" she said. "I have a lodger who will be leaving the Rectory. I sometimes play host to my teenage nephew in my home who rides a motorbike and enjoys the fact that the rectory is far enough away from neighbours so he can play his music at high volume. And in the privacy of my own home and under my direct supervision he and I have on occasions shared a beer."

"And is your lodger leaving because of your relationship?" It was the local journalist who asked the question, without a pausing for a moment. He didn't expect the sudden explosion of laughter that escaped from Charlotte.

Once she started she couldn't stop. Tears started rolling down her cheeks. The reporters looked at each other. Kate looked at her camera, but made no attempt to unleash its power. Surrounding Charlotte was shocked silence. Charlotte didn't even know herself whether she was laughing or crying but the release she felt was cathartic and the laughter and the tears continued.

The doorbell went.

Charlotte made no attempt to answer it, she didn't appear to even hear it.

The reporters had been stunned into inaction. And then the laughter stopped and Charlotte slumped onto the floor and dissolved into real tears, all the pent-up emotion of the past months flowing out in front of four reporters eager for a story. Now they had one.

The front door was unlocked and Linda let herself in. She would not normally arrive this early, but she had of course, seen the article. She had tried to ring her employer but receiving no answer had decided to turn up in person. She had passed a few people outside, who were out early walking dogs, or just out walking and who had decided to take a route past the Rectory. News travels fast in villages. It was just after 8am.

Linda heard the hysterical laughter and got to the kitchen door just in time to see Charlotte slump to the floor. She looked at the four people staring in shock at the spectacle in front of them. She saw the note pads and the pens. One had a Dictaphone that looked as if it was still recording.

One of the men stood as soon as Linda came in.

"If you are another reporter......"

"I'm Charlotte's secretary... what the hell........."

"It's alright," said the woman with the camera, "we're going, unless I can do anything."

"Looks like you've done enough." Linda was kneeling beside Charlotte, offering her some kitchen roll as a hanky.

"We weren't .... We're not vultures. Tell her we'll use the statement, that's all. But when she's feeling better perhaps we could come back and......" the look Linda gave stopped the young local reporter from saying anything more.

They all left.

Linda held Charlotte for several minutes before her sobs started to calm down. She said nothing, just kept Charlotte close, even when she gave a half-hearted attempt to pull away before giving in to Linda's care.

Eventually Charlotte became calm. She then returned Linda's hug. "I'm alright" she said.

"No, boss, you're not. And yes, I've heard about the article, so have half the village, probably all of the villages by now."

"Oh."

"Don't talk about it now, I'll make you some fresh coffee. Then I'm ringing Sam, he can take the funeral."

"No, it's his day off, he can't be expected to......"

"Don't underestimate him, it's about time he had a crisis to deal with!"

"Perhaps Roger....."

"Just for once, stop organising – I'm putting the coffee on, you are going to clean yourself up and I'm going to ring Sam. Then you and I can have a chat."

Charlotte simply looked at the younger woman who had been working for her for the past six years.

"Thank you" she said and went upstairs.

Charlotte felt utterly exhausted. She sat on the bed and lifted her hand up to her neck, slowly she slipped out the white piece of plastic from the cuff of fabric that held it there and undone her top button. Then she reached over for her mobile and rang Max's number.

Max answered immediately. "What's happening? Have they gone? Charlotte? ....Charlie? .... Darling say something."

"I've blown it," she blew out a stream of air and as her lungs emptied added "David will go ballistic." Max heard her partner take a deep breath.

"Are you on your own?" Max was anxious.

"No, Linda's here."

"I thought she'd have had more sense than turn up for work. What's she doing there so early?"

Charlotte felt as if she was trying to think behind a heavy fog but answered. "She was great Max. They've gone now, everything's gone."

"What are you talking about? Look I'll be over soon." She heard a click as Charlotte put down the phone. Max was worried. Charlie was the strong one she was always the cool headed one, always in control.

Charlotte heard Linda calling, "Charlotte, the coffee's ready."

Charlotte took off her smart black trousers and pulled on a pair of lose jeans. Her black clerical shirt hung outside, open at the neck. She went back downstairs passing the study she heard Linda's voice on the phone.

"Thank you, Sam. I'll let her know, I'm sure she'll speak to you later." Charlotte went to the kitchen and waited for Linda.

"Black and strong or white and sweet?" Charlotte hadn't even heard Linda come back in. But she did hear the phone ringing in the background, she started to stand up. "No you don't, either me or the answer phone will be screening all your calls from now on." Linda was suddenly taking control. She seemed quite good at it. The answer phone kicked in.

Without saying a word, or even waiting for an answer Linda busied herself and set down a strong black coffee in front of Charlotte and another for herself.

"And when is the owner of Patch and Stitch going to turn up and whisk you away from this circus?"

"What?" Charlotte looked straight at Linda.

"And when exactly, were you going to tell me that you've decided to leave?"

"I......." Charlotte couldn't find the words. Linda reached over and placed her hand on Charlottes arm.

"Why didn't you feel you could tell me? You trust me with all sorts of confidential information, and I've never once broken that confidentiality and for the record it wasn't me that gave the press some ridiculous story about you and Sasha."

"I..... what do you think you know?" Charlotte held her coffee in both hands, as if holding on to it was the only thing that kept her from falling deeper into whatever place she felt herself slipping.

"Charlotte my love, I'm not judging you. I think you are a fantastic priest. But if I'm honest I'm still trying to work out if I want a gay vicar."

"What?" Charlotte was stunned into one word replies.

"You keep on saying that. This thing isn't just about you, you know."

"What?"

"Straight talking, no more lies – oh sorry, excuse the pun – straight.... oh, never mind!"

"You know about me and Max?" Charlotte's eyes were wide in disbelief.

Linda nodded "It took a while for me to believe it. But I guess you and she are, well together. I must admit I thought it was Sash for a bit, but you two are just so different and I didn't actually think you'd be that stupid."

"Stupid?"

"To have your lover living with you."

"Oh."

"But those dogs are like your kids."

"Pardon?"

"Oh, come on, it's almost like a divorced couple sharing custody. Except that you two are as thick of thieves. I've not seen much of the two of you together – which, incidentally, made me even more suspicious. How can you look after a best friend's dogs so often, but hardly ever mention her? And Sasha is obviously friends with the both of you." Linda paused, looked directly at Charlotte and asked, "I'm not wrong, am I?"

"No."

Linda nodded again, as if confirming in her own mind what she had just heard. "So, what happens now?" She took a sip of coffee

"I'm leaving the ministry." Charlotte paused for a moment. "Announcements are being made at the annual meeting, or at least they were before all this happened." Charlotte waved her hand in the general direction of the newspaper.

"And when were you going to tell me I was out of a job?"

"You might not be. You are a parish employee, not mine." Charlotte's voice was very flat. She felt like an ashamed child who had been accused of playing some foolish prank.

"I happen to work in your house," said Linda.

"Yes, and we'll have to make other arrangements. The parish will need you to stay on."

"I guess there will be time to think about that – but what about you?"

"We need to call a Benefice Meeting, I was thinking about this, we need to get the Archdeacon. I'm the rural dean, so that's no good! Everyone needs to know the truth before all this gets out of hand."

"And are you under some impression that the truth will make everything alright?" Linda's voice was getting louder. "That you running off with Max and leaving the ministry will somehow be more acceptable behaviour than that of showing your lodger the door? Or entertaining rowdy young teenagers?"

"What?"

"Stop saying that. Like I said, we think you are a fantastic priest, well most of us any way, just deny the story and get back on with being our vicar. I'm not going to pass on what you've just told me. They'll be gossip there always is, but as long as you just do your job it won't matter – just don't, don't....." Linda stopped in her tracks, struggling to finish, struggling with the brutal honesty she was rallying against her priest and friend.

"Don't what Linda?"

"Don't shove it down our throats, there's no need for it – just keep your private life private that's all!"

Silence

"That's it?" Charlotte put down her mug, without really drinking any of the coffee.

Linda looked at Charlotte, but remained clutching her own mug.

"And this is the feeling of how many in our villagers?" Charlotte's voice had regained its strength and was almost accusing in its tone.

"I don't know."

"But you've got a good general idea. What has been said Linda? What have you not been telling me?"

"Nothing. Well a few bits of gossip that's all. Stupid talk. It's true there has been a lot of gossip about you and Sasha. I'm sorry I probably should have said something, but ignoring it seemed better somehow. Ignore the stories, they'll calm down and nobody gets hurt. Nobody really thought you were a bad priest. Mind you the best one was how they wondered if you and Sam could get together – I mean how many years difference?!" Linda snorted a little but was uncomfortable and rather embarrassed.

"I'm not hiding this away Linda. I can't. Before this whole press thing got lose, the Bishop and I had discussed at some length how I would quietly leave to pursue an alternative career."

"With Max?"

"Yes, with Max."

"And now what will happen?"

Charlotte didn't really want to be discussing all this with Linda. She certainly wasn't about to share all the things she and Max had planned, but she also felt she owed something to this dedicated friend, who had obviously been, rightly or wrongly, protecting her from village gossip for some time. She kept it work based.

"The first thing we have to do is to get a meeting sorted out, as quickly as possible. Linda, I know this is hard for you. And I'm sorry it has all turned out like this..."

Linda interrupted Charlotte's little speech. "Do you want to leave ministry Charlie?"

It was the first time Linda had ever addressed her boss with her nickname. Charlotte raised her eye brows. She felt exhausted by all the questions, but she answered Linda with absolute honesty. "No" she said. "But neither can I live a lie. I am who I am. I have to leave."

"No, you don't. Admittedly some people will leave the church after all this. Some are going to struggle for a bit, and they might leave, but they'll be back and others, well we'll just get on with it. Like I said, I'm still not quite sure about having a gay vicar, but I'd rather have you than some old cronnie, cos that's what these little villages will get. Stay. Please."

Charlotte just shook her head. "We've got work to do, but I need some pills, my head's pounding I'll see you in the study in a couple of minutes."

Chapter 22

Three days later two hundred people squeezed into the church of St Nicholas in Langford. The archdeacon, Venerable Clive King had cancelled an engagement with the greater chapter of Exeter Cathedral. Bishop David had said goodbye to his wife earlier that day before she drove up to Gloucester. He had arrived at 6pm and spent an hour with Charlotte and Max at the vicarage. Max was not going to the meeting. This had been a difficult concession for her to make, but all agreed that to have Max present would simply inflame a very sensitive meeting.

To have both men, the bishop, and the archdeacon present at such short notice, was nothing short of miraculous and only indicated the seriousness of the situation. Ironically the only other time they would normally be present would be at the beginning of ministry in a new parish, when a new priest is licensed, inducted and installed.

Annette, the diocesan press officer was also present, alongside a couple of local reporters, and a free-lance journalist looking for a follow up story for the nationals. The big papers hadn't bothered to send their own. The story hadn't appeared to catch the nation's attention but locally word had travelled fast.

Charlotte glanced out of the vestry door. She could see most of the packed church. Many faces she knew, but several were strangers to her. She wondered what the audience expected.

This was not a packed-out congregation waiting for their vicar to announce the first hymn. This was a gathering of curious people waiting for more information. She hoped this was a group of concerned people, waiting to know what was to happen next. But in all probability most were there for a good story to chew on for weeks, months possibly even years. And a few would be very sad about what they would hear.

'The only time we ever get these sort of numbers,' thought Charlotte 'was once a year at Christmas. The fact that I'm gay seems to have been the best form of outreach I've managed in all the time I've been here!'

"Charlotte..... I said we ought to get started." Bishop David had broken off his conversation with the archdeacon and gestured towards the open door.

Three chairs had been set out behind a trestle table. Music was playing in the background through the speakers. The rumble of voices gradually quietened as the three clerics took their places. The music ceased abruptly as the bishop stood to address the crowd.

"Ladies and gentlemen, you are all aware of the subject matter of tonight's meeting. I think it most appropriate that we begin by keeping a moment of quiet and I shall lead us in prayer."

Charlotte could feel her heart pounding. All heads were bowed in a dignified silence at the bidding of the bishop. The door of the church clanged open as a few late comers tried to enter without being noticed. Several people looked round at the young blond haired youth dressed in leathers and the slightly older woman dressed in a dark business suit. Just behind James and Sasha another figure crept in, quite tall, dressed in a long over coat, with the collar turned right up, a fringe covering the eyes and a woollen hat pulled down over the ears. Max had after all, not been able to stay away.

She melted into the crowd along with her two companions.

Charlotte was conscious of her hands trembling and the intense feeling of wanting to run away, her mouth was dry. She reached for the glass of water in front of her spilling a little as she took a sip.

"Let us pray." The bishop's voice was strong and confident. "...........and be guided by your Holy Spirit. Amen." Charlotte had not even heard the words.

"Can I invite the archdeacon to say a few words." The bishop was chairing the meeting, but Clive King had been given the task of addressing the meeting and setting out the agenda for the evening.

"Thank you, Bishop. Can I first thank the Church wardens and the parish staff for arranging this meeting at such short notice. I think we are all quite aware of why we are here."

Charlotte felt all eyes turn towards her.

"Certain allegations have been made in a recent newspaper article. This has caused some degree of distress for many concerned. Much of what has been written has been very misleading. With the agreement and full cooperation of Miss Northam, first I'd like to address the article and quite clearly state was is factual, and what is inaccurate."

Charlotte looked straight ahead. She focused on the top of the arch above the west window. She would not look down, she would not wring her hands, she would keep perfectly still, she would not lose the battle to keep the tears at bay, she would have to speak and when she did her voice would be strong and steady. This was what she was telling herself over and over again. She knew exactly where Max was standing, alongside her nephew and lodger. She was sure her heart had stopped when they walked in against all the advice of the Bishop. Very few people, she realised, actually knew them. Just a handful had ever seen

357

Sasha, a few had heard her nephew's motorbike but had never met him and apart from Linda, Charlotte didn't think any one had ever met Max. Yet according to the newspaper these were the subjects of binge drinking, sex orgies and all night raves. Charlotte fought to keep her mind on the meeting.

Clive took out the paper that they had prepared earlier that afternoon.

"We would like to make it quite clear that the Diocese has been fully aware that Miss Northam has played host to a lodger for some three years. This is not uncommon practice in large vicarages. A full tenancy agreement has been in operation throughout this period. A sum of rent is paid to the diocese by Miss Sasha Paynter each month. It is understood that Miss Paynter also pays towards the cost of heating bills and other such household costs." Clive glanced towards Charlotte who took her cue and gave a small nod.

A hand shot up from the back of the audience. Noticed by the archdeacon he addressed the owner of the hand and several others. "We appreciate that many of you may wish to ask questions and there will be an opportunity to do so in a few minutes, but first can I address other aspects of the report."

There was a murmur from the crowd as a few exchanges were made in response. "Ladies and gentlemen if I may continue. So far as we are aware, no complaints have ever been made either to Miss Northam, or the church wardens or to diocese with regard to excessive noise at the vicarage. These allegations appear to be unfounded."

"There's no smoke without fire!" An anonymous voice shouted from the south aisle.

Again, a murmured response rumbled across the church. Charlotte looked down to see both her hands formed into a tight fist, she released them.

Ignoring the outburst, the archdeacon continued. "The article suggests that Miss Paynter is soon to be evicted from the Rectory. It has been brought to our attention that Miss Paynter is looking for alternative accommodation due in part to her growing business commitments in other parts of the country." Clive then sat down.

Bishop David stood to again address the full church. "You may be aware that in recent months my family has faced a difficult time following a serious accident. Indeed, I was shocked to discover that news reports had reported my own involvement in the accident and I believe I may have been killed!" Embarrassed laughter was heard around the building. "I assure you I am very well, and doing what I can to support my son-in-law as he learns to walk again following this devastating incident. I would like to say again what I said several months ago, that my heart is with those families who lost loved ones during that dreadful night."

"What's this got to do with the vicar?" It was possibly the same man who had shouted out before, this time the whole church seemed to ssh him.

"Actually, my friend, I'm glad you asked me."

The bishop lifted his glass and took a sip of water.

"Through a rather bizarre set of coincidences the women sitting on my left has also been very involved in supporting my daughter and son-in-law through this difficult period."

Charlotte looked aghast at her bishop. This was not what they had discussed. The bishop was supposed to have simply stated that Charlotte had for some time been thinking of a career break, or words to that effect and gone on to explain the procedure for vacating the benefice and the process of finding a replacement and then time given for questions. The plan was to draw attention away from Charlotte's personal circumstances and more towards what would happen in the parish once she was gone.

"I have had the privilege of getting to know Charlotte as a friend in recent months. We have discovered a family connection that has for some years been hidden from us."

There was silence around the church. All eyes were on the bishop. The archdeacon was staring at David wondering where this was leading.

"A few months ago, I met with Reverend Northam to discuss an important post I wanted her to consider. The post of archdeacon was soon to become vacant in another part of the Diocese and I approached Charlotte to seriously consider applying for the post. She has the experience, she is an intelligent woman with good strategic capabilities and she has a pastoral heart which is a very important aspect of the role, even though one that is not often acquainted with the rather legalistic role of archdeacon. I would not have had this conversation with any one I was not totally confident in. This meeting was the same time my son-in-law met with his accident. Although neither one of us knew that at the time. The way that Charlotte supported my daughter through this time was second to none. Charlotte probably does not even realise how grateful I am to her and her partner."

A short gasp went up low voices whispered to each other, "Partner? She's got a boyfriend?" "Partner? What sort...."

Charlotte couldn't help but look in Max's direction. At first, she seemed to slink further down into her big coat and pulled her hat down further. But then, slowly as both Sasha and James looked on she took off her hat, pulled down the collar and unbuttoned a few buttons on the coat. Then without drawing attention to herself, she looked over to Charlotte and just nodded. James whispered something in Max's ear. Max shook her head but smiled.

"My friends," the bishop continued not noticing Max, "Charlotte is a good priest. She could continue to be a good priest, she could even be a very good archdeacon. I would have liked to have addressed you all today to announce that your Rector is leaving to take up this important role within the diocese, that you should be proud of her. In reality if that was the case I would not be here, Charlotte would have made that announcement herself. Instead......"

David's voice got louder and he spoke one word at a time, punching them out as if he was throwing each one at the gathered crowd. "Instead, we have this ridiculous situation because somebody decided they had a bit of juicy gossip to share with nation." David suddenly pounded his fist on the table, spilling the water. His anger had shocked all those present, especially Charlotte. The anger appeared to be aimed at the gossips, but Charlotte sensed some was directed at her. She knew the bishop has so wanted her to remain quiet, discreet and hidden.

David mopped up the water with his hanky. "Can I reiterate, that what has been written in the press, is largely fabricated nonsense. However tonight is not without a very important and a very difficult

361

announcement. Although the gossips may feel they have forced a decision, I'm afraid your power is not that great. The decision to be relayed to you this evening had already been made. The newspaper article has unfortunately forced our hand into making certain facts known to you sooner than anticipated. Reverend Northam."

Charlotte turned to the Bishop, puzzled. She wasn't sure what he wanted. David lowered his voice, "Tell them."

"Tell them what?"

"Tell them what you want. You wanted your moment."

"But..."

"I've had enough of this too, just tell them, you might as well."

The crowd was becoming restless waiting to be addressed by their Rector.

"Umm.....yes, thank you Bishop." One thing Charlotte hated was being caught off guard. She was not supposed to say anything apart from being available to answer factual questions. This was what had been agreed. She spotted the archdeacon whisper in David's ear. David just shrugged and turned slightly in his chair so he could see Charlotte better.

What was going on? Was this David's way of getting back at her? After putting him in this difficult situation, he had now turned the tables? Although it was true, she had wanted honesty.

There was increased shuffling and coughing in the audience. She had to speak. She felt dizzy, her heart pounding, but she would not be beaten. She caught Max's eye. Without even thinking she found herself beckoning her partner to the front. Max looked surprised and pointed at herself. Then she gestured towards Sasha and James, Charlotte nodded.

Slowly they made their way to the front. Charlotte could feel David looking at her intently trying to work out her intentions. She was still trying to do that for herself. Eyes had fallen on the three people approaching the table. They stopped just in front and faced the audience.

"I er, I'd like you to meet three people who you think you er.... know. The young man is my nephew, James. He rides a motorbike. James come up here for a moment will you."

As James came closer, Charlotte came out from behind the table and put her arm across her nephew's shoulders. "I am very proud to be James' aunty. As you know I haven't got children of my own, but I'm pleased that James feels he can come and see me any time. Sometimes he leaves it rather late in the day, and usually doesn't warn me he's coming."

Charlotte gave James a playful punch on his leather clad arm.

"But my nephew knows that my home is always open to him. I am also sometimes annoyed when he plays his music too loud and he gets a good telling off from time to time."

James looked down in a contrite way, but was smiling, at this moment he had never felt more proud of his aunt. "He also knows there is usually a beer in the fridge and at 17 will help himself, much to my annoyance. I sometimes join him. I'd rather he come to me and share his troubles than go out and get drunk with his mates."

There was a general murmur of agreement from anyone who had teenagers.

"It's not right though is it, he's under age" heckled a middle-aged man, who looked as if he enjoyed more than a pint or two.

363

"Shut up Geoff, no harm in the lad having a beer with his aunty, wish my son would do that with me."

"Yeah, what's wrong with that. Nothing, that's what, not in his own home. You go on Vicar."

"Er.... Thank you. And thank you James, go on back will you. Sasha, would you mind coming forward?"

It left Max standing alone, she took a step to the side, trying to look less conspicuous, then decided to crouch down beside one of the pews, declining the offer to squeeze in beside a rather large lady trying to be helpful, and realised she was the owner of a Collie she had treated the week before. "How do you know them?" the woman whispered. But Max didn't answer, Charlotte had started speaking again.

"Miss Paynter, Sasha, has been lodging with me for some time. I've known Sash for a number of years. More than anything, I was appalled by the allegation that I had thrown out a friend. I hope and pray that we will remain friends for many many years. Sasha is a very successful editor. Her work takes her all over the country. Sasha lives part of the time in London, but misses the countryside and finds the quiet of the Rectory an ideal place to work."

Sasha was nodding in agreement, wondering what Charlotte would say next. After all it was true she was moving out, and didn't really want to. "I have recently come to a decision that will probably mean that Sasha has to move out of the Rectory." Charlotte gave Sasha a nod indicating she too was 'dismissed' and could go back with James. Charlotte continued, hardly catching breath. "I have decided to leave my post."

There were more gasps around the church, this time they didn't subside but the noise grew as neighbours turned and nodded, or shook their heads "Told you she was." "Bet she's been forced." "See, truth in that article after all."

"Max, can you come up here please." Charlotte could feel both the bishop and the archdeacon behind her looking at her. She wondered for a moment if one of them would put a stop to what she was about to do, but they stayed glued to their seats. One female voice was heard from the middle of the church.

"Charlotte don't!" Linda has stood briefly, but sat down before most people spotted who it was. She buried her head in her hands.

"Max is...." But Charlotte was stopped abruptly in her tracks by the firm voice of her bishop.

"Maxine is my son-in-law's sister. Max and Charlotte have been supporting my family ever since the accident. I think Charlotte has spent nearly every one of her days off either visiting Mike in hospital or on occasions looking after his children so my daughter could spend time with him. When she couldn't go with Max she had the dogs so Max could be with her brother. And it was Charlotte who was the one person who had the courage to pray with my daughter, more than I could do. Charlotte and Max are committed to each other and deeply committed to their families. And what's more they are the better for it........" Bishop David's voice trailed off. He had said far too much.

After the briefest of pauses Charlotte added simply "Max is my partner."

Once again, her parishioners turned to each other, some whispering, some more vocal. Into the general grumble of voices the rather large outspoken gentleman stated the obvious. "She's a woman."

This outburst seemed to quell the voices and again Charlotte felt all eyes on her, waiting for another response.

"Yes....." for a moment Charlotte couldn't get her breath. Without thinking, but desperate for support Charlotte grasped Max's hand. Max shook it free. 'Don't....' she whispered, 'not yet' she added.

"I'm sorry." Charlotte found herself saying.

"You will be, you flippin' freak." The man, who Charlotte did not recognise, but was apparently called Geoff got up. At first, she thought he might be heading for the front of church, but he just stormed out, as others tried in vain to calm him down. At the door, he turned around. "You bloody well baptised my kid. Pervert!" Shock reverberated around the church.

Charlotte heard Clive speaking, "Perhaps we should all take a moment or two......."

"No Clive, give me a moment, will you?" Charlotte was shaking and pale, but she wanted to speak before this moment was lost.

"I will be leaving you. The archdeacon will explain in a moment exactly what will be happening over the coming weeks." Charlotte was surprised at the strength of her own voice. Max stayed beside her. "I am aware that for many of you this news is totally unexpected. Although it is obvious from the newspaper report that rumours had been circulating. Max and I have been together for some years."

Disbelief seemed to echo around the church. "It is quite clear that we have conducted our relationship in a discreet way. I have not been forced to share this information with you because of the newspaper report. As the bishop said, I had already decided that living a double life was dishonest to both myself and all of you." Charlotte took another sip of water.

The brief pause was long enough for somebody to ask. "But why are you leaving?" Several tuts and ssh's were heard, but no-one actually shouted down the questioner.

"I think our friend who has just left has answered your question," said Charlotte.

"He's just hot-headed" Somebody else spoke up.

"Sorry love, he 'ad a point, People round 'ere aren't ready for this sort 'o thing." Charlotte recognised one of the old farmers from the small congregation of St Hilda's. Somebody she had grown very fond of over the years. She hated the fact that he would be upset.

"Can I say something?" Max had been standing very quiet but now took a step forward. She wasn't asking Charlotte, she was addressing the whole church gathering.

"I also know some of you. I treat your cattle and your dogs. Some of you may be regretting that now, too." Max spotted a few of her regulars shaking their heads and one or two just looking away. "I have tried to persuade Charlie, er Charlotte not to take this decision. But just recently the strain has been huge. When she was asked to take promotion, if I can call it that, I was so proud. I knew it would be difficult, but I was prepared to support Charli..... Charlotte as best I could...... sorry, this isn't what I want to say. Charlie won't be a priest any more. She's giving up completely. I'm not sure that has actually been said this evening. This woman who has served you and served as a priest for nearly twenty years of her life is going to give it all up. Not for me, although it must seem that way, but because she is honest and can't stand the hypocrisy going on...."

"That's enough," whispered Charlotte, but Max's passion had been unleashed.

"... and I love her. And I hope that Charlie will never regret this decision. Some of you are shocked. Shocked because you didn't think priests could be gay; shocked because it never dawned on you that your priest may have a private life that you know nothing about; some of you may be shocked by none of those things, but because she's leaving you, and probably even more shocked because she's leaving the church completely. I hope you will find it in your hearts to do something about that." Max then looked towards the old farmer from St Hilda's. "I'm sorry Arthur," said Max, the use of his first name reminding Charlotte that many of those in the church also knew Max, as their vet, "but this sort of thing is as much part of round 'ere, as it is in the big cities. I'm sorry if I've shocked you."

"To be honest maid," replied Arthur in his broad Devonian dialect, "so longs you treat my heifers right I don't really care, but Vicars different, ain't right see." Arthur pulled himself up but sat down again as soon as he had finished.

"How's your brother?" this question came from the back and was directed at Max.

"He's er making good progress thanks," said Max, surprised at the sudden twist in the questioning.

"And does he know?" The questioner continued.

"If you refer to the relationship between myself and Charlotte, then yes."

"So, the bishop knew too then, he must 'ave, why leave it till now?" Max couldn't really see the questioner, but there was a smugness in her voice. So much so, that both Max and Charlotte were then surprised by what the questioner had to say next.

"Course that article had somethin' to do with it." She was looking at the bishop, not Max. "Stop trying to cover up the whole thing. You think we're stupid? When it was all quiet it was alright, no-one was getting hurt, but now, now you just need to get 'er out of the way. Too embarrassing for the poor ol' C of E, that's the problem." Then she turned slightly to get a better view of Charlotte "You're being forced out love, that's what this is. Now then lets 'ave the truth this time, and stop all this ruddy procrastination, get on with it."

Bishop David stood up again.

"No, let the vicar speak." Another woman had taken on the mantle. "Come on love tell us the truth, you being forced out or not? You been given the heave 'o?"

Standing beside Max, Charlotte again spoke. "I know it must seem like that. But that decision was made several months ago. I hope to take up a new post working with Max in her vet's practice in Okehampton. We're buying a house. I'm afraid the plans are well on the way."

"Why haven't you told us before then?" This time it was a man from the small community of St Judoc.

"Sir," Clive King interrupted and stood to address the questioner, "before any of this could be announced we had a number of legal processes to go through."

369

"Yeah, but most us couldn't care less whether she's gay, married, divorced or anything, she's a damn good priest, oh sorry, probably not the right word to use, but there you have it. If we want, can't she stay? We'll get a petition, I bet loads of people want her to stay. She's alright."

The man looked around for support. There was an uncomfortable murmur, but whether it was support or criticism was difficult to tell.

"Oh, shut up Ray," another man broke across the foray. "She's going and that's that. She's got her own life to lead."

"No she ain't she's a priest. Given 'er life to God," another parishioner chipped in, a young woman this time.

"Not for much longer, by the sounds of it." Another said

The gaggle of voices was rising. Some people still tried to shout above the noise.

"Too late now."

"She can't stay, not after this."

At the back of church where they had retreated a few minutes earlier, Sasha took James by the elbow, "Come on," she said, "I think it's time we went".

"No way Sash, Charlie and Max need us."

"No, they don't and I'm getting you home." They left by the side door without too many people noticing.

"Ladies and Gentlemen, please," Clive, the archdeacon had decided to try and regain some order. "Please can I have your attention."

Gradually the crowd calmed down and Clive could be heard. Charlotte and Max stepped to one side, but remained standing together.

"Thank you. You have all had to take in an incredible amount of information this evening. I'd just like to thank Bishop David for giving up his time to be with us. It is a most unusual event. Can I reiterate, exactly where we are. Reverend Northam has taken the decision to leave the ministry. This has nothing to do with recent events and is a decision she had made some time ago. I think we need to congratulate Miss Northam on her honesty."

Some people began to clap but it quickly died down as Clive continued.

"Bishop? Would you like to explain what will happen next?"

"Er, no you carry on." Said the Bishop.

"Well, Reverend Northam will take a period of leave and I shall be working closely with the assistant dean, the Church Wardens and the rest of the team. I believe we have a date for Charlotte's actual departure from the parish?"

The rest of the meeting was taken up with practical information. Max and Charlotte slipped quietly out to the vestry. Very few people seemed to notice.

"That's it then." Said Charlotte, her voice shaking.

"Is it what you expected?"

"I don't know. Funny, I'm not sure if there's support out there or not?"

Chapter 23

The next morning Sasha, James, Max and Charlotte were sat around the kitchen table when they heard the thump of newspapers coming through the door. No one spoke as James went to fetch them followed by Stitch and Patch.

"Somebody wanted us to know what had been written." James dumped a couple of nationals and the local paper down onto the table. The local radio was on in the background but nothing had been reported so far.

"Here's something," said Sasha flicking through one of the tabloids. "Says you've fled the parish......"

"Let's see." James took the paper and read out loud.

"'Once again, the sleepy villages on Dartmoor have had to cope with shock as their vicar the Reverend North,' couldn't even get your name right aunty, 'fled from a meeting in tears. Neither her or her partner Miss Paynter have been seen since." James stopped reading, "Oh good grief, can't they get any of the facts straight – you could sue, Sash for slander."

"Just read the stupid article," said Max.

"Er, OK..... seen since. It is confirmed that Rev North will be leaving the Church of England following her revelation at the public meeting where she declared that she and Miss Paynter were in a long-term relationship and intended to begin a new life together as soon as possible. A spokesman for the church said that Reverend North had made her own decision and they would not stand in her way. It also denied that a so-called witch hunt is being carried out to rid the church of gay clergy who refused to lead a life of celibacy. This is just another nail in the coffin of the established church who still struggles to gain relevance in modern society.'" He put down the paper. "What a stupid article, even the headline is rubbish, 'Love thy Lesbian'"

"Has a certain ring though." Charlotte hadn't picked up a paper but was sipping her coffee and stroking Patch.

"Here's one in the local paper," said Sasha. "At least they've bothered to be a bit more accurate. 'Three hundred people packed into the village church at Langford last night at a meeting attended by the Right Reverend David Graham, Bishop of Exeter and Very Reverend Clive King,' oh, that reminds me was Sam there?"

"I didn't see him," said Charlotte. The others shook their heads.

Sasha continued. "'The Bishop spoke warmly of the Reverend Northam,' Oh that's nice. 'However, the meeting was shocked to hear that Miss Northam had been conducting an affair with local vet Maxine Tannin,'"

"Oh great, well at least they've got my name right I suppose. Go on Sash."

"'The meeting was informed of Miss Northam's imminent departure not only from the Dartmoor group of parishes, but from the Church of England. She will renounce her orders as soon as certain legalities have been put into place. Local residents spoke of their disbelief and sadness. One local woman described seeing many villagers leaving the meeting in tears. Some gathered in the local pub after the meeting. One man expressed his anger at being misled by the church and his concerns for children in the area.' I bet that was that big fella, what was his name - Geoff? You baptised his kids."

373

"That's what he said, but I don't think he's been anywhere near church since."

"Typical though isn't it," said Max, "you'd expect people to have more sense in this day and age – risk to his kids, for pities sake, you are fantastic with the kiddies – wish we could adopt..."

"And you know where I draw the line on that one," interrupted Charlotte. "Go on what else is in there?" She felt uncannily calm.

"Well actually whoever wrote this, paints you in a good light, listen, 'such claims are totally unfounded and without any factual evidence. Other residents appeared shocked at such allegations and were full of admiration for their priest. It seems that Reverend Northam's departure will bring much heartache to the villages she serves.'"

"Hey, aunty, you've got an admirer there."

Charlotte remembered the young journalist from the paper. He had shown concern when she collapsed. The memory of it made her shudder. Perhaps he did have a heart.

"Don't get carried away Jimmy," added Sasha, "'Reverend Northam was seen fleeing from the church after the meeting in an attempt to avoid all contact with her parishioners. Her guilt is now out in the open and it seems all is not well with this once respected vicar.' Sorry."

"Well he's right. I can't stay here. Once I've seen Linda and spoken to the rest of the staff, Max and I will get going, which reminds me James you should have gone already, now get a move on you'll be late for college, don't get me into any more trouble."

"It's fine, aunty my first lecture is at eleven, plenty of time."

"Yeah, well, you'd best get going, I'm not sure what today will bring." And with that they heard the front door, it was not quite 8am.

Sasha answered the door.

It was Sam, looking as if he had slept in his clothes. "I've got to speak to Charlotte."

Sasha let him in calling to Charlotte that it was 'safe.'

In the hall, Charlotte started to apologise to her trainee curate.

"I'm sorry Sam, I've handled this all wrong, I should have spoken to you properly, but...."

"In private, please can I come in?" They went into the study and left the others sifting through the other articles.

"You do know, don't you?" asked a very flustered Sam "Look, I'm not like you, I'm not that brave, please don't make me, I'm not actually in a relationship."

"Whoa, slow down. Sam just calm down for a moment will you. You look as if you've hardly slept."

"Charlotte, I still want to be a priest, but I've never been honest about it, I can't I just can't, not even my parents know."

Charlotte frowned. "Are you gay?"

"Yes, of course I am, surely you know – I mean I've known about you but I never thought I'd have to..... never thought you would....."

"Sam, slow down. Come and sit down." They closed the door to the study and sat down. Charlotte surreptitiously switched off the phone. "Sam, I can see you are upset, but please hear me when I tell you that what you have just told me doesn't need to go anywhere. It never does, just keep your head down, stay out of trouble and be a good priest. That's how it works. And like you said you are not in a relationship. You are fine."

"But you've got this honesty drive. Can't stand the hypocrisy, you said."

"Well actually Max said.... Yes, you're right. I have decided to be honest. But that's my decision, and for the record no I didn't know about you. I don't go around with a radar, seeking out gays!"

"You don't?"

"Well may be a bit, but it's none of my business. I won't say a word. And I suggest, although I can't quite believe I'm saying this after all I'm supposed to be standing up for, but I suggest you keep quiet and keep your head down, well down for the time being. These little villages really would hit the headlines if the reporters found out there are two of us."

"So, I shouldn't go and see the Bishop?"

"NO!" Charlotte was startled. "Sorry that was a bit brusque. Look what you do is your decision, but don't just follow my lead. Sam, you are not alone. If all the gay clergy decided to resign, the church would probably fall apart. See I'm still a hypocrite!"

"There's a lot of people really admire what you've done. It's hit Facebook you know."

"No I didn't know and great! Do you want a coffee?"

"I think I'll just go back and get on with a few things?"

"And you'll be around later? The others are getting here at eleven."
Sam nodded.

"And you know I'm going away for a few days, not far just hiding out at Max's."

"I guessed you would."

"But you can ring me, if you need anything. On the mobile. I'm sorry, I'm really not handling this at all well, this must be so difficult for you. And I've kept you in the dark, not told you what was going on. And all the time you've been worried sick about your own career. I'm so sorry."

"It's fine. I'm glad we've talked a bit now. I just want you to know that I understand. One thing though. What about my curacy? I need to know what's going to happen."

"And I would have spoken to you, long before anything went public, but all this with the media just threw everything up in the air. It's on the agenda for me and the director of training to talk about. He will be in charge. You may need to work with somebody else in the deanery for a bit, but you can stay in the house. I'm truly sorry how all this has worked out Sam, really I am."

Sam left as Linda arrived.

"Charlotte!" She gave her boss a hug. "Don't say a word, please. I'll just get on."

She went straight into the study to pull up the rotas and prepared for the staff meeting.

Charlotte returned to the kitchen to discover Max had taken the dogs for their morning walk. Sasha was washing up and James was collecting his things ready to leave for college.

Another knock at the door. Sasha started to go, but Charlotte stopped her.

"Might as well face them, nothing to lose."

Charlotte opened the door to a large bouquet of flowers.

"Who are they from?" she asked the florist.

377

"Just an anonymous note miss," she said as she handed them to Charlotte.

It read 'I'm sorry'

"Well, er thank you."

And Charlotte took them into the kitchen to find a few vases.

"Wow, who are they from?" Sasha was now busying herself with the washing machine.

"No idea, look at the note."

"Weird. Somebody feeling guilt. Maybe it was the 'Gossip' and what the bishop said got to them."

"May be, but I'm not sure. Oh well. Don't suppose....."

"Leave them with me. I'll sort them out in a minute. You don't mind me staying by the way?" Asked Sasha, "I mean with you disappearing for a few days."

"I think you're brave, but no, it's your home too, well at the moment any way. I expect we've got about three months before I have to move out."

Charlotte went into the study armed with a large pot of coffee. Charlotte and Linda looked at the rotas and rearranged the parish services for the next three months. They were ready for the inevitably difficult meeting with church wardens and the rest of the staff team. If the team were not already aware they would soon discover that Charlotte had already ceased to exercise her duties in any public way. The parishes had now effectively been thrown into an emergency vacancy.

Chapter 24

Several days later, Charlie was still tucked away from sight staying with Max, still drawing a stipend and still plagued by huge swings of emotion.

The day after the parish meeting had been chaotic. Charlotte had been working non-stop with Linda both before and after the staff meeting. All through the day, Linda had fielded dozens of phone calls. She ensured Charlotte saw only emails that needed her immediate attention or the ones that offered messages of support. Some of them Linda did not mention to Charlotte, they were the most vial and upsetting. One in particular would haunt Linda for weeks to come. Most of the callers to the Rectory just wanted to know how their vicar was, but Linda only said she would pass on the message. She had sub-consciously taken on the role of guarding her friend. That evening Charlotte packed up her car and left.

Sasha would stay in the Rectory.

Nearly ten days later, early on a Tuesday morning Sasha was about to leave for London when she heard a loud thud against the rectory door. Her instinct was to open it. She didn't and that hesitation probably saved her life.

By the time the fire service arrived the heavy door had been burned through and flames were lapping around the hall. The whole of the front of the Rectory was charred. An upstairs window had been broken. The fire officer thought it was the heat that had blown it in, but when he and Sasha went into Charlotte's bedroom they found a large stone with a note tied around it. "GO TO HELL."

Sasha only returned to the Rectory once, just two days later to clear her room. She was to be met with heavy boards where the front door used to be and police tape cordoning off the front of the house. A police car was parked in the drive.

Inside the house, two police officers; one female one male, were interviewing Charlotte. Linda had arrived to collect the parish computer and a few files, she would set up a temporary office in her own home. She refused to be in the Rectory alone. One of the Church wardens was helping. A great heaviness hung over the once bubbling busy Rectory. Now it was lifeless, the object of grief and forgotten dreams.

•

PART TWO

Several months later

Chapter 25

"I definitely prefer the black."

"But it is so predictable. So masculine!"

"Rubbish, it will look fabulous."

"Please let's just look at the light wood and the white fronts."

"So, old fashioned."

"And would fit perfectly at the cottage." Charlie linked her arm into Max's and gently guided her back to the classic kitchen section of B&Q.

Eight months had passed since the Rectory had been damaged in the fire. It was to be sold and a new property brought for the next vicar; one that had less ground, better security, would be less draughty and much cheaper to run, although many thought it without the character of the old Rectory. Some felt that was a good thing, there had been far too much character in many ways.

This was no longer Charlotte's problem. Most of her belongings were now in storage waiting for the move into the cottage in Okehampton. Max's house would be rented out bringing in much needed extra income. The new veterinary practice was becoming established with Charlie proving that de-frocked vicars made excellent administrators.

It had not been without its struggles.

Charlie had collapsed when she heard about the fire. This time it took several days for her to recover. The strains and stresses had taken their toll and it was left to Max to gently coax Charlotte back to health.

James and his dad had helped Max organise the removal firm and had cleared the Rectory. Charlie had never returned. Several parishioners had approached the bishop wanting Charlie to have a final service but in the end, it had been too much. Despite such disappointment, the villagers had made a collection and a cheque of a staggering £5803 had been sent to Charlie via the bishops' office, as no-one really knew where to find her. At first Charlie had refused to accept it, had suggested it be given to charity, or be given back into church funds. Eventually she had been persuaded to read the letter that had accompanied the cheque.

Dear Charlotte and Max

This gift is to help you both, as you begin a new life together. One day we hope we can say a proper farewell to you but do understand totally why this is not possible at the moment. We know how difficult this has been for you, because we are finding it hard too. Charlotte, we appreciate all you have done for our parishes over the years, thank you for being there for us, when loved ones died, when we were sick, to marry us, to baptise our children. Thank you for the way you challenged us. You have challenged us now and many of us have had to think really hard, but I hope that the cheque shows you what most of us now feel. We were all really shocked about what happened at the Rectory, even those who were perhaps not too disappointed that you were leaving, (sorry.) Nobody should be treated like that. Max, you have a very special person, look after her for us and we hope that your future together will be 'lifelong and life giving.' We know that you may not wish to accept this gift but please do, because it really does come from our love for you. Look to your future, use it to make a fresh start in some small way and know that you will always have friends in the Dartmoor Group

With our love and Best Wishes

There followed several attached pages of signatures – around 500 in total, far more than the number of the Electoral Roll. It included names from the schools, from different community groups, all had pooled their gifts in this one united cheque.

After much soul-searching, the money would now be used for a brand-new kitchen.

"You thought any more about a house warming?" Max was checking the way the drawers slid in the guide-rails.

"Not really. We'll have the reception after the wedding in a few months' time."

"That's ages away."

"And you know how nervous I am about it."

"I know sweetheart" Max slipped her arm around Charlie's waist.

"Careful!"

"Why, no one's looking and any way it doesn't matter now – you're free."

"It's not that," Charlie shook Max's arm away, "We don't have to be, you know.... 'in yer face'"

Max stepped back with a sigh. "It's still going to take a while isn't it."

"Hey you two, decided yet?" Mike was pushing himself towards them with Joshua giggling in his lap, strapped in his harness on his father's lap.

"The Black" "The Wood" Charlie and Max called back together.

"Good that's settled then," grinned Mike. "Here take Josh a minute," he unclipped the harness and passed Joshua up to Charlie. Then he reached behind and pulled over his crutches, hauling himself up onto his one leg.

"I'm fine," he said as Max tried to help. "Just wish they'd get the falsey sorted out."

"Mike what are you doing?" Liz appeared with Heather in tow pushing a small push chair with her dolly half hanging out.

"I'm fine, will you ladies stop fussing and Heather rescue your doll before she head-buts someone's shin."

"You are supposed to be keeping your stump up, it'll never heal."

"I'll keep my stump up, once my bum has had a breather, if they'd fitted it right in the first place........"

"If you hadn't insisted it was fine......."

"And if you would both stop bickering!" interrupted Max. "Come on let's get a coffee or something, Heather you going to sit in daddy's chair? I'll push you. Here let's put dolly's push chair on the back, hold onto dolly. Wagons roll!"

And as Max pushed a gleeful Heather, Mike swung off on his crutches in hot pursuit of his daughter and sister.

"Decided?" asked Liz.

"I have, I just haven't quite persuaded Max."

"I didn't mean the kitchen."

"Hmmm, I guessed as much. Oh, I don't know. Funny I could always make decisions, but now. Why can't we just do it quietly? You and Mike, Maureen and Vince of course, the kids. James."

"Your sister. What about your friends in Plymouth?"

385

"You mean Jack and Gill."

"Are they really for real?"

"Fraid so. There will be Sasha of course."

"What about Dad?"

"Your father? You are kidding."

"No, I'm not. Have you spoken to him lately?" They were wandering towards the small coffee kiosk and could hear Heather giggling as Max whisked her round and round in her father's chair. Joshua was happily looking at the world from the safety of Charlie's arms.

"Goodness Joshy my boy, you are getting heavy."

"Don't change the subject, here let me take him for a bit." Liz held out her arms to her son.

"I can't invite him. That chapter is closed Lizzie," replied Charlie handing Joshua over to his mother.

"Since when? He still asks about you and Max. Joshua's christening is coming up soon, you'll see him then."

"Oh, yes I was going to speak to you about...."

"And we still want you and Max as godparents and before you say another word, this is not an argument for the middle of a DIY store!"

"That's put me in my place. But we need to know you are one hundred percent sure."

"Yes. Tea or coffee?"

Later that day back in Tavistock once both children were tucked up in bed the conversation once again came back to Charlotte and Max's civil partnership.

"We thought we'd wait for the dust to settle," said Max

"It's been eight months," said Mike

"And just when is our godson going to be baptised, come to that?" asked Max "I mean we'd hate to clash on dates."

"He'll be one in January so we thought we'd try for a date around then. I'd still like Dad to baptise him but he's really sensitive at treading on the local priest's toes. Shame you can't do it Charlie."

"Those days are long gone," said Charlotte as Max reached out and took her hand.

"Do you miss it?" asked Mike.

"Mike!" Liz shot her husband a glance, they had steered clear of this subject for months.

"No, it's OK Liz. Actually Mike, I think you might be able to understand more than most…."

Mike frowned and shifted in his chair becoming very attentive. He was not particularly religious, although he had a huge amount of respect for his in-laws.

"Forgive me if this sounds odd – but I could ask you Mike – Do you miss your leg?"

"Eh?" All eyes were now on Charlotte, it did seem an odd thing to say.

"It is," she continued, "as if priesthood was a crucial part of me. That sense of calling was with me for as long as I could remember, I even played at being a priest with my dolls and teddies, lining them all up in rows as I preached at them, or pouring water on them when I was in the bath and I'm sure mum must have wondered why so many had little juice stains round their mouths!"

The other three chuckled at the thought, but remained attentive.

"And now a bit of me is missing. I'm learning to function again without that part of me. I've got to learn a new way of being."

"What about the phantom pains?" Mike was trying to make a joke out of it, but actually they were a complete blot on his life.

"You know what Mike, I think they exist for me too. You've said that sometimes you forget you haven't got a leg and you reach down to rub the bit that's hurting but it isn't there, right?"

"That's about it, yes...... bloody annoying."

"Mike!" both Liz and Max said together.

Charlie ignored them, "Well the most painful bit for me, is when I hear about something happening in one of the parishes, or like the other day there was a really distressed women in the park and I was about to sit next to her and offer some support – and yes I could've done that, but I reached up to my neck, having to remind myself that the collar wasn't there. I was now just this random person, rather than easily identified as someone who might be expected to offer a bit of support. And I found myself just walking away. I'm just not sure how to function yet without that bit of me."

"I don't get the bit about the parishes," said Max, conscious that they had not sat down and talked in this way for months and glad that her brother and sister-in-law had breached the subject.

"I can't just stop caring. It may have been different if I'd left to become Archdeacon, to take up a different ministry. I guess I'm grieving for what I never had." Charlotte stopped for a moment. Max reached over to take Charlotte's hand. She knew Charlotte was still fragile. "I'm OK." Charlotte reassured her, "It's just I was thinking about Sam, and the other clergy. To be honest, I probably grieve more for what I never got chance to do, than for parish ministry. The bigger picture I suppose."

"And I still grieve for the loss of never getting the chance to play football with Joshy." Said Mike. "I know the false leg is pretty good, most of the time. I can manage a kick about with Heather, but that's cos she's little. But I can't imagine managing a proper game with Joshua and his friends when he's older. Ok, so you say it's like a bit of you is missing, have you thought about what might replace it – where's your false leg? The admin job? Cos I can't quite believe that."

"That's just it, the admin job is just a job. Don't get me wrong I do enjoy it..."

"And she's good at it too," interjected Max.

"Thank you sweetheart. But, however much I enjoy it – it can't replace that sense of calling – and that is what the priesthood was all about."

"So – any thoughts?" asked Mike

"Perhaps, but I don't want to replace it with a false calling."

"Yep, I see your point," said Mike, "after all, a calling shouldn't really be something you can take off if it gets a bit sore………." Mike tapped the space where his false leg would usually sit.

"I don't think I have lost the calling. Maybe I am still a priest, but not in the way the Church of England understands it."

"I've said before, we can emigrate!" Max sat up and like always when she broached the subject became very excited by the idea, "They need vets in San Francisco, same as they need priests and gay ones!"

"You serious?" asked Mike

"YES!" said Max

"NO!" said Charlie, both at the same time.

"No, not really," continued Max, as if her bubble had burst just as quickly as it was inflated. "Charlie thinks we have it good here with the business."

"And any way I do have a few thoughts about what I might do," said Charlie.

"What's that?" asked Liz, relieved that San Francisco was just a fantasy.

"A couple of gay Christian Groups have asked me to lead retreats and I've had a handful of people, mainly homosexuals, who've approached me about spiritual direction."

"Spiritual what?" asked Mike

"Kind of like counselling." answered Max. She too had been excited by these requests and had seen Charlie light up at the thought. "But my much beloved hasn't said yes yet."

"Why ever not, it sounds like a fantastic idea." Liz seemed genuinely pleased.

"I just think it is too soon," said Charlotte.

"To quote myself for the second time today – it's been eight months," said Liz.

"My thought's entirely," said Max

"I probably ought to get some sort of permission from your dad."

"What? Don't be crazy, you're free of all that now. It's not as of you are preaching about the value of homosexual sex from the pulpit or anything, or blessing a few gay marriages in the local parish church!" Liz was quite animated.

"You tell her Liz, I've been saying the same thing for over a fortnight," encouraged Max.

"Is the offer still on the table?" asked Mike

"I think so."

"Then go for it…… I know…. What do the 'phantom pains' do when you think about it?"

"That's a good question – and I'll answer it with another question for you – Are phantom pains always bad?"

"Ur. No not always, they kind of just occasionally feel comforting, kind of like feeling whole again."

"Hmmm well I think that's how I'm feeling. It feels painful to contemplate still having that sort of ministry, but when I do it also feels comforting."

"And, there is enough flexibility with the practice to give you the time to do it," added Max with an arm across Charlie's shoulders and a quick peck on her cheek to emphasise her support.

"I can see I'm outnumbered. I will follow it up and see what happens." Charlotte agreed.

"And before you two completely duck the question, what about solemnising your relationship?" asked Mike for the second time that evening.

Chapter 26

After several more weeks of discussion Max and Charlie finally sent out invitations to close family and friends to attend their civil partnership the following June. In the meantime, Mike and Liz got on with planning their son's christening.

When the day finally arrived, it was once again a cold grey day, not unlike the day a year ago, when Charlie travelled across the moor to meet her boss and give him her news. This time family and friends travelled north to Gloucester to the local parish church near to where Liz and Mike lived. It was to be part of the main Sunday morning service. Bishop David had been asked to preach, which he had reluctantly agreed to.

One area of the church was reserved for the baptismal party. Around forty had been invited including Max and Charlotte, who were to be godparents along with Liz's brother, John and another friend.

For the first time in months Charlotte found herself looking into the face of her former boss.

"How are you Charlotte?"

"I'm well thank you Bishop."

"I think you can call me David, after all you are about to become my grandson's godmother."

Charlotte looked for the sarcasm, or a hint of irony, but there was none. "And you're OK with that?"

"Why shouldn't I be? You are a lovely person and wonderful with the children. And any way..." David put his arm around Charlotte's shoulders and gently led her away from the milling congregation to a quiet side chapel, "…… how can I object to my daughter and son-in-law choosing a priest as godmother."

"That's not funny." Charlie was a bit shocked at the insensitive remark.

"Charlie, it's not meant to be. I'm handing in my resignation soon, well strictly speaking it's classed as retirement. I'm sixty-four so I'm not far off. But all this with you, it's made me stop and think. I just don't have the freedom to lead anymore, and seeing one of my best priests forced to give up, well it didn't sit lightly. If I was still in my fifties I would have stayed and fought for people like you, but I'll do it better from the outside now. No matter what legalities have been brought to the situation, it is God that calls us to priesthood, not a signature on a license. Not even a Bishop when he ordains you – God called you, and it's up to you what you do with that calling, in my eyes, you are still a priest."

He stepped back a little from Charlotte and straightened his back. "Now, let's get my Grandson baptised before he's big enough to run away!"

As David wandered off in search of the clergy vestry, Charlotte was left standing gob smacked at what she had just heard.

"Charlie, you coming to sit down?" Max was holding a wriggling Joshua. Aunty and nephew dressed in identical ivory waistcoats.

"Coming," but Charlie was distant.

"Wassup?" asked Max

"I'll tell you later. Now then young Joshy, will you keep still for one moment and let me put your shoe back on, how on earth you manage to kick them off so easily when it takes all my strength and skill to get them on you in the first place I'll never know."

Much later that evening back in their new home in Okehampton curled up on the battered old sofa that had once stood in the Rectory, Charlie tried to relay her conversation with David.

"I can't believe Mike and Liz never said that David was thinking of retiring," said Max, rubbing her feet on the back of Patch and Stitch, who were both very content in their new surroundings.

"I'm not convinced they know. David was so secretive, he didn't say keep it confidential, but I kind of got the feeling it wasn't common knowledge. Retiring Bishops usually make at least the local news."

"And he said it was because of you?"

"Sort of, but it won't just be that. I think he's just fed up with the whole system."

"But he'll still be a bishop."

"Uh huh, a retired bishop. He'll probably help out one in whichever diocese he decides to live."

"There's that thing about moving out of the Diocese isn't there? I wonder how Catrin is about all of this. What will she do, she has given her life to being a bishop's wife."

"She was very quiet at the Christening." Charlotte moved closer to Max.

"Not surprised," said Max as she wrapped herself around Charlie. "Do you think she'll ever except us?"

"No, not as a couple. But at least she isn't as jumpy when we're looking after the children."

"True. You know Lizzie had a go at her?"

"Mike told me. He sounded really proud of his wife. Can't be easy though. Not with the rest of the family being so accepting, Catrin is a bit out on a limb."

"So!" Said Max

"Don't be like that. Not everyone understands us. That's all."

"I know sweetheart. Their loss." Max tuned and kissed Charlotte's cheek. "I'm guessing they'll want to be nearer Liz and Mike, can't imagine him wanting to move London way. Do you know how long these things take?"

"Depends, six months, a year, why?"

"We've not got him on our invitation list yet – fancy a revision?"

Charlotte smiled and nodded her head in agreement, this time with no arguments and no reservations. If David felt he could attend, both he and a reluctant Catrin would be invited.

The end........ or a new beginning.

The author writes

I've wanted to write this book for some time. It is a book of fiction and any similarities to any of the characters in the book are purely coincidental. However, the book is written from real experiences. For many years gay priests have had to lead careful and often deceptive lives very similar to the experiences of Reverend Charlotte Northam. In the 21st *century, society's understanding of sexuality has changed. The church has been challenged to think through its understanding and teaching. Reports are coming in front of General Synod, that discuss our current thinking and to challenge previous intolerance.*

The current teaching is that the Church of England welcomes all people, regardless of sexuality. However, Church of England priests are not yet permitted to conduct the marriage of a gay couple, but can say quiet informal prayers of dedication over a committed relationship. Clergy are permitted to enter into a civil partnership but must declare that the relationship remains celibate. Gay clergy are not permitted to marry their partner. Those who do, face penalty under the clergy disciplinary measure.

The Church's current understanding is that marriage remains a union of one man and one woman. It also teaches that sexual intercourse remains within the context of a committed life-long union as in marriage. This may feel outdated by some in the wider society and yet stable monogamous relationships provide a life-long stability and emotional support. The challenge facing the church is whether doctrine can embrace that same commitment between same-sex couples and to open up this possibility to its clergy.

I hope this book of fiction will enable some to enjoy what, I hope, is a good read. I hope it may make some stop and ponder current teaching. I hope some may even be challenged.

Lightning Source UK Ltd.
Milton Keynes UK
UKOW03f1123180417

299344UK00001B/139/P